THE PR...

ULTIMATUM

6/18

DATE DUE FOR RETURN

THE **PRAGUE ULTIMATUM**

JAMES SILVESTER

⋃**RBANE**
Publications

urbanepublications.com

First published in Great Britain in 2017
by Urbane Publications Ltd
Suite 3, Brown Europe House, 33/34 Gleaming Wood Drive,
Chatham, Kent ME5 8RZ
Copyright © James Silvester, 2017

A CIP catalogue record for this book is available
from the British Library.

ISBN 978-1-911331-38-4
EPUB 978-1-911331-39-1
MOBI 978-1-911331-40-7

Design and Typeset by Michelle Morgan

Cover by Michelle Morgan

Printed and bound by CPI Group (UK) Ltd, Croydon, CR0 4YY

urbanepublications.com

For Mitchell Kevin Harrowell Lynn.
Always be Batman.

PROLOGUE

"TOMMY…? TOMMEEE…?"

The words floated ghoulishly on the bitter, raw night air, accosting Corporal Thomas Stone of the 4th Royal Tank Regiment and freezing him in his well-ordered tracks; his immaculately polished right boot hovering inches from the ground and his long-standing loathing of sentry duty rising familiarly in his gut.

It was the primary responsibility of Corporal Stone and the Armoured Regiments incumbent in The British Army of the Rhine, to deter incursion from Eastern forces, demonstrating an ability to deploy to forward positions with a high level of battle worthiness twenty-four hours a day, seven days a week. Theirs would be a symbolic sacrifice of course, the men knew as much. However brave, however well trained they may be – and were – it was common knowledge that the efforts of BAOR and their Western Allies would be wholly insufficient to quell a Russian invasion for any more than seventy-two hours. But they would be the most hellish seventy-two hours of the invaders' lives, Corporal Stone and his comrades in arms would make sure of that. He and the lads in 4RTR and throughout the Army had not been dragged up through the blood, toil, tears and sweat of a World War, only to back down when the call came. Corporal Stone was ready to do his duty and, if necessary, to die in the course of it. He was ready to do his best.

But heroic futility was not in the Corporal's immediate plans tonight. Tonight, his desire had been solely to complete his patrol with as little incident as possible, down a couple of beers with the boys and then throw himself on the sparse provision of the barracks at Fallingbostel; there to gnaw the cold from his fingers and plunge himself into dusty dreams of the squalid streets and dilapidated buildings of his childhood. The rubble and remains of neighbour's houses in the forgotten corner of Manchester derided by many as The Italian Quarter, had so often provided his playground and he longed only to play in them once more until the inescapable claw of reveille reached into his slumber and pulled him back to his post. But before he could retreat to his dreams, there was the matter of the words which so chilled him, and whichever ghoul had spoken them.

They were not aimed at him of course, not specifically at least, rather they carried the melancholy of a caller fully aware of the British patrols between themself and escape, and the haunted intensity of one determined to complete their journey. Patrols of the inner border between West Berlin and the forsaken East were common, and for more years than most could remember, some said as far back as the Peninsular Wars, the World knew every British soldier as Tommy Atkins. Corporal Stone knew this too, Corporal Stone was no fool, but this warmed him with little comfort when the Berlin night was at its blackest and the ghostly voices called his name. It was not only the words, but the spectral manner in which they reached him that unsettled the Corporal, whistling chillingly in his ears, just as the German bombs had done those nights he had stood vigil with his Mother, years before, wondering on the fate of his older brothers long since gone off to war. The sound was at once universal and particular, as though insistent that he feel some exclusive dread in the midst of its throes.

Rejecting the entrapment of memory, Corporal Stone called upon his military rationalism to dispense as best he could the threat of the supernatural. Crunching his wavering boot to the ground, he spun to face the direction of the words in one fluid movement. Swiftly, sublimely, he ran his numb hand up the sleeve of his dull green Great Coat until it met the varnished wooden barrel of the grimly reassuring A1L1 Self Loading Rifle hanging on his shoulder, sliding it down into readiness and opening his mouth to recite the time honoured cry of the sentry.

"Halt!" Corporal Stone barked, "Who g..."

His throat obstinately refused to release the words, mirroring instead his eye's surprise at the figure before him. Corporal Stone had sentried in Germany many times and was well used to the sight of people struggling to break free from the crumbling grey oppression of the East, and the desperation that so often fuelled them. Many had come on many previous nights, wretched, filthy, clothes and flesh torn by the jagged defiance of wire fences run through and crawled under in terror; the completion of their fear driven quests depending on escape through the British Tommies walking the line. Some offered chocolate, hoarded for the journey, some offered jewellery handed down through generations. Some offered themselves.

The Corporal's instructions were clear: to deter entry. Corporal Stone had balked when on his first patrol he had been handed the battered, worn axe handle and realised the implication of its purpose; his disgust palpably contributing to his hatred of sentry duty. The West was recovering slowly from the ravages of war, so the political mantra went, it couldn't accommodate everyone. Besides, how could they be sure which of the escapees were genuine and which harboured more nefarious intentions? Corporal Stone understood the argument, in his weaker moments he almost sympathised with it, but those who stood in The House and made it had seldom personally sentried the Divide and looked those people in the eye. Corporal Stone had, and he and his comrades had lost count of the occasions they had stooped to re-tie bootlaces, or suffered momentary loss of sight when the calls drifted over the fractured concrete and barbed wire, across the divide towards them.

Corporal Stone gathered himself and drank in the silhouette standing ossified to the spot a few yards ahead. A figure more than a boy but not quite a man stared back at the Corporal, almost as tall as he was painfully thin, the piercing white of his eyes and paleness of his flesh accentuated in the moonlight. It was those eyes which unsettled the soldier, they were pained and tired, too much so for one so young, as though something irrevocable was absent from the soul behind them. They bore through Corporal Stone, without malice or ferocity, but with an undeniable presence. His young face was gaunt and unsmiling, though not displaying a preoccupation with its own unhappiness, and his posture was devoid of the signs of desperate panic so typical in people scrambling towards the Lines.

"I am your friend, Tommy, though I have no password to give," the young voice was as emotionless as the face it came from, making its case simply and accordant with fact, "and I have no bribe to offer you. Will you let me through, Tommy?"

"You can't come through lad," Corporal Stone responded, still frozen into position and his voice not altogether as strong as he would have liked, "run along home now, your parents will be worried."

"My parents are dead."

"I'm sorry," Corporal Stone answered in sincerity.

"They died years ago, in the War. It was a long way from here."

"So who looks after you?"

"Those people..," the young figure answered, the slightest hint of hesitation in his voice, "they are dead as well now."

"Bloody hell," Corporal Stone cursed. The War had made losers of everyone, right the way across the continent and though it had finally ended some six years hence, the soldier could never quite get used to the totality of the misery it had caused. Nor, he hoped, would he ever.

"I really am sorry lad," he insisted, "but you won't find anything to make up for that this side of the fence. Whatever problems you're running from, you'll just find more here; the grass isn't always greener."

"They are coming for me."

"Who?"

"The Men."

"Why?"

No answer came. The figure simply remained standing, ghoulishly noiseless, his hands in his pockets, only the thin wire fence between them.

"I need to pass through, Tommy," the quiet voice eventually murmured.

"Why do you want to come here?"

"I am looking."

"For what?"

"Answers."

"There are no answers here, lad. There's a shed load of questions alright, but not too many answers."

Distant laughter behind him alerted Corporal Stone to his

impending relief and a momentary surge of alarm channelled through him. The boy still stood silent, ghostly; the intensity in his eyes a constant. He wasn't much younger than Corporal Stone's brothers had been years earlier, when they had left to fight the damn war with cheery promises of swift victory and imminent return, their faces full of an optimism they didn't truly feel. There was no such optimism in this boy's face.

"Will you let me through, Tommy?"

For an agonising and seemingly eternal instant, the Corporal stood, staring down the barrel of his rifle at this strange, emotionless boy whose future depended on the outcome to the conundrum playing out in the soldier's mind. And he wondered as he stared, if the German soldier had peered in equal hesitation on the day he took his brother from him; and pondered for the thousandth time whether he had in turn found himself at the end of an Allied rifle, or whether he had lived to cry regret into his glass in some post-War Bavarian beer house, for having allowed himself to be bullied by another's misguided sense of 'Duty' into acting against what his conscience told him was right.

He could only guess at the moral introspection of the wartime killers of yesteryear, but his own conscience was speaking to him now, loudly and clearly, and he knew very well which choice he believed to be right. With his heart full of family, Corporal Stone shouldered his rifle and turned away from the boy, swiftly and deliberately continuing his sentry along his side of the crumbling, grey concrete desert he was sworn to protect.

"Double Time, lad," he said, almost under his breath, "God bless."

The sound of quick, ferocious scrambling echoed in Corporal Stone's ears, followed by fast footsteps quickly fading into the black night behind him. He hadn't made much further progress on his path before a bellowing voice reached him from behind.

"Corporal Stone!"

"Sergeant Major!"

Corporal Stone threw himself to attention, a sinking dread taking hold of his stomach. The Badge, his Sergeant Major, had seen the whole exchange. Sure enough, the RSM, a barrel-chested giant of a man and a seasoned Warrant Officer who had stormed the beaches at Normandy, was striding imperiously towards the young soldier with purpose, his clipped moustache bristling above his fixed jaw. Rumours circulated among the men that the mere sight of him charging forward, bayonet fixed and battle cry bellowing had once been enough to convince a trio of German Paratroopers to surrender. Others scoffed at the suggestion and insisted the intimidation had been down to the ferocity of the profanities he screamed, and that it had been *five* men with the good sense to lay down arms. To cross this man was not to be advised and Corporal Stone began to inwardly prepare himself for the two weeks of jankers he could expect as a minimum punishment for his dereliction. To his surprise though, no vociferous volley was launched by the Sergeant Major when he drew alongside his subordinate, instead, Corporal Stone was greeted with a stern but fatherly stare from the older man.

"What was that, lad?"

"What was what, Sergeant Major?"

"I could have sworn I saw something coming through the fence and scurrying off just then."

Corporal Stone adopted an expression of supreme ignorance and shook his head, his eyes wide.

"Dunno Sergeant Major, must have been a fox or something, maybe?"

"A fox, eh?"

"Yes, Sergeant Major."

For all his fearsome reputation, the men knew their Warrant Officer to be an honourable man who had their backs, and by not having subjected him to an immediate dressing down, Corporal Stone knew he would escape the worst.

"When you finish here," the veteran soldier said, "collect my boots from outside the Doss House. I want them cleaned, shined and spic and span before reveille tomorrow, or I'll run a pole up your backside and have C Squadron use you as a flag. Plenty of Bull, understand?"

"Yes, Sergeant Major."

"Carry on, Corporal."

Corporal Stone turned on his heel and continued his patrol as his superior's boot steps receded back into the night. He had gotten away lightly he knew that, even if his bed would have to wait a little longer for him. He allowed a little pride to creep into his step; he was there to do his best and he'd done it, even if he had earned a mild punishment for his troubles. Someone had needed help and he'd given it, and maybe someone would have the chance of a better life because of it. He smiled at the thought of the strange youngster who had stood before him minutes earlier and wished him better times than those he had clearly experienced so far. While the War had stolen so much from so many, Corporal Stone always felt worse when the young were involved, and he hoped the boy would have a future free of the death, destruction and conflict which had robbed his eyes of their wonder. Content, he reassured himself that the boy would be fine and that he would have plenty of time in his life to reclaim the innocence in his soul and be happy; he was, after all, only a Child.

ONE

"THE GOLDEN ROOM IS CLOSED TODAY, I'm sorry," the woman behind the small, glass divide repeated her refusal for the third time, "you can join the regular tour at ten o'clock, but it will be a tight squeeze; this is the most visited castle in Czechoslovakia, sir."

Captain Lincoln Stone shifted his weight from one leg to the other, his irritation with both the woman's obstinacy and his own crouched stance at the low ticket office window fermenting steadily. Though the circumstances of his trade had well versed him in desert temperatures, the dry, burning sun and his own frustrations combined to break down his body's resistance and he felt the sweat begin to form atop his bald head; glistening droplets upon his smooth, dark skin. His face betrayed the baggage of military experience, but he wore it handsomely nonetheless and he was certainly leaner and fitter than most men in their mid-Fifties. A light, white cotton shirt hung open necked on his torso, above immaculate blue jeans and black shoes which glistened in the teasing sun. A light black jacket completed the ensemble, the finishing touch to a dashing, if imposing figure.

"Believe me, 'madam,'" Stone replied, countering her 'sir' with a barely supressed venom, "castles bore me, and I harbour no desire to tour one with a group of people more intrigued by my skin tone than the resilience of millennia old architecture. I've travelled a long way to get to this 'Golden Room', and whether you let me in willingly, or I kick down every door I see until I find it, that's where I'm going. Now if you can't help me with that, then please go and find someone who can."

The woman squirmed and vacated her seat, quickly scurrying through an inner door while Stone sought to rein in his seething. He instantly regretted his shortness with her, blaming everything from the heat to the circumstances for his display; and in truth, they were unusual circumstances, at least for him, and he moved to stand in the shade of the Castle gates while he reflected on them.

The envelope had dropped just days after the Hearing, along with the latest freebie rag, a couple of bills and the dying dregs of the hate mail the proceedings had briefly stirred up. A part of Stone suspected the mystery letter may too have formed part of the bile fuelled barrage, but instead he found inside a boarding pass from Liverpool to Bratislava for the following week in his name, connecting train tickets from the airport to the town of Prievidza, a ticket granting now disputed entry to Bojnice Castle's 'Golden Room' and a letter bearing the words 'Please attend promptly' above a flurry of official looking signatures. Only the grandest of these monikers persuaded him to comply.

"Captain Stone?"

Stone spun around to the voice's owner and accepted the hand of the woman before him. Young, probably mid-twenties Stone estimated, her long brown hair was pulled back into a severe pony tail which complimented the wholly professional look her white shirt and black suit afforded her. Her grip was strong, her tone commanding, with a military inflection. Stone immediately felt his frustrations retreat.

"It's a pleasure sir," the young woman continued, "this way if you please?"

Stone acquiesced and followed her through the courtyard, pleased at last for the return of a military rigidity to his situation.

"You're English?" He asked her, she nodding in response without breaking stride.

"Actually, Sir, I prefer to say British, while I still can anyway. My Mother is from East Kilbride and my Father from Bristol."

"Well that'd do it," Stone conceded, "at least until the next referendum muddies the water again."

They stopped at a large but inconspicuous wooden door, built into the solid stone wall of the castle and the young woman moved to knock, the Captain stopping her as she did so.

"He's in here is he?"

"Yes, sir."

"Who with?"

"Alone. You have been briefed haven't you sir?"

"I have not."

She frowned at the failure.

"Apologies sir, an oversight I'm sure. If you'd wait here a moment, I'll make sure he's ready for you."

"Thank you, erm....?"

"Moore, sir. Flight Lieutenant Charlotte Moore, 33 Squadron."

"You're a long way from RAF Benson."

"Special secondment, sir," she replied, "I looked after him during his last trip to Syria and he requested I be assigned to his personal detail."

"There seems to be a lot of that going on at the moment," he chuckled, somewhat cynically. "Thank you Flight Lieutenant Moore." Stone offered her a warm smile, his temperament at least partially restored by the familiarity of an efficient military persona.

She nodded a reciprocal smile, knocked on the door and went in, emerging a moment later to swing the heavy oak door fully open.

"The Foreign Secretary will see you now sir," she said, gesturing for the Captain to pass her and enter the room, before stepping out and closing it behind him.

On the other side, Stone found himself in surroundings which at once epitomised and undersold the description 'Golden Room'. Large, spacious, the room was carpeted with a thick red and black patterned shag, upon which stood all manner of grandly aurelian furniture, proudly beaconing its own ornateness to the newcomer. The walls, where not adorned with ancient portraits and lovingly preserved Coats of Arms, carried instead gilded patterns which intricately knitted brightly together the full height of the room and across the wooden ceiling. At the far end of this shining treasure cave sat a man, contrasted from his surroundings by the forebodingly dark suit which he wore tieless as he scribbled notes at the resplendent desk, his head down and revealing the tell-tale signs of a hairline beginning to thin. Stone recognised the man instantly, from TV reports, newspapers and from meticulously stage-managed war zone briefings to the troops: The Rt. Hon. Jonathan Greyson MP, Her Majesty's Foreign Secretary.

"What do you know of Oscar Myska, Captain?"

The heavy door swinging closed behind Stone had triggered the question, the politician's eyes remaining on his papers, his scribbling uninterrupted.

Stone frowned, sensing a return of his frustrations. While he had been unsure of the reasons behind his summoning, this was not the reception he had expected and he was loathe to remain in the dark playing twenty questions to a politician's rules.

"Only what I read online, *Sir*."

He spat the last word, in the time-honoured manner of a soldier wishing to apprise a superior of his contempt, hoping for a quick end to the charade.

"Not a fan of the papers eh?"

"You could say that after recent events. Neither am I a fan of having my time wasted. *Sir.*"

The last response had the desired effect, Greyson lifting up his head and offering Stone a small smile. Stone stood some feet away from the desk, taking in the man before him as he would an enemy in the field, and he quickly determined that this was no fellow warrior before him. The face was thin, carrying more lines than a man of Greyson's age may hope for, particularly across the forehead which furrowed with an obvious stress, betraying the attempted smile at the corners of his mouth.

"And nor should you be," the politician eventually conceded. Greyson gathered his papers into a shining leather briefcase and stood and walked out to face Stone, leaning on the desk in front of him.

"You're here Captain, because I need your help."

"My help, sir?"

"Your help."

"The help of a shamed man? Of a disgrace to the uniform, sir?"

The rich velvet of Stone's voice in no way diminished the bitter cynicism of the words he flung at Greyson, words which had been aimed at Stone by the Committee, days earlier. The Captain noted the embarrassed twinge on Greyson's face and enjoyed it, twisting the knife to see more.

"I'm at a loss to see how a fallen hero such as I could help you sir."

Captain Stone looked into Greyson's eyes and yearned to hate him, to see in them the reflections of the ignorantly self-righteous members of The Commons Defence Committee, who had hauled him over the coals days earlier, but he could not.

Then, Stone had sat resplendent in his dress uniform, his unparalleled collection of decorations capped by the dull crimson and bronze of the Victoria Cross earned through blood at Port Stanley, while his interrogators sought to eviscerate him. With a steady, unbreakable stare he had gauged them, not a single one escaping his disdain and each contemptible in their own way. Expensively attired Tory faux patriots, who would wrap themselves in the Union Flag before voting to slash the Forces, sat alongside Trotskyite Revolutionaries who hid their convictions and their hatred of the military behind tasteful suits and MPs' salaries. Each of them professed to know what was best for the defence of the country; none had ever served her at the front. Calmly, Stone had listened to their loaded questions, respectfully he had answered them, stoically he had refused to concede to their pointed twisting of his words as the journalists scribbled and the hot cameras whirred around him, as loud and as bright, it had seemed at that moment, as any battlefield explosion.

Did the Captain accept that he had wilfully disobeyed orders? Yes. Did he accept that his actions resulted in the tragedy? No. Would the Captain agree that his actions could be construed as cowardice? Emphatically not and were these the days of Wellington, such a question would result in the offer of a duel.

The barely concealed panic on the squirming MP's face as the comment was hastily withdrawn had briefly cheered Stone, thought it didn't halt the avalanche of arrogant condescension streaming from the Committee's lips. Try though he might, Stone saw none of the same arrogance in Greyson's eyes, only the strain of a man buckling under the weight of a thousand unspoken pressures.

"Oh come on man!" The exasperation in Greyson's voice was obvious and indicative of the stresses his face suggested he was under, "You can't have expected there not to have been an enquiry? London ground to a halt! The Markets, hardly at their most stable since Brexit, tumbled, share prices dropped, for God's sake, they were lying the dead out on pavements!"

Greyson covered his mouth as though offended by his own display of temper, and Stone grimaced in mute acceptance of the implied apology the politician waved at him.

"I expected an enquiry, sir, I expected hard questions. I did not expect to be scapegoated by my own country."

A cold silence, heavy with unspoken mutual accusation burned between them for a moment, neither man wishing it to break before emotions were better restrained.

Finally, quietly, with an air of tiredness in his voice, Greyson moved to speak.

"Well, successfully completing the job I have for you might go some way to compensating you for your trouble."

"I am not interested in compensation…" Stone began what he imagined was his predictable response, before an irritated Greyson cut him off.

"Exoneration," he snapped, "Full, complete. Re-instatement to active service with a promotion to Major, no more than you deserve with your history. God knows you've been a Captain long enough."

Stone's silence this time came from his shock at Greyson's words, rather than anger at the establishment he represented. He hadn't expected this, not after the bile flung at him by Committee, and he struggled for a moment to assimilate it. Promotion he could do without, but exoneration, the return of his honour was a priceless temptation; his son, his precious boy so opposed to the cruelties of modern war, could be proud of him again.

"I've no wish for a Majority," Stone finally said, honestly, "With all due respect I'd prefer to return to my Squadron."

"Out of the question," Greyson shook his head, "We can't have you running in and out of combat zones after what happened…"

"The men and women in that Squadron rely on me sir. Frankly after the way the committee went for me, I don't trust anyone else to take care of them in the aftermath. Important though exoneration is to me, if it were to come at the expense of those under my command then…"

"One month," Greyson interrupted, snapping, "one month with your Squadron, away from combat, then you accept promotion and take an administrative position at Sandhurst. Final offer."

Stone stared hard into Greyson's eyes, sure that this really was the final offer, but not wanting the politician's nerves to settle with an immediate acquiescence.

"So," the Captain eventually replied, "Oscar Myska."

The half-smile on Greyson's lips stretched fuller for a brief moment, before giving way to rigid professionalism as Stone continued.

"Half-British, half-Czech and a man with the dubious honour of being known as 'the respectable face of the extreme Right' across Europe. No criminal record, no history of violence and he's never been tainted by association with the skinheads or Neo Nazis, but he nonetheless professes a similarly unpleasant message."

"Quite." Greyson picked up the tale, arms folded, "Certain of his entourage have even been known to claim his direct, if illegitimate, lineage from Oswald Mosley, would you believe?"

"Is that true?"

"Anything's possible but it would be hard to prove. It certainly lends more credence to his 'One European Nation' platform though."

"One European Nation?"

Greyson turned to the crystal decanter on the desk, pouring generous measures from it into two glasses and handing one to Stone, who stepped forward to accept it.

"After the Second World War," Greyson began, "Europe's remnant fascist groups struggled to adapt to the continent's somewhat understandable rejection of their ideology. Many simply died a death or devolved into the insignificant groups of thugs you see today, beating up immigrants and painting swastikas on gravestones. Some though, Mosley being one, tried rebranding themselves under the principle of a Europe as one unified nation."

"And how successful was that?"

"Not very. Aside from the fact that none of the composite groups ever fully agreed with each other, once it became clear that their new vision was for an Aryan Europe with mass deportation of blacks and Jews, the novelty quickly wore off."

Stone knocked back his drink and placed the glass on the desk.

"I hadn't noticed any of that on Myska's website."

"No," Greyson agreed, "but he's clever, and he's played the migrant crisis like a dream. For the most part he's resisted attacking refugees themselves, he says it's all Europe and the World's fault for putting people into a position where they're forced to seek refuge within 'incompatible cultures'. His party have even set up charities in Libya and Syria among other places, ostensibly to help people stay and rebuild in their own countries, but in reality setting the scene for wholescale repatriation."

"How very noble," Stone replied.

"Quite. The effect being of course that he can distance himself from the more extreme vitriol out there and present himself as a kind of perverse humanitarian, while being sure that people know he hates any idea of diversification and that his core supporters will be busy putting his real message about in slightly less eloquent tones."

Stone grimaced, he knew the type well; the sneering face of middle class respectability who could spread hatred and fear so much more thoroughly with words than the average thug could with fists. It was the words of the so called 'mainstream' rather than the boots of criminals which kept this evil alive. Beautifully vocalised warnings of 'unknown hordes' and 'rivers of blood' created more panic than a dog turd through a letterbox ever could, because the educated, professional voices legitimised the fear, made it allowable, *desirable*, to mimic the intellectually determined cruelty. The first time the words were used against him in the playground, Stone had understood this, and since that day he had heard them used by embittered ideologues, backbench opportunists and boorish clowns in pinstripe suits. The only difference was the people they were aimed at.

"He sounds an unparalleled delight," Stone replied. "But with respect sir, why is this Britain's concern? The Article 50 process is under way, we're disengaging from Europe, why are we unduly Interested in the activities of a Czech MEP, however unpleasant he sounds?"

Greyson smiled his strained smile as though once more expecting Stone's objection.

"Because as far as British interests go Captain," he began, "the EU represents our very own Hotel California – we can check out any time we like, but we can never leave, not completely anyway. Our interests are inexorably intertwined with theirs, even if the more hard line of the government get their way."

"But surely Brexit…?"

"Brexit was our punishment," Greyson snapped in obvious irritation at the truth of the revelation.

"Three years ago, certain members of the government aided the Czechoslovak reunification campaign and helped prevent an assassination attempt on Miroslava Svobodova. As a result, you and I currently stand in a reunified country with Ms Svobodova at its Head. The Institute for European Harmony, the body responsible for the security of the Union, didn't take too kindly to our interference, hence the Prime Minister being forced into offering a referendum he would lose, compelling him to resign, banishing Britain from Membership and forcing us to deal with the economic and social fall out of the last couple of years."

As Greyson's matter of fact delivery sunk in, Stone felt the familiar rise of his contempt for the political class. He was a soldier, an honourable man, or at least he liked to think so, he faced his enemies head on, on the battlefield, where loyalty to one's comrades mattered and survival was far from assured. It was everything that politics wasn't. Backroom deals, dodgy dossiers, corrupted elections and now *assassinations*? The Captain reined in his anger to properly process Greyson's words.

"The Institute for European Harmony? Never heard of it."

"Not many have. Ostensibly it's a Think Tank, but you'd be better to think of it as sort of combined European FBI and CIA," Greyson agreed, smiling gently. "Far less official but every bit as far reaching. It's their job to keep Europe on track."

"So why would they throw Britain out, surely losing a member state weakens their overall position?"

"You'd think so, but like I said it's our punishment. We get economic turmoil and are still dependent on Europe, only now we have none of the power and no right to veto anything; the project can move on unhindered. But, we think they've miscalculated."

"How so?"

"Race." Greyson offered the word simply and quietly. "If Brexit has been successful at anything it's in galvanising the extreme Right both at home and across Europe, hence our interest in Myska. With the migrant crisis on-going and this latest bout of terrorist attacks across the continent, not least the attack last year in Prague, his sudden rise to prominence really couldn't have come at a worse time. We're worried that The Institute might try and use the instability to unseat Svobodova, or otherwise do away with her, and replace her with someone less favourable to Britain - God knows we need all the friends we can get these days. I need you to go to Prague, get a feel of the atmosphere, see if you can link Myska to any of the violence and unrest. If we can do that, we can discredit him and cut off the march of the extreme Right before it gathers any more momentum, and if we keep Svobodova in power we'll have an influential ally while we work out what the hell our Brexit economy is going to look like."

"That's it? Just go to Prague and see what I can find out?"

"For now. Think of it as reconnaissance work."

"With respect sir, I'm a soldier, I reconnoitre battlefields. Skulking around in dark street corners sounds more like a job for MI6."

"I can't trust MI6!" Greyson's irritation was palpable. "The Institute have been operating within government for years and frankly MI6 is compromised. The only operative they have who I can be sure of is already on the ground but I need more and have no-one else I can trust! I can't second a serving Officer to this kind of duty, it would be too suspicious, so that makes you, Captain, the ideal candidate for the job. And anyway, you'll still be reconnoitring a battlefield, just one of a different type."

There was a sincerity, almost a panic in Greyson's voice which overrode Stone's distaste, almost enough to sway him by itself, but the soldier's thoughts kept returning to his son and the restoration of his honour. Greyson was reaching out to him, the veins in his thin arm pronounced and strained, the palm open, desperate to clasp around Stone's. Shrugging away the last of his doubt, Stone obliged, shaking the politician's hand with a calculated and deliberate strength.

"How long?" he asked.

"It's in our interests to get this done quickly and quietly, so get to Prague and I'll be in touch."

"When do I leave?"

"Tonight. Flight Lieutenant Moore has your particulars."

The hand withdrew and the smile vanished, replaced by the deep furrows which clung once more to Greyson's face. He moved to close their meeting, picking up his briefcase and buttoning his jacket in swift, well-practiced movements.

"That's it, no codes, no passwords, no exploding keyrings," he said, "There's money in your account, enough for expenses and to rent an apartment; I'd suggest somewhere central, maybe somewhere on Pricna. Just get to Prague, find Myska, learn what you can and wait to be contacted by my man there; he's a bastard to be sure, but he's good."

"What about Svobodova?" Stone replied, annoyed at the lack of the type of specifics his military life had accustomed him to, "If she's the target why aren't I protecting her?"

"Leave Mirushka to me," Greyson commanded, turning on his heel and heading towards the elaborately framed inner door, "I have someone else taking care of her."

"Your man?"

"No," the politician replied over his shoulder as he disappeared into the corridor, the heavy door swinging slowly closed behind him, "my woman."

TWO

THE AGING COACH WHEEZED into the grimy, filth strewn parking bay, as tortuously exhausted as the passengers it ferried, it's front wheel juddering into a pothole causing the thin, brunette woman in seat 14b to cross her legs and pray for the resolve of her bladder. As the surly driver spent the first of several eternities on his, surely superfluous, inching of the ancient transport into place, she composed a mental checklist of people and objects connected to this journey to curse. The driver was pretty high up, second only in fact to the man who had pressured her into making these arrangements. Then came the dilapidated vehicle she sat on, which had ferried her and a motley collection of apparently unwashed young men (who also featured on the list) from Vienna with the on-board toilet requested at booking, stubbornly inoperable en route. She reserved a special mention for the overweight, middle aged Czech man sat beside her, who had spent the last few hours snoring contentedly into her ear.

Clambering achingly off the bus and taking a reluctant lungful of the sickly warm night air, she stretched the cricks from her back and neck before hopping from one foot to the other on the pavement as the driver heaved the collection of bags out of the storage bay. Collecting her own, she clutched it tightly to herself and took in her surroundings, a fresh wave of unease overcoming her as she began to understand the veracity of the reputation this place enjoyed. Florenc, the central bus and coach station in Prague, enjoyed none of the typical beauty of its host city. Dirty and poorly lit, collections of hooded youths sat shrouded in shadows on broken wooden benches along its bays, while groups of men prowled the concourse, smoking weed and filling fellow travellers with a perhaps unwarranted nervousness. She was an educated, civilised woman. She didn't give in to racial profiling or group fear mentalities, but nonetheless she found herself suddenly aware of her overdressed isolation, standing alone, away from the other travellers and attired in an expensive, if somewhat crumpled business jacket and skirt. Where was the car due to meet her? Again, she cursed the orchestrator of her discomfort and dragged her travel case along the cobbles, the wheels tripping and skipping behind her as she ducked into the small and frankly unclean toilet ahead.

Almost as soon as she had gone, a shining black limousine swept imperiously into the bay, ignoring the beeps of a multitude of coaches and impervious to the contemptuous glances of the Florenc hordes. A man, shaven headed with a neat, black goatee, stepped from the vehicle in time to see the woman emerge from the toilet and look thankfully in his direction.

"Professor Abelard?" the man asked in accented English.

"Yes?"

"Welcome to Prague."

"Fucking gypsies." The beauty of the young girl's face twisted away as she hatefully spat out the words, the instant metamorphosis in her demeanour stunning Stone like a shrill bullet in a silent Afghan night.

He had arrived, as Greyson had urged, that very night in Prague, at once disturbed that his soul had a price like any other and relieved that it could at least measured in honour, not silver. The exoneration promised by the politician was beyond priceless, offering not only the continuation of his hard-earned career, but the restoration of his reputation and proof of his blamelessness to the media, to the public, and most importantly to Stone, to his son.

The involuntary musings had refused to abate as he reclined in the back of his airport pick up, the oppressive frigidity of his mood resisting the stifling warmth of the Czech summer night, and growing colder still at the sight of the grey, imposing concrete housing blocks lining the highway from the airport to the city; having stubbornly refused to die with the empire which spawned them. Stone had seen such constructs before, often broken, desolate; he had crouched in their crumbling and precarious shelter as he surveyed the battlefield and directed his squadron forward. The graffiti which clung to the upright oblongs outside his cab window, offered no greater comfort than had the bullet holes in the buildings of the past.

The dullness gave way almost in an instant to a barrage of golden lights and illuminated grandeur, as though the City itself could sense the knot in the pit of Stone's stomach at the sight of the dull, grey plainness and so reached its fingers out to him, charming him with a more obvious and seductive nobility. As they entered the city's earnest embrace, his head was briefly turned by the shadowed outline of what looked very much like a tank, rooted to the pavement of a side road as the cab sped past. Though the silhouette brought a brief lift inside him, like a schoolkid excited at driving past their favourite footballer, he repressed the urge to query its presence and made a mental note to return to the scene the next day and confirm his sighting. The car had pulled to the side of a busy main road - the imposing, austere buildings which lined it seeming to beacon immense pride in their own architectural magnificence and crushing shame that so many of their number were now home only to liquor dens and sex shops.

Pulling his bag from the car, Stone handed a note to the driver and paused before entering the hotel apartment he had booked into en-route, choosing instead to try and grab some essentials from what looked like a tiny convenience store, wedged into the ground floor of the adjacent building.

Brimming over with all kinds of cheap snacks, every day convenience and tattered selection of tabloid newspapers, Stone had barely squeezed through the shop's door when a small, scruffy child pushed hurriedly passed him and ran out into the night, a tin of mushrooms quickly flung after him, narrowly missing Stone's face. The thrower immediately scrambled her apologies to Stone from behind the counter in fast Czech which went as far over his head as the can had near it. The young woman's stare was a little longer than comfortable as Stone stepped into the shop, he hoped not because of the shade of his skin, but the way her smile at his beautifully intoned English quickly twisted into the hateful condemnation of the Romani boy she had aimed at, implied otherwise.

"They get everywhere, little thieves. If it's not the gypsies it's the fucking Syrians; they never pay for anything. God knows why Svobodova keeps letting them in."

She was a young girl, too young, Stone thought, to be staffing such a shop on her own, but old enough to know better than to employ the kind of generalisations he was so sick of hearing in his own country. Having no wish to debate the matter, Stone quickly scanned the wares available, grabbing a few oddly labelled essentials and heading for the till.

Behind the girl lay row after row of spirit filled glass bottles of various shapes and sizes, most of dubious appeal, while stacks of pornographic magazines lay uncensored on the counter top. He gestured politely to one of the large Scotch bottles, whose brand he recognised amidst the unknown, and reached into his pocket to quickly assess which of the colourful notes that made up the unfamiliar currency would cover his bill.

The young woman, smiling again, quickly bagged up his goods and pointed to the appropriate note before handing him some equally baffling coinage as change.

"Sorry about that boy," the girl said as he pocketed the money, "You English did the right thing, getting out of the EU, taking back control of your borders."

The comment provoked a sigh that Stone struggled to internalise. A passionate European, he had long since grown tired of such comments, and while far from willing to again have the kind of conversations which had seen friendships disintegrate, the tug was sometimes too hard to resist.

"I'm not so sure that we did," he answered, finally giving in to the temptation to challenge her ignorance, "in terms of Britain's status in the world it seems to me that we've gone from having a little of the power to none of it. And personally, I've always found freedom of movement to be rather convenient."

"Well, for normal people," the girl sniffed, "but how are you supposed to stop terrorism with thousands of Muslims pouring in and out? It's crazy."

"There are thousands of car drivers in Europe, we've no idea which ones will drink and drive and kill someone as a result. Do we ban driving just in case? Millions of people across the continent enjoy a drink now and then; how do we know which ones will have too much and hurt someone?"

She squinted at him, a slight annoyance showing on her face at his lack of agreement with her philosophy.

"I still say it's crazy," she stubbornly repeated, "anyway Myska will sort them out."

The name pricked at Stone, focussing him at once on his new objective.

"Oskar Myska?" Stone raised his eyebrow, "I've heard he's a bit extreme isn't he?"

"He's a patriot, he just says what everyone else is thinking."

"Really?" Stone played dumb, "I thought people in this part of the world were behind Svobodova?"

Another sneer.

"It's one thing to reunite Czechoslovakia, but another to fill it with Syrians."

"It's hardly full," Stone countered, calmly, "and they have to go somewhere, the poor buggers."

"They can go somewhere else; either back home or to some island somewhere, we've no room for them here."

It was an argument, if you could call it that, Stone had heard many times before in his own country and it saddened him to hear it repeated here, his tiredness at his peculiar day a poor base from which to debate with a closed mind. Picking his bag from the counter and inwardly resolving to find himself a different store should he be in Prague much longer, he offered a thin smile to the frowning girl.

"Hmmm," Stone muttered, considering her last words, "It's a good job Nicholas Winton had a different idea in 1939."

With that, he turned on his heel, ignoring her open-mouthed expression and stepped out to walk the few paces to his new abode.

Quickly checking in, he stepped into the sleek glass lift which powered smoothly up through the middle of the ageing, concrete floors, stepping out at the door of his apartment. The bright modernity of its interior contrasted sharply with the gothic austerity of the building's facade, the Captain raising an appreciative eyebrow at the spacious comfort on offer.

Throwing his bag on the bed, opening it only to take out the simply framed photograph of himself and his son and placing it on the nightstand alongside his key, wallet and phone, he quickly undressed and stepped into the bathroom. The hot, soothing shower went some way to washing the tension from his muscles and the whirlwind confusion of the day's events from his mind. Stepping out, he threw a towel around himself and picked up the phone from the nightstand, scrolling through it until he reached the desired name.

The dial tone droned laboriously on, the interminable vibrations continuing until the disembodied voice of his son invited him to leave a message.

"Hi son, it's Dad…" Stone's voice hung inside him for an age, leaving him dripping in silence on the laminated floor. "Listen," he eventually mumbled, "I just wanted to let you know I got here; it's beautiful by the way, you'd love it, and I'll give you a call soon, ok? And I love you. I know, you don't like me saying that, but I do, I really do. And I miss you. Goodnight son."

Noting the threat of the crack in his voice, Stone shook his head a little and hung up the phone, delicately placing it on the pristine white cabinet beside his bed. Throwing the towel back over the rail, he reached into the bathroom and pulled a large, luxurious dressing gown from the door, allowing himself to surrender to the comfort.

Although the apartment's fridge was well stocked with alcohol, Stone resisted the additional expense and pulled the Scotch bottle from his plastic bag of assorted necessities and poured a large measure into a glass tumbler retrieved from the cupboard. Crossing barefoot to the large, grand window, he pulled back the thick, velveteen curtains guarding it and twisted open the small metal handle to take in the view.

Here, at last, was the Prague he had heard so much about: a golden city of spires, towers and bridges, cradled delicately by the majestic night, as warm and as beautiful as his encounter in the shop had been cold and harsh. Crowning the view were the illuminated spires of St Vitus's Cathedral, at once dominating and complimenting the famous castle atop the hill and shining, it seemed at that moment, just for Stone. Humouring his own superstition, Stone reached out of the window and raised his glass to the sight.

"Well, here's to you Prague," he said, "Let's see what we can do for each other."

It was a restless sleep, despite the comfort of the bed, punctuated with unpleasant memories and confusing dreams. In the time-honoured tradition of the soldier, his body was accustomed to taking advantage of whatever sleeping arrangements were available, without complaint, and these were certainly generous arrangements. That though was as far as the serenity went. Stone imagined himself running from something, as hard as he could down street after street of ancient cobbles while from windows high above, the laughing and pompous members of the Parliamentary Committee for Defence jeered and waved, hurling a combination of vile projectiles and viler abuse at his fleeing figure. Hard as he ran he couldn't escape them, their contemptuous sneering growing ever louder until he rounded the thousandth corner at speed, to run into the grinning figure of Greyson, grimly attired, eyes black and flesh eerily white, holding his hand up in the air, clasped in which was a tiny bell.

"It's time, Lincoln," the figure lamented, ringing the bell, impossibly loudly.

"What?"

The bell sounded once more and Stone sprang up in his bed, a deep and sharp intake of breath accompanying his waking. Blackness still engulfed the room and he blinked his eyes used to the lack of lighting as the bell continued to sound. Stepping naked from the bed, he fumbled in the open bag on the adjacent dresser, pulling out a pair of jogging pants and swiftly pulled them on and walked to the door, shaking the clutches of sleep from his mind.

"What is it?" Stone bellowed as he fumbled with the lock.

"Captain Stone?"

"Who wants to know at five o'clock in the morning?"

"Captain Lincoln Stone?" An unexpected Welsh lilt greeted Stone as he pulled open the door, coming from the equally unexpected, professionally attired and unsmiling woman before him.

"Yes?" he managed, frowning.

"Professor Natalie Abelard." She stuck out a thin hand, which nonetheless clasped his own with considerable strength, "I'm here to accompany you to your meeting with the Prime Minister, Ms Svobodova."

"I've no such meeting arranged," Stone objected.

"I arranged it," the face remained expressionless, "I'm Greyson's woman."

THREE

THE CITY STREETS BEGAN to crawl to life as Stone and his new companion were swept through them a short while later, the first light warming cobbles and illuminating the tips of spires, as door hinges and bones began creaking into use. Stone felt none of the empty suspicion of his journey from the airport the night before, the graffiti somehow less harsh, the atmosphere more bearable and the city itself altogether warmer, despite the somewhat cool silence of his travelling companion.

It was the Captain who ultimately broke the silence as the car glided past a rugged metal hulk, at once archaic and shining new, perched almost arrogantly atop a grassy, green roundabout, its long, cylindrical gun reaching deliberately out towards the oncoming traffic.

"That's a T54!" Stone exclaimed, twisting backwards to confirm his judgement.

"I never liked Terminator," came the disinterested response.

"No, the tank, there!" Stone articulated out of the window at the rapidly diminishing sight. "I thought I'd seen one last night on the way from the airport but didn't get a close enough view. But that's a Russian T54, one of the most durable and successful tank models in history."

"Most successful, really? Fascinating…"

"Well it is to me," Stone countered, "The equivalent of the British Centurion, they were used for years, incredible machines. What's it doing stuck on a roundabout? Odd place for a war memorial."

"It's probably there for the filming," Abelard said casually, her eyes focused on the papers in her briefcase.

"Filming?"

"Yes, the filming," the Professor sighed in frustration, and returned the papers to her folder. "The fiftieth anniversary of the '68 Russian invasion is coming up and they're making some big blockbuster about it."

"Who? Hollywood?"

"Yes, one of the big studios in partnership with a couple of smaller ones up here in Barrandov, with some extra funding coming from an EU cultural grant. It's been quite a big deal in the What's On papers."

"Has it? I've been trying to avoid the media recently."

Finally, the Professor's expression softened and she offered a smile to Stone.

"I'm sorry," she said, "I shouldn't take it out on you. It's just that running around Central Europe at the beck and call of my ex-husband isn't exactly my first choice of project assignments."

"You were Greyson's wife?" Stone struggled to contain the surprise in his voice and regretted the tone of his question instantly. He was relieved when it was met with a further smile.

"You really should read the odd paper you know?" She teased, "My name was in a few of them for a while, though fortunately they kept my face out. At least Jonathan and I could agree on telling the gossip rags where to go."

"So why are you here?"

"He asked me."

"Yeah, but…"

"Necessity. I'm a Professor of International Relations and Extremist Politics at the University of Vienna. It's a good role and I have a degree of freedom, but that's about as far as it goes in terms of an academic career. If I want to progress, to offer consultancy services to governments or private interests I need a track record to back up my expertise. Jonathan, for all his faults, and believe me I could tell you a few stories about them, knows how good I am and if this little project of his comes off then I have the background I need to boost my career."

"And what exactly is your role in the 'little project'?"

"Strategic," she replied, gazing out of the window as the car began to pull to a slow stop outside a grand gothic building. "I offer my advice to Svobodova on how to manage the extremist pockets in the country that have come out of the woodwork recently, and the best way for her to take on Myska, while you dig around and try to find any connection between him and some of the shadier characters in his movement. If we can use any information you find to wrong foot him while I look for ways to trip him up politically, we can put paid to threat he poses nice and quietly."

"How very neat," Stone said as the rear door was opened and the pair stepped into the courtyard of the imposing Prague Castle complex, each casting admiring glances at the impressive beauty of their surroundings while continuing their conversation.

"Yes, well I hope so anyway," Abelard agreed. "It might make up for being sent here in the first place. Let's just say Svobodova isn't someone I want to spend too much time around."

"Why not?"

"Because I think she's sleeping with my ex-husband."

Stone had no time to respond as they were swept through the building, arriving with smooth efficiency at the door of Svobodova's office, where they were asked to enter.

Despite the voluminous nature of the room, there was little pretentious or overtly grand about its contents. Svobodova's desk sat in the corner, adjacent to the clear windows overlooking Prague, while a couple of small sofas guarded a shorter table towards the middle of the room. Her desk, aside from official documents and office equipment was sparse, with few personal touches to admire, save for a small photo frame, inside which lay a wrinkled and torn page from a book, the writing on which was too small for Stone to read, and which was stained in what looked very like a deep, blood red.

Standing before them was Miroslava Svobodova herself. She was, thought Stone, as beautiful in real life as television presented her, her features mature, the stress of her job beginning to deepen the lines on her face, but her eyes full of strength and determination and her smile warm and genuine, if a little less full than the one worn in interviews and broadcasts. Her blouse sleeves rolled up to elbow length, her skirt black as was the tightly buttoned waistcoat from which a delicate gold watch chain eccentrically hung. Only the white, open necked shirt beneath it contrasted the dark shades, presenting, it seemed to the Captain, the image of a woman in mourning.

She strode across the room towards them and held her hand out to Stone who shook it firmly in response.

"Captain Stone," she said, "thank you so very much for coming, I know this is a difficult time for you."

"Happy to help," he replied brusquely, determined to avoid any display of sympathy, "this is Professor Abelard."

Svobodova turned to the Professor, her smile a notch thinner, not from coldness, it seemed to Stone, but more likely with a slight anxiety. Stepping closer, the Czechoslovak Premier offered a softer handshake to Abelard and her voice, when it came, lacked any trace of political bravado.

"Thank you, Professor," she said.

"My pleasure," Abelard responded, her own smile equally awkward, "and please, call me Natalie." Abelard's words were stiff and far from caked in sincerity, but the politician seemed keen to welcome any opportunity to break the ice between them, or at least chip it a little.

"Natalie," Svobodova held the Professor's hand a moment longer before stepping back and gesturing to them to come further into the room and sit down.

"I must apologise for the short notice of your invitations here," she said, joining them on the sofas, "and in the spirit of honesty let me admit straight away we've had reason to be suspicious of outside help in recent years and I was not immediately overjoyed with the idea of bringing you here; either of you."

"That's alright," Abelard answered, settling herself into her seat, "I know how persuasive Jonathan can be."

The barbed comment pricked any warmth from the room and an uncomfortable silence settled at once around the table.

This was not a situation Stone was either used to or desired to be in and he moved to limit the damage as quickly as possible.

"Anyway," he began, "the fact is we're here now and I presume our help is welcome."

"Absolutely," Svobodova confirmed.

"In which case, shall we get down to business? I took the liberty of reading up on our friend Mr Myska on the plane here, quite a colourful character in many ways, certainly in terms of his opinions, but I gather he wasn't front page news until after the bomb last year?"

The news at that time had been full of little else; a terrorist attack in the heart of Prague at Wenceslas Square itself. A young man, no more than a boy really, strode into one of the countless bars lining the famous tourist spot, with a suicide belt strapped around his waist. Luckily for the victims, if stupidly on the part of their attacker, he chose to detonate his device during the early hours of the morning, resulting in a much-reduced casualty list but one which nonetheless reached into double figures. After the initial panic and stutter in the flow of tourists, the City and the country had slowly returned to a semblance of normality, the media merely chalking up the attack alongside the similar occurrences in Paris, Brussels and elsewhere as the continent began to ease itself almost into a reluctant acceptance of such periodic atrocities, as though they were an occupational hazard.

"Precisely," nodded Svobodova. "After the business of reunification was settled, there were many who accused me of focussing too greatly on the plight of the dispossessed and disaffected in our society, but the bomb made them more vocal than ever before and Myska was the one who focussed that rage."

"What was his background?" Stone asked, "Where did he come from?"

"He was raised in London," Abelard interjected eagerly, apparently keen not to be excluded from a discussion involving her specialist subject. "He moved to his mother's home town in Moravia when he turned eighteen and got a job in a warehouse packing frozen food, eventually getting promoted to warehouse Manager before he got himself elected as an MEP a few years back."

"Unusual for an anonymous independent candidate to win election, isn't it?"

"It is, but he'd built up quite a following locally," the Professor continued. "There was heavy unemployment where he lived and he'd run campaigns and drawn attention to the problem. Local people saw him as 'one of them' and when he was elected it was a case of 'local boy done good,"

"Unfortunately," Svobodova said, taking up the tale, "his message didn't extend only to the well-being of the unemployed. He lived in an area with a large population of Romani, and very soon he began scapegoating that section of the community for the problems people were facing; employment, crime, you name it, he blamed it on them, but in such a way that he sounded as though he did so with genuine concern for their well-being as well as that of his white neighbours. He would speak at length about the incompatibility of the two cultures and the importance of allowing both the freedom and room to prosper. He never explicitly advocated apartheid, but everyone knew what lay behind his words."

"And since the bombing it's a theme he's returned to with relish," Abelard said, reclaiming the verbal baton from Svobodova, "only this time his focus is chiefly on Muslim immigrants from Syria, Libya and the like and after the bombing people are prepared to listen on a grand scale. He's been able to succeed where other Leaders have failed and essentially unite the European Far Right under his banner. The arrangement might be somewhat implied and informal at present, but it exists and for the moment at least, the other extremist groups across the continent are prepared to ride his coat tails to glory, as it were; they're making electoral inroads everywhere by mimicking his style and his message and the main Parties are negotiating a new grouping in the European Parliament as we speak."

Stone stopped himself from smiling at the game of verbal 'one-upmanship' the ladies were playing and focused on the veracity of their words.

"So," he mused, "Aside from the fact that technically speaking he could be accused of being an immigrant himself, and that he's not only riding the xenophobic band wagon across Europe, he driving the thing, what else do we have on him? Greyson seemed to think there's a possibility he's not as squeaky clean as everyone thinks, does he have any concrete grounds to do so?"

"Nothing definitive," Svobodova shook her head, "but Myska, for all his faults, is a clever man and any unsavoury connections he has, he's been sure to hide well, Jonathan knows that."

Abelard shot a look to Svobodova at the mention of Greyson and stayed silent, leaving the politician to continue the briefing.

"No-one can prove anything," she said, "so far as we've been able to tell, no-one in his movement has any criminal record or association with the more violent extremist groups; no-one officially on the payroll that is…"

"Meaning?"

Svobodova sighed deeply. "Well as you might have seen on the news, there have been several instances of unrest in the country; hate crimes have soared just as in Britain after your referencdum, attacks on immigrants and Romani are sadly far from uncommon at the moment. There have been 'sightings.'"

"Of?"

"Familiar faces, people in the crowd at Myska rallies showing up later at Crime Scenes, sometimes as witnesses, sometimes just… there."

"You suspect coordination?"

"We have no real proof, but it's not beyond the realms of possibility."

She stood and walked briskly over to her desk, opening the drawer and pulling out a thin black file, passing it to Stone who opened it and began to leaf through. Inside were a variety of photographs, some pulled from newspapers or online, others CCTV images, often grainy and unclear. Each held the image of a different face, alongside a few lines of text detailing any available extraneous information.

"And these people have all been present at both Myska rallies and trouble spots? To be honest that's not much to go on."

"I know," Svobodova agreed, sighing once more.

Stone slapped the book shut and looked up.

"Well I think the first thing I should do is get a feel of a Myska speech first hand."

"You're in luck," Abelard said, breaking her self-imposed silence, "he makes public appearances most days, usually in Prague. His website says he's at Náměstí Míru, that's the square by the Church of St Ludmila, later today."

"Not exactly appropriate," Svobodova replied, "in English the name translates to 'Peace Square.'"

"Well hopefully it'll be a peaceful day for the people he targets in his speeches."

"A fun day out for all the family," Stone replied. "That's settled then, I'll head over there and keep an eye out for any of these characters and see what I can pick up."

He leaned back slightly on the sofa and, with a first step in place, sought to break the ice a little more thoroughly than had been managed before.

"I must say," he smiled, "this all sounds small potatoes for the woman who reunified Czechoslovakia; surely that earned you sufficient stature to withstand any challenge from fly by night populists like Myska?"

Svobodova reciprocated his smile.

"Reunification was the easy part," she laughed without humour, "it was afterwards the problems started. He warned me that the Institute always had a plan B…"

She tailed off, lost for the briefest of moments in her own thoughts, looking, it seemed to Stone, as though she were fighting back tears.

"Who warned you?" He asked, frowning.

She shook her head quickly, as if to banish any surrender to emotion.

"It doesn't matter. Jonathan told you about The Institute…?"

"For European Harmony," Stone finished, "yes but only briefly. What exactly is their stake in all this?"

Svobodova's face betrayed the weight of the question and she took a deep breath before answering.

"The Institute were violently opposed to reunification, so I knew our doing so would be problematic, even more so when we merged the national banks and withdrew from the Eurozone, but the 'punishment' we expected has never come. Until now that is…"

"What punishment?" Abelard quizzed, meeting a wry smile from Svobodova in response.

"A motion is being raised in the Commission," she began, "on the legal status of Czechoslovakia's membership of the European Union."

"On what grounds?" came the Professor's surprised reply.

"On the grounds that Czechia and Slovakia joined the Union as independent nations that now, technically no longer exist and the new country which has replaced them has never formally applied for or been granted membership."

Although Stone was no lawyer, he frowned at the preposterousness of what Svobodova had said, hearing his own thoughts immediately echoed by Professor Abelard's exasperated objections.

"But that's ridiculous!" she exclaimed. "How can the merging of two States into one invalidate Membership? Not to mention how losing another Member State after Brexit would weaken them, the whole thing is an absurdity!"

"I agree," Svobodova nodded, "but the motion has nonetheless been raised and a vote on the matter is imminent."

"Forgive me," Stone interjected, "But why are you too concerned? If Europe, or at least this 'Institute' or whatever it's called, has been responsible for so much trouble in your country then wouldn't it be better for you to be outside? From what Greyson told me, I'd have thought Britain would willingly make closer ties with you."

"It's not that simple," Abelard snapped in apparent irritation at the thought of Greyson's 'closer ties' with Svobodova. "Britain has the luxury of its island status, but Czechoslovakia is landlocked with Russia on the doorstep. If they lose EU status, and worse, if NATO decides to take that as a legal precedent and also withdraw membership then…"

"We find ourselves very alone, very quickly," Svobodova said, her face grim. "And despite Britain's own predicament, Jonathan is very much a lone voice in his government in his support of Czechoslovakia."

"Lone voice?" Stone's voice betrayed his confused irritation, "I was under the impression this was a government sanctioned operation?"

Svobodova broke eye contact for the briefest of moments, in apparent acknowledgement of the exaggeration.

"Yes," she answered quietly, "And no. Jonathan barely hung onto his job as Foreign Secretary when the new Prime Minister chose her Cabinet; you wouldn't believe who she wanted to replace him with. He speaks in our favour but I'm led to believe The Institute's reach extends far into your new government."

"I was promised…." Stone's irritation began to bubble dangerously close to anger.

"Exoneration, I know," Svobodova finished, leaning forward and placing her hand warmly over Stone's own, "And it remains in his gift, he assures me. Complete your task here and you can return to Britain with your honour restored, and my eternal gratitude."

It was political charm she offered, Stone knew that, but there was a sincerity behind her eyes that calmed, a little at least, his desire to rage at the deception.

"How can I refuse?" he asked, sarcasm biting his tone.

"My gratitude is sincere," Svobodova reassured him, "to both of you. I realise you have your own priorities at present Captain, and Profess…. Natalie… I can well understand how uncomfortable this must be for you. But please be assured that I, and my country, are more thankful than you know for your assistance."

She stood up and moved to the window, gazing out across the City of a hundred spires as though she were a mother hen keeping watchful, loving eye of her chicks.

"I must admit," she said, "I thought we had seen the end of such extremist politics as Myska's as a major force, but when people are scared or circumstances less than perfect, they seem as eager as ever to find someone else to blame for their woes; the oppressed and the outsiders, whether our own Romani kin or the refugees from Syria and Libya, especially so if they happen to be Muslim. People willingly blind themselves to the real cause of their misery and the realities all around them. Take Russia for example; have you seen what they've done to the Ukraine in two years? And now they sit, just a few short miles from our border, goading us with their incessant 'military manoeuvres', while we rely on the security of an ally that hates us…"

"To be fair," Abelard countered, "a lot of that can be put down to the EU and America trying too hard to influence things in an unstable country. If NATO hadn't pushed so strongly for a presence in Ukraine, and if the EU hadn't essentially backed a coup, then it's doubtful Russia would have got their knickers in a twist the way they did."

"I know, I know," Svobodova replied, remembering how the internal dissent in the eastern country had led to its latest puppet President 'inviting' the Russian army to help restore order and precipitating the takeover, "Don't get me started on NATO at the moment, they're every bit as difficult as the bloody EU."

Svobodova exhaled and shook her head, walking to the window and gesturing out.

"You know? You should have a good look around our tourist spots while you're here," she said. "Every other bar or restaurant is owned by Russians, some of them far from reputable and with discreet connections to the Russian mafia. Russian gangs have added massively to our problems with organised crime, just last night there was another murder at Florenc, that's three this year, all gang related…"

"I was at Florenc last night!" squirmed Abelard, visibly shaken by the revelation.

"Then you are lucky to have missed it," Svobodova replied, her hands resting on her hips and her face thin with stress. "All those years we spent fighting them, trying anything and everything we could to resist their takeover of our way of life. How we celebrated when the Revolution came and we were rulers of our own destiny again, or so we thought, how we were free at last from Russia's rule. Only now, nearly thirty years later, Russia has practically taken over again and used Capitalism to do it, with everyone too busy hating Muslims and gypsies to notice, especially with Myska whipping up trouble at every turn."

The already tense atmosphere in the room was now doubly heavy with the added layer of moroseness ladled on by Svobodova's lamentations, and Stone sought to break it by excusing himself from the scene.

"Well," he began, "all thing's considered, I think Greyson would prefer I didn't get too involved in any more bouts of diplomacy with the Russians at present. If that's everything, I'll get myself ready for the rally."

"I'll have a driver take you back to your apartment," Svobodova offered.

"No need," he replied, "I need to get a feel of the city first and I'd rather do that under my own steam. It makes sense for me to keep a low profile too."

"Very well," Svobodova agreed. "When you head to the rally, you can take the underground to Náměstí Míru, the Church is just outside. Radoslav will provide you with papers on your way out. In the meantime, it would be helpful Natalie if we could discuss strategy, perhaps an analysis of our opponent's key positions?"

"Of course," the Professor responded stiffly, her discomfort evident in her inflection.

"Then good luck in your endeavors today, Captain Stone, I look forward to discussing your findings."

She stretched out her hand to him, clasping his in her now familiar grip and he stood to leave, smiling to his new associates and inwardly relieved that he could work alone, at least for the day.

"Mind you don't trip," Abelard said as he rose, "It's the deepest subway in Europe if I'm right?"

Svobodova nodded.

"Eighty-seven meters," she confirmed with a dash of pride.

"Then I'll try and land on my feet."

Stone afforded them both a respectful nod of the head and turned briskly on his heels, eager to do the best job he could as quickly as he could, return to Britain and his boy and hopefully put this experience a considerably long distance behind him.

FOUR

CONFUSING THOUGH THE INTRICACIES of Prague's transport threatened to be, Stone had negotiated worse and took his place on the crowded tube train to the accompaniment of several frowns and one or two audible sniffs at the presence of the well dressed and imposing Captain and, more particularly, his skin tone. Prague, Stone had been led to believe, was a vibrant and cosmopolitan city which not only tolerated the communities which composed it, but actively celebrated them, and in most parts of the City through which he had spent the morning walking to get his bearings, that impression had proven true. Nonetheless it still saddened him to witness the backward glances and distrustful stares in his direction as he made his way through certain other streets, which no doubt mirrored roads in every other city and town in Europe, his own included.

Since the EU referendum back home, Britain had never quite felt quite at ease with itself. The atmosphere was a shade nastier, the people just a degree colder; the new tensions accompanied by the return to the country's streets of the kind of open racial abuse that had blighted Stone's childhood and which he had long hoped was dead and not just sleeping in the nation's heart. And though these days it was 'them bleedin' Polish' and 'those fuckin' Muslims'

THE PRAGUE ULTIMATUM

who bore the brunt of the resurgence of hateful ignorance, Stone knew that he and anyone sharing his colour very much remained secondary targets, tolerated but never quite wholly accepted, even if they were, for now, superseded by others. If London, Manchester and so many other cities in the UK had succumbed to the symptoms of racism in these last years, Stone couldn't really expect that Prague, or indeed anywhere else, would remain immune, and deep down he knew that the contagion had spread far across the continent and even beyond. And while politicians continued to fuel displacement and migrant crises ballooned, Stone knew it was a disease that showed little sign of abating.

The train heaved into the stop and Stone stepped out with a trickle of others onto the platform, heading up the escalator which stretched as high above him as Abelard had opined, and he freed his mind from his musings on the state of the world and focused on the task in hand. Reaching the top of the escalator, he stepped out of the station and found himself in a scene of quiet tranquillity. An ancient, twin-spired church of ornate authenticity jealously commanded attention, guarded as it was by meticulous greenery and a litter-less path framed by black metallic benches. To his delighted surprise, across from the square stood the resolute shell of a further Russian T54 tank, regally poised as though resentful of the ignorance afforded it by a population used to its presence.

Checking his watch, Stone bounded over with a grin of boyish enthusiasm on his face, drinking in the dull and dusty green of its armour as though it were a cloak of sovereignty adorning some triumphant Monarch. It was the real thing, Stone realised, not a model or a reconstruction, but a genuine and veteran T54 with all the character and experience one would expect from such a machine seeping from its very frame. It was a thing of beauty,

Stone thought, and said as much out loud, ducking under the tape around it and reaching his hand to pat the dusty and worn caterpillar track, only for a shrill voice to halt his movement.

Frowning, he turned around to the source of the cry, to see a balding, slightly rotund, middle aged man, jogging up to him, the remnants of some sauce coated wrap dropping from his other hand to the pavement as he did so.

"Hey! Don't touch the props!"

Stone lifted his hand away and smiled at the newcomer who, judging by his accent was British, from somewhere below London.

"I'm sorry, I didn't mean to intrude. Are you filming here today?"

The man grumbled. "If they ever get here, it was supposed to be this morning but there's some big delay at the last location so we're pushed back to this afternoon. This old baby is too expensive to move and so we have to look after it until they are ready."

He gestured to a small collection of similarly dressed stage hands a few metres away accompanied by their larger set security colleagues, who looked over at Stone with an air of nonchalant indifference.

"And now we have to wait for this fucking idiot to talk to his sheep before we can shoot, which means we'll have to redress the whole square…"

He lapsed into a barrage of swearwords, Stone smiling in sympathy.

"Not a fan of Mr Myska's gang?"

"No," the man spat adamantly, "and you won't want to hang around here too much longer when this lot start to get wound up, you don't exactly fit their idea of the perfect resident, if you get my drift?"

"Thanks, but I can look after myself," Stone said. "Is there often trouble at these things?"

The man leaned closer and lowered his voice, flicking his eyes around him as he spoke.

"You don't want to know."

"Try me."

"Well, If you believe Myska, if you read his books or watch his speeches, he says he hates violence, he condemns anyone who uses it, he won't have those people in his movement. That's how he stays 'respectable'."

"But?"

He leaned closer still.

"These idiots I'm working with," he said, his voice almost a whisper, "some of them support him, I have to be careful what I say, they don't like when I talk bad about him, and what's more most of them are Russian…"

"But?"

"Well, see… I'm an ex-pat; been here for years, moved here after de-mob, met myself a nice Czech lady and until the fucking Brexit disaster and the arse fell out of the pound, I was living 'happily ever after' you know? Now all of a sudden my pension isn't worth as much and I have to make ends meet as a bloody roadie for the film crews."

"De-mob? You were a soldier?"

"Queen's Royal Hussars," the man said with pride, his back straightening in subconscious salute to his regiment's name, "Barry's the name, Barry Hendry, Sergeant as was."

"Lincoln Stone," came the response, the pair shaking hands in mutual respect, "Captain, RTR."

"Sir!" Barry clicked his heels, a smile on his face, which gave way to a gradual dawning.

"Hold, on… THE Captain Stone?"

The Officer nodded with a slight reluctance, unsure if his thus far warm reception would continue. He needn't have worried, Barry grabbing his hand once more and shaking it with a passionate ferocity.

"It's an honour sir, a real honour. It's a bloody disgrace what those bastards in Parliament and the Press have been saying about you; fucking cheek is what it is. How many of those bloody desk warmers have had to go through the shit we had to, eh? A bloody disgrace, a VC like you 'n all…"

Stone's appreciation of the warm words were genuine, but he balked at any notions of hero worship.

"I'll survive," he smiled, "if I could come through Afghanistan I can come through this. You were telling me about Myska?"

Barry's face turned serious again and he gestured subtly to the group of roadies he had come over from.

"You see the lad over there? The one with the goatee, a bit on the skinny side?"

"Yeah?"

"That's Petřík. I keep my eyes open for him, give him an arm around the shoulder when he needs it and a kick up the arse if the situation demands it, just like I did for all of my lads on the line back in the day. He's a good kid, hard worker, give you the shirt off his back he would, I mean really, no-one would say a bad word about him. But that was before."

Stone raised an inquizative eyebrow.

"Before what?"

"Young Petřík went and fell in love with an immigrant didn't he? The wrong kind of immigrant."

Stone grimaced, instinctively realising where the story was heading.

"The girl was from Libya, she came over to get away from all the chaos and shit after Gaddafi got done. Lovely girl, lovely," Barry shook his head, his eyes dropping for a moment as he recounted the painful memory. "When they got married, the whole village threw them a huge party; bugger me I got so drunk that night I could barely see the next morning..."

He began to stutter over his words, clearly troubled by something. Stone placed his hand on his shoulder and frowned in concern.

"What happened?" he softly pressed.

"They were attacked. Not long after the bomb, they were walking in Malá Strana, Myska had been speaking there earlier that day, making one of his big speeches about how it's impossible to tell which migrants are real and which are terrorists in disguise; the usual shite he spouts. Three men attacked them, young Petřík he tried to fight back but they knocked him out cold and with him out of the way, they... bloody hell, if only I'd been there." He gave in again to the lump in his throat, heaving a shaky breath into his lungs to counter it. "She'd been pregnant."

A torrent of revulsion enveloped Stone and he dropped his head, tensing his stomach to quell the rising pain the revelation had inspired.

Regaining his composure, the man nodded over to the Square, where people were beginning to mill about in anticipation of Myska's arrival.

"Look at them," he sneered. "Even if I could believe that Myska wasn't a violent man himself, that he thought he was doing the right thing and wasn't full of hatred, every word he says is sweet fucking honey to the people who are and he spends every day of his life making it worse."

Stone was lost for words. There were no remarks, no utterances he could make which could either express his sympathies or ease the young man or of his friend, Barry, and so, for a precious few moments, he simply stood with him, their heads respectively bowed as the bustle in the square grew louder.

A shout came over from the man's colleagues, gesturing for him to return to them and he straightened himself in readiness.

"I have to go," he said, "if you please sir, don't touch my tank and if you're taking an interest in that bastard, make sure you look after yourself."

"I will," Stone promised, "and it's Lincoln; I hope I bump into you again."

"Thank you, sir. I mean Lincoln," he answered, smiling again in appreciation, "if you're planning to be in town for a while pop along and watch one of the shoots if you like; they don't exactly stick to the schedule but if you hang around one of these beauties long enough we're bound to show up."

"I will, thanks. I can't say much but I'm taking a close look at our friend Mr. Myska, and I'll be doing everything I can to make sure shit like your friend has been through never happens again."

He offered his hand to the former Sergeant who took it and gave a professional, military nod of the head, before turning back to his work mates and walking away.

Stone watched him return then moved back across the Square, offering a last admiring glance to the tank as he went.

A group of people were gathering before a small and apparently hastily assembled wooden platform, their number added to by newcomers hurrying past Stone from the station behind him, and others scurrying from side streets in all directions, congregating before the makeshift stage. Stone estimated their number at around two hundred, and while slightly larger than most extremist gatherings he had heard of, the outward 'normality' of the people comprising it was unusual. Well-tailored and well groomed, the crowd was every bit a snapshot of everyday life; the expected loose assortment of tattooed skin heads and beer bellied malcontents nowhere to be seen, their places taken instead by fresh faces and apple pie smiles, eagerly awaiting the arrival of the man who justified their everyday prejudices. Far more of the usual suspects made up the counter demonstration held back by police, way across the other side of the square; an assortment of stark hair colours and starker slogans interspersed with everyday folk in jeans and trainers, typifying the predominantly young group who swore and gestured their contempt at the waiting listeners.

Stone hung back from both groups, idling over to an elaborate archway leading from the square, from where he could keep both groups in sight and leant against it. For an age, it seemed as though nothing would happen until a black, immaculately shining but unpretentious car sidled into view, slowing down as it passed the counter demonstrators as if to encourage their cries, before coming to a halt a short distance from stage. A security guard leapt from the passenger seat and stood by the rear door, holding it open as the occupant emerged to a cacophony of deafening applause, mixed with the boos and cries of the protestors further away.

Oscar Myska.

The politician paused for a while to work the crowd with a Barnumesque showmanship, his grin wide, his handshaking strong, the odd flattering word of thanks steeped in political sincerity, before he stepped up onto the platform and raised his hands to his supporters, urging them, not too forcefully, to stop their cheering.

Stone ignored the theatrics and assessed him coldly, as he had so many enemies before, and could not help but be impressed. He was a man still early enough into his forties to get away with being called young, though the flecks of grey in his otherwise dark brown and casually brushed hair added to an image of political maturity. He wore his collar open but, surprisingly to Stone, not tieless. Instead, a thin, knitted affair hung loosely under the open button which accentuated the casual 'everyman' look he pulled off so well, a look completed by the unbuttoned, off the peg Navy blue suit he wore. Everything about the man's image screamed that he was 'one of the people' a man reluctantly pressed into political life by the pressures of the modern world and the crises facing the continent. He was here, his image said, because he had to be, not because he wanted to be. He was not one of the well to do, privately tailored, political elite who ignored the concerns of the people while feathering their own nests. He was one of them, a Man of The People.

Stone half smiled as the words of his Colonel flitted through his memory. 'When the Devil shows up,' the grizzled old war horse used to say, warning his troops of the dangers of insurgents and suicide bombers, 'he won't be the horned red bloke walking around on goat legs. Evil is attractive, charming; it offers you what you think you want and makes you feel foolish for not taking it. Remember that'.

"Yes Sir," Stone said out loud, smiling as he repeated the mantra of old and acknowledging its appropriateness now.

The applause of the crowd gave way to a semblance of silence, interspersed with chanting from the protestors nearby, as the people gazed longingly upwards, yearning for the words of their hero who shushed them gently into silence and leant closer in to the microphone.

"Kamarádi," he began, " Nemohu vám dostatečně poděkovat za to, že jste!"

The crowd began to whoop and cheer, each round of applause serving only to widen the grin on the politician's face, while Stone laughed out loud at his sudden, delayed realisation that he had no idea what this man was saying. Shaking his head at the blind spot in his thinking, he reasoned that it wasn't quite the handicap he supposed; assuming Myska would be serving up a course of his regular diatribe, then his words themselves were not the most important thing to learn right now, much more so were the actions of the crowd and the Captain intensified his observations.

The speech droned on, interspersed with the regular cheers of Myska's devotees and the just as regular condemnation of the protestors, but free from anything that could be classed as a disturbance, which fitted Stone's expectations precisely. If Myska's modus operandi thus far was the avoidance of the grim pantomime which typically accompanied Far Right groupings, then his rallies were unlikely to involve anything more extreme than intense flag flying and a few verses of the National Anthem; it was the event's periphery which interested Stone.

An extended, semi-coital cheer signalled the end of the political orgy, and Myska stepped down from his box and moved deceptively speedily but thoroughly charmingly through the crowd, pausing occasionally to acquiesce to 'selfies' or accept adoringly vigorous handshakes. This was a showman, an illusionist at work; a ringmaster performing in the centre of his own personal circus; or more accurately, Stone thought, a man who truly understood and encouraged the decent of political leadership to the level of reality television. And, Stone understood, like all illusionists, the man in the middle was just the distraction, the eye-catcher designed to steal away focus from what was going on behind the curtain.

Stone hung back in the alcove, allowing his eyes to scan over the dispersing crowd as they shuffled and slunk back to their everyday lives, some hurling reciprocal abuse at the restrained protestors across the square, some fixing the Captain himself with brief, but hostile glances, the odd one lingering, too fuelled by alcohol to immediately disperse and looking to Stone as though they were in search of trouble, then looking away with the realisation that the silent Stone could likely provide too much of it. Such people were a nuisance but no more so than the average bar room drunk on a Saturday night and Stone thought it unlikely they could inflict the kind of damage that Barry had described if they were unable even to hold a gaze effectively.

One man though met Stone's eyes and didn't break away, and it was he who intrigued the soldier.

Stood away from Stone, across the square, similarly still and guarded, the man fixed his eyes on Stone's, a deliberate and unnerving smile forming on his bulky, cruel face. The man epitomised what Stone had expected to see when he agreed to attend the rally and he wondered when he had slunk onto the scene, realising too that the ugly, brutish face was one of those captured in Svobodova's folder. He was big and obviously strong, the lack of hair on his tattooed head compensated by the full, unwashed and untidy beard, itself matching the dirty black clothes the figure wore.

The stragglers finally beginning to shuffle on, Stone looked across to see a young Romani boy, of no more than ten or eleven years, heaving a bagful of shopping with him across the square, ducking and sliding through the dispersing crowd, a few of whom fixed him with hostile stares while a couple attempted to jostle and sneer at him as he made his way through, forcing him to seek his escape via the alleyway guarded by the bearded man. As the boy heaved past him, the bearded man's grin grew wider and he pointed at the scurrying figure, though his eyes remained fixed on Stone's, fierce, challenging, stirring memories in the Captain of the bullies and tormentors of his youth and awakening him immediately to the thug's intentions. In a heartbeat, the bearded man set off after the child, who dropped his bag in fear and fled, twisting down the cobbled streets rolling out in front of him. At once, Stone ran in pursuit, grim faced and determined, charging through the milling people in the square and spinning into the street the pair had run to.

Though his rival had a head start, Stone moved swiftly through the sparsely populated cobbled streets, his soldier's skill and reconnaissance experience overriding their unfamiliarity, his only surprise being the speed with which the bulky, unfit looking man was able to move. He spotted the youngster, weaving past the occasional bystanders and looking over his shoulder, his face etched into an expression of dread, before he finally rounded a corner and disappeared out of sight, followed by his would-be assaulter. Stone quickened his pace, feeling the burn of his thigh muscles as they screamed in resentment at his sudden break from the last few week's inactivity. Reaching the corner and skidding around it, Stone slowed his pace and looked around in frustration. He was back where he'd started, the Square stretching out before him, a grim-faced Barry and his more jovial colleagues away to the side, debating the intricacies of Myska's speech in the shadow of the imperious T54.

A sudden movement flitted past the corner of Stone's eye and he turned his head to see the youngster ducking into the entrance to the subway, and the Captain ran over in pursuit, scanning the entrance for sight of him. The bearded man was nowhere to be seen but Stone soon found the terrified boy pressing himself against the battered ticket machine that stood at the entrance to the station.

"Hey," Stone began quietly, cursing his lack of linguistic knowledge to calm the boy, "It's ok, it's alright." He walked slowly, arms outstretched towards the small, frightened child who pressed himself still further to the wall.

"Ne, ne, ne, ne!" The boy became hysterical as Stone approached, halting the Captain who tried again to placate the youngster.

"I'm not going to hurt you," he promised, raising his eyebrow as the boy shook his head.

"Not you," the boy finally shouted in heavily accented English, pointing behind Stone, "Him!"

Stone barely had time to curse his own stupidity before the heavy fist connected with his temple, stunning him and sending him backwards towards the noisy escalator. Grabbing the side rail, he tried to shake the scrambling from his brain and straighten up to face his foe, before a second fist sent him sprawling on the downward slope.

Stone scraped his fingers across the metal steps, flinging himself to the side to avoid the boot directed at his head. He stared up into the still grinning face of the bearded man, who raised his heavy leg once more to deliver the coup de grace. This time Stone was ready, and he grabbed the kicking limb, forcing its owner off balance and onto his back on the moving stairs. The attacker, though strong, was bulkier than Stone and struggled to rise as the Captain scrambled past him to the higher ground, aiming his own kick, which caught the assailant a glancing blow.

His senses returning, Stone took in the full length of the drop below them; what was it Abelard had said, the deepest subway in Europe? Stone remembered the escalator's length to be some eighty-seven metres, with most of those still below them, and he didn't fancy taking the fall to find out for sure. Dodging another heavy fist, Stone instinctively raised his arms, adopting the boxing stance of his military training, dodging the flying arms of his opponent and countering with hard strikes of his own, until the ox-like figure flung his whole self at Stone, knocking him on his back and crushing the breath from his body, all the time grinning his disgusting grin.

With the weight of his attacker bearing down on him and his strength depleting, Stone summoned the reserves of his energies and threw his head up, hard into his attacker's face, relishing the crunch of bone and splattering of warm blood the action brought. As the bearded man lurched backwards, reaching for his face, Stone wriggled his legs free of the giant frame and, with his feet on the bleeding man's belly, pushed with all his might, sending his attacker tumbling backwards down the moving stairwell, his beefy arms clawing fruitlessly for grip against the stainless steel sides, before landing with a crunch at the bottom, laying there sprawled and still.

Filling his assaulted lungs with the stale, warm air of the subway, Stone rose to his feet, brushing himself off and hopping over the fallen body as the escalator completed its decent. Crouching down, he reached out to check for a pulse, only to reel when a hand rose like lightening to clamp down on his wrist, while the other arm struck once more against the side of the Captain's head. Dazed, Stone felt himself dragged to the edge of the platform, the cold breeze from the tunnel bringing him to his senses. He was on his back, his head and shoulders hung over the edge of the platform, the still grinning bearded man straddling his legs and holding his arms tightly down. In the distance he could hear the approach of the train, and he fought to stop panic clouding his mind.

Stone was not afraid to die, far from it; he had faced that final journey to the Greenfields countless times and called it a career. But he couldn't die here, now…. He frantically wriggled under the stronger man's hold, his eyes darting around searching desperately for something, anything to help him, until the twin beams of the oncoming train burst through the blackness of the tunnel and into his face, accompanied by the angry howling of its horn and the laughter of his grinning murderer. There was no escape, none. No, NO! His boy…!

With the horns at their loudest and the train as close as it could be, Stone felt the weight of his assailant lifted, the man suddenly falling over his head, and himself pulled sharply back from the platform's edge. He watched for a brief eternity as the bearded man's grin turned to a look of abject horror as he dropped onto the tracks to be instantly pounced on by the roaring train, his cry accompanied by the impotent screech of futile brakes.

Stone bolted upright, confused and unsure. A bony hand reached out, helping him to his feet and he stared into the eyes of a wrinkled, dishevelled man with unkempt grey hair and eyes as fierce as any Stone could remember.

"You've been fucking spotted mate," the man hissed. "Get the fuck out of here before they start asking questions." He nodded over to the train where Stone saw a shocked and pale driver radioing the incident while stuck passengers stared through dirty Perspex windows at him.

"But wait, who…?" Stone turned back but the stranger was gone, the platform deserted. As angry passengers began to bang on the still closed doors of the train, desperate to get out, Stone turned to the upwards escalator, leaping up the steps three at a time, gasping fresher air into his lungs with each bound. At the top, the boy he'd sought to rescue was nowhere to be seen and Stone tried his best to appear relaxed and decided to get back to his apartment and figure out what had happened. He hadn't gone more than three steps before a figure stepped into his path, causing him once more to recoil in readiness for violence.

"Captain? Captain Stone?"

The delicate Welsh lilt at once brought him back from the edge and he smiled into the concerned face of Professor Abelard.

"Professor," he breathed, "what are you doing here?"

"Never mind me, what about you? You look like you've been in the wars."

"Not my usual kind of battlefield," he laughed, "but just as dangerous."

The concern on Abelard's face was joined by a quizzical eyebrow, eventually giving way to a smile.

"Really?" she grinned. "Tell me over a drink?"

FIVE

IT WAS ONLY A SHORT WHILE LATER that Stone had relayed his tale to Abelard before reclining back in his seat on the edge of the beautiful Old Town Square. Contrary to his expectation, the news seemed to bring her to life, the contrast to her persona earlier in the day stark to say the least, and she quizzed him with eagerness and no trace of fear on the details of his fight and rescue by the strange bedraggled man, until he had to almost insist upon changing the subject. His telephone conversation with Radoslav had been entirely different, curt to the point of irritability. The young officer had insisted on only the facts before bluntly assuring him that CCTV records would be taken care of, a call to the police was not necessary and that the Captain should present himself at Svobodova's office later that afternoon, ready to explain in person.

Not far from them, a multitude of accents and skin tones bustled in the hourly tourist ritual to witness Death tolling his bell to the procession of dead souls guarding the Astronomical clock face high above. Not a single cry of 'scum', 'immigrant' or profane demands to leave accompanied their presence. As cameras flashed sightseers cooed at the foot of the tourist trap.

Abelard returned to the table from freshening up and gave the Captain a warmer smile than he had previously had from her, lifting her glass towards him.

"Well, here's to working together, Captain Stone," she grinned.

"I'm enjoying it already, Professor Abelard," he smiled back, grateful for the easing of tensions between them. In truth, he thought, she seemed like a different person to the rigid professional who had woken him that morning and resisted his attempts at conversation on the journey to meet Svobodova. Whereas then her face had been stern and her voice austere, there was a bright openness to her demeanour now, as though her 'business' character was an uncomfortable item of clothing she dressed in each morning and was keen to discard as quickly as possible.

"I suppose I should toast Jonathan for making it happen, too."

"I don't envy you," Stone said, at the mention of Greyson, "working for your ex can't be easy."

She huffed.

"Well, at least he's not here to rub my nose in it," she said distractedly, "unlike a certain Prime Minister of our acquaintance."

"What makes you think they're sleeping together?"

"Intuition," she said. "He's forever making trips to this part of the world, or 'bumping into her' at conferences the world over, it's become a joke now."

"It could just be a coincidence," Stone suggested, "they are both 'world leaders' after all, and Greyson needs to drum up all the support for Britain he can get after Brexit."

"I might believe that if he didn't have form," she replied, cynicism poisoning her accent. "You know his junior minister, the one who died?"

"Yeah, she dropped dead of a drug overdose, if I remember rightly, what was her name?"

"Caroline Bland," she spat, the bitterness still apparent. "That was here, in Prague. I'd suspected it for months and he always denied it, but after she died he finally admitted he'd been fucking her. That's why I divorced him; the lecherous git's just like his Dad…"

Stone, no stranger to broken relationships had few words to offer other than the standard issue perfunctory 'sorry' which he duly offered, only for her to shake her head and smile.

"I'm not stupid," she said, "I know what goes on when you mix with the political class, but actually being faced with the reality of it still hurts. Ah, what's the bloody point? I don't even know why I'm bothered, he's free and single and he can get his leg over with whoever he likes. And what about you? Any lady back home eagerly awaiting your return?"

Stone laughed at her change of tack.

"Ha! If only. No, I'm a single Dad, my wife left years ago and I can't honestly say I've been in much of a rush to get involved again, not seriously anyway."

Her eyes narrowed slightly, catching him a little off guard before she picked up.

"Sorry to hear that, do you mind if I ask what happened?" She asked the question gently, non-judgementally and to his surprise Stone found himself answering.

"She met someone whose battles weren't fought in deserts or fields thousands of miles away." He grimaced slightly, taking another mouthful of ale. "I can't really blame her, being partnered to a professional soldier must be hard and I was frequently not there, even when I was, if you know what I mean."

"Forgive me," Abelard replied, "but it's unusual for a mum to leave her child, isn't it? From what I've heard it's usually the other way around."

"I won't blame her for her choices." Stone was adamant. "That she left meant I got to keep him and that boy is the single most important thing in my entire existence, even if he is a pain in the arse." He placed his glass back on the table and focused on Abelard with honesty in his eyes. "He's my reason for living."

She smiled back, awkwardly, seemingly stuck for something to say, and Stone's chivalrous instinct kicked in, pushing him to pick up the conversation.

"Anyway," he smiled, "it seems heartbreak and separation are two things we have in common."

"Divorcees of the world unite," she laughed back.

"It was all a long time ago anyway," he said, "I'm quite happy without her but I'll admit that every now and then I'll catch myself thinking about her, sometimes hoping she spares me a thought from time to time."

"Bullshit."

The word pricked the bubble of delicate melancholy that had swollen around their conversation, at first causing Stone's eyebrow to rise in surprise, before he felt a snigger begin to rise from inside, quickly becoming a laugh.

"Bullshit?"

"Bullshit!"

Abelard echoed his laughter, tilting her glass to her lips before elaborating on her exclamation.

"You don't hope she 'spares you a thought from time to time,' that's just what you tell yourself. What you really hope, deep down, is that one day she'll look in the mirror and ask herself why the fuck she ever let you go, then spend every day for the rest of her life wishing and praying that she was lying in bed next to you, instead of whichever lightweight façade she's really waking up to. You loved her so much that losing her damn near destroyed you and deep down you want her to go through the same. Not out of cruelty mind, but because true love brings us all to the edge of destruction and if she goes through that too, then it means she really did love you after all."

Stone continued to grin at the bluntness of the Professor's words, nodding along in faux acceptance of her analysis.

"So, you're saying I love her enough to bring her to the edge of destruction?"

"If you like."

The Professor's response was as cold and concise as Stone imagined her lectures were, devoid of the joviality that had marked their conversation to that point and, he supposed, offering a glimpse of the anguish gone through during her own divorce and her own current feelings about Greyson. He ignored the new inflection, eager to extend the relief from tension their exchange had granted him.

"Well each man kills the thing he loves, or so Oscar Wilde reckoned," Stone chuckled.

"Maybe not quite kill, but nearly."

"And I thought I was supposed to be the morose one," he laughed, tipping his own glass to his lips.

"It's true though," she grinned in return, "That's why human beings hate to be single; no matter how many family or friends we might have around us, without a partner, or 'significant other' or whatever, we can never truly shake the feeling that if we disappeared into the ether, it really wouldn't take too long for everyone to get over us and get on with their lives, maybe occasionally 'sparing us a thought'. When what we really want, if we're honest with ourselves, is for our loss to mean something terrible, something devastating; maybe even so devastating it could destroy."

Though her smile had returned, it remained several degrees below warm and Stone felt the focus in her eyes drifting, enough to make him seek to regain her attention by clinking his glass loudly to the table.

"Not the most selfless of adverts for romantic love," he quietly responded, mirroring her smile's reduction in width, though unwilling to match its new coldness.

"No," she agreed, "but near destruction can be a good thing. It allows one to rebuild; create something stronger from the same raw materials, something better...I must admit though, I was always terrified of getting my heart broken, I suppose I'm lucky I made it this far before it happened."

"You should never be scared of a broken heart," Stone responded, "pain just reminds you you're alive, builds character."

"So it damn well should build character," she snapped the words, "it crushes the old one after all. I'm not the woman I used to be. I'm not even sure I know who I am anymore...so much for love."

Stone smiled warmly back at her. That this woman who only a few hours ago was so cold and yet was now so open puzzled him, as did his own willingness to respond in kind when he would typically dry up and retreat within himself rather than engage in such conversations. This had been a strange couple of days, stranger no doubt for the Professor with her added emotional involvement. He supposed that her recognising him as a kindred fish out of the bowl and latching onto him was essentially a coping mechanism to get through an uncomfortable assignment. Well that was fine with him, it seemed like a damn fine strategy given the circumstances and despite himself, Stone was beginning to greatly enjoy her company and saw no reason to limit it when they would likely be stuck here for God knows how long.

Draining the last of his drink, he met her eyes.

"Maybe you're right, maybe love and romance is intrinsically selfish, but that doesn't mean all love is."

"No?"

"No. Parental love, when it's done right, is just about the most selfless emotion you can experience."

She laughed at his remark, though a little cheekily and without condescension.

"Really? I don't know, I've always thought that people have children because they want them; it seems a pretty selfish desire to me, to force existence on someone without their consent, just because you like to cuddle babies or fancy a spare kidney on hand in your old age."

He smiled his own melancholic smile in response, his rich voice deep and soft, but his brow betraying his intensity.

"Well maybe you're right, but I swear, once that child is born and it looks at you with pure, utter trust in its eyes, you realise that everything you thought was love before was nothing compared to this, this wondrous, terrifying feeling that grabs hold of you and won't let go."

He kept his eyes on hers, to enforce the passion of his gentle words.

"It's all consuming, it burns perpetually inside every inch, every fibre of you. Marriages can break up, relationships crumble but nothing, no slight, no wrong, no insult, no argument, no betrayal will ever diminish the love you have for this beautiful child. And when they grow and they want to spread their wings, ignore you, when you for a time stop being their most valued source of guidance and encouragement, it never stops for you. And even when, in their youthful, righteous passion they lash out against you and the things they think you've stood and fought for, when they reject you in some impetuous rush to find their 'own way' in the world, even then, there is not one torture, not one solitary agony you would not eternally endure, just to save them a moment of pain…"

Stone paused to quell the lump rising in his throat and blink away the threat of tears.

"And that's real love."

Her eyes hadn't moved from his as he spoke and she remained in silence for what seemed like an age, as though she was mulling over some great conundrum, the corner of her mouth raising slightly as she stared. Eventually, she picked up her glass and drained it of the last vestiges before standing and throwing her light jacket over her shoulders.

"Come along Captain," she quietly said. "We don't want to keep the Prime Minister waiting."

The veil of professional silence which the Professor had worn earlier in the day enveloped her once more as they journeyed together to Svobodova's office, reinforcing Stone's view of his companion's coping strategies. Not that he minded the silence, it gave him chance to mentally prepare his report on the day's events in a more concise and orderly fashion in readiness for what he expected would not be so avuncular an inquisition as he had just enjoyed with Abelard. His apprehension proved well founded as he sat before Svobodova's desk recounting the tale of the bearded man and his ill-fated attempt on Stone's life with military precision, devoid of emotion or exaggeration, while Svobodova herself listened intently, exhaustion deeply apparent in her eyes.

"I must apologise Captain," she began after pausing for a moment to collect her thoughts, "for your less than warm welcome to our country. You are injured?"

"I've had worse," he answered. "What hurts more is not knowing who he was, other than recognising him from your folder. It does though tell me straight away that Myska isn't quite the squeaky-clean man of the people he makes himself out to be."

"You're sure Myska is connected to him?"

"Undoubtedly. I doubt very much that this guy was the only muscle on the scene, looking for undesirables. I suppose the best word for them is 'bouncers.'"

"That would be pretty standard for any extremist movement," Abelard interceded from her chair alongside Stone. "In the old days, they'd be wearing black shirts and jackboots but it makes sense in a movement that defines itself as separate to and above all that kind of thing to make their security arrangements more 'unofficial.'"

"That old 'plausible deniability' chestnut again," Stone added.

"Korva..," Svobodova swore under her breath, "More's the pity you couldn't bring him in for questioning, if we could have established that link between Myska and the violence…"

"I didn't kill him," Stone snapped a little too defensively, "and there was no way for me to stop the man who did."

"I know, I know, I'm not blaming you Captain Stone." Svobodova stood up from behind her desk and opened the cabinet behind her, taking out a glass bottle and three small shot glasses, deftly pouring the clear liquid from the bottle into each of them. "Believe me, I've already viewed the CCTV footage, you had a lucky escape."

She handed a glass each to Stone and Abelard and knocked her own straight back in one go. Stone did likewise and grimaced at the unfamiliar, harsh taste burning its way down his throat, while a quick glance at the Professor confirmed her similar reaction.

"But it begs the question, not only who was your assailant, but who was your guardian angel?"

"Greyson said he had a man, an operative on the ground here, does it look like him?"

"Jonathan isn't in the habit of introducing me to his agents," Svobodova shook her head, "save for seeking my consent for their presence, but as far as I'm aware he is in Brno investigating Myska's Party funding..."

"Well whoever he is he must have been tailing me since I arrived last night, which means both he and Myska know I'm here and presumably why. My late bearded friend had me marked from the start and not just because of my colour."

"You don't think...?"

They turned to Professor Abelard who shook her head at her own brief words.

"Go on," Svobodova urged, gently.

"I was going to suggest the man who saved you could belong to The Institute."

Stone raised his eyebrow at the possibility while Svobodova sat heavily back into her chair as though mention of The Institute swept a fresh wave of melancholy over her tired features.

"Think about it," Abelard continued, "we know The Institute uses operatives from all over Europe, we know they've tried to interfere in Czechoslovak affairs before. Is it beyond the realms of possibility that they are equally concerned about what Myska might be up to and have their own man on the scene?"

"Why would he interfere to save me?" Stone queried.

"Well from the way Jonathan described them to me, and from you own experiences Ma'am," she nodded to Svobodova, "they sound essentially pragmatic in nature within the boundaries of their overall objectives. If you're here doing the legwork for them, why would they hinder you? And for that matter why would they let anyone else hinder you? Far better from their point of view to let you get on with digging the dirt while they watch from the sidelines."

Svobodova refilled her glass, smiling slightly at both Stone's and Abelard's polite refusal of a second drink.

"Well it's a theory, certainly," she mused, "and one that fits the facts as we have them. You might very well have your own Institute Protector, Captain Stone."

"I've had more comforting thoughts," Stone huffed, "but who knows? Maybe he'll get the chance to save my life again; Institute Guardian or not, I have to get closer to Myska, find some way of getting you that positive link if I've any hope of Greyson making good on his promises."

Svobodova's eyes dropped to her desk at the frustration in Stone's voice and the military man shot a glance to Abelard, whose own gaze had likewise dropped, instantly regretting allowing his annoyance to show. Though they had been in his life for only a few hours, Stone had instantly respected and admired Svobodova and Abelard for their respective strength and intelligence and he had no wish to add further discomfort to what must be a difficult situation for both women.

"Anyway," he said, breaking the awkward silence, "enough of that for now, it's been a long day."

"Yes, of course, you must be exhausted. You get some sleep and we can talk again in the morning."

She walked them both to her office door, her smile returning. "And thank you both of you again for all your help today, I can't express how much I appreciate it."

"It's nothing," Stone said quietly, ducking through the grand door, "Good evening."

He turned back in time to see Svobodova stopping Abelard by the door and clasping her warmly by the hand. The Professor reciprocated and smiled back at the politician, the two women briefly pausing in an unspoken moment of understanding before Svobodova delicately pulled away and retreated behind the closed door of her office.

"Well," Abelard began, her professional persona beginning to melt once more as she caught up with Stone, "an interesting first day on the job. I suppose I'd better find a supermarket and get some supplies in; we might be here a while."

"You can't have had much sleep," Stone responded, "early night for you, is it?"

"Actually," Abelard countered, her wicked smile beginning to show itself, "I wondered if you fancied getting another drink?"

SIX

AFTER BRIEFLY PARTING TO FRESHEN UP at their respective abodes, the pair had returned to the gothic beauty of an Old Town Square, nervous laughter punctuating their ill-informed debate as to which of the myriad of narrow cobbled streets they should elect to explore. The Professor sported a knee length black cocktail dress, perfect for the warm Prague night, while Stone himself was dressed in dark jeans and a casual jacket over a navy blue cotton shirt. The nervous laughter continued as they walked, arms linked, past an array of gaudy souvenir shops, offering a seemingly infinite assortment of crystal ornaments, amber jewellery and painted wooden marionettes in between the racks of t-shirts, towels and postcards, all stamped with the unmistakeable image of the Prague skyline under stylized Czech lettering. All around them, the early evening streets offered the delights of tourist friendly consumerism; stalls, eateries and museums of everything from Communism and sex to medieval torture.

They had continued walking until the river was in sight, the foreboding majesty of the imperious Tower guarding the entrance to the Charles Bridge just across the road from them.

Running out of choices as they neared the end of the street, Stone had spotted the elaborately framed and inviting entrance of what looked like a wine bar, tucked discreetly between buildings, lights illuminating its four-storey stretch to the sky.

Stepping through the door, Stone took in the bustling ambience of the small bar area and the fully occupied tables around it. The white walls were adorned with a variety of racks, each housing a multitude of bottles of various shades of red, while corners and crevices were filled with deep, tall refrigerators housing an array of whites, roses and champagne.

Touching the Professor's waist, Stone began to guide her further into the bar, only to be stopped in his tracks by the protestations of an immaculately dressed waiter who moved quickly towards them, waving his arms.

"No room, sorry!" A tinge of desperation was evident in the waiter's voice as he approached them.

"You must have something," Stone offered his most charming smile and his hand to the waiter, who swiftly and surreptitiously pocketed the note it contained.

"You wait downstairs," he smiled, "in the club. I call you, twenty minutes."

He gestured towards an alcove away from the bar, through which Stone saw a deep staircase descending into blackness.

Nodding his agreement, Stone and the Professor made for the steps, thumping dance music greeting their descent, and they emerged from a small stone tunnel into a vast basement area, filled with an ambience and a clientele totally at odds with the venue they had stepped down from seconds earlier. A bar, fully stocked with a wide array of beers and spirits stood at the back of the main room, while alcoves in the wall offered views of a stage in a lower basement a few steps away, around which casually dressed and highly inebriated punters were eagerly gathering.

Stone smiled at the contrast with the upper level and was pleased to see his expression mirrored in the Professor's face.

"Well, twenty minutes shouldn't be too long," he grinned, shouting over the thump of what was evidently passing for music.

"A lot can happen in twenty minutes," Abelard grinned, mischievously, "I'll have a spritzer please."

Stone returned from the bar to find Abelard seated in one of the alcoves overlooking the stage and passed the glass to her as he sat down.

"Cheers!" The Captain clinked his pint glass against the spritzer and shouted the word, just in time for the tuneless noise to stop, giving way to murmured chatter and the drunken laughter.

"Well thank God for that," he laughed.

"Not a music fan then?"

"Oh, that was music?" Stone replied, "I thought someone had just had a stroke and collapsed on a mixing desk."

She laughed at his comment and took a sip from her drink.

"Not quite your cup of tea, in other words," she grinned, "maybe the younger generation would appreciate it a little more."

Stone's smile dipped a little and he dropped his eyes to his drink for a moment.

"I'm sure my lad would love it," he sighed.

Abelard's face betrayed her concern and she reached out to put a hand on his knee.

"You're too hard on yourself," she said gently. "A single dad, trying to balance parenthood with a military career? It can't have been easy. You should give yourself more credit."

He patted her hand in return, looking up again and smiling.

"No-one will ever convince me I was a good enough father," he sighed, "you try your best, you work hard at it, you do everything because you think it's the right way to do it, or hope that it is, but really you haven't a clue, you're just winging it."

"If you ask me, that's true of the whole adult world," Abelard laughed, "we're all just winging it."

It's funny," he said, "I used to have all these grand designs of what I'd be like as a parent, I'd always imagined I'd be like one of those hippy parents you see around, you know? No slapped backsides, no raised voices... But it didn't turn out that way. I've slapped when a stern word would do, shouted when a hug was needed and I'm not sure I ever learned from my mistakes. I was every bit the disciplinarian old bastard I always swore I wouldn't be."

"That's the soldier in you," Abelard replied cheekily, her reciprocal smile helping Stone relax further into her company, countering the unwelcome memories which scurried cruelly through his mind.

"Ah, the soldier in me..." He looked at her, suddenly intensively, eager to ensure her full understanding. "Did you know I've been a soldier since the Falklands? That's when they pinned the Victoria Cross to my chest and called me a hero. I've lost comrades, lost blood on more battlefields than I can remember. In the old days, it was the thought of honouring my father that got me through, but then, *he* was born. And every tour, every conflict that came along, was only tolerable by the thought of going home to see him, my darling boy. And finally I'd return home from the fight, every vein just bursting with the urge to hold him, love him, but all I'd end up doing is shouting, disciplining him, trying almost desperately to make sure he 'grew up right'..."

Abelard countered his intensity, spreading her warm smile wider.

"You're not alone there," she began, "I have a friend who does exactly the same; she gets so worried about the state of the world that she lays it on thick to her daughter to make sure she's ready to face it. And she's no soldier, she works for the Council!"

Her grin was infectious and Stone acknowledged her efforts.

"We all have our own battlefields," he said. "There was one time, I remember it like it was yesterday. He had got his school report and it was brilliant, I mean he's always been clever, but this time it was really, really good. I was on a tour, but managed to ring to congratulate him and tell him how proud I was of him."

Stone raised his glass and drew deeply from it, shaking his head just slightly at the rawness of the memory, his eyes lost somewhere over Abelard's shoulder.

"I ended up shouting at him, pissed off by some trivial comeback he'd made, or for the way he made it, I don't even remember."

Emptying the heavy glass, he softly replaced it on the table, his grip refusing to slip from it as his thoughts continued on their trail.

"I always wanted him to be a rebel, to question authority, just…"

"Not yours."

"…Yeah."

"I was the same, I suppose," she mused, "in terms of my marriage I mean. I was so scared of being one of those possessive, harridan wives of old that I went too far the other way. Jonathan was in politics, I knew he'd be away a lot of the time and I had my own career to focus on so it didn't seem to matter at first that we spent so little time together. It turns out that kind of relationship only works when you can trust your partner…"

She tailed off as she relayed the memories, Stone offering her a sympathetic smile.

The brief silence between them was broken by the resumption of the rhythmic booming and the roar of the drunken crowd, as a pair of long legged women, one blonde, one brunette, strode onto the stage below them to the whooping of the mixed crowd below.

"Looks like the show's about to start," shouted Abelard over the music.

"What, a dance show?"

"Erm... you could say that," the Professor said, "in a manner of speaking."

Stone looked up at her wide-eyed expression, then down to the stage upon which the two 'dancers' had quickly undressed themselves and opened up a box containing an array of objects and devices, the sight of which caused Stone's own eyes to bulge and the crowd around the stage to whoop and applaud.

"Tell me," Stone began, inwardly cringing at the situation, "do you think the weather's nice enough tonight for a river cruise?"

It wasn't long before the pair were sat by the window of an almost empty river boat, having walked stiffly and briskly away from the unexpected 'entertainment' and towards the adjacent Vltava, where dinner boats and jazz cruises patiently waited, the mutual eruption of their previously stifled laughter causing the few other diners to tut and frown at their uncouth display.

"So, tell me Captain," Abelard grinned as the boat set off past the glowing lights and architectural magnificence of the Prague riverside, "do you make a habit of having lady friends accompany you to erotic shows on first dates?"

"Regimental tradition," he grinned back. "I trust this is adequate recompense?"

"First class Captain, first class."

Stone felt his tensions ease as they ate and was delighted to find that his enjoyment of the Professor's - of *Natalie's* - company was every bit as strong as his admiration for her intellect, which likewise grew as they discussed the political scene they had stepped into this last manic day. Before long, they had moved on deck and sat watching the skyline together, as the boat slid elegantly through the tranquil water. As a gentle but determined breeze blew across them, Stone felt her nestling close to him for warmth and he lifted his arm around her shoulders in response.

"So, what did happen in Syria, I mean really happen?"

The question caught Stone off guard.

"Don't you trust the media?" he half-smiled, trying to deflect the question as lightly as he could.

"I trust you..."

The words stabbed at Stone, causing for just a moment, the now familiar lump to flirt in his throat, before disappearing as his soldier's instincts chased it away.

"If you believe the papers, the TV and the Parliamentary Defence Committee, then it's all quite simple," he began as she snuggled closer into his chest.

"After everything kicked off again in Syria, I was OF-2 of one of the first Units on the scene, trying to recapture ground from the militants in North Damascus while keeping as far away as possible from the Russian Units who were doing the same thing from the South. We had a rebel cell locked down in Sarouja, that's just north of the Old City. Orders came through to take them out and I refused to engage. Consequently, the Russians captured the town and a number of the cell were able to escape, later posing as refugees to flee the country. It's speculated that this cell was behind the attack in London."

"I see," Abelard finished, the news having been full of little else during that time. "But there was no real proof of that, if I'm right? It's all speculation and paper talk?"

"Who needs proof in today's world?" Stone huffed. "Pick a scapegoat, place a few un-sourced 'quotes' in the press and a couple of well worded threads on Twitter and let innuendo do its worst. Once everyone's clicked 'like and share' very few are interested in the truth."

"Which is?"

Stone looked defiantly out at the Vltava, weighing up the likely reception of his words. His thumb beginning to gently rub Natalie's bare shoulder, he sighed.

"The Russians had got there before us."

His face was grim and his words every bit as cold as the waters they sailed through.

"The MI6 intelligence was flawed and we thought the Russians were further away than they were. Although there were a few fanatical stragglers still in the town, it was occupied by Russian forces, apart from a small portion in the East. I relayed that to command and was informed that their orders stood; they wanted me to go in and capture the town anyway."

Natalie frowned at the tale.

"Wait," she began, "they wanted you to actually engage the Russian forces in combat?"

Stone nodded.

"The perils of taking orders from politicians, I'm afraid. America saw the capture of Sarouja as a key PR stepping stone in the battle against extremism and the Ministry of Defence had already prepared a statement to the effect that British forces had captured the area; neither wanted to lose face."

"So you refused."

"I moved the unit into the unoccupied territory but I told command there was no way in Hell I was going to start World War Three for them. I met with the Russian commander and shared a drink with him in a bombed-out hospital; I proposed to honour the existing partition, that we'd defend the portion of the town we'd taken but wouldn't encroach further and he agreed to do the same. He wasn't in any mood to start an armed conflict between East and West any more than I was; I hope he came out of it better than I did. The whole thing passed almost in a daze; it was certainly the most surreal experience of my life. But we just got on with it; stiff upper lip and all that."

Stone felt Natalie's hand on his, gripping it in concerned affection, willing him to continue.

"The Americans wanted me relieved of command but my squadron threatened to lay down arms if I was replaced. Fortunately, my Colonel and General had my back and agreed with my judgement, which pretty much forced the UN to agree to joint occupation of the town. Needless to say, my squadron was soon replaced on the ground."

"They replaced you for doing the right thing? Bastards."

"I could have lived with that. My parents taught me to accept responsibility for my actions and I knew there were bound to be consequences, and at first they were pretty light ones, including dangling a promotion in front of me."

"Which you didn't accept?"

Stone smiled wistfully.

"Being a Captain meant the world to me," he said, "it still does. I joined up as a Squaddie and spent my career with the Royal Tank Regiment, in one form or another. My Dad, my adoptive dad that is, was in 4RTR in the Fifties and it meant the world to me to be following in his footsteps. I applied for an extension to my service once I turned forty, then five years later applied to be commissioned and they made me a Captain."

"So why turn down Major after such a long career?" Natalie asked, confusion evident in her voice.

"I wanted to stay in the field," he mused. "That's what soldiering was all about for me. To take Major, to push for Lieutenant Colonel, yes it might have been nice, but I wouldn't have been a soldier anymore, not really. I'd spent my career in battlefields and that's where I wanted to stay. I was lucky to be there anyway, promotees from the Ranks are usually assigned administrative duties like Quartermaster but because of my reputation in the field, and possibly for political reasons too, I was given command of Dreadnought, the Battalion's Command and Reconnaissance Squadron. It was the proudest moment of my professional life; we were a family, I looked after them like they were my kids…"

Stone heard his voice beginning to drift and was pulled back to the present by Natalie's probing.

"Political reasons?" he heard her ask, "Such as?"

He pulled her tighter to him and allowed a cynical smile to take root on his face.

"Let's just say there have been more than a couple of politicians over the years eager for their photo opportunity with the Black Hero." He laughed contemptuously at the memories of so many saccharine smiles, so many half-hearted handshakes.

"Man did that change quickly…"

"The Enquiry?"

Stone breathed deeply before continuing, realising inwardly that this was the first time he had voiced these frustrations and that the pain and anger they provoked were still fresh.

"The London attack gave that lot exactly the excuse they needed to hang me out to dry. They needed a scapegoat to explain away the security failure and I was the perfect fit: the Officer who refused an order to take out an insurgent stronghold, allowing them to escape to Europe by posing as refugees and carry out carnage in Britain. The way it was spun, some of the Red Tops pretty much accused me of killing the victims myself. The government emerged blameless, as did MI6, and the papers had a real physical person to unleash their anger on, with the added bonus that the anti-immigration headlines guaranteed good copy. Everyone's a winner baby."

He felt the squeeze of her hand and patted her shoulder in return, attempting to assure her of his resolve as his eyes drifted over the illuminated majesty alongside the river.

"But you'll be exonerated now, surely? Jonathan promised."

"The word of a politician?" The cynicism left Stone's face and he smiled gently down at her. "You'll forgive me if I don't get too excited. Even if he comes through, things won't be the same, the price of exoneration is accepting that damn promotion and being shuffled off to Sandhurst. My career in the field is over, but at least I'll be able to show him I wasn't a coward, that I tried to do the right thing…"

"Show who?"

"My son." Stone looked down again to see tears welling in Natalie's eyes and her delicate mouth hanging slightly open, as if she were searching for words that wouldn't come.

"Hey," he whispered, brushing her cheek with his thumb, "it's ok."

He pulled her closer to him, leaning his face towards hers as the breeze continued to caress them. And it was then, just as he felt the brush of this woman's lips on his own, as he emptied his mind for the first time in so long of all thoughts of bombs, and death and terror, that the grandiose opulence of the domed Rudolfinum, the most beautiful of the city's theatres convulsed into a frenzied plume of raging flame.

SEVEN

STONE PUSHED HIS WAY onto the bow of the boat, willing it to make port faster, before finally leaping to the dock as the vessel laboriously brought itself alongside. Quickly steadying himself, the Captain ran along the bank into the nightmare of Jan Palach Square, the clatter of his shoes on the cobbles drowned out by the chaotic cries of the injured, the screams of the crowd and the wail of sirens both distant and near.

Flashing his pass, he sped past the stunned young police officer who had moved to stop him, and into the centre of the flaming and bloody sonata playing out under the moonlight before him. Carnage awaited him, but Stone had seen carnage before and fell back on his professional stoicism and combat experience to survey the situation, his eyes steely, flicking back and forth as his soldier's mind assessed the situation. Of the three blasts, he surmised that one had been in the entrance of The Rudolfinum, its magnificence now burning and tarnished with the blood of those come to seek the solace of music within its walls, and the other two in the gardens the crowd had fled to, past the statue of Antonín Dvořák, which stared grimly at the horrors before it.

"Bastards," he whispered, tempted to allow his anger and his hatred of the cowardliness and deliberate cruelty of attacks of this nature. He quickly pushed such thoughts to the back of his mind to focus on the realities around him, for there was work to be done.

He sped to the flaming entrance, from which stragglers still hesitantly stumbled, clamping his eyes shut in inadequate preparation as he ran through and into the smoke-filled disorder of the inner hall.

Smoke eagerly and instantly filling his lungs and stinging his useless eyes, Stone reached around, grabbing, fumbling for the source of the screams he could hear around him, latching eventually on to a flailing arm and dragging it towards him. With one arm locked around the waist of his quarry, he pulled them hard towards where instinct told him was the door, collapsing through it and heaving the fresher, if only slightly, air into his burning lungs.

In one movement, he handed his rescuee into the arms of a waiting fire fighter, resisting her attempts to take him too to safety. Instead he stumbled, almost falling down the steps towards the green, where a fresh pair of arms impeded him.

"Lincoln!"

He blinked again, clearing his sore eyes and focusing on the face of his accoster, though her voice had ensured instant recognition.

"Lincoln!" Natalie shouted again, almost shaking the soldier into cognisance.

"Natalie! You need to go!"

"I'm not going without you!"

"You have to!" His senses returned, Stone was not about to risk the first woman he had felt close to for more years than he could remember and his tone took on the military inflection that had served him so well throughout his life.

"It's not a suggestion!" He moved her toward the periphery. "I'll be fine, this is the day job for me. Go to your hotel and I'll see you tomorrow."

He fumbled in his pocket, pulling out his phone and handing it to her.

"If you want to help, you can do me a favour and call my boy, let him know I'm ok."

"What?"

She screwed her face in frustrated confusion as Stone began to extract himself from her arms.

"Just call him!" He repeated his request, almost commanding her. "I'll see you tomorrow, I promise!"

With that he pulled himself out of her arms and ran back towards the congregating wounded and fearful on the adjacent green.

On the grass around him, people lay scattered and broken, some attended by weeping relatives, others by harassed medics. Firefighters ran through flames to search for more to add to their number and overstretched police linked arms to keep onlookers from the perimeter. Some of those lying alone screamed for Stone's help, but he knew that the silent ones required more immediate attention. Though more sirens were drawing near, Stone's experience demanded he react now, lest it be too late for someone. A man, middle aged and apparently alone, lay silent a few yards from the Captain, who bound over to him, instantly spotting the bleed from under the man's jacket. Pulling it open he located the deep wound in the man's stomach, pushing his hand onto it and shouting vainly for a medic.

The click of a camera accompanied by the cry of a young voice distracted Stone and he turned to see a child, a girl of no more than ten or eleven years weeping and looking around her, shouting loudly for 'Mama', while a thin man in his twenties clicked pictures of her despair, apparently unfazed by the scene he stood in. His anger bubbling, Stone opened his mouth to deliver a tirade, before a woman, her dress once elegant but now tattered, ran past him and embraced the child who wrapped her arms tightly around her mother's neck, the pair sobbing uncontrollably into each other. The reunion was nectar to the photographer, whose clicks grew faster the longer they embraced.

Stone spun swiftly in disgust, pulling the offending object from the astonished man and hurling it as far as he could, then clamping down onto his arm, dragging him alongside the prostrate victim. Stone forced the man's hand over the gaping wound and pushed down hard.

"Keep it there," he ordered, his tone implicitly warning of the dangers of refusal.

"But, but I'm a photographer!"

"I couldn't give a shit if you're Robert Frank, this man's life is more important than your fucking Pulitzer Prize, right?!"

Scared, the newcomer nodded, Stone's glare sufficient to warn him of the consequences of doing otherwise. The Captain himself ran to the new paramedics jogging through the cordon, stopping one and pointing to the stricken man, before his eyes were drawn to the imposing black car sweeping onto the scene. The rear door flew open to reveal Miroslava Svobodova, who ran with a determination Stone was sure would have taken her into the flames themselves had she not been pulled back by the ever-reliable Radoslav.

The Captain ran over to her, holding his hands up to further block her movement.

"What the fuck are you doing here?!" He bellowed at Svobodova who stared defiantly back at him, un-intimidated by the voice which had frozen troops and halted enemy in their tracks.

"I came to help!"

"By getting yourself killed? You shouldn't be here!"

"My place is with my people," she exclaimed, every bit as forcefully as he, "I'm going nowhere!"

As she spoke, a fresh hell ripped forth from an ignored dustbin across the square, sending debris far and wide and consuming the closest bystanders in its flames. A twisted piece of jagged, hot metal skimmed between the Captain and the Prime Minister, slicing slightly but painfully across the military man's temple, causing him to clasp his hand to the wound and curse, his profanity lost in revived chaos and renewed screams.

"Wrong!" Stone's voice was authority itself, invested with years of command, "Rado!"

Almost as soon as the explosion had sounded, the operative and his team had thrown their bodies around Svobodova, shielding her from any possible injury, and on Stone's word they bundled the defiant and still protesting politician back into her waiting car which sped immediately from the scene.

Breathing a sigh of relief, Stone wiped the blood from the side of his head, catching a glimpse in his eye of a man. Standing outside the cordon, grey hair straggled across his wrinkled face and hawkish eyes stared silently and directly into his own. Stone knew him immediately as the man from the tube station, the man who had saved his life. The view was blocked, only for an instant by a fleeing victim, but it was long enough for the stranger to have slunk from the scene. Stone cursed but knew he could ill afford to give chase now. Looking around to take in the new terror before him and, with a soldier's courage, he turned and ran straight and steady into the midst of chaos.

The trickle of blood had long since dried, etching a stubborn path through the caked cement dust sticking to, and crudely contrasting with the exhausted Stone's flesh. He had lost count of the minutes since the fire crews took control of the blaze and the police sealed the scene, leaving him faced with the gruelling walk back to his apartment far away on the other side of town. The further away from the scene he walked, the more casually news of the event was being taken, the minds of the people reluctant to be rescued from the drink, drugs and dancing they had paid good money for if the threat wasn't immediately in front of them. Retreating into the closed fortress of his mind, Stone ploughed on, almost ready to fall as he stepped through the lobby and into the glass lift, barely able to wave an acknowledgment to the concerned night porter at the desk.

As the lift pinged and the glass slid back, the sight of the woman crouched, shivering outside his door dragged alertness back to his mind, and he stepped out to see Natalie staring up at him, her eyes puffy and red.

"Did you take care of it?"

"I did what I could, it wasn't enough. It never is."

He slid and sat on the floor alongside her, their backs against the white painted wood of the door, both looking straight ahead into nothing.

"And what about you?" He asked.

"I started to go back to the hotel, but then I heard the other explosion and I realised..."

"Realised what?"

"you," she said. "You were running in and out of burning buildings, rescuing people, 'taking care of it', but who takes care of you?"

Stone had no answer. He turned to face her, meeting her eyes and gently shaking his head.

"The only person I need is back home and calls me 'Dad', there's no-one here or now that I need," he whispered.

"Everyone needs someone, even if just for right here and now." She reached up her arm, brushing his cheek with a dusty, dirty thumb.

"Let me take care of you tonight."

She took his hand and pulled him up to open the door, leading him inside to the bathroom. Utterly drained and somehow standing through his exhaustion, he offered no resistance as she delicately and carefully unbuttoned and unzipped him from his clothes before joining him in nakedness and stepping into the hot shower, pulling him gently by the hand behind her. He closed his eyes in surrender to the tenderness of her touch as her graceful fingers wiped away the grime and dirt from his tired, aching body, as soothing and relaxing as the flow of hot water streaming over them. While his body relaxed, the tension in his mind rose, his eyes squinting tightly closed until she moved her thumbs to them, lightly opening his lids, inviting him to accept her naked vulnerability.

"I'm sorry," he whispered, as though close to tears, "this isn't me, I don't do the whole 'one night thing', I shouldn't have taken advantage..."

She pressed her finger gently to his lips, the water running sensually down her arm.

"You didn't," she smiled. "And who said it was for one night?"

The shower water masked the tears beginning to form in his eyes and he smiled joyfully at the beautiful woman before him, taking her hand from his lips and kissing it, and surrendering once more, wholly now, into her warm embrace.

EIGHT

LATER, THEY LAY TOGETHER in the dark, his arm protectively around her as she nuzzled into him.

"I don't understand," she mused, delicately running her fingers across his chest.

"Understand what?"

She perched herself up on one elbow, looking into him, her face concerned.

"Tonight you ran into a burning building, again and again, dragging people to safety before running back in and searching for others you couldn't even be sure were there. And your service history, the VC in the Falklands, the CGC in Iraq; how could anyone ever suspect, let alone accuse you, of cowardice?"

The question was unexpected and Stone at first worried how to answer, but the ease and comfort which his new partner exuded was enough to dispel his concerns.

"Something happened a few years back, after Kosovo." He sighed, moving his eyes to the ceiling, as though the white plaster was a screen upon which his memories played out.

"When I returned from my tour, I wasn't well, it was like I couldn't process it all as easily as before. I'd seen plenty of conflict before then, too much some would say, but there was something different that time. Some of the things I saw… it was as though I brought it back home with me, I just couldn't disengage in the way I'd done before. And it affected me I think, affected the way I was with people, I had trouble sleeping for a while. I wasn't exactly waking up screaming every night but the nightmares were so real, so vivid, it was as though I was still there."

Natalie stroked his cheek in loving concern.

"It must have been terrible," she said. "Did you get help?"

Stone laughed quietly. "I was never exactly of that generation," he said, "I thought that given time I'd get over it and things would be back to normal."

"And were they?"

"Eventually," he answered. "But some people noted the change in me and others saw the chance to spread a few rumours, tried to put it about that I was burning out, that my combat days were behind me."

"Why would they do that?"

"Those 'political reasons' again," Stone shrugged. "There'd always been one or two who thought I was the token minority soldier, pushed through the ranks into Officer class and handed gongs because of what I looked like rather than what I'd done."

"Arseholes," Natalie spat.

"Quite," Stone grinned, "It's ok, I learned a long time ago not to let that shit trouble me. But still, that was the first time they offered to make me Major and assign me elsewhere, away from combat. I refused."

"And went on to serve in Afghanistan, Iraq and now Syria…"

"Exactly," Stone nodded. "Sometimes I wonder if I kept volunteering just to keep proving to myself, to everyone, that I could still do it, that I hadn't grown soft and I could still do my duty."

She leant forward and kissed his brow, he tenderly caressing her back in response.

"Looking back, I made the wrong choice," he mused. "It's only now I realise what was going on with me and it was the people around me who suffered, my boy especially. I'd take out all of these emotions I couldn't handle on him, my punishments got more severe, I was shouting at him as though he were one of my troops, bellowing at him for the slightest infraction… I think that was the seed of what was to come. And it wasn't helped that by me gallivanting off to fight in every war declared on some kind of 'mission' to prove myself, when I should have been at home, fighting for my relationship with him."

Another kiss from the gentle woman alongside him, another stroked cheek.

"I'm sure he understood, forgave you," she offered, meeting another soft laugh in response.

"Maybe," Stone answered softly. "As he got older he started hating military actions, joining in some of the protests against them, Iraq in particular. As I was leaving to go on my tour there he told me he hated me for being a part of it. I justified it with the WMD threat and tried to explain that I was fighting to help make a better, more peaceful world. Look how that turned out…"

He let his eyes flick across the ceiling, jumping forwards to new memories on the reel of his life.

"It got better," he said, his voice suddenly optimistic. "We really started to turn a corner and when I got back from Syria, he was the only one to really have my back. It was as if being scapegoated by the government brought me back from beyond the pale in his eyes. Then there was the attack… but I'm fine though now, I'm fine."

The cheer disappeared from his voice as instantly as it had arrived, replaced with gloomy melancholia. He felt her embrace tightening in response, enough to break his stare from the ceiling and look into her wide, beautiful eyes. It had been so very long since he had seen that look in a woman's face and it amazed him at least as much as it must her that they had met only that very morning; two damaged strangers thrust together into a strange land and who now clung to each other as if they offered some mutual best hope of getting out of this bizarre situation in one piece. And while the rational strategist in his head warned him of the dangers of this kind of battlefield romance, for once, Stone preferred to follow the yearnings of his heart. He lowered himself back alongside her in the bed and cupped her face in his strong hand.

"I'm more than fine."

Stone awoke early the next morning to an empty space alongside him and the smell of frying eggs and grilled bacon drifting in from the kitchen. Throwing his dressing gown around him he stepped through the bedroom door to find Natalie at the cooker, her hair tied back into a loose ponytail and dressed in Stone's own jogging bottoms and T-shirt which hung voluminously on the attractive young woman.

"Morning sleepy head," she said over her shoulder, the Welsh tint in her voice by far more appealing this morning than it had sounded when she'd rung his bell the previous day. "I hope you don't mind me nicking your togs but I didn't think a dirty cocktail dress was appropriate attire to go buying essentials in. Sit down."

Stone obeyed, sitting at the adjacent wooden dining table and watching her as she plated up their breakfasts.

"Where did you go for it?

"Shop just outside," she answered. "I'm not sure I'll be going there again mind, the girl at the counter was rather keen on giving me her opinions on gypsies."

"Oh, so you've met our local charmer then?"

"That's one word for her!"

Natalie placed the plates on the table and slid into a chair alongside him.

"Are you ok?"

Her voice was soft and a little uncertain, as though conveying the natural awkwardness that typically greeted such 'morning after' conversations, and Stone felt compelled to offer reassurance.

"Absolutely," he replied just as softly. And, he silently realised, he was ok, absolutely ok. He'd had so long dwelling on the tragedies and catastrophes of his recent past that he hadn't registered just how miserable and insular he had allowed himself to become until the woman next to him had coaxed him from his shell. He reached across and placed his hand gently on hers, giving it an affectionate squeeze.

"I promise."

His gesture seemed to satisfy her and she returned quickly to the matter in hand, her customary confidence returned to her voice.

"They didn't have any sausages other than chorizo," she chirped, "and I didn't really fancy the sound of that this early in the morning, and I'm not too sure about this bacon either to tell you the truth, but you can't go wrong with eggs, beans, tomatoes and toast."

She tucked ravenously in, speaking the last words through a half-full mouth, Stone grinning in response.

"How do you stay so thin?" he joked.

"Gym twice a week and a metabolism like a furnace," she grinned back, "Oh, there's no HP either."

"I'll live."

Stone started work on his own plate as his thoughts returned to the horrors of the previous evening. Reaching for the TV remote on the table he flicked on the news and spent a few moments taking in what he could of the reports.

"We'll need to see Svobodova today, as soon as we can," the Captain said. "Myska is bound to make capital out of last night and she needs to move quickly to get ahead of the game."

"I'll advise her to get to the hospital to see the victims and visit the scene as soon as the police say it's safe to do so. She'll need to get working on a way to counter whatever response Myska makes... I'd hate to be part of the refugee community this morning, that's for sure; his followers will be like caged animals right now even if he plays the Statesman himself."

"Yeah, and for what it's worth, I think their rage will be misdirected..."

"What do you mean?"

Stone flicked the TV off and turned back to Natalie.

"Something's bothering me about last night," he said. "The first three detonations were suicide, one inside the theatre entrance itself, the other two in the crowd as they ran for safety. That's a familiar pattern, it sits comfortably with established modus operandi in attacks of this kind, but the fourth..."

"The bomb in the bin?"

"Exactly, where I got this beauty," he tapped the fresh scar on his temple. "Suicide bombers walk into a crowd, they try to spread fear and panic, to take as many people with them as possible. Leaving a timed explosive in a bin to go off after they'd killed themselves just doesn't fit the profile; they'd have no way of knowing if anyone would be near it when it went off, let alone if it would kill anyone..."

His voice began to tail off and he pulled himself back to the present before his mind could surrender to preoccupation, turning back to Natalie who sat, looking at his plate with a smile on her face.

"That is a work of art," she laughed.

Looking down, Stone realised he had obliviously piled the food on his plate onto an enormous sandwich which he now held a few inches from his mouth, the odd bean dripping from it back to the plate.

"Another of those Regimental traditions," he grinned back at her and took a big bite.

From the bedroom, a muffled mobile phone ring tone began to sound, causing Natalie to scramble to her feet.

"Shit, that must be yours, I forgot to give it back to you last night."

"Did you ring my boy? What did he say?"

"What?" She shook her head in confusion, "No, I…"

"It doesn't matter," Stone reassured without irritation. He reached out his hand for the phone and she passed it to him. He frowned at the name on the display and swiped it with a greasy thumb.

"Yes, Prime Minister?"

A short time later, after a brief detour to Natalie's apartment to allow her to change her clothes, the pair stood outside Svobodova's office door, before they were directed downstairs and into a waiting limousine which swept them instantly into Prague's busy and still recovering streets.

"Good morning to you both."

Svobodova's words were business like and devoid of the warmth and charm which had typified their meeting the previous day, instead infused with an exhausted irritability.

"I apologise for my short sightedness last night," Svobodova said, addressing Stone. "You were right of course that my presence was inappropriate. It's just that it is important to me that my people should not face any danger that I myself shy away from."

"And I apologise for my rudeness," Stone reciprocated, "I congratulate you on your country's extremely well trained emergency services, they did you and your people proud."

The niceties over, Stone acknowledged to himself how the tiredness in Svobodova's eyes seemed to have doubled since the previous day.

"Where are we heading?" Professor Abelard asked, her voice at its most polished.

"The Rudolfinum."

"The police have declared it safe?"

"I've no idea, we're going anyway."

"Are you sure that's wise?" Stone queried, the Professor leaning forward in support.

"Maybe a visit to the hospital would be more prudent until the area is secure…"

"I've already done that," Svobodova snapped, "last night."

The Captain looked closely at her in her seat across from them, with a mixture of admiration and frustration. She was clearly exhausted, drained even, the warmth in her face from the previous day gone entirely and her eyes a tell-tale red.

"You haven't slept in a long time," Stone said softly, a statement rather than a question.

"I needed to be with my people," she replied in a reflective tone, only half-addressing the Captain, "and then I spent the rest of the night fielding calls from the damn Americans, demanding they be allowed to conduct the investigation..."

Abelard shifted in her seat next to Stone and took a deep breath.

"Please forgive the insensitivity of this question, but were the cameras at the hospital with you?"

"What? No!" Svobodova screwed her face up in distaste.

"I'm sorry, but Myska is riding high in the polls and will use this attack to make the lives of immigrants and refugees in this country and across Europe hell. You have to use anything you can to get in front."

Svobodova leaned forward, the resolve in her tired features apparent.

"I will not exploit the victims of terror to boost my poll ratings."

"I respect your principles," Abelard said, her own resolve equally strong, "but Myska will have no such hesitation, and his message will spread all the more clearly because of that."

An icy tension descended on the occupants of the car as it continued on its way, the two women embarked on a silent battle of wills. Each was formidable in her own way, thought Stone, and while he agreed with the strategic logic of his new lover, he saw in Svobodova a desire to be someone different to the cloned, standard issue politicians occupying the conveyor belt of power the world over; a desire he more than respected.

The car pulled to a halt, the door opening for Svobodova, who stepped out, closely followed by Abelard and Stone, small pools of filthy, spent hose water lapping at their shoes as they stood at the barrier to the site, drinking in the nauseous image of beauty corrupted. Though the billowing smoke of the previous night was gone, its stench clung defiantly to the charred and battered surroundings, lending a malodorous accompaniment to the images of scattered debris and dark red stains tarnishing the ancient beauty of the grand old building.

Svobodova had brought with her a large, but not exorbitant bouquet of lilies, which she placed on the ground in front of the yellow tape barring entry to the scene, before stepping back and bowing her head, her eyes reverentially closed. Stone, no stranger to such ceremonies, mimicked the gesture along with Abelard, the pair hanging back from the Prime Minister as much to avoid the encroaching cameras as to respect her moment of solace; the buzzing of the gathered platoons of journalists rising in intensity with Svobodova's arrival.

It was the noise of the buzz rising further still which caused him to open his eyes a moment later, accompanied by the sound of rubber tyres breaking softly on wet cobbles and the opening of a car door. He glanced over his shoulder and grimaced; the sight before him as unwelcome as it was expected: Myska.

The MEP cut every inch the figure of the sincere mourner, adorned in an immaculate black suit and tie, every trace of the casualness in his demeanour and hair which Stone had perceived the previous day now brushed professionally away and replaced with a look of Statesmanlike distress. Carrying a similar bouquet, he passed through the clawing rabble of reporters and cameras, moving to lay it alongside Svobodova's before taking up position alongside her so immaculately that the assembled press could be forgiven for believing the entire event to be choreographed.

If Svobodova was shocked by the unexpected appearance of her rival, no such emotion played on her face, which remained reverent and respectful, her open eyes remaining fixed upon the sight before her. Closest to the pair, Stone pricked up his ears to catch the words of the populist politician, who leaned subtly, almost imperceptibly closer to Svobodova, clearly determined to take every advantage of the situation. His efforts were in vain as what words the Captain could strain to hear were in any case whispered in Czech and uttered too quietly for him to discern. Instead he settled back into the posture of a background guard, his gaze determinedly locked onto Myska.

Almost as soon as etiquette allowed, the young politician raised his head and half-turned towards Svobodova, glancing quickly at Stone before turning back to her, an expression of pained sympathy on his face. He spoke again, just a fraction louder but clear enough for Stone to hear and in and English which left no doubt as to his intended audience.

"A word of advice, Prime Minister," Myska hissed quietly, "charming specimen though he is, keep your new monkey off my back and well in his cage, otherwise he's likely to require the services of a vet."

With that, he stepped away from the barrier and took up position a few steps away, a chunk of the journalistic horde following him, questions spewing forth from their lips as soon as they were mere steps from the scene, as though they an orchestra desperate for him to take up the baton.

Stone and Abelard stepped up alongside Svobodova who continued her vigil, obviously struggling to swallow the pointed racial barb her rival had made.

"Bastard," whispered the Professor, while Myska's voice began to sound through the boom mics yards behind, "promoting himself and making speeches before they've even cleaned the blood off the floor. What's he saying?"

Svobodova paused before responding, allowing Myska's condemnations to echo in her ears as a grim soundtrack to the devastation before her, eventually speaking with a voice coated in tiredness and resignation.

"He's saying that this is the outcome of a political class that ignores its people and dismisses their concerns as 'racism', that appeasement today means bloodshed tomorrow and that this is further proof that two such radically different cultures cannot live side by side in peace."

"So he's a tasteless bastard too," Abelard spat.

"It is the way the world of politics turns," Svobodova bemoaned, "but it is one I refuse to endorse."

"Maybe you should."

Both ladies turned to the hitherto silent Captain Stone, whose face was creased into a ferocious scowl.

"If you're happy for him to make speeches all day long he will do; he'll get the upper hand in the argument and you'll look like you're on the defensive. Take the fight to him for a change."

The anger in Stone's hissed words was obvious and he continued through gritted teeth.

"Let the monkey loose on his back for once."

It had been a long time since Stone had allowed himself to give in to the anger born of the type of comment Myska had aimed at him. And while he cursed himself for doing so, he remained rational enough to know that what he had suggested to Svobodova was right: Myska must be challenged.

With respect to the Captain," Abelard began, "I disagree. You've already made your statement to the press, respond to his goading now and you're dancing to his tune. Believe it or not, from a PR perspective you're already ahead of Myska after your hospital visit last night, not to mention your pit stop at the scene of the attack."

"But there were no cameras?"

"There were no TV crews to capture you, no, but this is 2018, there's no-one out there without a smart phone or a tablet; the second you showed your face it was uploaded to YouTube and shared the world over. Believe me, I checked in the car; you're trending."

"What?" Svobodova frowned.

"It's precisely the lack of TV crews that tells people your concern, your worry is genuine. You were prepared to put yourself in danger, you spent the night in the hospital with the victims, then a couple of hours later you were here paying respects. All that speaks louder than any speech Myska can make."

"That's all very well," hissed Stone, his irritation growing, "but while you're busy taking the high ground that bastard will be spreading his filth all over the country and God knows how many people are going to suffer for it. When your opponent wants a street fight, sometimes you just have to take off your jacket and get down to it."

He could feel the eyes of both women on him and he latched onto their concern to stop the anger from clouding his mind. Natalie's interjection had stung, not least because he knew she was right. Svobodova's whole career, her 'mission' since taking office, was to do things differently to other politicians; to be not just a symbol of political change but an embodiment of it, and submitting to Myska's forced popularity contest was no way to do that. But Stone was right too. Myska was the type of bully who would go on causing harm until the day his victim stood up and punched him squarely in the face and by not rising to the challenge, Svobodova was effectively allowing him the run of the playground.

The unexpected touch of Svobodova's hand on his arm pulled him from his train of thought and he turned his head to meet hers; her eyes wide and sympathetic under a furrowed brow, but possessed of a steadfast determination to proceed on her chosen path.

"Captain Stone, Lincoln," her voice was soft and sincere, "I accept the veracity of your sentiment, believe me I share your desire to take on his poison, and I'm sorry, truly. But I will not use the site of an atrocity to beg for the approval of voters."

She deftly allowed her hand to drop and turned back towards the car, ignoring the pleas of the horde to respond to Myska's brutish assessment. Abelard hung back, looking nervously at Stone, who swallowed the temptation to feel personally slighted by the Professor's advice.

"Are you coming Lincoln?" she asked, gesturing to the waiting car.

"I'd prefer to be alone," he snapped, instantly regretting his response, shaking his head in flustered apology.

"I'm sorry," he said, "I appreciate the offer but I'm afraid I wouldn't be very good company right now, I just need to clear my head for a while."

The faint smile on her face wasn't enough to mask her concern, though sufficient resentment played in his system for him to resist immediately alleviating it.

"Ok," she eventually replied, the worry in her eyes evident. "Call me, alright? When you want to."

"I will," he nodded, forcing a thin smile to his lips, "I promise."

She remained for a moment and Stone briefly pondered whether he should lean forward and give her a kiss, but decided this was hardly an appropriate setting to do so. Instead she smiled awkwardly and followed Svobodova's footsteps to the car, Stone turning in the opposite direction, and walking a short distance away before finding a suitable alcove from which to keep the still bleating Myska in his line of vision.

"Captain Stone, isn't it?" The unmistakeable inflection of North America rung in Stone's ears and he turned at the mention of his name to find a well-groomed and expensively suited man standing by his shoulder, staring intently past Stone at the eulogising Myska.

"Never heard of him," the Captain answered, turning his head back to the cameras.

"Oh, come now Captain, don't be modest. You've made quite a name for yourself recently; a British war hero, a VC no less, allowing a terrorist cell to escape and wreak havoc rather than order an advance? Must be kinda hard to live with, especially considering who the victims were… now wait friend, I don't want any trouble!"

Stone had spun around and stepped toe-to-toe with the newcomer, who couldn't hope to match the military man for height or build, and who put his hands up at the reaction.

"Well I suggest, *friend*, that you be careful to whom you repeat the shit you read in the papers, otherwise 'trouble' may be precisely what you get."

"Oh, point taken Captain, point taken," the American twang was dripping with fake sincerity, the words clambering cynically through over-bleached teeth set behind a fixed, disingenuous grin. "Believe me I understand how frustrating the media can be, particularly when it comes to reporting attacks such as last night's. That's why I'm here: to help."

Stone stepped back from the charmless grin, the sickening thought that this was Greyson's vaunted 'Man' making contact beginning to gnaw at him.

"Help how?" he ventured, almost dreading the answer, "and who?"

"Madame, Prime Minister of course," came the condescending reply, Stone remaining silent at the answer. "You have influence with Svobodova," the man pressed on.

"Do I?"

"Yes. And more than you think. It's been a long time since she let 'outsiders' advise her; you and the good Professor should feel privileged."

"I don't know what you're talking about," Stone unconvincingly replied, prompting an abrasive laugh from the American, whose seemingly permanent grin lent it a sinister quality.

"Yes, you do. And you're going to tell Svobodova she should really accept the help that's on offer to her and allow US agencies to conduct the investigation. She respects you, she'll listen."

"I think you've overestimated my importance," The Captain said, defiantly resentful of the insight this stranger appeared to possess, "Svobodova is her own woman, she doesn't need to listen to me."

The man straightened up and began to step away from Stone, who kept his eyes fixed on him and his hands ready for possible conflict.

"Oh Captain, my Captain," he brushed down his immaculate suit jacket and adjusted a loose cufflink, Stone clenching his fists in readiness for a conflict he almost hoped would come but which his mind restrained him from instigating, "you're more important than you realise. If you advise her to do a deal with America, she'll pick up the phone for sure. She needs friends and lots of 'em. See that guy over there?" He gestured to where Myska was wrapping up his rhetoric and making his way back to his own vehicle. "He's a major league asshole for sure, but he's winning votes. If Madame Prime Minister were seen to be co-operating in a high-profile crackdown on international terrorism, alongside her US partners, it can only be good for her image, I'd guess. And it would be far better for her health should she move to bring us on board while she, you know, still has a choice in the matter."

The words were said with an air of blasé nonchalance, the unsettling, baleful smile growing wider as he let them hang in the air while he began to move away from the soldier.

"Meaning what, exactly?" Stone shouted after him.

The American halted for a brief moment and looked back over his shoulder at Stone.

"Don't make me spell it out to you, you're too intelligent for that; even if you are a national disgrace."

"You fucking…"

Stone lurched forwards, grabbing the man by his needlessly expensive lapels; the twisted smile not leaving the American's face.

"Temper, temper Captain," lectured the stranger, "a British Officer suspended for suspected dereliction found beating a US diplomat in the street just across the road from the cameras in Czechoslovakia? You don't really want to become an internet sensation, do you?"

The Captain, with painful reluctance, allowed this new tormentor to slip free from his hands while the darkest of scowls radiated the depths of his contempt.

"Be seeing you," smirked the man.

And he was gone, slipping quickly but unhurriedly through the growing mass of people coming to pay their respects and let their emotions flow.

It would be frivolous to follow him Stone realised; even if he were to successfully give chase, accosting him would only lead to more problems for Svobodova than she currently had and he had no wish to add to her stresses, despite the frustration still throbbing within him at her refusal to tackle Myska head on.

Heading nowhere in particular but as far away as he could, Stone picked a direction and walked in it. Choosing streets at random, he found himself passing designer boutiques and glass fronted emporiums, tastefully built into the typically eerie allure of the architecture he had come to expect and admire in his short time in the city.

He drew a lungful of warm, summer breath into his lungs as he walked, willing the stresses of this manic couple of days out with the spent air he exhaled and cursing himself for his unsoldierly display of petulance in front of Svobodova and Natalie. Stone could forgive anyone for an emotional reaction in the aftermath of the previous night's attack, the scenes had after all been horrendous, but he was not anyone, and had borne witness to countless similar spectacles and worse in his long career. It had been Svobodova's stance which had disappointed him, and though he knew it unfair, he found himself blaming her for a lifetime of political disenchantment, as the shining dawns, bright new eras and sunlit uplands promised by so many successively failed to materialise. Svobodova was a good leader, that much was obvious, and she was a strong woman, too strong, Stone thought, to have backed down to Myska's challenge, regardless of her stance on not providing him with the 'oxygen of publicity'. He already had the publicity; the challenge now surely was to counter what he did with it. Stone had grown up listening to the eloquent prejudices of respectable men, and it pained and angered him to hear them spoken of again so many years hence. Some of his earliest childhood memories were the twisted faces of his neighbours and the sneers of passers-by in the aftermath of 'old Enoch's' speech. And seeing the rising tensions in Britain mirrored here in Prague brought the fear that the infamous 'Rivers of Blood' may one day appear if the extremists were left unchallenged.

And then there was Natalie. Here he was not only enjoying the company of this woman but relishing it, and it seemed by her actions that the feeling was very much reciprocated. He had lost count of the number of times over the years that he had pushed women away, or been pushed away by them, as soon as the issue of his son came up, and it was as unsettling as it was welcome to find that not to be the case with her.

He stopped to gather his bearings, the thought of Natalie lingering and a buzz of nervous anticipation playing in his stomach as he contemplated their first meeting. Enjoying the unfamiliar excitement, he took in his surroundings; the street having led him to the edge of the Old Town Square, a grand, baroque Church in white stone, its twin towers capped in green alongside him. Pausing to take in the panoramic beauty, the Captain froze as his gaze fell on a bedraggled, untidy figure, standing motionless under the shadow of the ancient Clock Tower, his wide eyes fixed on Stone. It was the same man who had silently watched him the previous night and who had saved his life in the subway; and Stone was damned if he wasn't going to get one of these underhand bastards to stay still long enough to answer his questions.

The Captain ignored the creek of his knees as he pushed himself into action, quickly pulling his frame up to a full sprint towards the mystery man, who without even a suggestion of panic, slid into the throng of tourists clambering around the ornate pillar. Stone emerged on the other side of the tower with the tattered stranger nowhere to be seen.

"Damn!" hissed Stone to himself, vainly scouring the milling swarm for any sign of the unknown figure. He began to traverse the perimeter of the Square, surely an impossible task given the multitudes within it, his annoyed expression eliciting the occasional mocking glance from the more inebriated members of the local custom as he continued on his fruitless patrol.

The shrill ring from his mobile phone broke Stone from his obsession and a small and brief wave of excitement washed over him as he pulled the phone from his pocket in the hope his boy was returning his call. The disappointment that it was not his son's name on the display was quickly quelled by the appearance of Natalie's moniker, and he pressed the device to his ear, his eyes still flicking through the crowd.

"Lincoln?"

"Yes."

"Are you alright?"

"Yes, why?" he answered distractedly. "I mean, yes, I'm fine Natalie, thank you. Look, I'm sorry about earlier, I just think she'd have been better taking him on there and then, and then when you back her up…"

"Where are you?" she interrupted.

"In the Square, by the Clock Tower," he answered, puzzled by her tone, "I thought I saw…"

"Get to a bar, quickly," she interrupted.

"What?"

"Get to a bar, a British one with a news channel, you need to see this."

There was a desperation in her voice which spurred him into action. Listening for the sound of British voices, Stone heard a collective roar from an inebriated stag group sat outside a pub wedged into the alcove of one of the Square's side streets close to where he was standing. Jogging over, he squeezed past the drunkards and headed inside, phone still in hand, to the dark bar area, illuminated only by the light of a half dozen fruit machines and a hat trick of TV screens, all tuned to football updates. The unpalatable smell of stale alcohol greeted the Captain; the chipped, varnished wood of the bar sticky with uncleaned spillages upon which the remnants of cigarette ash and the occasional stub had been dumped. Stone grimaced as his palm pressed onto a cold and tacky deposit of spent gum, spread across the unpolished brass bar rail, and he hastily wiped his hand on the not altogether cleaner towel while trying to catch the attention of the disinterested teenager manning the fort.

"Hey," Stone gestured to him, "can you switch the news on mate?"

"Are you drinking?"

"Fine," he answered in frustration, "I'll have a pint of whatever's on draft. News please?"

The bored youth slunk a thick pint glass underneath a plastic tap and flicked the lever down, before taking what seemed like a deliberate age to locate the TV remote from behind hanging bags of cheese and onion crisps and dry roasted peanuts, eventually knocking the TV closest to the bar onto the European news.

"Have you got it?"

Stone heard Abelard's voice through the phone and he pressed it again to his ear.

"Ok, I'm here, what am I looking for?"

"It's Jonathan," came the voice, "he's…"

"Yes, I know," Stone's face plummeted low, matching the hollowness he felt in his stomach as he watched the words flash up in stark, white capital letters against a sensationalist red background complimenting the looped video of Jonathan Greyson stepping from the doorway of Ten Downing Street and waving briefly to the camera before sliding into the waiting limousine. Were this any other time, or any other politician, Stone would have hopped straight to another channel without batting so much as a politically disengaged eyelid, but instead he stood rooted and open mouthed as the listless barkeep placed the crudely drawn beer on a mat in front of him, with a simultaneous demand for 48

Crowns. Stone made no move for his wallet, as the shot cut back to the studio for analysis, the lurid headline following.

'FOREIGN SECRETARY DISMISSED' read the banner, before a string of noble words and commendations from the usual band of rent-a-quote talking heads spewed under them across the screen like a stock market ticker tape.

"He's gone," Stone murmured into the phone, odium engulfing him as the knowledge that the departing MP carried with him in his soon to be relinquished Ministerial limo, any and all hope of Stone's promised exoneration. "He's bloody gone."

NINE

THROUGHOUT THE MANY BATTLES in his extended career, Captain Stone had always found it easy to adapt to whatever challenge was thrown at him; his enemies and his goals had always been clear, allowing him to focus his energies on overcoming the problem and pressing on. Would that his situation in these last days was so transparent; instead he found his enemies faceless and his goal, the exoneration he so desperately sought, had been pulled from his grasp, an apparent casualty of political score settling, leaving him devoid of objective and, more importantly of hope. It was that, far more than the unfamiliarity of the streets he pounded, that encouraged his adoption of the mantle of 'stranger in a strange land'.

Since the news of Greyson's dismissal broke, it was as if Stone had been stupefied; his routine over the last couple of days involving little more than walking the streets and drinking in whichever bars he fell into before staggering back to his apartment and passing out, his phone in one hand and his son's picture in the other. Ah, his boy, *his* boy! The thought of going home with his record expunged, his son being able to tell his friends that his Dad was a hero again and not the villain of the piece, had obsessed him now for so long that being robbed of that outcome had left a cavernous vacuum which the Captain was unable to fill. It was more for his son than himself that he yearned for absolution and each night since the sacking, he lay drunkenly maudlin on his bed, unable to dial his son's number to break the news. Twice he had even made it to the airport, fully intending to board the first plane home, wrap the boy in his arms and confess all, but the fear of the disappointment it would bring him always made Stone turn back to the bar in search of a liquid courage which wouldn't come. He was falling into a dangerous cycle, from which he needed to escape, but with his objective gone, he struggled to find the motivation to do it. Abelard had tried to help but Stone had refused, declining all invitations to meet and denying even Svobodova's requests for meetings. He had likely offended Natalie in the process despite his efforts to remain polite, and with few others in this city likely to be interested, it was a mystery to him how he would break free.

The conundrum still pecked at Stone as he made his way back to his apartment later that night, his mind unceasingly occupied as he jumped onto the cobbled street from the tram, swaying a little as the union of alcohol and night air began to flirt with his senses. The wide-open street was practically deserted, save for a scattered few mid-week tourists staggering towards whichever bars would allow them entry; their journeys illuminated by the bright lights of fast food joints, underground clubs and dank, corner house gambling dens, whose slot machines and roulette tables sang to the drunkards like world weary electronic Sirens.

The seductive intoxication spurring him on, Stone felt in his pocket for any remaining crowns and quickly assessed their worth, heading towards another of the seemingly infinite number of convenience stores peppered into the streets in this part of town. After much pointing at the selection of bottles behind the counter, the ancient Vietnamese woman at the till, who insisted on shouting at him with all the linguistic intricacies of her mother tongue, passed Stone two dark bottles of some Bohemian mixture. He slapped the money down on the counter and slipped the bottles up his coat sleeves, stepping out of the door and yearning now for the sanctity of his apartment as the alcohol continued to claim his senses.

He set off on the road leading to Pricna, not travelling far before an accented voice called out to him

"Hey, English!"

"Oh, fuck," he sighed.

The voice cut sneeringly through the night towards him, muffled a little by the speeding taxis and thud of basement club beats, but unquestionably aimed at Stone. The Captain knew what to expect and cursed himself for allowing his defences to drop and leaving him underprepared. From the shadows in front of him, stepped a young girl, no more than twenty, her clothes dirty and ill fitting, her smile insincere.

"Hey, English, you want have a sex? Have a good time?"

"Maybe another night," Stone answered, trying to retain at least a semblance of his usual eloquence.

"Oh, another night?" The unsettling smile grew wider, displaying poorly maintained teeth which blighted her potentially attractive face, "I think tonight, come on English."

She was stood before him blocking his path, and now moved closer, taking him in an embrace and running her hands over his body, dipping her fingers deftly into each of his pockets in turn.

He pulled himself free and stepped backwards, the adrenaline helping him to focus his drink addled mind.

"Keep your hands to yourself and back the fuck off," Stone commanded, hoping to God the words didn't sound as slurred out loud as they did in his head.

"A problem here, English?"

Another voice, this time from behind him, joined the conversation and Stone quickly turned to take in the newcomer.

"I know you, don't I English?"

The new voice belonged to a man, not much cleaner than the girl and of a similar age, but bigger and stronger; the overpowering stench of rotten breath coming from his maliciously grinning mouth.

"I don't believe I've had the pleasure," Stone hissed.

"Oh yes," said the newcomer, "I see you around town, following Myska, he makes good speeches, no?"

"I wouldn't know; my Czech could use a little brush up."

"Ah," the young man laughed, "well, I can translate for you?"

"No thanks."

"I insist! It's no problem!"

The man stepped closer, taking his hands from his pockets. His breath cut through Stone's intoxication and he could feel the woman inching closer to him from behind, his body tensing in readiness for a confrontation but hampered by the day's drink.

"All Myska wants, *really* wants, is for people to be happy again."

"Really?" Stone's voice was etched in sarcasm.

"Really. All Czechoslovak people, that is."

"I see, and what's this got to do with me?"

The man began to look around in exaggerated fashion, as though trying to prove some point.

"Well," he said, looking around him, "I don't see many Czechoslovakians around here quite like you, you know what I mean? So to see you here, there, wherever Myska goes, it makes me nervous, makes me think that maybe you don't like him very much, no?"

"I'm sure he's a positive delight." Stone's voice was as cold and hard as his name, and he defied his eyes' lingering desire to blur, to stare into the young man's face.

"Absolutely," he confirmed through the unsettling grin on his thin face, "he's a good guy, a man of the people. So, there's no need for you or any more of the Whore's little band of foreigners to come to any more meetings, ok?"

"And supposing I feel compelled to enjoy his oratory again?"

"Then watch him on YouTube," came the contemptuous response, "or buy his DVD. Either way, keep your ugly, angry, black face the fuck away from us, or I'll carve you a matching scar on the other side of your head."

A dull but unmistakeable click sounded, eliciting a snigger from the woman behind him and dragging the soldier's mind fully home to sobriety. His muscles tensed as he registered the new development, not letting his now fully focused eyes drop from those of his opponent and permitting a thin but confident smile of his own to form on his face.

"Young man," the Captain calmly said, "if you don't promptly put your toy away and apologise for that remark, then this ugly, angry, black face smiling goodbye to you as the light fades is the last thing you'll ever see."

A sneering laugh came from the man with the knife, echoed by the woman.

"Really?" came the mocking tone, "Well maybe you need a little taste in advance."

His senses proved as faithful in the street as they had on the battlefield, overriding the day's booze and fuelling his reaction to the man's quickly raising knife hand. The Captain swiftly and calmly slid sideways, before the hand of the woman behind him poised and ready to push him into the blade could make contact, causing it instead to meet the knife as it swished across her palm.

She yelped in pain while Stone's enraged attacker lurched and veered towards him.

The bottles still held securely in his sleeves, the soldier's arm swung fast, windmill like, connecting with the young man's head with a sickening clunk and crack, dropping him to the pavement with blood issuing forth from the deep cut on his temple. Stone too winced as the Moravian wine coating his forearm mingled with blood from his own laceration, and he shook the fractured remnants of the bottle from his sleeve. The woman, crouched next to her fallen partner in crime, used Stone's momentary weakness to scramble forth and scrape the dropped knife from the pavement with the fingers of her other hand, fury engraved on her dirty, unhealthy looking face.

Spotting her lunge, the crouched Stone rolled to the side, her attack finding only thin air, before he picked up the largest of the broken shards around him, raising up on one knee and holding it steadily towards her.

"Don't think for one moment you'd be the first woman I've had to kill," he said, his stare as hard as his voice and as steady as his arm.

For a moment she looked from the jagged glass bottle to his face and back again, as if weighing up her chances against a man who had so easily felled her accomplice. When after a few seconds had passed, Stone half-heartedly thrust the craggy glass towards her, the wounded assailant turned at once on her heel and fled from the blackness and down the street towards the neon lights and milling drinkers.

Stone too heaved himself upwards and ran the short distance to Pricna, hurrying through the doors and climbing the stairwell to his apartment with only a cursory nod to Honza, the regular night manager. He slammed the door behind him and collapsed against it, sliding down until he sat on the laminated floor, pulling his stained coat from his back and tossing it into the corner, the remaining unbroken bottle atop it, and cursing himself as he examined the cuts on his arm. While he could hardly have prevented the targeted assault, he could have at least been better prepared for it by keeping his mind clear instead of pickling it in drink like a sulking teenager. He might even have escaped the encounter without the gash in his forearm he was examining now.

The adrenaline was beginning to leave his system and encroaching tiredness replaced it, the Captain yawning widely as his eyelids began to droop. It would be another night without a call home, but the soldier reasoned it was better that than attempt an exhausted explanation of events through an unrested mind. He knew he should shuffle to the bathroom to clean his arm, but fatigue had him in its grip and he gave in to the heaviness in his eyes, his head dropping forward as the unfamiliar stresses of the past days caught up with him. Greyson might have disappeared but there was still a job to be done which he'd given Svobodova his word he'd help to fix, and he wasn't going to be able to do that from the bottom of a pint glass. Tomorrow he would start putting things right, whether exoneration was on the cards or not he'd make his lad proud of him.

"Night, night mate," he whispered as blackness rolled in, "God bless, see you in the morning."

TEN

HE JERKED AWAKE EARLY THE NEXT MORNING, his mouth rough and waterless and his throat swollen from a night's snoring. He was still in the same position against the door and as the aches began to toy their way through his body, Stone dreaded for a moment the prospect of shifting his legs and inviting the worryingly familiar pangs into his battle worn knees and ankles. Braving the twangs, he pulled himself upright and headed into the bathroom, throwing his blooded and wine-stained clothes into the corner and stepping into the hot, purifying torrent, willing it to bring him back to some form of life. On closer inspection, his fresh scars were not as intense or deep as they may have been and after cleaning them in the water he sufficed himself with a quick, homemade bandage from the First Aid box stashed under the kitchen sink.

His arm dressed, though the rest of him was not, he quickly threw on fresh jeans and a white cotton shirt, his black overcoat flung over the chair to pick up on the way out; early morning chills still enough to aggravate an unprotected chest before the summer sun could take firm hold. Sliding his phone's music app into service he breakfasted simply on toast with butter and jam and as big a cup as he could find of hot tea, frowning only slightly at the creamier taste of the Czechoslovak milk, while the timeless melodic tones of Beethoven's Moonlight Sonata played over him. He sought to give a mental acknowledgement to the fact that while in this part of the world he should be listening to a Dvořák or a Smetana, but those names merely served to remind him of the carnage of a few nights ago and he was determined to keep his mind in a calmer state today. In the dark days after his return from Kosovar, Stone's mind had been restless, emotional; his aggression crouching in a persistent state of readiness just beneath his skin. It had been after one typically charged and stupidly trivial breakfast time confrontation over the failure of his son to place dirty pots in the sink, the youngster had fled to the sanctuary of his room, seeking to control his own temper by playing Beethoven's masterpiece. Then, the damaged father and son had wept their apologies to each other, clinging tightly to their only refuge from the insanity of life and never wanting to let go. Stone, for his part had lamented that while he had frequently chastised his boy for failing to learn his lesson, in truth it was he himself who seemed incapable of learning and he'd promised then to make amends in future. From that day on, this had been 'their tune', their shared method to take the stress from a situation and relax their minds; and the stresses of Stone's present situation were too high for any substitute to be worthwhile.

The stirred familial memories sent a twinge of guilt in the soldier's gut for having been incommunicado for the past few days and he quickly rattled off a text to his boy in apology alongside the usual but sincere declaration of love. Taking a deep, lungful of breath as the melody came to its gentle conclusion, Stone allowed himself a brief smile then jumped to his feet and flung the waiting coat over his shoulders, heading out of the apartment. He directed a cheery 'dobrý deň' to the young girl on reception who smiled warmly back at the handsome military man who stepped out onto the street.

He headed down past the scene of his altercation the previous night, the sunshine robbing the more nefarious of darkened alleyways to hide in but unsavoury characters aplenty still occupied the streets, waiting for the opportunities the day would surely bring them. Stone clocked one or two more poisonous glances in his direction, but fresh, rested and his head clear of booze, he presented too much of a challenge for the average street thug, and he merely scanned their faces for any recognisable visage, although frustratingly none met his gaze. A few shards of broken glass remained in the spot at which he'd been attacked, which he casually brushed to the side with his shoe, while the wide, dark red stain on the pavement was being greedily dried by the emerging sun.

The street before him, he'd learned, would lead him to the bottom of Wenceslas Square which, with its over abundance of branded shops, franchised eateries and rowdier bars hedonistically defying the beauty of the location, Stone had long since decided to avoid. Despite his reluctance, he followed the road, reasoning that the Square would be relatively free from the clogging of tourists and hollers of street vendors this early in the morning. He could stretch his tight muscles with a brisk walk across the bottom of the Square and down through the increasingly recognisable maze of Old Town, before catching the train at Náměstí Republiky and heading through to Jinonice, where the internet told him filming was due to take place that morning for the much vaunted movie. Since speaking with Barry on his first day in the country, a nagging itch had played in Stone's mind which he suspected the friendly roadie could help scratch. Whatever information he could glean would aid him in making his apologies to Svobodova later that day, and then he'd be free to attempt the most likely more difficult task of reconciling with Abelard. Though it hadn't been his intent, he knew his sour demeanour so soon after spending the night with her had caused her pain, and he cursed himself for the dark mood swings which had plagued so many of his relationships with family and lovers alike; yearning for the simpler days when he could carry the weight of the world into battle without feeling even a fraction of the pressure an ignorant word or a badly parked car could cause him today. The Greyson situation was hardly of her making and surely no easier for her to deal with and he squirmed in embarrassment at his own selfish reaction to it over these past days.

Allowing his mind to dwell a little longer than perhaps he should on the thought of Greyson, the Captain chastised himself for letting his brighter start to the morning cloud, if even slightly; but even as he tried to push them back, they would return to consume his reasoning with a vengeance barely a few steps later, as he rounded an ancient building dressed in fading, crumbling yellow. There before him, stood among the cobbles like a spectral portent of mocking tribulation, was the wraithlike figure of Jonathan Greyson himself. His cheeks sallow, his features almost skeletal, but his gaze strong and the hint of a smile, however cruel, still playing on his lips.

"Good morning, Captain," the figure said, unperturbed by the tourists heading past the soldier and himself and tutting at the blockage to their ambling.

"You..." Stone quietly whispered, a moment of confusion captured on his face.

Greyson pulled his hands from his coat pockets and held them out to Stone in a stance of apology. The soldier though, his resentment restored, marched up to him and grabbed him, subtly but firmly by his coat, and began ushering him away from the tourists and down a narrow, isolated alley.

"You lying bastard!"

The alleyway was decorated with more than its share of abusive words and pictures, crudely sprayed onto the walls, and stunk of a potent mixture of stale urine and spent joints. Stone flung the politician in front of him, a punch to the head knocking him to the filthy ground and stood above him to block any possibility of escape, although the sprawling MP in truth showed few signs of wishing to.

"Ok, yes; I lied." Greyson rose shakily to his feet, his voice groggy but calm in spite of the assault. "I needed someone on the ground I could trust not to give up on the job. Who better than a man trying to clear his name for the sake of his child? I just thought I had more time to get everything in place."

"Like my exoneration?" Stone icily asked, "Or your next political appointment? Well you can exonerate this!"

The sum of Stone's rage and frustration flooded into his coiled arm, as though revelling in its own potency, robbing the seasoned professional of every trace of his hard-learned discipline and fuelling the irresistible urge to strike the passive figure. Greyson himself was swaying, his body limp in Stone's grip, his eyes betraying the tell-tale bewilderment of a beaten man, and offering little resistance to the soldier's onslaught. The unwillingness of his quarry to fight back in no way diminished Stone's desire to continue and he swung the powerful arm down, eager for the satisfying smack of fist upon cheek and the electrifying surge of pain through the hand that offered the congenial signal of victory.

The arm swung uselessly through the air, inches from Greyson's face. Stone twisted in confusion, feeling himself yanked backwards, hard, knocking him off balance and away from the politician. He spun to face the unknown threat, ready to employ the still swelling rage against whoever the mystery newcomer was but stopped, instinctively and barely in time, as the familiar prick of a knife's blade touched the skin of his throat. The sensation allowed reason to return to Stone's mind, although the reluctance to back down from the ecstatic pursuit was physical, the built-up energies, desperate for their own climactic expenditure, screaming through Stone's body as he sought to return himself to normal.

He followed the knife with his eyes, steadfastly guarding his neck, down the bony hand which held it, taking in the figure that stood before him, in all its inelegant glory. A thin - almost painfully so - figure stood at the end of the arm, bedecked in an oversized, frayed and weathered, grey pea coat, hanging over a faded t-shirt; Stone's mystery guardian angel, there before him in the flesh. He looked old, his unkempt hair grey, his skin thin and wrinkled, yet the defiance in his eyes leaving Stone in no doubt that he was both able and willing to use the weapon at his disposal, should Stone be foolish enough to struggle. It was the seriousness in those eyes that persuaded him. This man was a killer.

Despite the certainty of the threat, Stone's normalising mind deduced the unlikeliness that murder was the newcomer's primary concern, the knife having remained immobile since pressing his skin. Once more in control of his senses, Stone sought a way to likewise regain control of the situation, raising an eyebrow at the strange figure before him.

"It seems you have me at a disadvantage," he opened.

"Good," said the figure, a faint Scottish hint to the voice, with no other feature on the figure moving. "Now far be it from me to intrude on your lover's tiff," he nodded to the recovering Greyson behind the Captain, "but I'm thirsty and one of you fuckers is about to buy me a drink."

He whisked the knife back from Stone's throat, deftly closing and pocketing it in one swift, refined movement which defied his outward appearance.

"What?" Stone frowned in puzzlement, rubbing his neck, while Greyson hauled himself to his feet and stood between the pair.

"You took your time," Greyson said, groggily, "how long were you watching?"

"Long enough," came the reply, "I had a bet with myself you could get a punch in before he knocked you out. You lost. That's a scotch you owe me."

Stone felt his feral aggression quickly replaced with an equally severe confusion, coupled with a frustration that Greyson was regaining the advantage. As though sensing the soldier's emotions, the faintest of smirks formed at the corner of Greyson's mouth.

"Captain Stone," he began, "Allow me to introduce a man as unwelcome in the grounds of MI6, as you are with the Parliamentary Committee for Defence: Mr Williams, my own, personal bastard."

ELEVEN

THEIR JOURNEY TO THE PUB in whose garden they now sat had been lengthy in distance but passed quickly, though in complete silence.

The entrance to the bar seemed as dishevelled as this 'Williams' character, paint peeling from the dry wooden doorframe and old pictures of guest ales and promotional bottles faded to insignificance as they adorned the crumbling concrete of the outer wall. Leading them down a steep stone staircase, Williams strode through the almost empty, dark room, uttering a few words to the man behind the bar before exiting into an adjacent beer garden, enclosed all around with high metallic fencing and attached to what looked like an enormous outdoor cage, filled with shrubs, trees and greenery. Stone sat down on the hot wooden bench, and leaned on the table, staring in silence at Williams, the scent of stale beer mats and unknown dishes from the kitchen invading his nostrils. Williams, for his part, stared back, unblinking and eyes furrowed, seemingly sizing Stone up, while Greyson quickly excused himself and moved to the far edge of the enclosed garden, whispering into his phone. A tattooed and pink haired waitress brought a tray to the table, leaving three tall glasses of cold beer and a bowl of some kind of soup which Williams took possession of. Offering her a few quiet words of impeccable Czech, Williams took the soup and dropped his eyes to it, spooning it into his mouth without a thought for etiquette.

As Williams tore a slice of bread in two and began dipping it in his soup, Stone saw the blackness and filth of his hands, which suggested to him that his new counterpart had spent more than a couple of nights sleeping rough. He reached into his pocket and pulled out a small bottle of hand sanitizer, rarely used but bought for him as a joke by his son some months before and kept since as a memento. He held it out to the dishevelled man who stared at it for a brief second before returning to his bowl.

"If you want to go through the day smelling like a fucking flower that's your business," Williams said, "as for me I'll make do with soap and water."

Tiring of games, Stone was eager to understand what was happening, refusing to let this strange figure return to his angry silence.

"So why does he call you a bastard?"

"Why did the kids in the playground call you a nigger?"

The retort was matter of fact, delivered between mouthfuls of soup by the scruffy figure, who sat pointedly unfazed by the visible contempt it elicited in his companion and carried on, answering his own question.

"Because they were small minded people telling you something intrinsic about yourself in a particularly cuntish way."

Stone's stare hardened, his rich voice dropping deeper in disgust at the word Williams had employed.

"I'd hardly call it the same thing."

"No? Well, being a bastard comes as naturally to me as wearing my fucking skin, so…," he spooned the last drops of liquid into his mouth and pushed the bowl to the side, "I beg to differ."

He looked up, finally, his grey eyes meeting Stone's, offering neither fear nor defiance, merely cold indifference; an attitude the Captain didn't so much mind as long as it accompanied a general willingness to answer questions.

"How long have you been following me?"

"Since you arrived."

"That easy to find was I?"

"What? Finding a black guy in Myska's Prague? That's like trying to find a Magic 8 ball in a bowl of porridge."

Stone grabbed the man's arm as he raised it to his lips, spilling the soup from the spoon it held onto the table.

"Mr Williams," he quietly intoned, "if you'd rather continue this conversation from a hospital bed while being fed on a drip then by all means, carry on with your repertoire of Seventies brand jokes - I've a lot of pent up frustration to release today."

Williams made no move to pull his hand free, instead reaching over with his left hand and plucking the spoon from the restrained appendage, taking another mouthful while keeping his eyes on Stone's, who couldn't help but smile at the gesture.

"Captain Stone," he mimicked, setting the spoon to the table and letting his arm slip from Stone's released grip. "if you invested as much energy in staying undercover as you do in reacting to my more unsophisticated humour, you might have gone longer than ten minutes in this country without being tailed by the very people you'd come to observe."

Stone's frown deepened at the implication.

"Meaning?"

"You were spotted at the airport," Williams confirmed exasperatedly, "and not just by me. They had your flight, your description and a pretty fucking good idea of what you were up to. Which is why I was shadowing your arse at Náměstí Míru - you're welcome by the way - and why I've been sleeping on the street outside your apartment for the last couple of nights; although a lot of that has to do with the petrol bomb thrown through my flat window."

"Petrol bomb? I never heard about that?"

"Well it wasn't likely to make the front page. I got back from Brno earlier than expected to find the place gutted. It seems they're onto me too now, although in fairness it could just as easily have been thrown by my 'colleagues' in MI6. When Greyson finally reappeared from up his own backside it was time to meet properly."

Stone quickly assimilated the information Williams was throwing at him.

"Wait a minute," he interrupted, "how could they know I'd be arriving? That'd mean…"

"It means we have a leak," Greyson dragged a rickety wooden stool up to the table and sat alongside the mismatched pair, his voice not quite as grim as the inference it contained, "and considering our band of Merry Men is finitely small, I'd say it was a pretty fucking catastrophic leak."

The politician took a drink from the beer in front of him and continued. "And before we go any further, yes Captain Stone, I apologise for lying to you, but exoneration is still on the cards if we play this right."

"You'll forgive me for not being too optimistic," the Captain responded, "from where I'm sitting you have decidedly less influence with the Committee than apparent at our previous meeting."

"You know what they say about a week in politics," came the response, "it's all a game of musical chairs and the final round is still in play; we get this right and we can all end up in the comfy seats at the end and make sure the right people end up on their arses when the music stops."

Though his distaste at the political chicanery on display was profound, Stone swallowed any remaining temptation to give in to his aggressions, theorising that however unpleasant, these two sat with him remained his best and only chance of achieving the outcome he had come for.

"Go on," he said quietly.

Greyson took another drink, clearly revelling in his role of story-teller.

"You saw the details of my dismissal on the news?" he asked rhetorically, Stone nodding affirmatively none the less. "Ostensibly due to irrevocable differences with the Prime Minister on post Brexit foreign policy. In reality it was due to my comments on the night of the attack here; I told the press that Britain stood with their Czechoslovak brethren in horror at the events and were prepared to fully support them in their quest to uncover the truth of what happened."

"Very statesmanlike, I'm sure," remarked Stone, to his surprise bringing a snort from the still eating Williams.

"Oh I was," Greyson replied, ignoring the intended barb, "but what I was supposed to express along with my heartfelt regrets was the hope that Czechoslovakia would welcome their allies, specifically America, into the investigation. Coming from me it was supposed to be a signal to Svobodova that Britain would withdraw from recent agreements should she choose not to co-operate. I decided not to go along with that."

Despite his lingering antagonism, Stone felt a reluctant pang of admiration for Greyson's choice and willingness to accept the consequences of his actions, but questions still plagued him, not least the government's willingness to side with America over their alleged allies Czechoslovakia and the insistence of American operatives that the investigation be surrendered to them. The MP shrugged at the question.

"I think loyalties are beginning to get mixed," he said. "I'd known for a long time that most of the government and certainly a large part of the security services were being unduly influenced by The Institute for European Harmony, but as I understood it The Institute and the Americans haven't exactly been on the same page since reunification. It's possible some of the government have had their heads turned by Washington…"

"And is it possible that any of the government are actually interested in working for the people who elected them?"

Greyson gave in to a brief but audible laugh.

"I'm afraid Captain that the first duty of most politicians these days is to their own career, with country coming in some way behind that and Party in their list of considerations; surely the referendum would have convinced you of that."

"Well then how lucky I am to be sharing a table with the one incorruptible example." Stone drank deeply from his own beer, Williams allowing himself a brief cynical smirk at the Captain's remark.

"Indeed," nodded Greyson with ill-disguised sarcasm, his ego quite obviously far from pricked.

Williams clattered his spoon into his empty bowl, pushed it across the wooden table, took a mouthful of ale and pulled a cigarette from his pocket, lighting it and drawing the smoke deeply into his lungs.

"You're always so busy worrying about the fucking Yanks," he said with disdain, "I'm telling you The Institute is the problem here."

"Look," interjected Stone, "you obviously still need me involved in this or we wouldn't be sat here now. I need to know who and what I'm up against and what precisely you want me to do about it; not some vague statement about 'observing' some Czech MEP, but actually what you want me to do, and what exactly this Institute is."

The billowing stench from William's cigarette enveloped Stone, his brow furrowing to protect his eyes from the sting.

"And haven't you ever heard of electronic cigarettes?" he coughed.

"If I wanted to walk around spaced out with a dildo hanging out of my mouth, I'd take a rohypnol and make a pass at a lesbian. I've seen people sucking on less comical bongs."

The wrinkled man emphasised his point, drawing in a huge chest full and exhaling luxuriously.

"Besides," he said, nodding towards Greyson "it's only fair to let the cancer have as equal a chance of finishing me off as this prick."

"Charming to the last, Mr Williams," grinned Greyson, "although I think you're wrong about The Institute on this occasion."

"Whether he is or not," said a frustrated Stone, "I'd like to know more about this 'Institute'; for starters who's behind it?"

A flutter of discomfort flitted across Greyson's face, cracking the veneer of confidence he had projected to that point.

"Like I told you in Bojnice," he began, "The Institute is a clandestine grouping aimed at ensuring the security of the Union; the person with the most direct control over it is a man known as 'The Child'. There's very little known about him other than the fact that he's ruthless in the pursuit of his goals, which he considers to be for the greater good; he's not interested in money, power or personal empire building as such, just in the continued unity of Europe. He must be a fair age by now...

"That sounds about as blank a canvas as you can get. Is there anything we do know about him?"

Greyson shrugged, dragging on his own cigarette; appearance no longer dictating he conceal the habit, and paused for a moment to savour the burn in his lungs.

"There's very little documented," he finally ventured, "my Dad kept some papers, diaries and the like from his career, I've been going through them since his death, this 'Child' is mentioned a few times."

Stone nodded in a brief display of respect, remembering the Headlines when Sir Roger McShade, a controversial figure and Greyson's largely absent father had died, ironically enough in Prague, a few years back. Suicide so the papers had claimed, but something in Greyson's face brought a flicker of doubt to Stone's mind as to the cause.

"What do they say?" the soldier finally asked.

Greyson exhaled, shaking his head. "It's mostly anecdotal from various sources over the years. We know he came over from East Germany in the Fifties, we're not sure exactly when. There were rumours he murdered his adoptive parents before he ran, though they were never corroborated. Intelligence at the time was somewhat patchy and the Stasi files uncovered since the Wall came down are only so useful."

"Murdered his parents?" Stone frowned, almost as much because the others present did not share his instinctive revulsion, as because of the revelation itself.

"So they say," Greyson nodded, apparently revelling once more in his role as gruesome story teller, "But if it's any consolation they wouldn't have been very nice people. He was a Lidice child, you know? It was one of the Czech villages that was destroyed by the Nazis during the war after Operation Anthropoid. Ležáky was another one. That's where he gets his name from; he was selected for 'Ayranisation' and sent to a suitably loyal SS family to raise him. After the war, the Red Cross set about finding the kids and returning them to what was left of their real families, they were very successful too, in all but one case."

"No prizes for guessing which," Stone remarked.

"Quite. It's not too much of a stretch of the imagination to think that one day he found out the truth."

"Well aside from an unlikeliness he'll attend any cosy family get togethers in Bavaria, that doesn't tell us much." Williams pulled the spent cigarette from his own mouth, stubbing it in the rapidly filling ash tray under his nose.

"No," Greyson agreed. "After that he went under the radar for a while, eventually wound up with the reputation for doing the kind of dirty work in West Germany that made him the front runner when The Institute was being created. He was instrumental in bringing down the Wall and there are certain references to his activities here during the Velvet Revolution. There's even a suggestion he was involved with Richard Grave for a while…"

"Grave, the defector?" Stone raised his eyebrow at the name, remembering the whispered stories of 'The Grave Affair' from his youth, while Williams' scowl further deepened.

"The same," Greyson confirmed, "but Dad's notes from that period are pretty sporadic. That was in 1989, and then the notes become more sporadic throughout the Nineties. When Dad left the Commons in 1997 the references dried up completely, but what is obvious is that The Institute went undercover, fast becoming autonomous and separated from the intelligence agencies that spawned it. Before long they'd begun infiltrating the host agencies of each Member State and took a de facto control of European Affairs. To this day, those politicians that know about it generally choose to go along with their objectives, or else ignore it and try to convince themselves it doesn't exist."

"Why so keen?"

"Let's just say there's been some tremendously bad luck when it comes to 'unfortunate accidents' among a fair few of the elite over the past decades," Greyson sighed.

"Accidents my arse," scowled Williams.

"Quite. But as I said, I think the Institute have miscalculated in their rush to unsettle Mirush... I mean Svobodova; Myska's plans are hardly what you'd call 'in line' with The Child's. They might both want a united Europe, but Myska's slightly more Aryan tastes are the antithesis of what The Institute claims to stand for; whatever else The Child might be, he's no racial demagogue. I'm far more concerned that they'll use the crisis to simply cut Czechoslovakia loose."

"What do you mean?"

"The Institute survives on discipline and fear; Czechoslovakia went against them with the decision to reunify hence their efforts to undermine Svobodova. But if it looks like the only beneficiary of that action will be the Far Right, then it might make more sense to simply let Russia subsume them all over again."

Stone's contemplation of the words was interrupted by a graceful but sudden and unexpected movement in the corner of his eye. A feline shape, silver grey, elegant and just large enough to brush an average man's hip hopped down from a stool by the bar and strode into the light of the beer garden, idling past Stone's leg and through a small metal flap in the caged area behind him, disappearing nonchalantly into the greenery.

"Was that a puma?" Stone asked, puzzled at the lack of reaction from his two companions, "what's the owner doing giving it free rein of a bar?"

"That's nothing," said Williams, drawing on his fresh cigarette, "you should see the reaction when he takes it to Tesco."

He swallowed large gulps of his ale, wiping his mouth with a dirty sleeve.

"Whichever way you look at it," he intoned, without looking at anyone in particular, as though he were debating with the dark recesses of his own consciousness, "the Institute are losing their grip; at one time arseholes like Myska would have been only slightly more irritating than a blocked toilet in need of a plunger while the refugee crisis would never have got this far. In the old days, The Child would have knocked some heads together and found a solution, but today's summit meetings resemble a convention for late middle aged parents still discussing how to programme the VCR when everyone else has moved onto the Cloud. If you ask me, The Child's lost the fucking plot."

"That's as maybe," Greyson conceded, "but if true only makes Czechoslovakia's situation worse; there's no telling what the old bastard will do if he thinks he's backed into a corner."

"Well rather than wait to find out, it's even more important that we dig up some hard evidence connecting Myska to the violence. Everything I've seen so far is screaming 'Red Flag Op' to me; a fucking terrorist attack just when it would benefit Myska? Rather convenient, wouldn't you say?"

"Convenient it might be, but it doesn't automatically point to a Red Flag," Stone responded, thoughtfully. "The terrorists goal, assuming they are genuine terrorists for a moment, is chaos and war; they're not interested in seeing tolerant, inclusive politicians elected, they've no interest in dialogue or compromise. A divisive leader like Myska is exactly what they want and need to keep the flames of division burning; every word that comes out of their mouths only helps the poison spread further."

"You said 'assuming they're genuine,'" Greyson cut in, frowning, "why wouldn't we make such an assumption?"

"The methods are different this time," Stone answered, touching the scar on his temple. "The bomb in the bin at the concert for example and even going back to the first attack last year; I find it hard to believe that a genuine fundamentalist of the kind I've experienced would get their timing so badly wrong as to allow a building full of potential victims to escape. Something just doesn't stack up right for me. And there's something else, I just can't quite put my finger on…"

"All the more reason to suspect Red Flag!" Williams' frustration was abundantly clear to his colleagues, the Scotsman spitting the words in almost a fury. "And while you're scrambling around looking for somewhere to put your finger, The Great White Hope is out there planning his next big event." He nodded his frowning head towards Greyson. "Can you not persuade your girlfriend to allow some evidence to be 'creatively manufactured'?"

"Ha!" Greyson laughed out loud, inadvertently spitting his mouthful of beer back into his glass. "Hardly," he answered, "I'm rather afraid Mirushka is the very essence of political morality; if she's to take punitive action she demands evidence. And in any event, she isn't my girlfriend."

The MP flashed a hint of what looked like a bashful grin, before catching Stone's eye and sheepishly looking down to reorder his demeanour.

"How has she been holding up in all this?" Greyson eventually returned his, somewhat hesitant, eyes to the level of the Captain's, who offered him nothing in the way of sympathy with the intensity of his stare.

"Mirushka?"

Stone employed Svobodova's nickname with a voice dripping with enough scorn that even Williams stifled a wicked grin.

"Svobodova," Greyson answered, clearly resentful of the joke at his expense.

"Well, considering," Stone answered, narrowing his brow, "and it can't have been easy. I'm told that tourism is holding up reasonably well and there aren't exactly reams of people waiting to cancel their bookings, but it's fair to say there's a great deal more tension in the country, here particularly, than I'm led to believe is usually the case. At least, that's what Natalie told me."

Stone's mention of Professor Abelard was deliberate and even, he thought, a little cruel, but no more so than the man before him deserved, even if the only chance, however slight, of the soldier's exoneration lay in the politician's hand.

"Natalie?"

Greyson quietly repeated the name, a shade of resentment at Stone's obvious familiarity visible on his features.

"Yes, she told me over breakfast the other morning," Stone drove the dagger home, his affections for the woman who had provided him a brief glimpse of the damage this man had caused her overriding his sense of fair play, until he remembered his own less than chivalrous behaviour over the past couple of days. "She'd gone over the reports from the Tourism and Heritage Ministry. And of course, the filming is keeping the country firmly in the international eye; although we're told that given some of the attacks recently they're taking on extra security."

"I doubt they'll bring on enough people to keep history secure from the fucking film studios."

Stone and Greyson turned their eyes to Williams who had voiced the contemptuous words while balancing a stained beermat on the edge of the wooden table, flicking it upwards and catching it in his thin, cadaverous fingers.

"What the fuck do Yanks know about history?" the untidy man grumbled as he flicked his beermat again. "The complete span of their fucking country is two hundred years; I've had longer fucking bowel movements."

"Anyway," Greyson frowned, "might I suggest that the two of you become better acquainted and co-ordinate your efforts?" He stood to leave, picking up and finishing his glass. "I'll be getting in touch with Mirush---, Ms Svobodova, later today." He shot another awkward glance to Stone who stared back with all his years of military deference. "It's safer for all concerned if I stay out of the limelight for a while; there's no need to fan the flames any harder."

"I need a new flat." Williams piped up, ignoring the conversation's change in direction and introducing his own, "I don't want to have to bunk up with Captain Marvel and his Professor friend, I'd feel left out."

This time Greyson refused to rise to the bait, briskly responding by confirming that there would be funds in his account before the end of the day and he should make his own arrangements from there before linking up again with the Captain.

"Actually, speaking of the film, there's one or two things I wanted to check with the crew. I'll check the location diary, perhaps we can meet there later?" Stone asked the question with a certain degree of awkwardness, at Williams' casual exposition of the Captain's recent sleeping arrangements.

"Agreed," the Scot nodded. "Here's my number, bell me when you want to get down there."

He slid from between the Soldier and the former Secretary of State and without another word, disappeared into the dimly lit bar interior; the click of his shoes on the steps assuring them of his ascent to the street.

Stone moved to follow but Greyson caught him gently by the arm; the soldier pausing to observe the MP, his head tilted to the side.

"Captain Stone, a question if I may?"

"Yes?"

"Professor Abelard, Natalie. Are you sleeping with her?"

The bluntness of Greyson's question surprised Stone, but not enough that he didn't know how to answer.

"I'm not sure where you learned your manners, Mr Greyson," he said, "but it was evidently at a different establishment than I."

He moved to leave once more but was again stopped.

"You realise she's my ex-wife?"

Stone could see no aggression or even hostility on the politician's face, but neither was there any trace of warmth, and while the question was not exactly wholly unexpected, he was damned if he was about to dignify it with an answer.

"Then I would have thought that your divorce renders her social calendar little of your business."

The suggestion of a half-smile arose, though Greyson's eyes remained resolute.

"An honourable man," he said, "and entirely correct of course. But a word of warning Captain: these are dangerous times and you are observing some particularly foul people. I don't think there's any need for her to become too involved in your investigations; after all I'd be greatly displeased were anything untoward to happen to her."

"Whereas I am conveniently expendable, I presume?"

"I didn't say that," Greyson replied, "you're every bit as vital to completing the objectives…"

"Yes, well, Natalie is her own person," Stone interrupted, eager to save himself from any more guarded political platitudes, "she makes her own decisions and she'll be every bit as involved in 'completing the objectives' as she chooses to be. And from what I know of her, God help anyone who suggested otherwise. I will say this though…"

He leaned closer in, speaking softly into Greyson's ear, his words delicate but delivered with just a subtle hint of threat, enough to make Greyson know where he stood.

"Natalie was brought onto this merry-go-round by you, Mr Greyson and you alone, presumably using the same mixture of duty and emotional blackmail you used to bring me here. And while I would move heaven and earth trying to prevent anything from 'happening to her', as I'm sure she would for me, it would be worth remembering who persuaded her to take her seat in the first place; just as it would prove useful to understand that concern for a person's welfare is perhaps best expressed before they've made the decision to leave you."

Stone didn't wait for an answer, turning immediately away from Greyson and heading into the pub and up the steep angled steps into the hot afternoon. He disliked cruelty and he knew it was unwise to bite the hand that still offered to feed him, questionable pickings though they currently were. But what drove Stone to do so, even more than the patchy details Natalie had offered of their life together, was the shame he still felt at having not made the effort to prevent his own marriage from collapsing; a mistake he felt he was in danger of repeating through his behaviour in recent days. And with Williams' chief concern at the moment being a new roof over his head, Stone had the time to rectify his mistake; if, that was, the Professor was still ready and willing to talk to him.

TWELVE

IT TOOK STONE SO LONG to find Abelard, even following her tersely texted directions, that he could be forgiven for imagining the confirmation of his fears - and while that would be painful he could certainly understand why. From his admittedly limited experience of the Professor thus far, she struck him as the kind of woman ill-prepared to take much in the way of disrespect from her gentleman friends and he hoped that his alcohol fuelled self-absorption would not be taken as such. Nonetheless, he eventually found the almost unnoticeable gate on the slope of Petřín Hill which led to the small but intensely beautiful Vrtba Garden, in the shadow of the Palace. Pausing for the briefest of moments to admire the baroque finery he ventured in, finding the picturesque venue mercifully free of tourists.

He soon saw her, sitting on a stone bench, her face away from him, taking in the majesty of the grandly constructed St Nicholas Cathedral. He approached her with the stealthy subtlety of a soldier as he struggled to make his opening gambit; the instinctive spontaneity which served him so well in combat leaving him floundering now.

"I'm sorry," he said at last, his hands in his pockets and sincerity on the face she was turned away from, "I was an arse."

No answer came, the Professor continuing to stare ahead. Breathing deeply, he spoke again, attempting an explanation of his morning with Greyson and his Bastard, to who Stone somewhat resentfully owed his life.

"Greyson's in town," he said simply, opting to avoid any flowery lead-in to a topic which was bound to unsettle her. "He surprised me this morning while I was walking in Old Town; he and the man who saved me in the tube station, Williams he's called."

"Is that why you're here?"

She snapped the question with an obvious pain in her voice, repressed as best she could but inescapably present.

"You haven't wanted anything to do with me for the last few days, but all of a sudden Jonathan comes to town and you think I'll go scurrying back to him if you don't make a move, is that it? Am I supposed to take that as another Regimental tradition? The military equivalent of raising your leg and pissing all over whatever you consider to be your property."

"No," Stone moved to stand beside her, joining her in looking out at the Cathedral, "no, that's not it. You can believe it or not but I was coming to see you anyway before he found me. I got jumped last night by a couple of Myska's goons."

"Are you ok?"

She spun around instantly, her wide eyes checking him for any sign of physical impairment.

"I'm fine, honestly I'm fine," he reassured her, though she scanned him thoroughly before returning her stare to the Cathedral.

"They were just a couple of scrotes trying to put the frighteners on me, that's all, they came off worse. But it was enough for me to get my head out of my arse and start realising what my priorities should be again."

"Well I'm glad you're ok."

Her words were sincere but almost whispered, a clear indication to the Captain that his behaviour was not yet entirely excused.

"Look, I know it's not been easy for you, this assignment, and my recent attitude hasn't helped matters, but I am truly sorry. On the morning of the attack it seemed like I was fighting all the old battles again when Svobodova took your advice over mine, and then finding out about Greyson's sacking just tipped me over the edge. The only reason I agreed to come here in the first place was for the exoneration he offered me, and it felt like the rug was being pulled out from under me when I saw his face plastered all over the news. And it's not about marking my territory or anything like that; if you want to tell me to get on my bike now then I will. But once I learned he was in town I figured you wouldn't take it too well and I wanted to be the one who broke the news of his arrival to you. I didn't want you to walk into a meeting one morning and find him sat at the head of the table with a croissant, coffee and a condescending smile."

"I already knew," Natalie spoke again with less anger in her voice, "Svobodova told me, she said it was 'only fair.'"

He slowly lowered himself beside her on the cold, hard seat, deeply exhaling and shaking his head, no words coming to his mind to support her in her confused emotion. Though her gaze remained fixed ahead and her body language tense, Stone felt a part of her relax into his presence, her head hovering just a few millimetres above his shoulder, not quite low enough to fully break the tension.

"Why did you get divorced?" she suddenly asked, out of the blue, the Captain frowning in response at the unexpected enquiry.

"I told you," he stiffly answered, "she got tired of being a soldier's wife, that's all."

"No," Natalie pressed, "I mean, what was the straw that broke the back? What made you both realise that you just didn't want to fight anymore?"

The probing question didn't offend Stone, but he struggled to know how to answer it, his mind raking over memories long since dormant and less than a delight to re-live. Nonetheless he began to relax, his tautness dissipating as he pondered out loud.

"I don't know," he sighed gently, "everything was so easy in the early days, you know? I loved her, truly and thought we'd be together forever. And for what it's worth, I believe to this day that she genuinely felt the same way about me. But slowly things began to unravel. I think when our son was born she wanted, or maybe expected me, to give up the Army, find something else to do with my life."

"But you couldn't do that, could you?"

"No way. I mean I thought about it, but being a soldier, it's just who I am. I joined up the day I turned eighteen. My Dad, my adoptive dad, took so much stick for having taken us in, a black single mother and her son; he was the best man I'd ever known and from an early age I swore I'd follow in his footsteps, be the type of man he was. There was no way you could ever get me in a shirt and tie doing a nine to five. I thought I could provide the best example for my son; boy did I get that one wrong."

Their eyes still on the Cathedral, Stone felt her fingers reach deliberately between his, squeezing her affection and support as he continued.

"After that things started to get worse. She'd forever be accusing me of having affairs, of sleeping with women in the forces or knocking around with prozzies while away on duty, all stuff I never did and never even occurred to me. I ended up sinking so deep within myself that I stopped communicating with her almost entirely; I didn't ask her advice on anything, never talked about my work and basically just grunted responses when there was no alternative but to talk to her. When I was home I used to take her out, just the two of us, trying to recapture some of that earlier passion, but every time it became a disaster. She'd have too much to drink and start screaming at me that I was a lying, unfaithful cheat, then I'd shout back that she was crazy and making my life hell. We said some pretty horrible things to each other before we'd stagger home, pissed out of our heads shouting all the way... In the morning we'd make up, do our best to laugh it off as being down to the drink or the stress or not getting to see each other as much as we'd like and we'd get on with the day, only for exactly the same thing to happen the next time we went out. I suppose we were cheaper than cabaret for a lot of people around that time."

He blinked away the dampness in his eyes and returned the squeeze of Abelard's hand before continuing.

"Things just got worse from there. Eventually, the rows became longer and the making up less sincere; we stopped laughing it off the morning after, just hugging each other wordlessly instead, and pretty soon the hugs became shorter and more awkward, until finally even those stopped - but the arguing continued and the name calling got worse. One night, after she'd called me a filthy liar one too many times, I turned around and told her she was a shit mother who cared more for getting pissed and screaming at me than for her boy sat at home wondering why his parents didn't get on. It was a fucking horrible thing to say, whatever the provocation and I certainly didn't mean it, but the damage was done. I wanted to apologise but by then I was so sick of the constant fighting that I didn't find it in me to. The next day there was no apology, no hug, not even a smile; she just kissed her boy goodbye and walked out the door. Barring solicitor's letters, that was the last I heard from her; I thought we'd have a protracted battle for custody but the fight never came."

"You never saw her again?"

"She'd write letters to him, send presents for birthdays and Christmases, but until recently that was it."

"Until recently?"

Stone nodded, the words coming more easily than he'd imagined, while Natalie's hand continued to squeeze his.

"She found him on Facebook one day, started to e-mail him and asked to see him. I'd just been suspended after the Syria Incident, so I was at home with him. He asked me about it and I said it was up to him, I had no right to try and block anything."

"And did he meet her?"

He collected his thoughts again, a loving smile spreading on his lined face.

"He was so worried about meeting her that day," he mused, "it was almost like he was getting ready for a first date, never mind a reunion with a parent; 'how do I look Dad? What do you think of this shirt? Should I shave? Is this too causal? Is that too formal?'"

The Captain grew misty eyed at the memory.

"I just laughed and said he was perfect however he chose to look and he should just go, be himself and see what happened. He was still nervous so I offered to ride on the Tube with him to go and meet her. I felt closer to him that day than any day in my life; it was as though none of the stuff we'd ever argued or rowed about in the past mattered anymore, not that it ever did, not really. I was so proud of him, and I'd like to think he felt the same about me…"

Natalie's lips pressing softly on his own gently pulled him from the melancholia which threatened to overwhelm him, and he returned her kiss enthusiastically, accepting the forgiveness she offered.

"I know he did," she whispered as their lips parted, the warmth flooding back into her demeanour with each passing second, "and so do I."

THIRTEEN

"HI MATEY, ARE YOU OK?"

Stone gasped to regulate his breathing, having awoken to the sound of his mobile phone and sprung up quickly. He blinked his eyes to become accustomed to the dark and looked around at the bedroom of his apartment. Natalie was still there, curled up beside him and locked securely in the depths of sleep. They had returned directly from the Palace gardens to the apartment, making up in the time-honoured way. A Trail of untidily deposited clothing marked their stumbling path from the main door to the bedroom, where the tension, stress and pain of their situation broke, relaxed and poured away in the ecstasy of their love making, before they had drifted into carefree and appreciative sleep. Barely one shrill ring from the telephone had been enough to wrench the Captain from his rest, and now he sat, upright with the phone glued to his ear, hoping for the expected sound of his son's voice, in one of his typical late night/early morning calls.

"I'm fine thank you honey bunch," came the cheerily sarcastic reply in inescapably Scottish tones, "how are you?"

"Williams," sighed Stone, rubbing his hand over his tired, sore eyes, "aren't you supposed to be out finding somewhere to sleep?"

"Aye, I have done," came the answer, "by chance the apartment below yours was free so I've taken that."

"Oh, bollocks."

"Ah, don't be like that Captain," the river of sarcasm continued to flow, "we're all one big happy family now."

"Williams, do you have any idea what time it is?"

"Of course I fucking do, why else do you think I'm calling now? I was trying to get my head down before but you and the Good Professor were banging away so hard I thought I'd developed tinnitus; at one point I was looking up the Czech word for 'Plasterer' in case you came through the fucking ceiling. Ringing you in the middle of the night is the only way I could pay you back."

"Piss off."

"Hang on!" Stone moved to hang up the mobile, but something in Williams' tone compelled him not to. "Don't get precious on me Captain," the aging voice chastised him, "that isn't my only reason for calling."

"And what is the real reason?"

"You have an early start tomorrow."

"Oh yes?"

"Remember you said you wanted to catch up with the film crew? Well now you have the perfect opportunity; one of them has been murdered."

Stone reached the scene even before the sun had grazed the roofs of the multi-coloured baroque buildings lining the streets of Malá Strana, a black overcoat shielding him from the early morning chills and accompanied on one side by a grim faced Radoslav and on the other by the furrowed wrinkles of Williams. Another of the tanks stood silently and archaically majestic upon the cobbles, it's turret pointed upwards as if in salute to the bloodied and battered body that lay a few steps in front of it, being brought almost lovingly into focus as the creeping sun leaked light onto the bloodstained path. A small cordon of police vehicles and a surely redundant ambulance encircled the scene, complimented by the fluttering of yellow police tape, steadfastly prohibiting the encroachment of the gradually increasing bystanders.

A police officer, evidently tired and overdue for relief held up a hand to the approaching trio, backed by his superior who took issue with Rado's flashing of his credentials and proceeded to argue the necessity of his presence.

"What's she saying?" Stone quizzed, frustrated in his desire to examine the scene.

"Oh, it's just the old 'jurisdiction' chestnut," Williams explained, translating the terse exchange with ease. "She's wondering why a security operative like young Radoslav is interested in a run of the mill murder scene. Plus, she doesn't like the look of us two."

"Doesn't she now?"

"I can't say I blame her, we look like the fucking villains on a shit crime drama. Still, like us or no, she'll have to let us in. Rado's Full House beats her Pair."

Stone scowled in distaste at what he was beginning to realise was Williams' deliberately provocative humour, while as if sensing the disapproval, the seasoned Spook grinned widely to himself.

"Come on now, quick as you like…at last! Thank you!"

A thunderous expression on the detective's face, she finally, if somewhat reluctantly, bowed to bureaucratic reality and waved the three of them through the yellow paper barrier and into the scene. Stone headed to where the victim lay and crouched down, shaking his head sadly as the sickening outcome he had half expected since William's call a couple of hours earlier was proven true.

Barry Hendry, Sergeant, late of The Queen's Royal Hussars lay with his head on the kerb, the impact with which had, according to the attending mortician, killed him outright. There was certainly enough blood to verify a massive head injury, while the look of surprise on the dead man's face added credence to the explanation, but it did little to satisfy Stone.

"How do you know it was murder?" he snapped loudly and to no-one in particular. A uniformed officer stood close by taking it upon himself to answer the question in Stone's own language.

"Witnesses," the young police officer said, "several. They say a fight broke out and this man was punched to the ground, he hit his head and that was that."

"You have the attacker in custody?" Williams quizzed, receiving a shaken headed response.

"His name was Sergeant Hendry," Stone barked, "not 'this man'. He was a soldier, he gave his all for his country and he deserved a damn sight more than to die like this in a street fight."

Radoslav placed a hand on Stone's shoulder, firmly but without condescension.

"Captain," he softly intoned.

"I'm sorry." Stone shook his head again and gave one last look of respect to the fallen comrade.

"At ease, Sergeant Hendry."

Straightening up he spoke again to the young cop, though in altogether softer tones.

"The witnesses you mentioned, are any still here?"

The officer nodded and gestured over to where a young man with a goatee beard and deathly pale skin shivered in the open back door of a squad car, a towel hanging pathetically around his shoulders. Stone saw enough to know both that the man was in deep shock, and that he was Petřík, the young man with the tragic past whom the late Sergeant had pointed out days earlier while Stone had been admiring the beauty of the Russian tank. The Captain walked slowly over and leant close to the man, searching his mind for a some comforting word to offer and finding nothing but blanket apologies instead.

"Petřík?" Stone tried to tease some words from the shaking youngster but seemingly to no avail, Petřík simply rocking back and forth. The young face was bruised and swollen, contusions evidencing the beaten he had taken.

"What happened Petřík? What happened to Barry?"

For the briefest of moments, the frightened eyes turned towards Stone and the mouth hung open just slightly, as though he were being consumed from within by information he yearned to share but which would not come. And then, almost as soon as he had looked up, his stare became sightless again, returning to the ground before him while his rocking continued apace.

Stone straightened and turned away, cursing. He had no evidence at all but the stench of Myska's hand permeated the crime scene and it was the singular lack of evidence that caused him to swear out loud as he walked away from the recovering witness, gripped by an unfamiliar and wholly unwelcome sense of impotence.

"Are you alright?"

Williams' voice never seemed too far away from a cynical incline, it seemed to Stone, but the man's eyes at least displayed an apparently genuine concern, the weathered spy appearing alongside him unexpectedly.

"Yeah, fine," Stone lied. "It's just, he was a soldier, he risked himself in combat his whole life and managed to come through unscathed. It's not right that anyone should die like this, but for someone who's dodged bullets for his country to be sucker punched in a street fight…"

"You haven't heard the worst of it yet."

"There are other witnesses here?"

"No, but I've just read a couple of statements. It seems the late Sergeant Hendry and your friend with the shakes over there got wind that some of the crew were heading out last night on 'Terror Patrol'. "

Stone grimaced at the expression, having heard similar stories from other parts of the world.

"Terror Patrol," he spat.

"Aye, a few of them suited and booted in their best Army Surplus fatigues, stocked to the gills with knuckle dusters and night sticks, roaming the streets looking for 'terrorists', or anyone who fits the general shade on their colour chart. Your comrade in arms and his mate found out about it and went out to challenge them, getting a sound beating for their trouble, with the Sergeant coming off worst of all."

Stone gave up any effort to contain his anger as he assimilated William's words and he swung his fist against the tank's metal shell, cursing at once as the pain surged through his arm.

"I want every one of the bastards in chains and charged as accessories to murder!" He shouted his demands in the general direction of the still angered Detective, who glared fiercely back at the Captain, while Williams gave a short contemptuous laugh.

"Yeah? And I want to be rocked to sleep every night in the bosom of a Valkyrie Maiden with a bottle of single malt plugged intravenously into my veins. You have no fucking power to demand anything here, Captain Marvel, so just keep your fucking emotions in check."

Stone glowered at the Scot and opened his mouth to angrily retort but was cut short before he could begin.

"Emotions man," Williams scolded, "that's not why we're here! You said you had suspicions about the crew, does this bear them out and is it useful to us?"

"I don't know, maybe… yes."

Stone filled his lungs, trying to balance out his chemistry and regain composure while a short man dressed in khaki pants and a short-sleeved shirt opened almost to his slightly rotund belly broke free from the crowd and headed towards them, bellowing at the pair.

"Hey! Hey, you!"

Stone and Williams crossed to the barrier as he approached, Rado falling in behind them as they took in the sight of the curious newcomer in all his perverse glory.

"Are you in charge here?" the squat man asked with an unmistakeably American inflection. "How long are you guys gonna be?"

Stone balked at the blatant disrespect on show and stepped forward to offer his own choice remonstrations, but met with the surprisingly gentle touch of Williams' hand on his arm, the Scotsman greeting the man with an enormous smile.

"I'm sorry, sir," he intoned with breath-taking sincerity, "this road is likely to be closed to tourists for the rest of the day at least; we've had a murder here you see? The guy on the floor over there isn't just lying down on the job while using a bottle of ketchup as a pillow, so unfortunately that means you and whichever entourage you're touring with will have to find a different part of the city to be insufferable in today, ok?"

The angered face turned a glorious shade of crimson at Williams' condescension, but no indication its owner was prepared to back down.

"You have no idea who I am, do you?"

"Oh, now give me a minute," Williams eagerly replied like a moth to the proverbial flame, "you *look* like you could find work as a stunt double for Michael Moore, even with your designer specs which you probably don't even need, but you *sound* more like that blustering, uncultured noise my car makes when it backfires… Got it! You're Fred Flintstone's less successful brother!"

"Very, fucking funny," the man slowly intoned, his grip on his anger evidently not very strong and his gaze fixed firmly on Williams. "Just in case the Entertainment News reaches as far as Scotland, you might recognise my name: Jonah P. Reynard."

Stone knew the name well, as did many people with an interest in film; Jonah P. Reynard, one of the brightest directing talents to emerge from Hollywood in the past ten years; a visionary radical, with a string of successes behind him, only inches separated them now as the film maker assimilated Williams' barrage.

"The Director?" Williams looked around, shock on his lined face, "Well thank God you're here! You really couldn't have come at a better time Jonah, you see, there's a movie being filmed in Prague right now as it happens and by all accounts it's going to be shit."

"Shit, huh?" Jonah repeated, a sarcastic smile on his face. "Well then I'd better get to work improving it. I have two trucks full of equipment stuck up the road, waiting to be unloaded and a coach full of actors who get paid for every day over schedule that this movie lasts. You guys are in the way of my shoot and you are costing me time and money."

"This is a murder investigation."

"There's nothing to fucking investigate!" Jonah's voice rose, his anger finally overcoming his restraint. "A couple of guys had a fight, one ended up with his ticket punched instead of just his head. You have witnesses, you know who you're looking for, so get the stiff in the ambulance, clean up the cobbles and open the fucking scene, I have a film to make!"

Williams shook his head and lowered his voice.

"You know, I've never been one for public displays of emotion or an abundance of sympathy, but you sir, are one insensitive bastard. That's your employee lying dead there."

"And there's plenty more where he came from," Jonah replied in an equally quiet tone. "Look, if a couple of guys on the crew want to get themselves wasted and fight to the death on some backstreet in Prague, that's their business; I don't expect it to interfere with my film."

"Where did you source the tanks?"

"What?"

Jonah looked towards Stone, hitherto silent but who now repeated his question accompanied by a frown of fearsome intensity.

"The tanks, where did you find them?"

"I don't know, that was down to props; they came from a few places I think; museums, private collections, a few brought over from Russia…"

"How many?"

"What?"

"How many tanks? I've seen at least seven since I've been in the city, how many do you have in total?"

"What does it matter? Twenty-five, I think. Look, when can you open the street for filming?"

Stone weighed up the man before him and the callous disregard he displayed for the dead Sergeant Hendry, screwing his face up as he replied.

"I don't know," he spat, "it could be days."

"Days?! Come on man, we're making history here!"

"Well you're certainly not presenting it," Williams interjected again, his mischievously cruel smile returning.

"Excuse me?" Jonah snapped, taking the bait in full.

"Well everyone knows that accuracy is the first victim of most Hollywood epics," Williams grinned, "How does this one end for example? Does the US Cavalry leap across the Vltava and rout the invading forces?"

The Director stepped closer, his face a curious shade of red, his finger pointing into Williams' still benevolently smiling face.

"Now you look h…,"

"What's next on the filming agenda? A Waterloo spectacular with Wellington's army rescued at the last minute by a fleet of Apache helicopters? Or maybe a Biblical Epic, with a group of daring young Americans nailed to a cross for our sins?"

Williams' smile was sincerity itself and Stone could no longer resist his own grin, which pulled defiantly at the corners of his mouth, looking across to see Rado struggling with a similar concern. The short man in front of them narrowed his eyes, chewing on his gum slowly.

"Ok," he said, "I get it. Everyone loves a comedian. You just be sure to go back and tell your bosses that I have millions of dollars in people and props tied into this movie, and I intend to suit for full recovery of any overspend we incur as a result of your 'investigation', ok?"

"Oh, the bosses will be delighted to help," Williams smirked.

"Will they?" snarled Jonah. "Well I'm sure they'll be equally delighted to foot the bill for the additional security the Producers and I are gonna draft in to protect our investment; all of a sudden this place doesn't feel too safe, you know what I mean?"

Spitting his gum to the ground at Williams' feet, Jonah turned on his heel and swaggered back towards his turf, plunging into the still growing crowd and heading back towards the sanctuary of his entourage.

The smile dropped instantly from Williams' face, reverting to is default setting of generalised wrinkled contempt.

"Fucking Yanks," he spat.

The duel over, Stone turned away and headed back through the police line and up to cross the Vltava, Williams and Rado following swiftly.

"Did you find the information you wanted Captain?" The emotionless security man quizzed as they walked, Stone shaking his head in reply.

"If only," he sighed, "the man I came to speak to is the one that's lying dead on the pavement. Do you think you can have a word with police? Make sure anyone involved in this 'Anti-Terror Patrol' last night is hauled in? If they're made to feel a bit uncomfortable then maybe we can dissuade anyone else from trying the same trick."

"I'll see what I can do," the professional young man nodded. "If that's all for now, it's time I returned to my duties. Sir."

He offered a respectful incline of the head towards the pair and split away, speaking quickly into a radio that had appeared in his hand.

"Damn it, Williams, I thought I was onto something," Stone cursed, "I thought today was Jackpot day."

"Yeah," nodded the Scot, "a bit like betting your savings on the Grand National only for your horse to die at the first fence."

"Have a word with yourself," Stone chastised the callous Spook, "a man's dead back there; you don't need to be a crass bastard your whole life."

"I'd rather have a word with Myska," Williams responded, unperturbed by Stone's disdain and stopping the Captain in his tracks.

"Oh really?" he answered, "and say what exactly? 'Good Morning you fascistic sack of shite; we think the violence in this city all leads back to you'?"

"You sound like my fucking Mum," Williams retorted with feigned surprise on his face, "and why the hell not? You'd be surprised what a good old fashioned beating can produce if you put your mind to it."

"A confession under duress is no confession at all."

"So you say, but it's worked like a dream elsewhere; you and me go over to Myska's Party Headquarters, have a wee chat with the horse's mouth then we kick seven shades of shit out of it and ask again."

"I'm a soldier, not a damn spook; that's not how we do things."

Stone turned away, almost feeling Williams' scowl on his back as he shouted after him.

"Well excuse me, Captain fucking Britain," he sneered, "don't let an escalating crisis we have no leads on how to prevent sway you towards understanding the necessity of cruelty. Is it two sugars you take with your cup of self fucking righteousness in the morning? Shit's hitting the fan here and you and me need to find out what's going on and how to stop it and if that means a wee game of fisticuffs with a Blackshirt then all the fucking better!"

"We have no evidence!" Stone span around, exasperation on his face and his arms spread out wide as though proving to Williams that he held none on his person. "And if we go roughing Myska up without any and he walks straight in front of the cameras saying 'look what Svobodova's street squad did to me', or worse 'look what those damn immigrants did to me', what do you think will happen?! You think the shit's hitting the fan now? If I let you march into his office with your bony fists flying, you'll make it a thousand times worse!"

"If you 'let me'?" Williams screwed up his face at Stone's phraseology. "Listen, my morally untarnished friend, you have absolutely no fucking power over me…"

He was stopped mid rant by the ring of Stone's mobile phone and the Captain raising his hand while he answered it, the Scotsman's well furrowed brow creasing further still in frustration at his wait.

"Well," Stone began finally, after bidding signalling his agreement to the caller and pocketing his phone, "not that this hasn't been a delightful chat but we'll have to pick this up again later. I'll call you; try not to beat anyone up in the meantime."

He turned away from the belligerent older man, picking out his landmark and planning a route.

"Where are you going?"

"To the Castle," Stone answered over his shoulder, "I've been invited to an audience with the President."

FOURTEEN

THE PAINFUL CREAK in the old man's knees was obvious to all in the room, but none allowed their concern to display visibly on their faces.

As soon as he had arrived at the Prague Castle gates, Captain Stone had been ushered through a myriad of corridors and levels by efficient if unsmiling security, until he stood outside an imposing, grand doorway, upon which his escort knocked reverentially.

Bade entry, Stone had stepped into a voluminous suite which reminded him instantly of the glittering opulence of the Golden Room in which he had first met Greyson, although the finery of this environment was arguably more tastefully understated. In front of him to his left he saw Svobodova and Natalie rising from their chairs to acknowledge his presence, while behind the expansive desk of varnished oak directly ahead sat a groomed and well-tailored figure of venerable dignity: Karol Černý. A leading figure of the Reunification movement several years earlier, and a one-time rival of Svobodova for the Party Leadership, he was known by all today as her staunchest ally in domestic politics as well as for his status as the wise and noble President of the new Czechoslovakia.

In truth, Černý's visage was one with which Stone had long been familiar; it having adorned numerous black and white photographs from the 1968 invasion, facing down Russian tanks alongside the late Herbert Biely. Though elderly now and visibly frail, the man was a genuine holder of the overused label of 'hero', and the Statesman's insistence on rising to his feet to greet the Captain made the soldier shift uncomfortably.

"Please, Sir," Stone began, "there's no need to stand on my account."

Černý paid no heed, walking with an unsuccessfully disguised discomfort towards the soldier, his hand painfully extended towards him; Stone grasping it in sincere gratitude.

"There is every need Captain, when it is to welcome a new friend. I thank you for your efforts to help my country."

"I'm grateful for your sentiment, sir," answered Stone, uncomfortably, "but I'm unsure as to how much help I've actually been."

"Nonsense Captain," the old man spoke in beautifully accented English, his smile paternal and almost affectionate, "Madam Prime Minister has impressed upon me the value of your advice, even when another path is preferred."

Stone felt a pang on embarrassment and shot a look at Svobodova, who smiled in return; a silent reassurance that no ill feeling remained after their disagreement at the Rudolfinum.

The aged President gestured for Stone to fully enter the room and sit down, then returned to his desk, standing at the window behind it which overlooked the City as it basked in the glorious rays of the mid-morning sun; every one of the spires within the ancient conurbation stretching high, as if in silent competition with each other to touch the highest cloud or stroke the belly of the sun.

"I am an old man, Captain Stone," Černý mused, gazing out at the sight, "and with advanced age come long memories and deeply held fears. Did you know that in just a few short days it will be exactly fifty years since the Russians came to end our Spring?"

"I did, Sir," Stone confirmed, "I doubt history will ever forget it."

A gentle laugh issued forth from the old man, unaccompanied by condescension.

"History may not forget it Captain," he agreed, "but I fear that too many of the people of today have forgotten about history. Time and again, throughout the world, the same mistakes that brought so much pain in the past are repeated by new generations; bringing misery anew to so many, but still the lesson is never fully learned."

"We are at a crisis point, Captain Stone," Svobodova spoke up from her chair alongside him, "the murder scene you attended this morning was only the tip of last night's iceberg; these 'anti-terror patrols' have been appearing all over the country, attacking anyone who 'fits the profile'. And more worrying still is the intimidation. There is a refugee hostel in Poprad; last night it was surrounded by men wearing camouflage and ski masks, who just stood there, in silence, staring in through the windows…"

"Didn't the police put a stop to it?"

"They dispersed them eventually, but they are becoming over stretched; if the number of incidents continues to rise then it raises the grim prospect of our having to call in the armed forces to keep control of the streets."

"Which, of course is exactly what Myska wants," interjected Abelard, "so he can use it to make the case that the government cares more about the well-being of immigrants than it does its own people."

Stone shook his head as he felt his anger begin to rise.

"And with so many incidents, we still can't prove the connection to Myska's campaign? Unbelievable."

"It's not that simple," Svobodova replied, "we have a number of people in custody who we know show up at his rallies; those faces in the folders I showed you. But they aren't official Party members so even when I go on camera and condemn his message for attracting this type of person, he can legitimately say it's nothing to do with him or his Party."

She lifted the shot glass she held to her lips and knocked it back.

"Sometimes it's hard to think just how much the mood has changed in only three years; our reunification, the Czechs and Slovaks brought back together as family. It was supposed to be the start of something wonderful and instead…"

She trailed off, as though her voice were fearful of breaking if it continued, an awkward and uncomfortable silence descending, contrasting with the elegance of the room the company sat in.

"Striving to reach the gates of the Promised Land is difficult enough," Černý opined, breaking the quiet with his gentle charm, "but it isn't until one walks through them that the work really begins."

He continued to look out at his City, his people; the others mulling on his Presidential wisdom.

"So many people fall into the trap of believing that the New Dawn itself is the goal; the objective we fight for, when in reality it is merely the beginning of the challenge. There are precious few who understand that even Utopias will die if their people fail to transpose the passion that built them into a passion to preserve them."

Černý's eyes remained fixed on the glistening spires as he mulled the query aloud.

"So many become transfixed with the glory of the 'event' that they begin to believe that in itself will solve their problems. And then they awake the next morning to the unpaid bill on the mat, to the sick child crying, to the senile parent and the empty bank account and all at once they lose their fight, their passion! They see only that the magic words they thought they believed in did not work, that the promises they thought they heard were broken and they give up their desire for cynicism; until history repeats again."

A telephone on Černý's desk began to ring, saving the room from the descent of another awkward silence, the President lifting the receiver and listening intently to the speaker, before responding in quickly spoken Czech which Stone was unable to understand.

"Excuse us," he said to Stone and Abelard, gesturing for Svobodova to accompany him as he replaced the receiver. "Miroslava, perhaps we should initially take this call in the ante-room? Would you please both remain here?"

The two politicians crossed the room and exited through a small door, leaving Stone feeling temporarily at least more relaxed, a sensation the Professor obviously shared, exhaling and pushing herself to her feet.

"I'm sorry about Sergeant Hendry," she said to him, her concern visible on her face, "I was with Svobodova when Rado phoned in; it can't have been a pleasant job."

"It's ok," he reassured her quietly, "I barely knew the guy, I'd only met him once, it's just… well he seemed a decent man, that's all."

"And a soldier."

"Yeah," nodded Stone, "and a soldier."

She sat again alongside him, reaching her arm across his shoulders in comfort.

"This life," she said, "the Army; it means the world to you, doesn't it?"

Stone smiled, reaching up to stroke the fingers she'd draped on his shoulder.

"I told you, didn't I, that my Dad was a soldier? An NCO in 4RTR in the Fifties and Sixties."

"The family business?"

"Yes, if you like," Stone laughed. "I'd just turned two when I met Dad for the first time. He was home on leave from the Regiment when he met my Mum and they hit it off straight away. I remember being at the front door, my big sister next to me, looking up at this giant man standing in front of me, he had these enormous hands like shovels, but his eyes were so kind... He knelt down and took my tiny palm in his huge one and shook it gently. 'Hello' he said, 'I'm Tom.'"

He smiled warmly at the memory and she squeezed his fingers tighter as he spoke.

"He lost everything when he took us in," he continued, his smile dropping now, "thank God these days most people wouldn't bat an eyelid, but back then a white man marrying a black single mother? Everyone had to have their say."

"Not exactly society's finest hour..." Natalie responded, almost whispering.

"Quite," Stone agreed. "It cost him family, friends... and you can imagine the things he was called and what used to come through the letterbox, cries of 'Here come the Black and White Minstrels' whenever we went for a walk together. But he never let any of that worry him, he had us and we had him and that was all we needed. When I grew up I decided that if the Army could make me half the man he was then it was a good way to start repaying him. He was my hero. And then, when the kid was born, there was a big part of me that thought I could be his hero too…"

He looked up to see her eyes glistening and she quickly turned to blink it away just as the inner door opened and Svobodova leant out.

"Professor, Captain; would you join us please?"

They both stood and hurried to the room, emerging into a smaller, but still spacious conference room, in the centre of which stood an oblong oak table surrounded by high backed leather chairs, of which only one was occupied, by the wizened President Černý, who's attention appeared focussed on an elaborate spider phone in the centre of the table. The three of them quickly took seats and joined the old man in his expectant stare at the device.

"Thank you Rado," Svobodova spoke in English, "if you could please say that again for the benefit of our guests."

"Yes Ma'am," came the voice of the security officer through the speaker, "There's been another attack."

"Oh, God," Stone blasphemed, while the colour drained at once from Abelard's face, as though a light had been turned off in her soul, "where?"

"Old Town Square," came the immediate response, "there's been a mass demonstration there this morning; when it got out that police were arresting members of the Anti-Terror Squads, Myska held an impromptu rally in the middle of the square. A counter demonstration immediately started and riot police were called to contain the crowd. Two men in suicide belts tried to detonate themselves in the middle."

Stone looked over at Svobodova in deep concern. He didn't need to vocalise what a disaster this was; not only another terrorist attack but one which would give Myska and his followers all the excuse they needed to start an all-out internal war. To his surprise, the Prime Minister remained motionless and he imagined that for a moment she had allowed herself to buckle under the momentous strain she was under; her grim determination uncharacteristically marginalised.

Thinking to save her any embarrassment and to ensure the crisis was actioned, his leadership instincts kicked in and he leant closer to the spider phone.

"Alright," he said, "get down to the scene and liaise with emergency services and remember to comb the area for secondary devices. The Prime Minister will be en route to the hospital…"

"No, Captain, it's alright!"

Rado's voice was calmness itself, cutting Stone off in mid flow.

"How is it alright, what do you mean?" The lines on his brow deepened as he furrowed it in confusion.

"The devices didn't explode," Rado explained. "I've had operatives tailing the Myska appearances for days. They spotted these two on the fringes of the crowd and challenged them; one of them is dead, shot."

Blood slowly began to fill Abelard's cheeks once more as the opiate of relief spread between the academic and the soldier, Svobodova muttering a not entirely inaudible prayer under her breath.

"Not that I am not grateful," the Prime Minister began, "but who authorised you to shadow Mr Myska's events?"

A brief silence came from the other end of the line before Rado spoke again.

"It was Captain Stone's suggestion," he said, "after the concert attack he thought it prudent to monitor the crowds for regular faces, troublemakers. It worked."

Svobodova smiled gently across the table at him.

"It seems I have you to thank again, Captain Stone."

"Never mind that," Stone responded, eager to dispel any misplaced notions of excessive gratitude, "what about the other guy, the one who didn't get shot?"

"Well that's the best news of all," came Radoslav's response, "we have him."

FIFTEEN

THEY HAD HIM INDEED. Abdul Salam, a young man, almost a boy, who the media speedily determined had fled to Czechoslovakia from Syria, enrolled in a college at which he excelled in science, and who had no previously known deep religious conviction, was now sitting alone in a heavily guarded police cell somewhere in Prague.

TV screens and social media were full of little else but the images of the two young men, two such young men, mingling with the band of protestors who jeered and mocked Myska's speech, before calmly and deliberately dis-attaching themselves and disappearing from view, only to return moments later on the other side of Old Town Square at the edge of the politician's crowd of admirers. CCTV had captured in glorious detail the moment sinking trepidation descended on the faces of the assemblage, as the first of the men had opened his unseasonably warm coat to reveal the explosives cradling his body in a cadaverous embrace. The ossified terror had grown quickly into blind panic as black-suited operatives appeared in an instant around him, weapons drawn and barking commands to raise his arms; commands which were quickly defied by the would-be killer's move to trigger his device and the hail of bullets which sent him bloodied and sprawling to the floor. His comrade, hitherto unexposed, had then run deeper into the scattering crowd and reached the detonator of his own device which had steadfastly refused to ignite. Only the proximity of so many innocents had spared him the fate of his partner, two of the operatives hurling themselves upon him and dragging him down in a selfless act which both saved lives and earned the pair their own hashtag.

But while catastrophe had been averted, storms of equal intensity had quickly brewed. Myska, as was to be expected had embarked upon an unfaltering tour of the TV studios from almost the moment his felled attacker was packed off to the morgue and his associate to his cell, defiantly asserting that the assault proved nothing but the validity of his message; a line with which the evening editions of most newspapers agreed, if some reluctantly. And with Myska himself targeted, some of the less savoury of his supporters grasped their opportunity to revenge themselves upon the weak, the scared and the different, with many a running battle being fought in the ancient cobbled streets until the police could contain the aftermath.

It was everything the populist Leader could have wished for. An assassination attempt on himself and his followers from which all walked away unscathed, save for a few rattled nerves, committed by a Syrian Muslim ushered into Czechoslovakia by the excessively liberal regime of his rival. And it was precisely that convenience that had turned Svobodova's initial relief at the lack of casualties and delight at the capture of the perpetrator into the swell of teeth grinding frustration growing within her, as she held the telephone receiver to her ear and struggled visibly to contain her temper.

Stone observed her silently from his seat across her office

and marvelled at the diplomatic restraint she showed before her patience finally wore thin and she interrupted the incessant tirade coming from the other end of the line.

"Mr Ambassador," she interjected tersely, "as I have expressed on many previous occasions, both I and Czechoslovakia have been and remain grateful both for the friendship of the United States and for her generous offer of assistance in our investigations. Suffice to say I have every faith in our own security services and every confidence they will extract any and all pertinent information from the suspect in custody without the need for us to take advantage of your said offer, and certainly not in the immediate future. Now, as I'm sure you appreciate, I have a great many things to attend to at this time, not least reassuring the people that it is safe to go about their daily business. That being the case I will wish you good day and I look forward to our next meeting."

She slammed the receiver down with more force than was perhaps appropriate and stood up behind her desk, inhaling deeply with her eyes clamped shut. When she finally moved over to where Stone and Abelard sat, she clutched the now familiar bottle in her hand; three shot glasses gripped tightly in the fingers of her other.

"The Americans aren't happy," she said, clinking the glasses to the table and pouring a large shot into each.

"Are they ever?" sniffed Stone.

"Well even less so than usual," she replied, acknowledging his sarcasm with the hint of a wry smile. "They want me to waive extradition proceedings and release the suspect to American custody immediately on charges of international terrorism, or at least be permitted to conduct an interrogation themselves."

"On what grounds?" frowned Abelard.

"They're claiming he's linked to cells responsible for attacks on US troops."

"That's supposition of the wildest kind," the Professor protested, "how can they possibly back up such a claim?"

"They can't," Stone said, picking up his glass from the table and knocking it back, his stomach slowly becoming accustomed to the severe taste, "it's just a conjuring trick, an illusion for the electorate. Dragging a terrorist suspect in front of the TV screens for a show trial will be good for keeping any number of uncomfortable stories out of the press and for making the President look effective. It's all just politics."

"Yes," Svobodova sighed sadly, "politics…"

Stone admonished himself for encouraging melancholy in the room and he pressed her for an action.

"In any event," he said, "you can't give in to such a demand."

"Absolutely not," echoed Abelard. "Politically that would play right into the image Myska wants to convey of you as a weak leader, bullied by so-called friends, and frankly morally speaking it'd just be plain wrong."

"I know, I know," Svobodova asserted, holding her hands in the air. "Believe me, I have no intention of giving in; the prisoner is a resident of this country, arrested while attempting to attack this country's citizens. He will be interrogated and tried here. But I find myself increasingly isolated in the matter. Germany, France, Belgium, Spain, even Britain since Jonathan's departure, all have publically advised me to accept US help in completing the investigation."

Abelard inhaled deeply and quickly emptied her own glass, grimacing as it went down.

"I can't believe I'm about to suggest this," she said, "but maybe Jonathan could help you? He may no longer be in government but he still has influence."

Svobodova offered the woman a small but sincere smile at the suggestion.

"I'm afraid Jonathan has to keep a very low profile at present; I'm led to believe he is persona-non-grata at Parliament and having presently been dismissed as Foreign Secretary it is inadvisable he should be seen to be publicly interfering in foreign affairs."

"But he's here, in the country," the least he can do is get his hands dirty."

"No," Stone interrupted, "if he comes out publicly then Myska proves you're under the influence of foreign governments; it's best to keep him out of sight. Sorry." He turned to Abelard as he added the final word of apology, not wishing to appear unsupportive in a matter she was so personally involved in.

"Agreed, Captain," Svobodova nodded. "Now if you'll both excuse me, I am scheduled for interview and I want to be sure I get my side of the story out before the next Myska rally."

They all stood and Svobodova moved to leave, stopping only due to the audible 'tutting' noise made by Stone.

He made no effort to disguise the disappointment on his face as she turned around at his display of petulance, her own offended expression matched by the look of surprise on Abelard.

"I beg your pardon Captain Stone, what was that?"

Knowing that etiquette and common courtesy demanded he bite his tongue, the resentment he had felt growing within him since even before his arrival in the city had matured within him and he realised that this was the time for the tasting, refusing to drop his eyes from the politician's.

"You know, it's funny," he began, "I've only been in the country a few days but if there's one thing I'm sick and tired of worrying about it's the 'next' Myska rally. You're supposed to be the Prime

Minister of this country, but I don't think I've heard you give one speech since I've been here that actually calls that fascistic bastard out on his horse shit."

"Lincoln!"

He raised his palm, urging Natalie not to intercede, while resentment quickly grew in Svobodova's own face.

"Then I suggest, Captain, that you spend less time in the bars and clubs of the City and more time reviewing the current affairs discussion shows; I have been interviewed daily..."

"Yeah, yeah, very interesting," Stone interrupted with intentional rudeness, "for the forty-three people in the country that watch that crap. But the millions who don't think you've got nothing to say. Now, I wasn't here at the time but I'm told you were the People's Heroine during reunification, that your rallies were legendary, that you could bring people together with just a few choice words, stood on a soapbox on a cobbled street. Where the hell is that Svobodova? Because I've never met her!"

She opened her mouth to protest but before she could he had dived in again.

"Where the hell was she the morning after the Rudolfinum blew up? At home in bed? Myska was there; oh, that guy wasn't going to miss a chance to spread his poison but the woman with the antidote was nowhere to be found!"

His could feel his anger grow with each word spoken and he relished the sensation it brought him; like charging into combat against a dozen enemy soldiers with only his rifle, his wits and his passion to aid him. He saw that anger mirrored in her own eyes; his apoplexy reigniting the passion behind her Prime Minsiterial smile.

"I will not use the suffering of my people for political advantage!" she hollered loudly, her face reddening and her frown growing deeper with each word.

"No-one was suggesting you should!" Stone shouted back with equal venom, "and while you dithered, that arsehole was paving the way for more of your people to suffer!"

He stopped for a moment, breathing deeply.

"Ever since the 1930's," he began again, his voice calmer, "the Far Right has been hated and castigated the continent over, damned by history and condemned by the present, despised by every right-minded person who ever drew breath. And yet it never quite dies, it never quite goes away, not forever. A few twisted devotees keep the flame alive, however faintly it might flicker until somewhere, when people are desperate, angry, looking for someone or something to blame, it raises its head above the parapet once again and starts whispering. It starts pointing the finger, it tells people they shouldn't have to live like this, that it isn't fair the way life's treated them, that if it weren't for the Jews, or the Pakis...if not for the 'fucking Muslims pouring in' or 'the bloody Polish taking all the jobs', then things would be better, more than that things would be perfect. They'd be 'Great Again', they'd 'Get their Country Back'. And you know why it keeps growing? Because the politicians, the 'Mainstream', people like you Prime Minister, gloss over it, never accepting that their message, however loathsome it is, might just be what disenfranchised, disaffected people want to hear. So instead of confronting the filth, instead of telling those people that there is a different, better way, instead of accepting where governments have failed and working to put things right, instead of fighting lies with truth, you ignore them, you put your hands over your ears and pretend you can't hear them. So, when the bigots tell the people their concerns are being ignored, that the political classes don't care, you're doing a pretty damn fine job of proving them right instead of doing what you should do! And so every generation it comes back and none of us can ever truly rest easily, we can never know for sure that the shit we went through in our lives won't be re-visited tenfold on our kids, or on their kids, and all because a bunch of politicians are too scared to go over the top in into the battlefield and win the damn war!"

Stone turned away and leaned on the desk, his eyes glued to the papers upon it, the rise and fall of his shoulders betraying the heavy breathing brought on by his tirade. He instantly regretted the outburst; not the content, which he was sure needed saying, but certainly his tone, and he remained in his position, awaiting the inevitable admonishing.

It didn't come. Instead he felt Natalie's soft palm covering his own, squeezing it with the same understanding affection he had come to expect from her. And while her touch began to ease the tensions from his body, he heard Svobodova behind him, taking a step closer.

"And which battlefield, Captain," she began, her voice understanding and devoid of resentment, "should people like me be walking into?"

Stone straightened up and turned around to face her, keeping hold of Natalie's hand as he did so.

"Fight them, Prime Minister," he replied simply. "Take the fight to them, on their own turf, their own battleground. Meet on television, on the hustings, on their own damn doorsteps. Take each and every untruth they can throw at you and show them up for the lies they are. Don't deny these bastards the oxygen of publicity; give it to them in droves and then see them choke to death on it when they're exposed for the liars they are. If Myska's making ground because he's good TV then be better TV, that's the only way to beat him: at his own game."

The hint of a smile brushed Svobodova's lips, her eyes steadfastly on the Captain's own.

"I take it Captain," she began softly, "that you have such a battlefield in mind?"

"Indeed I do, Madam Prime Minister," he smiled back, "but if you'll forgive me, I'd like something in return."

SIXTEEN

IT WAS A MESMERIC PERFORMANCE from Svobodova; one which had her supporters on the streets cheering, the journalists drooling and Stone himself relishing a burning sense of pride. She had done precisely as he'd hoped and confronted Myska, unannounced at the scene of the latest bungled terror attack itself.

The self-styled Man of The People had, as expected, basked in the opportunity to bring others to his cause, condemning the folly of allowing refugees shelter within a culture they couldn't adapt to, attacking the inherent brutality of the Islamic faith and extolling the virtues of a thoroughly Westernised European Union to all who would listen, and that number continued to grow, boosted by the whir of the cameras which captured his every move. Only when, from his vantage point on the ridge of the Jan Hus Memorial, he saw the crowd part and a figure walking through it did he begin to falter; the appearance of Miroslava Svobodova herself approaching him and stepping up to join him on the plinth, robbing him of his compassionately phrased - if hate filled - crescendo. He had tried to continue, but the momentum was ers, as was the attention of the cameras and the crowd, some of whom spat boorish insults which she simply laughed away, but most would be abusers stunned into reluctantly respectful silence while her supporters beamed up to her with unabashed pride. She had spoken in passionate Czech to the people, holding them in her palm as she had done years before and, stood away from the crowd, Stone felt the emotion pouring from her body and spreading through so many of those present; some who would in any case call themselves her champions, but others swayed by the intensity of her delivery and her irrefutable logic. Time and again, Myska raised myth after long debunked myth about the evils of immigration, the conspiracy of multiculturalism and the incompatibility of Middle Eastern traditions with those of central Europe, only for Svobodova to effortlessly bat them aside, until the characteristic unflappable charm began to twist into uncomfortable frustration. By the time of her final vehement appeal to the crowd, Myska had no answers to give save for the repeating of soundbites and slogans.

He had taken in the performance a second time later that night, with an equally excited Natalie in his arms, as Svobodova's dramatic appearance was repeated on the news bulletins and discussion shows, her vehement defence of herself, her philosophy and those who sought shelter under her country's protection subtitled for people across the globe to watch and admire.

"It took us twenty-three years to remember that we are a family," Svobodova had declared to the crowd in her final address, "after listening for so long to men who told us we were different, so different that we should be kept apart, that our lives should be separated by borders and regulations; relations reduced to the status of barely welcome visitor in each other's lands. Twenty-three years before we came to our senses and realised that our bond, our familial unity, our common humanity was and is so much greater than any division the world wants us to live through from time to time. Yes, these are challenging days, many would say terrible; the world seems abundant with evil people committing evil acts. But if Mr Myska succeeds in convincing you to follow his dream, his path towards a Europe united in race only, for let us be honest with ourselves, that is the essence behind his charms, do any of you think that those evil acts will end? Of course they will not! Only who will you have to blame then? How long before the Leaders of this glorious future label you as the next great threat? Since human life first crawled out of the sea, there have been those inclined to visit horror upon their brethren; whether their justification was philosophical, political or religious, they were and are united in their desire to commit evil. Let us now be united in our desire to overcome it, together, to counter terror with love. My friends, it took twenty-three years for us to remember we are one Czechoslovak family; I pray nightly and I beg you now that it will not take another twenty-three to remember we share that relationship with the World."

Her words had been spontaneous and heartfelt, and as soon as they were spoken she had stepped down from the plinth and walked back through the crowd whence she came, as the crowd cheered her and headline writers went into overdrive.

The warmth in Stone's chest grew with each viewing, until Natalie's hand reached across to the remote he held in his and flicked the screen to blank.

"You were right," she said, stroking his chin, "she should have done that a long time ago."

"Maybe," Stone smiled, resisting the playful urge to give the time-honoured riposte of 'I told you so', "but maybe now was the perfect time."

"Well the reaction has been positive to say the least; the speech coming on the back of the arrest is going down well in the country.

If we can keep things looking positive until the service next week we might just have turned the corner and taken back a bit of momentum."

Stone grimaced in distaste. The plan for the great and good of the world to fly in for a choreographed show of 'solidarity' in the wake of the attacks - but what was to the more cynical a glorified publicity shot for the elite - had been agreed earlier that morning, and it was not one which pleased the Captain. He had attended more than sufficient stage-managed conflict zone appearances in his career, by politicians who flew in under heavy cover and promptly flew out again of the battlefields they had helped create, after a few perfunctory handshakes and heroic poses with the latest hardware. This was simply more of the same; a theatrical appearance by a political class who despite for the most part despising each others' politics, all shared the same burning ambition of power for its own sake and possessing of a keen awareness of what they needed to do to wield it. Attacks of the type suffered by Prague and throughout Europe in recent years, while causing loss of life and temporary chaos, nonetheless offered the silver lining of opportunities such as this to link arms and light candles in unison, while looking sombre and statesmanlike for The People, many of whom would unwittingly buy into the charade with a hashtag or two; all a refreshing distraction from whichever domestic catastrophes they sought to divert attention from. Stone had long since tired of such parlour tricks, even before his public disgracing, and knowing that both Svobodova and the increasingly world weary President Černý were likewise opposed to it was small comfort, given that they had accepted the political necessity of jumping through this particular hoop.

"I can't wait," the Captain grumbled, "remind me to come down with diarrhoea that day."

"I'll send out for beer and burritos the night before," Natalie laughed.

"Anyway," Stone continued, "I'm hoping to have something more substantial to cheer about by then anyway."

"Ah," his lover nodded, "your 'something in return.'"

"Yep."

"When are you doing it?"

"Tomorrow." Stone took a sip from the glass of water next to the bed and yawned, shuffling down between the crisp, fresh sheets and closing his eyes, the pressures of recent days beginning to catch up with him physically. "I'm meeting Williams at six at Zlatý kůň Hill and then the day is ours; aside from a few ground rules we've pretty much been given carte blanche."

Her fingers began to stroke gracefully against him, Natalie exquisitely tracing the outline of his face with the tip of her finger.

"So, you'll be wanting a good night's sleep then?" she asked, a hint of mischief in her voice.

"Mm-hmm," he confirmed, trying to resist his body's reaction to the finely moving fingertip, "a particularly deep one."

"Ok," she replied, "I understand. Of course, you know that the best way to be sure of a truly great night's sleep is to make sure you're extra tired beforehand?"

"Is that a fact?" he grinned, his eyes still playfully closed, "and where did you learn that?"

"They don't make people Professors for nothing. In fact, I think it would be best if you were positively exhausted…"

Stone opened his eyes and his grin widened, reaching over to embrace her fully in his arms.

"Oh really?" he chuckled, pulling the sheet over them as she settled into his arms, "well who am I to argue with a Professor?"

SEVENTEEN

"IS HE IN THERE?"

The sun was beginning a lethargic ascent as Captain Stone arrived in front of the typically scowling Williams just before six that morning, climbing just high enough to glint across the triangular roof which adorned the commanding tower of the nearby Karlštejn Castle.

"Aye," confirmed the Scotsman, "Rado's lot picked him up just before four, he's been down there by himself for a while now; he must be nicely uncomfortable."

"Let's hope. After you Mr Williams."

"Oh, no," Williams demurred theatrically, "I wouldn't dream of it, after you, Captain."

Moments later, the pair were descending down a winding metal staircase, built into the very earth itself, emerging at last into a damp, dimly lit but expansive cavern, decorated from head to toe in majestic drip stone formations of varying length but equal magnificence. The uneven footing only added to the abundance of just visible natural beauty around them which seemed only to grow in intensity the deeper into the cave they walked, as if the cavern were displaying itself with the self-confident audacity of a

Peacock, almost daring the newcomers to find a rock out of place or a stalagmite of anything less than breath-taking resplendence.

While the perfection of the rock formations was indisputable, the Captain and his companion soon came across something that was indeed out of place, if not wholly unexpected. Reaching the edge of one runway, illuminated by the lights wired into the pathway, a figure came into view; unkempt, lolling slightly against the ropes that bound him to the chair which sat at the very edge of the path, inches from the sheer drop to the next level beneath him. Here at last was Stone's 'something in return'. Though the restrained figure sat with his back to the newcomers, the Captain knew exactly what he looked like: skeletally thin, unhealthily so especially for one so young, with a short beard protruding from his chin. Here sat the second of the would-be bombers; the one whose belt had failed to detonate and whose face had since been shared across every news channel in the West and across countless social media accounts in the intervening couple of days.

Abdul Salam.

As they drew up behind him, Stone winced. The caves were cold, damp air permeating even his well-guarded lungs, but the young man was sat wearing only a thin t-shirt and shorts, his shivering obvious from some distance away.

"For fuck's sake," he cursed under his breath to Williams, "I didn't say he was to be tortured, did I?"

"Yeah, sorry about that," Williams answered insincerely, "I must have got giddy and embellished your instructions a bit."

The Spook strode ahead, grabbing hold of the chair and scraping it around and towards them, pulling the prisoner back into consciousness as he did so; the young man blinking the mistiness from his eyes and straining to focus on the duo.

"Who are you?"

A second chair stood to the side and Williams pulled it in front of the bound figure, sitting down with an almost jolly aplomb.

"Who, us?" he smiled, "oh, we're just your friendly neighbourhood infidels; it was such a beautiful morning we thought we'd stop by for a chat and show you the sights. These are the Koněprusy Caves, do you like them?" He gestured expansively around, his unsettling smile still on his face. "They form the largest cave system in Bohemia, you know, and the funny thing is no-one knew a thing about them until about ooh, 1950 or so. The Communists were still in charge here back then; they were a funny lot, very irreligious. You'd have had a whale of a time running around blowing up the unbelievers then, I can tell you... well, maybe just the once actually. But anyway, the Caves! Fascinating tale; a bunch of quarry workers were carrying out a controlled explosion on the south-eastern side of the hill up there, and they only went and blew an entranceway to these beauties right there in the quarry wall. They spent all their spare time crawling through these caves, one metre at a time until finally one day, they found the main cavern, the one back there. Brilliant eh?"

Salam simply stared, his lips remaining defiantly closed and his body trying to supress the shivers running through it.

Williams feigned disappointment at the lack of response and shrugged.

"No? Well, I guess you had to be there. But you know the moral of the story is that explosions can sometimes have unintended consequences, even ones that don't manage to go off correctly."

Williams sprang forward, gripping Salam by his t-shirt and tipping him forward so that his face drew close to the Scotsman's own, which twisted instantly into a mask of angry ferocity.

"Now you listen to me you little shit," he snarled, "you might be too fucking dumb to know how to work a trigger properly, but as far as I'm concerned you're still a murdering wee bastard who should be hung out to fucking dry. We're giving you one fucking chance to answer each and every question we put to you, or I will personally drop you over the side of this rock and take great pleasure in watching you break apart across millennia old stalagmites, do you comprehend me?"

"Williams!"

Stone, appalled, pulled his colleague away from the prisoner, whose chair rocked back upright.

"What the fuck do you think…"

"This is MY interrogation Mr Williams," Stone cut him off, "and you are here at MY invitation. We'll be doing things my way for the duration, is that understood?"

Though used to the spy's cool demeanour, the stare he now gave the Captain was soaked in a new level of icy hostility, almost as though he was struggling to restrain himself from physically attacking Stone. After an age, Williams nodded softly, his unbreakable stare not leaving Stone.

"Aye," he quietly intoned, "I understand. The floor is yours Captain."

With a sweeping movement, Williams presented the prisoner to Stone and moved in an instant to the side, as though absorbed by the cave wall he leant against.

"So much for the Bad Cop," coughed Salam, the hint of a sneer on his face.

Stone sat down on the abandoned chair, rocking it gently forward and back for a few seconds as he sized up the prisoner before him.

"I'm sorry they left you like this," he said dispassionately, "this wasn't entirely what I had in mind."

"And here comes the Good Cop. Well don't worry, I couldn't care less." Salam spat his response, defiantly, although the wideness of his flickering eyes betrayed his fearful lack of confidence. "I hope you have better conversation than your friend."

"We're not cops," Stone answered.

"Spies then, agents."

"Try soldier."

"Soldier?"

"Yes, at least I am. Captain Lincoln Stone VC, Her Majesty's Royal Tank Regiment, at your service."

The sound of raking phlegm echoed through the cavern and Stone lifted his hand to wipe the spit from his face, swallowing with great difficulty the urge to pick up where Williams left off and drop this murderous imbecile over the edge of the chasm himself, managing with great effort to keep his voice level and calm.

"Not a fan of the Forces I take it?"

"Should I be? After they spend decades fighting my people."

"The only people I fight are those fighting me," Stone answered, meeting a contemptuous stare for his trouble.

"You have denied me my prayer time; my devotion."

"I've done no such thing, pray away, I'll wait; I've got all the time in the world."

"Not like this," Salam hissed, looking down at his ropes, "not restrained."

"Ah..." Stone mused for a moment before making his decision. "No can do I'm afraid," he finally said, "Not until you've answered a few questions for me anyway."

"You cannot deny me..."

"I can deny you whatever hell I like!"

Stone bellowed the words which reverberated around the

cavern and shocked the young prisoner into a stunned silence and brought even Williams to attention.

"You rigged yourself up to explode in a crowd of innocent people yesterday; tourists with kids just wandering around looking for a good place to take a selfie, old people struggling home with their arms full of shopping bags, people out to listen to democracy in action right there on the streets. Civilians," he said, his voice beginning to break, "innocents."

The Captain stood and kicked the char to the side, his struggle to contain his outburst becoming more obvious with each passing word.

"If you'd had your way yesterday a lot of people would be dead now, including you, so as far as I'm concerned I can deny you pretty much everything and anything I can think of. Now you play ball with me and give me the answers I need, then I might just see my way clear to returning the favour, but if you don't, then I walk back up to the surface and leave you in the company of my Scottish friend here, and let him take out his fourteen centuries of pent up frustration on you. Is that fucking understood?"

In truth, he was as shocked by his outburst as the person on the end of it, though having given in to his aggression he saw no reason to acknowledge the regret. Stone had had his fill of Militants; he had fought them hand-to-hand across deserts and battle grounds ever since that first disastrous decision to move the troops to Afghanistan. Some were powerful, some were weak; some seemed imbibed with some fanatical belief in their own invulnerability, the certainty of reward for their martyrdom or both, but all possessed one shared characteristic; their eyes. A true fanatic of any persuasion, bore their twisted devotion in their eyes; a subconscious warning to any enemy stupid enough to get close that there would be no negotiation, no surrender; indeed there could not. At first disturbing, Stone had seen sufficient examples to no longer fear the sight. But what disturbed him now even more was the lack of such conviction in the eyes of the prisoner.

"Here's how it's going to go," Stone began, in control of his voice once more. "Between you and me I have no power here, no jurisdiction. But what I do have is the ear of the President, the Prime Minister and the Head of the Security Services. You answer my questions truthfully, thoroughly; or I pass you to the care of a prison system that makes Guantanamo Bay look like a fucking holiday camp."

"A question for a question?"

"What?"

Salam looked into Stone's eyes almost with earnest as he repeated his question.

"I don't care if they kill me," he said, "I ask for no leniency, only the chance to ask you a question. Soldier to soldier."

"I wasn't aware you fit that description."

"Soldier to soldier," the youngster repeated, staring intently, his head on one side. There was an almost ethereal quality to the gaze and Stone found himself acquiescing to the unusual request.

"You answer my questions first. I don't release any sensitive information and if I don't like the sound of something you get no answer, ok?"

"Ok."

With the surreal arrangements in place, Stone began his inquisition. Where did Salam come from? Syria. Which cell did he belong to? None. Who was his accomplice killed in the Square? A friend and fellow student now enjoying the reward for his devotion. On and on Stone pressed; each question fully responded to but telling him little that he didn't already know, until finally, one question met only silence.

"I repeat," said Stone, "you took refuge in Czechoslovakia, you enrolled in University. By all accounts you were initially a sociable guy before withdrawing in on himself, no strong political convictions other than regarding Assad, and no mention of profound religious beliefs, certainly nothing to put you in the category of potential suicide bomber at least. I want to know what turned Abdul Salam the frightened refugee into Abdul Salam the attempted murderer?"

Again the ethereal stare, the unbalanced head, the disturbed expression.

"What made you go into battle for the first time, Captain?"

"We haven't got to me yet," Stone shook his head, "answer my question."

"Divinity," he snapped quickly, as though the answer mattered little to him, "a response from Heaven to my devotion. Now please; when your country sent you to wars you knew were wrong, what made you stay and fight? Duty? Honour? God?"

The prisoner shivered and strained against his bonds giving Stone every bit the impression that he really did *need* to know. He sat upright against the back of the chair and narrowed his eyes, the limp necked prisoner firmly in his view.

"Ok," Stone almost whispered, "I'll tell you. In the Falklands I was defending my countrymen from invasion, in Kuwait I repelled attacks on innocents and in Kosovar I helped keep the peace. But by the time of Afghanistan, Iraq, Syria… by the time they came along I was so damn tired of it all. Some of the lads still had their heads full of that Queen and Country bullshit but I was all out of that, there was no romance left to soldiering for me. I knew it was all bollocks; that we'd been lied to and the intelligence was shit, but I was used to politicians lying; my trust extended as far as my own command chain because no-one else was going to make sure I had boots on my feet and food in my belly. But as we were stuck there anyway, I aimed to be as professional as possible, be nice to the civilians we were trying to help, look after the innocents and my Squadron and pray that we'd all get out of it alive. And if I found some bastard shooting at me I made damn sure I shot him first. Yes, I knew it was dodgy, but when you're there on active service you live in a bubble; the reasons for being there aren't important anymore, you just get the job done, keep your conscience as clean as you can and get home. The biggest philosophical question every day is what the mess will serve up for tea. But in that bubble with you are people who still feel the romance, who still think it's an adventure. They're your Squadron, your kids, you have a burden of responsibility, you can't abandon them. So you stay and fight, and hope that however wrong the war might be, the people you're fighting are worse."

Stone closed his eyes and exhaled, as though his speech exorcised a thousand demons within him.

"That's what made me stay and fight and that's why I stay in the Army to this day; I have a responsibility to my Regiment."

No answer came from the prisoner, only a gentle nod of his lop-sided head and a continuing stare from the wide eyes.

It was Williams, pulling away from the cave wall with sheer exasperation on his face who finally broke the silence.

"Not that I'm not loving all this profound introspection," he said, discarding the luxury of his vantage point and moving briskly behind the captive figure whose hands were bound, clenched in impotent defiance, "but I've got a box set of *Chicago Fire* to watch tonight and I don't want to be up too late, or I'll be all cranky in the morning."

The lightening alacrity which subdued Stone in the alley returned, as the gleam of Williams' blade flashed almost imperceptibly behind the prisoner, accompanied by the restrained man's cry.

"I've just slit your wrists," Williams said nonchalantly, walking from behind the man and towards the mouth of the cavern. "It's not too warm in here, that'll buy you some time. I reckon you've got about an hour, maybe two before you bleed out; plenty of time to have a think about whether you want to talk to us or not."

"You think I'm scared of dying?" The bleeding man's voice tried to convey its typical mocking tone, but was tinged with an undisguisable confusion.

"I don't think you're scared of the kind of death you want, no. You know the kind? You looking all heroic and commanding in your military fatigues before blowing yourself and a restaurant full of kids to Kingdom Come on your way to meet your seventy-two virgins. But bleeding slowly to a very lonely, painful and pointless death, miles away from the TV crews before I dress you in a crop top and hotpants, and bury you in a fucking pig carcass, is a very different prospect."

Stone's face was one of incredulous fury and he gripped the striding Williams by the arm, spinning him around to face him.

"This isn't how it's done, you can't do this!"

"Oh yes I can fucking do this!" Williams yelled back, stepping closer into Stone, their rage filled faces barely inches apart.

"I didn't come here for a philosophy lecture, and I couldn't give two shits what keeps you motivated enough to shoot bad guys in the desert; I came here for answers! That guy dripping on the floor is the only way I'm going to get them, and if all he's going to do is put everything down to 'divine inspiration' then I'm just wasting my time."

"He was talking to me!"

"About what? I'm trying to find a link to these bombings and stop anyone else from dying; you're stuck on some sort of fucking grand voyage of self-discovery! If you want to find yourself, go talk to a Priest or a psychiatrist, and stay the fuck away from my fucking prisoners!"

He pulled his arm free from Stone's hand and resumed his stride into the black tunnel, glancing back over his shoulder as he disappeared into the darkness.

"He said he's happy to die, let him get on with it."

Stone followed in his wake, his anger building exponentially, emerging in a dimly lit tunnel away from the main cavern.

"We're not leaving him to die man," Stone hissed as Williams slowed his pace and turned back to him, "I don't give a fuck if he's a terrorist, we do things differently where I come from."

Williams looked heavenward in exaggerated frustration.

"Look at him, he's no fucking terrorist. For fuck's sake man, you've done enough tours in that part of the world to know a genuine Jihadist when you see one!"

"I know."

"Do you?!"

"Of course I bloody know!" Stone hissed his angered frustration at the wrinkled Scot, glaring into him with menace. "I've fought with enough rogues, militants, whatever you want to call them to know when someone's the real deal. It's in the eyes, that's where all the righteous anger and hatred shows itself, in everyone, and that's the problem! He's no terrorist, he's a kid! There's no hatred in his eyes, there's nothing, just…"

"Drugs."

"What?"

"Drugs!" Williams shrugged, a condescending smile forming on his face in response to Stone's puzzlement. "Think about it, it's more common than you realise. Look back over some of these so called 'terrorist attacks' in recent years; some are the real hard core fanatics, some are even strategically organised with access to weaponry and an unshakeable certainty that paradise awaits them for taking out the number 47 from Croydon; but how often do you read about some atrocity or other committed by a normal, young kid, with no previous indicators? Kids exactly like our friend through there."

"Radicalisation, or so the papers say."

"Oh and you believe the media do you? 'Cos they really treated you fairly didn't they? Yeah, some radicalisation goes on, but for a lot of these attacks you need to look further than your local mosque for your brainwasher."

"Where? Why would anyone need to brainwash kids into committing terrorist acts when there's plenty of terrorists to go around?"

"The same reason people hang highly decorated career soldiers out to dry when the need takes them: scapegoating. Why advertise your targets when a conveniently placed terrorist will take them out for you?"

"But the true fanatics desire chaos, why would they submit to being part of an organised attack?"

Williams grinned widely.

"That's where the drugs come in," he said, "come on and follow my lead."

Together they walked back into the alcove, the dim light illuminating them like ghoulishly distasteful decorations.

Williams leaned against the damp cave wall, glancing over at the tethered would-be killer, who stared back defiantly. The condescension was gone from the older man's face and replaced with a weathered weariness, his voice quiet and contemplative, as Stone watched.

"Say you wanted to commit an act of violence against someone or something, but you don't want to advertise your own responsibility."

The boy gritted his teeth in resentment but silently listened to the Scotsman's quiet voice.

"Sure, you could try and persuade a fanatic to do it for you and hope for the best, but fanatics are pretty unreliable, so instead you make your own, well, what should we call him? Stooge? No, how about Fuckwit? You find a kid, a bit of a loner, lacking in confidence, keeps himself to himself you know? He's the kind of kid who everyone regards as 'normal', or 'average' whatever the fuck that means, but he's from a minority group, preferably one of the brown ones, he has a latent connection to his parent's faith and he's not happy about the latest illegal invasion of wherever and the demonising of his people's religion. Now you befriend that kid, encourage his weed habit and make sure he has enough of the stronger stuff to make him just paranoid enough to start believing the bullshit you feed him, maybe slip him a tab or two of LSD at prayer time to make him think he's on some grand fucking voyage of spiritual enlightenment, and..."

"Bingo," finished Stone, sadly, "You've got your very own fanatic, easy to handle, dependant on you and willing to blow themselves up on your say so, to earn their one way ticket to Paradise."

"Drop a few electronic paper trails on the right web sites and everyone's happy." Williams picked up the thread, clearly relishing the interplay between himself and the soldier. "Your Fuckwit gets martyred, conveniently taking all evidence of you with him, the media have an excuse to ramp up the anti-Muslim headlines and you can carry on whatever your real agenda is completely unsuspected, everyone's a winner."

"Apart from the poor sods the stooge takes with him."

"Ah, well, collateral damage you see? The more carnage the better, it adds to the panic, adds to the fear!"

The aged spy's voice grew louder with each word, his wiry frame punctuating his theories in a mania which Stone began to infectiously feel taunting him too.

"Indeed," the Captain agreed, "But speaking of collateral damage, the Stooge kind of qualifies on that score too, don't you think?"

"I thought we were calling him Fuckwit?"

"Potato, Potahto," Stone shrugged, "But imagine going through all that, believing you were doing God's will only to find out afterwards that it was all for nothing when your bomb belt doesn't go off? That your spiritual experience was really a drugged-up stupor and your guide on your religious journey was a fraud?"

"Oh, well that'd certainly be a bit of a pain in the arse," Williams nodded sagely, "And it would take a special kind of Fuckwit to screw up a belt bomb. A Fuckwit, just like you."

Williams pulled away from the wall and sat in front of his prisoner, his face a hair's breadth away. "I've seen the videos, the mugshots and read the reports; when you were picked up, your pupils were wider than my ex-wife's legs at Hogmany; I'm guessing you were tripping when you tried your rendezvous with Major Tom; what was that, about forty-eight hours ago?"

"LSD normally leaves the body in around six to twelve hours," Stone picked up his colleague's trail, hanging further back than the older man, staring down at the frustrated martyr from above. "But that depends on your metabolism, your weight, how much of the stuff you've had lately... You're only a skinny guy, but even if it stayed with you a bit longer, you must be running on fumes now."

"You know? I'd almost feel sorry for you, if it weren't for the whole you being a murdering cunt thing." Williams' hawkish eyes burrowed deep into the boy's, searching, Stone thought, scouring for confirmation of his dread. "Here you are; a warrior, a soldier for the cause. But you're a blind soldier, you're going around thinking you're fighting the good fight but in reality, you're blowing shit up in the name of causes you don't even fucking know exist!"

"We want a name," Stone cut in, his demeanour demanding and fierce, "we want to know who took you on your journey from ordinary guy to wannabe killer. Believe me, whoever he is has no interest in you or the ideal you think you hold. I'm not promising anything but if you tell us what we need to know maybe we can cut some kind of deal."

"My wrists…"

"Name, arsehole!" Williams snarled, Salam looking up blankly in return as though he were struggling to assimilate or counter the pair's version of his story.

"Divinity," he eventually muttered, "my devotion."

EIGHTEEN

"OUR ONLY MOTIVATION is to offer moral support and practical assistance to a valued ally in the War Against Terror."

Benjamin Scarlet, US Ambassador to Czechoslovakia spoke with the same political sincerity in person as he demonstrated on the phone; and it was precisely because she had proven so difficult recently to reach on said device, Svobodova supposed, that he had taken the step of an impromptu visit to her private office, where he now sat comfortably, enjoying her diplomatic hospitality.

"Your support is very much appreciated and your assistance unnecessary. What's your real reason for being here, Benjamin?"

Scarlet remained silent for a moment, his eyes remaining on Svobodova's as he raised his china cup to his lips and quietly drained his coffee.

"We want him."

"Who?"

"You know who."

Svobodova's cynicism displayed on her face in a wry smile and she looked away, shaking her head at her guest's arrogance.

"He's our prisoner, captured by our own security…"

"People are dying, Madam Prime Minister," Scarlet's voice

raised slightly over Svobodova's own, drowning out her words while his posture remained determinedly still. "American people are dying, here and now in your country. They died in the bar, they died at the concert and my government is keen to avoid any more deaths within your borders, even despite your 'increased security'.

"Are you implying...?"

"What I'm implying is that it will go some way to repairing the relationship between our two countries if America sees the willingness of the Czechoslovak government to release a killer of American civilians, who may well come from the same cell as other killers of American civilians, to face justice in the country he hates."

Svobodova's eyes remained on him as she raised her coffee cup to her lips. To dominate a discussion without obvious rudeness was an art and he was far from being the only person to attempt it with her. Few had ever succeeded.

"I was not aware that our relationship had been imperilled in such a way," she replied. "You'll recall Benjamin, I asked you for the real reason."

Scarlet gave a half smile, acknowledging her wiliness.

"The President is down in the polls, much farther than anyone expected. The interrogation and trial of a terrorist would be very good publicity, particularly one from the cell which caused the deaths of so many Americans."

"I haven't been advised that such a link is confirmed."

"Neither have I, but that's what the cameras will see."

Svobodova mustered the vestiges of her diplomacy to banish the grimace which threatened to claim her features.

"You're talking about a show trial," she said, the hint of disgust in her voice undisguisable.

"I'm talking about the media," Scarlet replied, "I'm talking about public retribution, about showing the American people that their government will ensure those who would do them harm will be held accountable for their actions."

"Does that include members of their own government?"

Her barb hung accusingly between them, adding a thin level of frosted ice to the tension enveloping the room. For a moment, she thought he might retaliate with a choice implication of his own, but instead he remained silent, the familiar derisive half-smile twisting onto his face as he drained the last drops of coffee from his cup.

"Los Andes, huh?" he queried, reading the logo on his cup.

"It's Columbian," she answered, matching his tone, "a small business run by a couple of friends of mine."

"Well, it's excellent," he answered. "These friends of yours, they're Columbian too?"

She nodded.

"And there-in lies your problem, Madam Prime Minister," Scarlet gave an exaggerated sigh, clinking his cup to its saucer, "you've always been a little too friendly with a few too many of the wrong type of people."

"Wrong type of people?"

She repeated the words slowly and deliberately, as if she wanted to have misheard him and his sinister implication, though the hardness in his eyes told her otherwise.

"You know what I mean," he quietly said. "This guy Myska is calling you out on it and that's why you're stuck with the problems you have right now. Acquiescing to our request will help you go some way to pulling the rug from under him; you realise that don't you? You'll be seen as tough, taking a stand on Islamic terrorism, instead of soft and weak like you look right now."

She replaced her own cup on the table, keeping her eyes firmly on his as she mulled over his words. There was no denying the veracity of at least some of what he said; large chunks of the electorate were indeed frustrated with her multi-racial idealism and reluctance to counter the attacks of the past months with knee-jerk reactions and draconian restrictions of rights for the groups the attackers had come from. But despite her political struggles, she had no desire to avoid or ease them by enabling another government to use someone as a tool to lie to its people, even a person as odious as the man in custody must surely be.

"As ever, Benjamin," she eventually began, "I appreciate your forthrightness and honesty, and I shall give your proposal the most urgent consideration."

She stood up gracefully and gestured politely with her arm; a clear invitation to step to the door ahead of her. Scarlet instead though remained in his seat, his smirk still defiantly perched on his face; he removed his glasses and played idly with the frame, looking up at her with an accustomed arrogance.

"You know," he said, "in recognition of the mutually beneficial arrangements our countries have enjoyed in recent years, I'm going to lay it on the line for you as clearly as possible. It isn't always just our enemies that do us harm, sometimes, even with the best of intentions, our allies do as well. Your reluctance to allow us into the investigation is harming us and we will simply not allow that to continue. Support for US military action in the Middle East has never been lower, not just abroad but at home. People are tired of seeing their sons and daughters brought home in body bags draped in the Stars and Stripes; they figure all this has been going on for too long, that it's too far away to really matter to them anymore. Reports are being published by the month that condemn our attacks on Iraq and Afghanistan, while most people couldn't even find Syria on a map let alone tell you why we're fighting there. And so we need someone, a symbol, a scapegoat, call it what you will; something to reassure the people that their sacrifices haven't been in vain, something to remind them why the War on Terror costs so much by way of dollars and lives. Bin Laden's death is a fading memory and any ISIS Leaders coming to prominence get taken out by drones; we need a real, flesh and blood 'Monster of the Week' to take the fall publically on their behalf. Abdul Salam is to be that Monster."

"Our investigation is still ongoing..."

"I really couldn't care less about your investigation. Neither will the President and neither will NATO. This man is connected to people responsible for the deaths of Americans right across this continent and one way or another he will take the fall."

"If a jury of his peers determines his guilt, he will indeed take the fall, here, in Czechoslovakia where the alleged crimes took place, and I will not abandon the rule of law, even for one accused of such crimes as he, to provide a propaganda victory for our allies, however valued and close they might be!"

Svobodova's tone rose with each word, defying Scarlet's attempts to shout over here and drown her out. Instead, he remained silent for a few brief moments, allowing his own frustrations to cool.

"Madam Prime Minister," he looked at her with narrowed, almost sinister eyes, every portion of his features conveying the implicit hostility behind the façade, "America has a need right now, a need to show purpose to the sacrifices made since the turn of the century. Czechoslovakia likewise has a need: it needs friends. Russia is already at your doorstep, it's peeking through your curtains while you bathe. The European Union is poised to throw you out in the cold and abandon you; do you really want NATO to follow suit?

Svobodova's heart sunk at his words and she strained to prevent it displaying on her face, instead merely raising a cynical eyebrow to the threat, while Scarlet revelled in his role as enforcer.

"We can announce it sensitively, call it a joint investigation or whatever you want. But we'll tie him in to a bagful of unsolved cases back in the US and he'll quickly be sent packing there. Otherwise, you and your people may just find out how lonely it can be in the middle of Central Europe, when all your friends are gone."

He let the last words hang in the air, then stood swiftly and quietly to leave.

"Madam Prime Minister," he acknowledged as he opened the door, "please do give my offer your most thorough and immediate attention."

"With respect, Mr Ambassador," Svobodova answered, her countenance strong, "this is no offer; it has all the hallmarks of a threat."

Scarlet stopped in the doorway, turning back towards her, the sarcastic smile which had adorned his features replaced with an incredulous irritation.

"This is no threat," he replied, with something approaching offence in his voice, "this is international politics. The world is a small place, there's no halfway house anymore and there's nowhere to hide. You've stepped up to be a piece on the board and like it or not the only freedom you have is choosing which of the players you prefer to be used by, Them or Us, and you live or die by that choice. You can sulk all you like, you can shout and cry about the unfairness of it all and say you don't want to play anymore, but if you do, you'll find yourself very quickly advanced into pretty precarious territory, and maybe your Player won't try all that hard to protect you from being taken by the other side. Your noble little vision of a planet filled with people gloriously at peace with each other will never amount to shit, your grand ideals can never change the world, because the world doesn't want to be changed;

it likes the way it is, it enjoys the game. And if you refuse to see the nature of the world as it really is then it will turn on you and devour you before you can say Utopia. That's the choice you have Madam Prime Minister, that's your ultimatum; you, like everyone, are trapped in a world that hates you and you can either have a seat with the big boys and enjoy the view, or watch in chains as the game plays out without you. You will either authorise an immediate extradition and allow your prisoner to be tried in the US, or we will be forced to support a motion suspending Czechoslovakia's membership of NATO, which with Russia's hands all over your ass at the border isn't something I think you'd appreciate."

He paused for a moment, silhouetted in the doorway like an immaculately tailored harbinger of misfortune, his stare meeting hers and his silence reinforcing his message.

"It's time to make your choice," he said softly, before turning away and letting the door close behind him. And as it finally did, a cold draft blew over the beleaguered Svobodova, who standing alone in the centre of her room, began to feel the unwelcome torment of a new depth of isolation.

NINETEEN

STONE FELT THE WARMTH FADE from his face as the sun's rays dipped over the hillside to be replaced by the evening's familiar cool breeze. Stretching the cricks from his back as he pushed against the hill, the Captain stared out, trying to ignore the footsteps, and the person they belonged to, approaching him from his right.

"You look like you could use a drink."

"I'm not convinced I want to have it with you."

"Oh for fuck's sake man, just take the bottle."

Stone looked up, the cynically delivered profanity almost raising a smile, to see Williams alongside him, holding out a glass bottle of Czech ale with one hand, while swigging from his own. Giving in to the peace offering, he accepted it, clinked it against Williams' own and took a deep drink.

"I thought we did alright in there, to be honest," Williams said, joining the Captain in looking out at the silhouetted Karlštejn Castle, "eventually anyway. I don't know what you're moping about; after what happened to you I wouldn't have thought you'd have much sympathy for terrorist bombers, coerced or otherwise."

"Ah, he was just a kid," Stone sighed, "but a kid willing to go out and kill. He just got me thinking a little bit, that's all."

"About?"

"About why I do it, while I still do it; spend all my time fighting politicians' wars, looking after my squaddies when I had a boy back home who needed his dad. Do you ever read Oscar Wilde?"

"Not recently."

"You should. He said that children begin by loving their parents, after a time they judge them. Rarely do they forgive them."

Williams frowned, unsettled. "Rarely doesn't mean never."

"Kids like Salam," Stone continued to muse, "so many of them are so angry with the mess the parents, the grown-ups have made of the world that they think going out and killing innocents is a better way. Did we really get things so wrong?"

"Stop that shit right there!" Williams forcefully demanded. "You and I have enough things to blame ourselves for without feeling responsible every time some fucked up psycho wanders onto a train and blows himself up. A: That wasn't your fucking fault and B: the kid in the cave was doped up. End of story."

"If you say so," said Stone, raising the bottle to his lips.

Williams sighed loudly, as though unable to cope with Stone's insistence on examining the state of his soul.

"Go on then, tell me," he reluctantly said, "why do you still get your kicks dodging bullets?"

Still the Captain kept his eyes straight ahead on the busily setting sun, allowing the gentle coolness its disappearance set in to compliment the cold beer chilling his insides.

"Because it felt like I was doing something worthwhile," he finally said. "I wasn't fighting to oppress, I wasn't fighting to conquer someone's land, but everywhere I went I met people who were desperate for some kind of freedom from the people who were oppressing or conquering them. So while I was there, I fought for them, because no-one else would, and I let the politicians sort out the diplomacy afterwards."

Taking a large swig from his bottle, Williams pondered Stone's words for a moment.

"Look, I know what you think of me," he said, gazing at the castle, as it settled comfortably into dusk, "and I can't blame you for it. You're a soldier, it's your job to see things in black and white; you've a defined enemy, a clear battleground. You go in, fight like hell, move when you're told to move. Basically, you're a pawn."

Stone felt his smile growing, despite himself, and he laughed.

"Is this you trying to make me feel good about myself?"

"Maybe I'm not a very tactful guy," Williams conceded, "but it's true. I'm a pawn too, just a different kind. My battlefield is everywhere, my enemies not so clearly defined. An ally watching my back one day could be stabbing me in it the next. There's not much by the way of honour or valour on my battlefield, Captain, all I can do is keep sight of the objective and hope I have stomach enough to reach it, and if I'm not prepared to limbo under the bar of morality on occasion then I won't."

Stone took in Williams' words, spoken in an almost resigned despondency, but with a simultaneous resentful disdain for any condemnation the Captain might respond with. In the end, the military man simply shook his head, a wry smile forming at his lips.

"The ends justify the means, eh?"

"I don't know anymore," Williams sighed, swigging from his half-spent bottle. "In the old days I used to think so, like the objective was something worth fighting for. But the older you get, you realise that there is no shining utopia, no happy ever after and that you've spent so long complaining about the other side's smell that you don't notice the stench coming from your own."

He knocked his grey head back, pushing the last of the ale down his wrinkled throat, toying with the top of the empty bottle in his hand.

"So why do you go on?" Stone asked gently, sincerely, his own stare joining his grim colleague's.

Williams shrugged. "You can't survive in this world if you look at it like some deontological minefield to be carefully negotiated for fear of making the 'wrong' choice. It's the same for everyone these days in any walk of life. I mean, look at the state of elections in the past couple of years; it's got to the stage where voting is pretty much just an exercise in deciding which politician you'd prefer to be fucked by. They all promise you the moon, you know? But all the manifestos and slogans all boil down to saying the same thing: Our guy isn't quite as big a cunt as theirs. At the end of the day, all we guys and gals in the middle can do is pick whichever side looks slightly less shit than the other and hope for the best. But even that gets more difficult the more mind numbingly stupid the electorate continues to prove itself to be."

The bitterness underscoring Williams' melancholia was obvious to Stone, despite its delivery with the Scotsman's typical nonchalance, and it was an emotion with which the Captain could sympathise. He had long since tired both of the gloating of the 'Brexiteers' in the aftermath of the referendum a couple of years previously, and that so many continued to use the result as a means to vindicate their own long held hatreds. It wasn't that Stone had thought the EU perfect, far from it in fact, but the willingness of the elite to pin the blame for their own failings on it while affecting a concern for the poor and dispossessed riled him intensely. Successive governments of every shade had perpetuated all manner of inequalities in Britain for as long as Stone could remember; chronically under-investing in the areas that needed it most and which ironically would have the most to lose by withdrawal from Europe, as they were now discovering, alas too late. Likewise, it wasn't that Stone had trouble accepting that rational, sensible arguments existed for withdrawal; it was more that he had so rarely heard them used, with the default position of most he had debated with ultimately revealed as there being 'too many bloody foreigners' or some equally ineloquent riposte. But since his arrival in Prague and the references Williams and others had made to this 'Institute for European Harmony', even his own staunchly European passions had been rocked.

"Franz Kafka spent time around these parts, didn't he?" Stone asked.

"Yeah, why?" Williams frowned.

"Because I'm beginning to feel like I'm trapped in one of his nightmares," Stone laughed. "We're struggling to keep the country inside the boundaries of a political Union that resents its very existence and actively works against it. Did I turn over two pages at once?"

"It's The Institute we're fighting," Williams replied, "not the body of the EU itself. Just because the bureaucracy is against us doesn't mean the principle isn't worth fighting for; if we can neuter The Institute, chop the head off the snake, we stand a good chance of re-shaping the Union, getting rid of the shite and baggage. We might even stand a chance of getting Britain back inside before the economy well and truly dies on its isolationist backside."

Stone laughed. "If the papers back home heard you they'd accuse you of being a bitter Remainer unable to accept the democratic will of the people."

The barb, light hearted though its delivery was, irked the Scotsman, who turned his ferocious gaze on the Captain.

"This might be a hard concept for the military mind to understand, Captain, but it is entirely possible to both accept something and to loathe and despise it utterly at the same time. I accept Brexit like I accepted my cancer diagnosis: I might have to acknowledge its existence but it doesn't mean I have to wave a Union Flag and sing Rule Britannia while it fucking eats me alive."

Stone struggled to contain his laughter at Williams' choice of words, holding his hand up in mock surrender to the foul-mouthed tirade.

"And in any case," Williams continued, "democracy only works when your population doesn't know more about the cast of the latest reality TV show than it does about the fucking issues it's voting on."

Stone guffawed out loud, Williams too eventually allowing his misanthropy to crack into mirth, as though the pair were the only two capable of seeing the ludicrousness of the world they found themselves trapped in.

"Mind you," Stone laughed, "given some of the candidates we've seen recently, democracy has practically become the new reality TV."

"Aye," Williams nodded, with something approaching sadness in his eyes and his brief moment of laughter subsiding, "you're right."

He straightened up and stretched the stresses of the day from his back, a deep and lengthy yawn overcoming him.

"But at least," he began, as the pair shuffled away down the path, "with our friend Mr Salam in custody, we can give the viewers a hell of a show."

TWENTY

"THERE WAS NOTHING ELSE she could do, they had her over a barrel and she knew it."

A quiet bitterness haunted Captain Stone's voice which the sincerity of his words did little to counter. There had indeed been nothing Svobodova could do in the face of the 'give in or be given up' ultimatum delivered by her American friends, but that knowledge in no way masked the astringent flavour of the pill she, and by extension he, were now swallowing. The headlines screamed it, the TV reports debated it and Stone watched it unfold from his vantage point in the south east of the city, where the dirty, white walls of the High Court stood, topped with its orange roof and connected via secure, underground tunnel to the bustling and overcrowded Pankrác Prison; the prisoner was to be transferred to American custody. No extradition hearing was required, the US media stated, as the agent who took the prisoner down was part of a pre-arranged joint operation between Czechoslovakia and the US. A useful little lie which Svobodova had little choice but to back up.

"Fucking Yanks."

Stone almost allowed himself to smile at Williams' now familiar display of contempt, but his own impotent frustrations kept his face defiantly rigid.

"He was mine, I had him," the Scotsman continued sourly, "I just needed more time."

"We got some leads out of him," Stone tried to placate his associate, somewhat insincerely as they stood in the car park of the court, away from the jostling and jeering crowd of protestors, awaiting the prisoner's journey through the tunnel and out of the court to the waiting transport, "the Myska connection looks a hell of a lot more provable now."

"With the only witness strapped up and on his way to enjoy trial by TV in America? Fat lot of good that'll do us. By the time he's wearing his orange jumpsuit and having his face plastered on trailers between re-runs of Columbo and Desperate fucking Housewives, Svobodova will be out of power, the lunatics will have taken over the asylum and European governments will start toppling like a game of Domino Rally. A couple more days and I could have got the whole damn story from him!"

Williams' indignation was as passionate and deeply felt as the Captain's own and it had burned since Svobodova's intervention the previous evening which repeated through his mind now. He and Williams had returned the prisoner to his solitary cell at Pankrác, his wrists freshly stitched and bandaged from the MI6 man's assault, to find Abelard looking pensive and Svobodova herself waiting there in the shadows. Her face had displayed none of the stresses Stone had become accustomed to, but neither was there any trace of the warmth he had all too briefly glimpsed, instead her features were cradled by a mask of grim resignation.

Pausing only to briefly and tersely express her distaste at the sight of the bandages, she had overridden the objections of the pair and her security detail and insisted on speaking privately with the prisoner in his cell. The duo, joined by an angered Radoslav and frustrated Professor Abelard had watched intently on the monitors as she had stood in accusatory silence mere yards apart from the man who had tried to kill so many of her people, with only a solitary guard outside the door. The tension in the cramped control room had been almost opaque; a ghost-like atmosphere enveloping all present as they waited for the Prime Minister to fracture her silence with her country's erstwhile attacker. The only words had been a whispered warning from the Professor that they would not like what Svobodova had to say, as she slipped her fingers into Stone's.

The politician had eventually spoken, explaining to the man that she had wanted to look into the eyes of someone who could attempt such an act as he, and try to determine if any trace of humanity lay behind them. She had told him he was not the first killer she had met, but he was the first to look at her with only emptiness in his face; no fear, no regret, no hatred, just a desperate nothingness. And it was then she had dropped her bombshell; with the briefest of apologies and a lament that there was nothing that could be done, she had explained that the prisoner was to be handed over to American authorities and transferred to the United States, whereupon a link to active terrorist cells would be proven and he would doubtless be convicted of innumerous crimes against that country. She had delivered her news frostily, her message to the point and un-conversational, and once delivered she had turned on her heel and exited, not caring to observe the failed killer's reactions.

She had exited the cell and walked directly into a verbal barrage from the furious trio; a storm she had weathered with typical stoicism.

"Madame Prime Minister, I really must object," Stone had begun, before being interrupted by the glaring Williams.

"That's putting it fucking mildly!" The Scotsman had been apoplectic and paid little heed to deference or the level of her office. "I really must tell you you're being a fucking idiot! After all your services went through to capture him, and after the fucking day from hell the good Captain and I have been through today, you're going to hand him over to that fucking trigger happy band of rent-a-smile morons to be tried in front of a studio audience with a lawyer sponsored by Doritos? It's fucking lunacy What a fantastic arrangement, what leadership, what..."

"Mr. Williams!" She had interjected, cutting him off in mid-flow, the fierceness in her voice matched by the expression she adopted, "you do not have to like the arrangement..."

"I don't!"

"But neither do you have any need to discuss it. For the record, I did not like the arrangement between Jonathan Greyson and yourself to have me believe you were in Brno when you were in fact shadowing Captain Stone all over the city. The decision is made and tomorrow morning the prisoner will be transported from here to the US Embassy for formal handover. I am grateful for your efforts in gathering information from him and ask that you kindly use it to further your investigations with Captain Stone, now if there is nothing else gentlemen, I think this is a suitable moment for us all to get some sleep."

She had turned to leave, Radoslav falling dutifully into place behind her while scowling his displeasure to Stone who nodded in reciprocation.

"Prime Minister," he'd called after her.

"Not now, Captain Stone, thank you," she'd replied without breaking her step.

"Miroslava!"

The presumption had had the desired effect of stopping her in her tracks and she had paced slowly back towards the military man, who walked forward to meet her, leaving the silently fuming Williams and the worried Abelard behind him.

"You don't have to do this, you know," he'd earnestly whispered, "you don't have to give in to them, you could make a stand, you could…"

"I know," she'd answered in similarly quiet tones, the look of resignation returned to her face, "and were it as simple as that and I were the only one to suffer the consequences of such an action, then I would do it without reservation. But reality is hard, and I will not allow my people to fall back into adversity because of my own intransigence."

She had looked past him at Williams and Abelard, the Scotsman muttering profanities not entirely under his breath and casting occasional glances of frustrated impotence at the politician. Her eyes back on the Captain, he had seen a desperation in her eyes, as though pleading for understanding and he began to feel his anger slowly dissipate in response.

"I am sorry," she had whispered, "truly, I am.

"But why? Why now?"

If Stone hadn't had known better, he would have sworn he'd seen tears in her eyes as she'd weighed up her answer before replying with sincere candor.

"Because when they point the gun at me, I am strong enough to resist them still, but when they turn it on my people, I am as helpless as a Mother desperate to protect her children."

With that she had turned swiftly on her heel and set off down the corridor, leaving only the sound of her footsteps and William's cursing to play in his ears.

Stone had replayed the conversation over and over in his head after returning to his apartment, his desire to curse the bad luck which seemed intent on pushing away every chance of achieving his aim almost as soon as it arrived, delaying his yearned for reunion with his boy, somewhat alleviated by the presence of Natalie. She had spent what seemed an age massaging the stressful aches from his shoulders while whispering sweet words of reassurance to him, the gentle intensity of their lovemaking emphasising her palpable concern for him which he hoped she knew was reciprocated. That morning they had risen, showered and dressed quickly, Natalie taking a piece of toast on the go while Stone left a quick voicemail for his son before they had descended together in the lift and stepped out to the reluctantly awakening street and heading to their separate duties; Natalie's involving another early start with Svobodova while Stone had met with Williams and travelled to the prison.

"It's time."

"What?" said Stone, his mind returning to the present.

"Salam," answered Williams, the spite heavy in his voice, "he's on the move."

Stone looked to where the Prison transport truck, unceremonious and grim in its dull off white, replete with superfluous green stripe began to back towards the steps of the High Court building to the accompanying jeers of the spectators. The main doors to the court opened and black suited operatives took up position on either side as though preparing the way for royalty. Stone frowned when the prisoner did not immediately appear; the wrinkles deepening further still when a stretcher was carried into the view, down the steps with Salam strapped securely onto it, his face underneath the obligatory towel such occasions demanded.

As the stretcher was hauled down the steps towards the waiting truck's open rear doors, Stone jogged over, Williams close behind him.

"What the hell is this?" the Captain demanded, approaching the lead operative at his position by the truck doors, "he isn't Hannibal bloody Lecter."

"The Americans insisted on it," the begrudging response came as Salam's stretcher was firmly slotted into place. "They want to be sure he doesn't escape."

The straps were so tight there would be little chance of that, and the gurney was quickly secured in place and sealed behind the heavy metal doors; the gates of the courtyard opening to allow the truck to take its place in the bizarre cortege that awaited it. Shining new police cars took up their positions at the head and rear of the procession with the truck in between, flanked by sleek and quick police motorcycles; the jeering of the amassed crowd quickly drowned out by the passionately whining sirens. Stone accepted the offer of a ride in Williams car, every bit as aged and weathered as the spy who drove it, to follow the transport and ensure no chance of escape, and they pulled swiftly onto the road behind it.

The journey from the prison to the US Embassy in Malá Strana was a twenty-minute ride in good conditions and the route had been cleared in advance, but the grim parade had travelled for significantly less than that when Stone first noticed the problem. An innocuous family car, insignificant in a rusting dull blue came into view as the procession approached the turn for the Mánes Bridge and kept a respectful distance until the first police car began to turn.

Stone, with the observation skills so necessary for his trade, saw the car begin to pick up speed, and in his mind he saw what was about to happen before it did, his body having time only to mouth a useless expletive before the bland, inoffensive vehicle struck the police escort smack in the side, hard. Chaos ensued as the truck swerved to avoid the twisted mass of metal, only for the rear door of the blue car to kick open and a masked, black clothed man lean out, a shotgun firmly in his hand.

The first blast tore its way through the front driver's side wheel of the tuck, sending it into a hazardous skid. A second blast dealt with the rear wheel and the truck tipped at speed onto its side, the screech of speeding metal across tarmac drowning out the screams of onlookers who ran panicking in every direction, inhibiting the aim of the armed police escorts who ran towards the disabled truck. One of the police had leapt from his motorbike, bravely attempting to tackle the gunman, only for its butt to be swung against the side of his head by the attacker, who clambered onto the felled vehicle and fired a third heavy shot into the small and thinly barred tinted windows, peppering the air with shattered glass and twisted metal.

As soon as the car had struck, Williams had accelerated into the scene, while the remaining police threw themselves into the battle, two managing finally to wrestle the gunman onto the ground, only for a further attacker to run from the neglected wreckage, a glass bottle in his hand from which a flaming rag trailed. Throwing himself from William's car, Stone pounded behind him, hurling himself at the attacker's legs in a rugby tackle the lads in RTR would have been proud of and bringing the man to a fall on the hard surface. He was just too late; the toppling figure having hurled the bottle into the hole blasted into the truck's window by his associate moments before and from which a plume of smoke and flame now burst. Scrambling to his feet, the Captain ran to the felled truck, pulling uselessly at the locked rear doors while the flames grew wilder.

"Fucking open!" he screamed at them, they defiantly refusing his order. Still he pulled until Williams appeared behind him, his bony fingers digging into him and pulling him away.

"Come on man!" Williams was shouting, "it's gonna go!"

With a climactic, anguished bellow of rage, Stone ran with his colleague away from the spreading flames, the pair throwing themselves to the ground as the prison transport finally exploded in wrathful, incandescent fury. Pulling himself up to his knees, Stone grimaced at the burning shell in front of him, the thought of the dead prisoner inside it and the transfer which would never now happen. This was a catastrophe, and even as the two men who had caused it were dragged unceremoniously into custody to the sound of screams and sirens, Stone realised that even the heat of the explosion would be no match for the rage of the Americans that would shortly be visited upon Svobodova. And he hoped against hope that Czechoslovakia would survive the fall out.

TWENTY-ONE

"AND SO THE EXCUSES ARE MADE. Ladies and Gentlemen; we are alone."

And alone they were. President Černý's words may have been tinged with a melancholic dramatism, but it was one which was sorely deserved.

The response of the World to the attack on the bridge had been as instant and severe as anyone could have expected; as though Czechoslovakia were a habitually errant child who had tried the patience of its parents once too often and was now suffering the consequences. Scarlet's threat or ultimatum, call it what you will, was as good as implemented the moment the blue car revved its engine; NATO announcing formally that Czechoslovakia's membership was suspended with immediate effect pending legal scrutiny. The move was mirrored instantly by the EU; the Institute for European Harmony, Svobodova supposed, taking full advantage of its opportunity to inflict further punishment. Both moves were presented to the media as unconnected to the Abdul Salam issue, their timing purely coincidental. Whether or not anyone believed that was immaterial; nothing could alter the fact of the country's new found isolation.

Myska, of course, took full advantage of the situation,

condemning Svobodova for her refusal to accept the incompatibleness of Islam with European tradition, while Stone and Williams conducted several fruitless searches for the individual named by Salam as his 'spiritual guide' in their interrogation in the cave. But still more distressing news was to come, which would fill the hearts of all involved with dread.

It came in the form of an offer, a telephone call to Svobodova from, of all places, Moscow. The call was terse and brief, devoid of small talk or pleasantries of any kind. The President of the Russian Federation, so the caller said, was gravely concerned by the problems its close ally was facing and was determined to ensure the region remained stable and free from the ravages of Far Right extremism. To that end, The President was offering his 'help' to support Svobodova in her efforts to contain the threat and restore order to the streets. Military help. And furthermore, in expectation of her acquiescence, the Armed Forces currently engaged in maneuvers in the Ukraine, would henceforth relocate to the Ukraine/Slovak border, in readiness to accept her invitation to cross and support the administration's fight against extremism. When the call ended, Svobodova was as morose and ashen faced as Stone had, in their short acquaintance, seen her, and she wordlessly dismissed the company from her office to tackle the conundrum in solitude.

Stone, with the sixth sense of a professional soldier, could smell impending battle in the warm, summer air as he walked the ever bustling ancient, gothic streets, at once despairing and envious of the blissful ignorance with which the tourists continued to mill, as though subconsciously believing themselves wrapped in some impenetrable shell of invulnerability, immunising them from the kind of terror which stalked the rest of the world. Stag groups still staggered from bar to bar, globetrotters still trotted from shop to store, searching for the perfect gift to take home; none acknowledging or even registering the heavily armoured threat currently rumbling towards the border.

The continued absence of Greyson in all this disturbed him and he set his mind to reaching him through Williams and finding out precisely what effect this new development would have on their agreement, when he was distracted by a message on his phone from Svobodova. No pleasantries, no exposition, just an address and a time, under the header 'Meeting'.

Were it not for the presence of Abelard outside the stated address when he approached it some hours later, after negotiating the labyrinthine streets behind the fiercely imposing Church of Our Lady, the Captain would have thought he was in the wrong place.

"What the hell are we doing here?" Stone asked in incredulity, leaning forward to kiss his lover and accept the de-stressing bliss of her embrace. And he could be forgiven for asking, for it was no office or conference center they stood before; rather the fading yellow walls and battered wooden doors of a music joint, a painted wooden sign proclaiming it to be 'The Smokin' Hot Blues Bar and Restaurant' swinging gently in the slight breeze.

"Beats me," shrugged the Professor, "but she's in there, talking with some big Czech bloke; she looks happier than I've ever seen her. Your friend Mr. Williams is there too, although decidedly less impressed looking than Svobodova. Shall we?"

The pair joined hands and walked through the double doors and into the small but intimate bar area to their right. The place was deserted of customers, though Williams sat scowling at a corner table, nursing a glass of some strangely coloured spirit and a young, pleasant looking man dried glasses behind the well-stocked bar. At a table in the middle of the room, laughing with an abandon which drowned out the slow blues playing over the speakers, sat Svobodova, her clothing as casual as her demeanour and just as unexpected. Across from her, dressed in a once black, now dark grey t-shirt and jeans, a small but noticeable crucifix around his neck, sat a heavy set Czech man with a round, cheery face, who Stone imagined it was impossible not to like.

All eyes turned to the Captain and Abelard as they entered.

"Captain Stone, welcome! Please, come in, come in. I'll be with you all in a moment. And don't look so scared Captain, all will be revealed."

Though he could almost feel the confusion on his face, he acquiesced and moved with Abelard uncertainly to join Williams; the barman immediately bringing over a tray of drinks.

"Welcome to the briefing," Williams said, raising what was clearly not his first glass of the evening to the pair in mock salute.

"What's going on?" quizzed the Captain.

"Tonight we are merry," the spook replied, "for tomorrow we go to war."

"War?" Abelard's voice carried every bit of the concern etched onto her face.

"Aye," he confirmed, knocking his drink back and reaching for the next one on the tray. "She's mobilised the troops; the Czechoslovak Armed Forces are presently en route to the Ukrainian border to prevent Mother Russia from entering uninvited. Mother Russia of course, never one to stand on ceremony, will enter regardless and, given their somewhat hefty numerical advantage, will eventually break through the lines and that, my friends, will be check-fucking-mate."

"They can't do that," Abelard protested, "there'll be international uproar; the invasion of a sovereign State…"

Williams took another glass from the tray and handed it to her while interrupting.

"Yeah, because it's not like the West haven't set a precedent for doing that in recent years is it? Any 'objection' from anyone involved in any of the Afghan, Iraqi, Libyan or Syrian cock ups will carry all the moral authority of a peadophile history teacher bollocking the sixth form for shagging behind the bike sheds. Relax Professor, it'll all be over soon. MI6 will forcibly retire me, most likely with their preferred pension plan of a bullet to the skull, the Captain here can skulk back to national ignominy, you can go back to shuffling papers for academics and Svobodova can look forward to her specially arranged 'disappearance'. Merry fucking Christmas all."

Abelard continued to protest but Stone said nothing, turning instead to take in Svobodova, so relaxed here, so happy, despite the enormous burden she carried on her shoulders, just glad to be in the company of her friend. As he watched, the man, whose name Stone quickly learned was Rasti, reached into a pocket of the leather jacket hung over the back of his chair.

"I found a photograph I wanted to give you."

"Of Peter?"

The hope in her voice was unguarded and impossible to disguise, her optimism apparently dashed a little when her companion briefly exposed the back of a tattered old photo holding it tightly to his chest

"I need to explain it first," he said.

"Well that sounds intriguing…"

"Did I tell you about the flood?"

Rasti's voice was light and typically disarming, though not far from breaking, it seemed to Stone, who twisted his neck sideways to hear the story the big Czech was so obviously desperate to tell.

"No," Svobodova grinned, her own voice likewise close to its breaking point.

Her reassurance seemed to imbibe Rasti with a new confidence and he swallowed the bulk of his pint before continuing, a warm smile upon his lips.

"Well," he began loudly, his relishing of his position at centre court exemplified by his continued oration in English, "You remember when the Vltava burst its banks in 2005? The whole of Old Town was completely flooded, everywhere literally knee deep in water. Well mercifully the waters didn't reach us here on Jakubska, at least not too heavily and as fate turned out, we were the only restaurant in the area who could stay open. Brilliant, you'd think, only I had no staff to cope with the wave of tourists flocking to the only open venue this side of Prague! I was sweating my bollocks off in the kitchen and I had one waitress running around all the tables, with a queue of people at the door and nobody manning the bar. I couldn't turn people away so I had no choice but to press gang one of the regulars into service."

"Let me guess," Svobodova interrupted, "Peter?"

"The man himself," Rasti grinned, "But the problem was he'd come to the bar straight from work and was so pissed he hadn't even realised there was a flood, he just thought it had been raining particularly heavily… But I filled him full of coffee and sandwiches and managed to stand him upright at the bar with his best smile and I hoped for the best."

"And…?"

"To begin with it was all going well, he didn't punch anyone and I'd come to accept that every shot ordered by a customer was accompanied with one for Peter, but by that stage I didn't care. Anyway, it was soon all over the news that the flood had reached the zoo and animals were being washed out of their paddocks…"

"Yes, I remember that," Svobodova replied, "they found some washed up in Austria didn't they?"

"They did indeed," Rasti nodded, "but some stayed a bit more local. It must have been getting on for closing time when I came out to check Peter was ok and see how many customers were left. Then out of the blue we heard this slapping sound coming from the main door."

Rasti articulated his tale with a slow, heavy hand slapping down on the table as he spoke.

"We couldn't work out what the fuck it was, so I went to look and opened the inner door, only for the biggest bloody seal you've ever seen in your life slide past me like some kind of royalty and hop up to the bar! I just stood there, my mouth on the floor, while Peter, as pissed as the day is long but somehow still standing, just blinked at it, shook his head and said, 'Looking a bit rough tonight, Rob, usual is it?'"

Svobodova screamed at the story and laughed loudly until tears began to stream down her face, joined in mirth and pain by the tale's teller who gave a last loving look to the picture and held it out to her.

Svobodova looked down at the crumpled photo; a younger and trimmer, if decidedly tired Rasti, looking back at her, joined by a dishevelled and obviously drunk, but happily smiling Peter, a particularly large black seal between them.

Svobodova reached across the table and stroked Rasti's hand affectionately.

"Thank you," she said, simply and sincerely, taking another loving look at the picture and placing it in the inner pocket of her overcoat. The moment passed, she stood up and called for the others to give her a few moments; the barman lowering the music while she spoke.

"Thank you for coming," she said. "As I'm sure Mr. Williams has told you, tomorrow promises to be a momentous day in the history of this country. Russia has made clear its interest in returning our relationship to that of the old days and, after consulting with President Černý today, I have decided that the only way to dissuade a bully from attacking you is to show one's own strength in return. And so as I speak, our Armed Forces are moving towards the border with the Ukraine, where tomorrow I will join them."

"You can't go the Front!" Stone objected fiercely.

"I'm afraid Captain that that is the only place I can be," Svobodova responded, "the President agrees with me that a politician who orders their country's forces into conflict should be prepared to face those same horrors themselves. Tomorrow morning I shall visit Vyšehrad Cemetery, and from there travel to the border where I have arranged to meet with the Russian Deputy Premier and, together, we shall see what terms we are able to come to. Captain Stone and Mr. Williams, it is now more imperative than ever that Myska not make political Capital out of chaos. I would ask that tomorrow you move to action whatever evidence you may have against him."

Both men remained silent, nodding a simple agreement to her request.

"Thank you," she responded. "Now as for tonight, I invite you to join me in raising a glass."

She lifted her own glass, containing the familiar clear spirit she had introduced them to in her office. Behind her, Rasti stood up, somewhat unsteadily, raising his own beer and even Rado, stoic as ever and loyally in place by the door, broke his position to join the toast. The three at the table followed suit, Stone recognising Svobodova's gesture as her version of the ancient maritime tradition in which a Captain would tour their ship on the eve of battle.

"To Czechoslovakia," Svobodova began, "to Freedom; and whatever fate tomorrow brings us, may we each find our own peace."

It was an unusual, almost fatalistic toast, Stone thought, but he nonetheless drank to it and offered the beleaguered Prime Minister the most reassuring of smiles he could muster.

Her glass drained, Svobodova visibly relaxed, almost flopping back down to the table with Rasti, while the music returned to its previous volume.

"Well," Stone said, looking at Williams, "it looks like you'll get to work your charms on Myska after all."

"Aye," Williams agreed. "At least that means I should be nice and tired by bedtime."

Stone grunted a reluctant laugh and turned towards the pale looking Natalie.

"Hey," he said gently, placing his hand on her shoulder, "it'll be ok. We'll figure something out, Svobodova will work out some kind of Treaty and old misery guts here and me will smooth things over back here."

"Sure," she whispered, unconvinced. "I just hope that by the end of the day the rest of us aren't joining Svobodova on a trip to the cemetery."

Stone frowned a little, his vast experience of steadying troops before a battle of little use when it came to reassuring a civilian, particularly one who had revived the kind of feelings within him that Natalie had. Rather than trying and failing to give a calming word, Stone opted to turn the subject away from the fear of impending battle and he tried as subtly as he could to steer her remark in another direction.

"Yeah, what was all that about the cemetery, just paying respects?"

Natalie smiled, acknowledging her man's distraction technique.

"Have you ever noticed," Natalie began, taking a glass of wine from the tray and taking a sip, "how in graveyards, if you look close enough, you'll sometimes find fresh flowers on old graves, too old you'd think for anyone to be tending them?"

"I suppose so," Stone smiled gently back at her, "I'd never really thought about it."

"Well then I suppose you've also never thought about who leaves them there; the flowers I mean."

"No."

Natalie's eyes began to wander, as though her mind were flirting at the edge of age old memories.

"I have," she said, "since I was a girl. I used to love walking through cemeteries, everything seemed so peaceful there, serene. I'd see these fresh flowers, sometimes in bouquets, sometimes alone and I'd wonder... did distant descendants put them there, or kindly passers-by, or maybe the fairies?"

She grinned, as much to herself as to Stone, "But I was wrong. It was people like her," she nodded over to where Svobodova sat with Rasti, the pair laughing through melancholic tears together.

"People who've lost someone, someone they love and care deeply about, but who have no grave or marker of their own to pay respects by. So, instead, they walk among the headstones, finding one that looks neglected, forgotten, and they lay their flowers there instead."

Natalie's eyes were beginning to dampen and Stone placed his hands over hers, encouraging her to continue.

"She lost someone, Svobodova, someone very special to her. Jonathan told me."

"Who was he?"

"I don't know for sure, someone who helped her during

the election; a man called Peter something. He worked for this 'Institute' and was supposed to kill her, but fell in love with her and vowed to protect her instead."

"And what happened to him?"

"Guess," she replied darkly, her fears resurfacing. "But since then you can often find her, when the cameras aren't looking, standing alone in a graveyard, placing a flower on the shrine."

The sympathy Stone felt for the Premier increased with Natalie's words; a sentiment evidently not shared by Williams whose dismissive scowl dug new depths on his face.

"She certainly shared a lot with Greyson," Stone opined before grimacing in recognition of his own insensitivity.

"Sorry," he quickly uttered, only for her to laugh in reply.

"It's ok," she quickly reassured him, "I made my peace with that a long time ago; at least it sounds like they didn't have boring pillow talk."

"Well at least you'll have something to talk about with the Ex when he gets here," Williams nonchalantly supposed.

"Jonathan's coming? Here?"

"He just texted me," said the spy, "he's on his way."

She looked panicked at the news and stood to leave, collecting her phone and purse from the table top and depositing them back inside her bag.

"Look, don't go," pleaded Stone, "you don't have to go anywhere near him, we can…"

"I can't be in the same room as him," she snapped, her voice flustered, "not right now. Tell him…"

"Tell him what?" quizzed Stone.

"Just tell him I'm getting my roots done."

She stood quickly and headed for the door, stopped only by Svobodova's voice as she reached it.

"Natalie?"

Stone, behind the Professor, put a hand on her shoulder in support, which the politician noted and smiled gently at.

"You're leaving?"

"Yes," replied Abelard, "I've no wish to be around Jonathan any more than I need to be. I'm sorry."

"I understand," said Svobodova with what looked like regret in her eyes, "but before you go, I just wanted to tell you that it really wasn't like that at all."

She reached forward and took Natalie's fingers in her own as she spoke.

"I realise I am not your favourite person," she began, dismissing Natalie's half-heartedly shaken head, "and I realise that I spent far too long in your husband's company than any wife could feel comfortable with. But I assure you, those days, those visits, they were never for anything other than political business. I was the Leader of a newly unified country, Jonathan was trying to forge a path for Britain's international cooperation after Brexit; we were open to each other, we built strong agreements and we worked well together. I knew that Jonathan came with a reputation and I admit there were occasions when he made clear his willingness to take the relationship in a different direction. I must also admit that there were times Natalie, when I was tempted to accept."

Stone saw the slightest flash of anger in Abelard's eyes at Svobodova's words, but she made no attempt to remove her hand.

"But," Svobodova continued, "I am a woman; a woman who has herself been betrayed and who remains in mourning for the love of her life. However charming Jonathan could be, however attractive he surely is and however much I enjoyed his company; it wasn't enough to overcome those things. I didn't want you to go without knowing that."

She finished her unexpected confession and a brief silence hung between them while the Professor took in all that was said. After a brief moment, Stone saw her gently squeeze Svobodova's fingers in return, stroking her hands with her thumbs.

"Thank you," she said, her voice soft and sincere, "Miroslava."

The women shared a smile, before Svobodova eased her hands away and returned to the inner sanctuary of the bar; Abelard relaxing into Stone's protecting embrace.

"Are you ok?"

"Yes," she exhaled, truthfully, "I think I am. Goodnight Lincoln; call me in the morning please? It' sounds like tomorrow's challenges are going to be pretty unique, and I'd like to help if I can."

"Of course," he replied as she turned back to the door, "Natalie wait…"

She stopped in the doorway and he stepped closer to her.

"Listen, Natalie," he stuttered, "you've been brilliant to me since we wound up here, more brilliant than I think anyone has before, or at least in a bloody long time… Shit, I'm not very good at this am I?"

"You're doing better than you think," she laughed.

"Well I just want you to know, in case anything happens tomorrow, that, well, I…"

She stepped forward, pressing her lips warmly against his.

"I love you too."

She quickly went through the doors, affording him a brief, but sincere smile over her shoulder, reassuring him of the truthfulness of her words as she disappeared into the darkness of the street; the Captain's elation stumbling as Williams bounded up to him.

"Captain," he said, touching Stone's arm discreetly, "a word."

Stone followed him out of the building and looked up at the

illuminated spires towering above and illuminating the streets of Old Town, Williams claiming his attention once more with a curt grunt.

"Listen, you heard what she said in there; tomorrow, you and me are paying a visit to the friendly neighbourhood fascist, right?"

"Right?"

"Well I need to know you're not going to pussy out on me when we get there."

Stone's face displayed his instant resentment at Williams' insinuation and when he replied his voice low and growling.

"I didn't 'pussy out' in Syria, Mr. Williams," he snarled, "nor in Iraq, nor in Afghanistan, nor in any of the God forsaken shit holes I was sent to on the back of 'intelligence' from the likes of you; right back to the Falklands where I fought so damn hard they pinned medals to my chest after 'intelligence' said Argentina wouldn't dare invade."

"Oh yes, very impressive," Williams sneered dismissively. "Listen; I'm not arsed about how hard you fight when your uniform's on and your arm's too tired to wank at night because of all the saluting. Tomorrow we're not doing things by the book with a nod to Queen and Country. I need to know you've got the balls to beat a confession out of an unarmed man because that's what the world needs you to do. Well?"

Stone's anger turned quickly into a contemptuous laugh.

"You fucking spies," he spat, "Christ knows how any of you on whichever side ever sleep at night. Do any of you have the first fucking idea what it means to face your enemy with honour, on a level playing field? None of this shit was in the deal the Magical Disappearing Greyson put on the table to me. Simple reconnaissance was my role, enough to give Svobodova something on Myska and help stabilise her position, then I was supposed to be back home with my boy by my side, toasting my exoneration. I was an idiot to think it would be as simple as that with you cloak and dagger bastards running the show."

Though Stone kept his back to Williams, he could feel the Scotsman's indignation grow with every passing second until his lament had finished.

"Oh, well my apologies Captain, Sir!" The typical thick sarcasm in the voice was joined with a heavy mixture of resentment and pent up aggression, as its owner stepped close into Stone's shoulder to project his venom at close range. "It completely passed me by that I was dealing with the elevated ideals of the mighty; don't let me stand in your way, by all means fuck right off back to Syria and have your arse blown off for Britain with your conscience clear of difficult decisions, pragmatic reasoning and any and all fucking responsibility! Off you pop now, go fade into irrelevance with the rest of your squaddie chums."

"Excuse me?"

Stone turned his head at the barb, observing the raging spy in his peripheral vision.

"You fucking heard me," he said, "you might have had a genuine role once but all you are these days is a representation of the Prime Ministerial bollocks."

With precipitate alacrity, the Captain reeled around, clasping his abuser by the throat and thrusting him against the crumbling concrete of the wall behind him, holding him there in an inflexible posture, and staring into the older man's eyes with a ferocity which would halt the hounds of hell in their tracks.

"Between you and me," Stone seethed, "I'm getting a bit sick of your opinion of Her Majesty's Armed Forces. Would you care to re-phrase your last comment?"

If there was fear or even discomfort inside Williams he refused to allow it to display on his face, his own equally combative eyes resolutely returning Stone's glare, before being complimented by a cynical, almost malicious grin.

"You," he began quietly and patiently as though lecturing a small child, "and your comrades in arms, are the equivalent of the Prime Minister's fucking testicles."

He was rewarded with a renewed squeeze around his neck and the sight of Captain Stone's other arm coiling ready to deliver what would surely be a knockout blow, but if the military man's intention was to intimidate, it was a sadly fruitless hope as William's unsettling grin became a disturbing, almost unbalanced laugh, distracting Stone long enough to delay his assault.

"You really are one arrogant prick, you now that?" he chuckled. "Don't get me wrong, so am I, but at least I'm not labouring under the misapprehension that I'm any better or worse than you."

"It was people like you, you fucking Spooks with your worthless intelligence that got us stuck in Iraq for eight years," Stone spat with unbridled enmity, "that kept me away from my boy when it mattered most, beached in Middle Eastern deserts looking for WMD instead of holding his hand on the way to school."

Stone unleashed his fury on his quarry as though the throwaway comment had burst the damn of his pent up rage and he was unable and unwilling to stem the flow.

"And it was people like you, *bastards like you*, who told us the Russians were miles behind in Syria when the call came in to take the town, then washed their hands and disappeared when everything went tits up. And now, again, all you wannabe James Bonds have had us obsessing over terrorists, some real and most imaginary, while all the time the threat was coming from elsewhere and now another country is about to fall into war because of it. All you and your kind know how to do is deceive, twist, obscure, like this is all some big fucking game to you. I'm a soldier, I face my enemy on the battlefield, one on one, I look them in the eye when I kill them and if I make any kind of mistake on the ground, you can bet your wrinkled arse I will damn well stick around to sort it out. And the truth is I've more in common with each and every enemy soldier I've taken down over the years than I ever had, than I ever *could* have, with a fucking Spook."

His energy spent from his verbal assault, Stone closed his eyes and heaved air into his lungs, the outpouring ending as suddenly as it began. He uncoiled his arm and dropped his clasp from Williams's throat, joining him against the wall, both men sliding down the graffiti adorned structure until they sat at its base, their legs stretching out across the cobbles.

"You're shouting at the wrong guy," Williams sighed quietly, watching the tourists mill, far away towards the square. "You didn't need to keep volunteering for duty; you can't blame your parenting hang-ups on me. Believe it or not, I really am on your side, and like it or not this all is some kind of game, that's exactly what it is. But it's not Spooks making the moves, it's not soldiers either, we're both just the fucking pawns, launching ourselves against the onslaught and hoping for the best. I'm no better than you, I'm no worse either; we're both just beholden to the Puppet Master."

"Maybe we should run for office," Stone pondered aloud, only half joking. It might be nice to rub shoulders with the Mighty for a change."

"Oh, they wouldn't let the likes of you in," Stone replied, with an equal degree of seriousness, "and not because of your skin tone either. That's why I called you lot the PM's balls, you know?"

"Go on then," Stone smiled despite himself, "explain away."

"Well war is how these fucking elitist career politicians measure their masculinity these days, isn't it? They all want the glamour of military success but the prospect of actually serving on the front isn't too appealing, so when the press start questioning if they have the stomach for the job, not least when there's a woman in charge, they all start voting for wars they'll never have to fight in. They spread a bit of fear, throw around a few vague warnings of 'foiled attacks' to get everyone nicely onside, then they get their armies out for the lads and to hell with the consequences, and everyone stands back and admires how strong they are. It's kind of like gambling with someone else's money."

Stone nodded slowly, accepting the logic of the Scotsman's argument.

"Makes sense," he acknowledged.

"Ah, but nowadays, it's not so easy. People have long memories, even the Reality TV loving morons back home. They know Iraq and Afghanistan cost a lot in money and lives, some of them pay attention to words like 'War Crimes' and some have even latched onto the fact that if we start bombing the likes of Syria and Libya, then more of those brown people with the funny clothes and the unreasonable goals of fleeing death start turning up and there's not as many free seats on the bus. It's harder to start a war, but governments still need to spread the fear; it keeps people nicely in check. What's the next best thing? Trident. A placebo which we can never use without killing ourselves but we absolutely must have because, you now, the world is a dangerous place and all that. And so the elite have a new toy, the people are nicely subdued and you my friend are slowly replaced in the thrills department by a Two Hundred Billion pound vibrator."

The chuckle in Stone's tired throat grew into a hearty laugh which Williams eventually joined in; the pair sat untidily on the street, enjoying their moment of self-mockery.

"You've not much faith in 'The People' seeing through all this, then?"

Williams scoffed. "Ha! If only," he said. "The only real difference between the governments you despise and these 'The People' you venerate is degree. What's the difference between a government announcing the abolition of jury trial and the presumption of innocence, and your average Joe in the street sharing some poor fucker's picture all over social media because a bloke in Cleethorpes he cut up at the lights claims they're a pedo? Or a horde of keyboard warriors forcing some girl out of business because a Trophy Wife in Ealing says she looked at her dog funny? Ask yourself that the next time you click like & share."

The Scotsman heaved himself to his feet and offered a hand to the Captain, pulling him up alongside him.

"Fuck it, I'm going to get some sleep. We've a battle on our hands tomorrow Captain; best not to face it tired."

"Few die well that die in a battle," Stone smiled as he turned away to head back inside the bar, "Goodnight you old bastard."

TWENTY-TWO

THE NEXT MORNING BEGAN EARLY, with Stone's head a little light from the perhaps one too many shots he'd enjoyed the previous night, and he re-capped events as he stood in the shower, the hot downpour washing the dizziness from his brain. Greyson had indeed arrived, silently and without ceremony, and after the most uncomfortable of handshakes with the Captain had joined Svobodova at her table. The two instantly engaged in heated discussion, leading Stone to head outside for a sobering blast of fresh air. Alas, he hadn't found the solitude he craved but instead was joined by the bar's peculiar owner, Rasti, who'd seemed pleasant enough company until the fact of his previous career as a priest came up; Stone insisting it was nothing personal, but that his recent experience with priests hadn't filled him with comfort. Rasti likewise insisted no offence was taken and that he had similar reservations about soldiers, but was pleased now to have an opportunity to amend his opinion. As they'd talked, Stone found himself warming greatly to the gentle man with his self-deprecating humour, who hadn't even balked when the Captain explained that two decades of fighting extremists in deserts had left him somewhat suspicious of religion, a suspicion only exacerbated by the placard waving imbeciles back home who preached little but hell fire and condemnation.

"Oh, I agree, absolutely," Rasti had nodded, "believing in some big magic guy in the clouds is completely fucking illogical if you ask me."

Stone followed up by quizzing if he'd left the priesthood after losing his faith, and was somewhat surprised when the answer came that no, he'd left because he'd found it. He'd realised one day that he was so busy trying to do things the priesthood's way, ascribing to traditions and rituals that he'd taken his eyes off God, and so he'd left and confined himself to trying to live for his faith and not his religion, because faith wasn't about logic, and that he got it wrong plenty of times on the way.

Enjoying his new friend's tale, Stone had lamented that so few chaplains in his experience could demonstrate in a month of Sundays the wisdom Rasti had in five minutes, preferring instead to condemn those who didn't believe exactly as they did. Rasti's answer of, "Sheep and goats," had surprised him, before the chef elaborated.

"It's from the gospel of Matthew," Rasti had begun, nestling himself comfortably against the wall of his bar. "At the Last Judgement, Christ separates all the people of the world into the 'sheep' and the 'goats', the sheep being 'the Righteous', those who fed and watered Him when He was hungry and clothed and sheltered Him etc., and the goats being those who didn't. Now, the Righteous are confused and ask when it was they fed or clothed Him, and the un-Righteous ask when they didn't do the same, and Christ says to them, 'any time you did these things for the least of my brothers, you did it for me.' Or not."

"Nice story," Stone had answered softly.

"I always had trouble with the idea of God banishing all

unbelievers when I was a young man. I worried what would happen to my friends, to my family if they weren't as pious as me, you know? And then reading that passage one day I started to think that maybe I didn't have to get so bogged down in doctrine and theology to do God's work, maybe it was more important to just live for Him, to get out there and just try my best. Maybe there are more people than the churches or the synagogues or the mosques or wherever realise, who are getting to Heaven ahead of them by doing that; just trying their best to live right. And when I started to think that, I felt warm and clear for the first time in a long time, and I began to realise that those friends and family I worried so hard about would be alright, that they'd be waiting for me at the end."

Against all his expectations, the conversation cheered Stone and he'd walked back to the apartment that night with his mind and heart clearer than they'd been in some time, before slipping into a deep, if slightly intoxicated sleep before his early morning alarm had awoken him to his dizziness. Now dressed and his head settled, Stone lifted the picture of his son to his lips and set out into the early morning blackness; the final vestiges of night jealously defying the impending onset of the sun's warming rays. Williams was already outside and the two of them travelled together to collect Professor Abelard from her own apartment before they continued on towards Prague Six and the headquarters of Oscar Myska and The Slavic Party for Europe. The building itself was far from the most impressive in the City; a simple, bland affair, nestled in the bosom of Pod kaštany, across the street from the foreboding Russian Embassy. It was made all the more threatening by the presence of a twin pair of T54 tanks taking pride of place outside the main Embassy gates, around which a tired looking production crew were busily setting up for a shoot; the surly Director of a few days previously stomping around the scene and barking orders.

As the sun decisively won its battle with the night, the trio breakfasted in a small bakery down the street; the pit of Stone's stomach churning at the thought of food so early in the day and confining him to the consumption of strong, black coffee of which he drank several. They stayed there in silence for over an hour, observing several arrivals and departures but no sign of the man himself. Until at last, after what seemed a coffee fueled eternity, the familiar black car crept into view, pulling up outside the building, with Oscar Myska stepping from the back, giving a brief glance over to the film crew and heading inside. The arrival initially sparked only the order of a further round of coffee and croissants as they allowed the politician to settle into his daily routine, before Williams eventually rose from the table, wiping pastry crumbs from his mouth and washing them down with the last of his coffee.

"Right then," he said quietly, "let's tear this bastard a new arsehole."

Stone and Abelard shared a brief raised eyebrow at their colleague's words and fell in behind him as they walked across the street to the Party Office.

Their actual entry into the building was a lot smoother than any of them had thought it would be, Abelard making the initial approach to reception, her polite tones asking to speak with Mr. Myska rebuffed before Stone and Williams joined her in making them. Muscular looking security had then invited them to a waiting room on the first floor where they waited for an age before Williams attracted further attention by standing up and heaving the table in the middle of the expansive, sparsely decorated room onto its side. When the muscular operative returned, Stone blocked his entry to the room, demanding Myska's immediate attention and telling him to pass on the message that they had come to talk about Abdul Salam.

Sure enough, they found themselves attended moments later by the populist leader himself, Oscar Myska, who, unfazed by the obvious animosity towards him, still smiled at them with the typical magnetism for which he was famous.

It was an impressive act, Stone inwardly conceded; political charm without smarm was a tough ask and Myska pulled it off with aplomb, appearing almost statesmanlike before them as he fielded their questions patiently; defending and justifying his Party's position, his attack dog minder behind him, until Williams' thin patience finally snapped.

"Alright you little shit, that's enough of the party political. The Russians are about to roll the clock back thirty years by riding the coat tails of so called terrorist attacks that I think you know far more about than you're letting on."

Myska adopted an expression of what anyone would consider sincere offence.

"And how could anyone think that? I have dedicated my life to standing up for my people against the terrorists; to taking back control for my country..."

"Abdul Salam," Stone interrupted, his face displaying all the solid dependability his name implied. Salam's name elicited a momentary flicker across the politician's face; just the slight squint of an eye betraying a disguised concern.

"The man who tried to kill me and a crowd of loyal patriots," he said, guardedly, "the very man who you and our paper Prime Minister allowed to be blown to his death on the bridge; not that I mourn him for a moment."

"The very same," answered Stone. "He was on the verge of telling us something, of giving someone up, before the convoy was attacked."

"Then you have my condolences that his demise occurred

before you could get all you required from him."

Myska's voice was low and burned with an obvious contempt, mirrored by the intensity of his stare.

"Thank you," Stone answered back in a similar tone. "Rather conveniently timed, his death, for the people he was protecting, wouldn't you say?"

"I wouldn't know," came the reply. "But what I do know is that those men arrested are nothing to do with my organisation; the police have confirmed as much. And furthermore I know that you, Captain, are a disgraced man for your actions in Syria, allowing a terrorist cell to escape disguised as refugees. I should thank you Captain, for proving my case for me, even if your error did nearly cost me my life."

"Ah well, that's the thing you see," Williams said, walking nonchalantly around the room, "I've just got a new phone, it's brilliant, do you like it?"

He held up the device to the room, the widest, most unsettling smile on his face.

"I think it's great and I just can't keep off YouTube, you know? I've seen the footage of the fucking Marx Brothers' answer to terrorism and their failure to launch so many times over the past few days and do you know what I notice? Everyone in that shot looks scared. The crowd are scared, the bombers are scared; even the security agents look less than happy; in fact the only person who doesn't look scared on that clip, Myska, is you."

He held up the phone again zooming in on the politician's reaction which was significantly calmer than those around him.

"In fact, my fascistic little friend, the word I'd use to describe your reaction is 'disappointed'. The last time I saw an expression like that, Miss Marple was attending a social gathering and nobody died."

Abelard picked up the thread, while Myska remained still, keeping them all in his line of sight.

"It's almost as if," she began, "you were expecting a disturbance; that either you knew the blast wouldn't reach you or that the belts themselves would fail to ignite."

"And that," Stone intoned, "would be another amazing coincidence."

A few moments of tense stillness were broken by Myska's guard slipping his hand into his inner jacket pocket, holding it there in readiness for the order, while the man himself allowed all pretense to drop from his features.

"As you say," he quietly began, "astounding coincidences. And now, would you believe, we are about to witness another? All three of you disappearing on the same day; though mind you, with the chaos today is about to bring, I doubt anybody will notice."

He nodded to his guard who pulled the gun swiftly from its holster, a silenced shot whooshing between Williams and Stone. Stone threw himself forward, knocking the big man to the floor and the gun from his hand, before Abelard picked up a decorative, modern vase from the window ledge and cracked it hard across the man's head; his consciousness fleeing on impact.

"Hell of a shot, Natalie," Stone grinned in surprise.

"Born in Cardiff," she grinned back.

Myska was reeling from the blow to the head delivered by Williams, who pulled a flex of telephone wire from the wall, pushed the politician backwards into a chair and tied him roughly to it. A swift flicking sound signaled the presence of Williams' knife and Stone knew from experience he was prepared to use it.

"Alright you little bastard, exactly what 'chaos' are you talking about? Another bomb?"

"I have no idea what you mean," the restrained leader grinned, his senses returning.

"Enough of the games," Abelard piped up, "we know all about how you've targeted unstable people and used drugs to make them think they were religiously inspired and part of a cell; how you've manipulated them into killing God knows how many people by blowing themselves up for you."

"Not forgetting the added insurances like the bomb in the bin," Stone added. "And all so you could march all over Czechoslovakia claiming the Muslims are out to get you all and Europe needed to be rid of them."

"So where next?" Williams snarled, "first the bar in Wenceslas Square, then the concert, then the no show in Old Town; which tourist trap are you after next?"

"Tourist trap?" Myska answered innocently, "You misunderstand."

Williams scowl plunged to new depths as he glared at the populist with fury.

"I've never misunderstood anything in my life," he hissed, before pausing for a moment, looking up at a map of the city on the wall behind Myska.

"Unless…" he stared intently at the diagram, his widening eyes signalling the dawn of realisation. "Unless we were wrong about the target!"

A sudden anxiety captured the Scotsman's voice and he slapped his hand against his forehead, cursing his own blindness with an apoplectic rage. With a hefty boot, he kicked the restrained Myska hard in the middle of his chest, tipping the chair backwards until it crashed on the floor, then knelt at the politician's side, the familiar switchblade in his hand and pressed to the squirming man's neck.

"Where's next, you Nazi bastard? Where's next?!"

"For God's sake Williams!" Abelard's shouted objections to his actions went ignored, Williams continuing to bellow his abusive question at Myska, who simply grinned his malicious grin back into the wrinkled face.

"What is it? What have you seen?" shouted Stone, his own temper rising.

"Look at it!"

Williams ripped the map from the wall, screwing it up and and throwing it towards Stone, who caught and swiftly un-crumpled it.

"It's a map of the attacks," he said, confused, "there's nothing we don't already know."

"Oh yes there is," Williams countered, his fierce eyes not leaving Myska's, "something obvious that's been staring us in our stupid, dense faces since the start! Look at the locations!"

"We know the locations," shouted Abelard, "the bar, the concert and the Square, so what?"

"Forget the Square; that was just window dressing. Who owned the bar?" Williams growled, "Who was playing at the concert?"

The pit of Stone's stomach churned nauseously as his understanding unclouded irrefutably before him in an instant. The bar, the performer and material at the concert; all had one thing in common.

"Oh, shit," he exclaimed, looking from the map to Williams, "the Russians...?"

"We were supposed to think Muslim terrorists were blowing up Western tourists," the aging spy spat, "but they were never the target, it was the fucking Cossacks all the time."

He let his blade pierce the skin of the wriggling Myska, who winced but kept the taunting, mocking smile on his face.

"Where next you little shit?!"

Stone put his foot on the rim of the chair, flipping it back upright and jarring the smirk from the MEP's face and bringing it face to face with his captor's.

"Tell him," Stone softly intoned, "or I'll gut you myself."

"Oh you're going to find out very soon now," Myska sneered.

"I'm going to find out right now."

"Oh, Captain," he whispered, the diseased smile returned to the twisted face, "you don't know how right you are…"

At that moment, a thunderous booming erupted from across the street, spreading in all directions and sending shards of broken glass over Stone, Abelard and Williams who ducked for cover at the sound of the blast. Myska too sat rigidly upright, strapped immovably to his chair, his neck turned away from the windows and his eyes clamped shut.

At the sound of the explosion, Stone had covered Abelard and he gently eased her to her feet as it subsided, replaced by the even more horrible pandemonium of aftermath; the screams, the alarms and the ever nearer cry of the sirens.

"Are you hurt?"

"No, I'm fine," Abelard answered, dusting herself off and moving to the window. "That must have come from across the street at…"

"The Embassy," Williams finished, brushing broken glass from his frayed coat, his face a portrait in anger. "We were too fucking late, they've only gone and bombed the Russian fucking Embassy; now the shit's going to hit the fan!"

From the window, Stone witnessed the film crew panic and run, the Director screaming at them to stay and film, before realisation hit him and he threw himself into the backseat of a taxi that screeched to a halt for a handful of his colleagues, before high tailing away into the distance.

Smoke was pouring from the destroyed roof of the Embassy;

certainly an internal blast, Stone thought, but there was also a cavernous opening in the road in front of the Embassy gates. The smoke plume and pattern of debris indicated something had blown upwards from beneath the ground, and the Captain strained his eyes to make out the unclear shapes moving around.

First one, then another, then a continuous flow of men, uniformed, armed men stepped out of the smoke and into the anxious street, lining up in formation as they emerged. Out into the street they poured, as though from the bowels of an earth spewing out its dead for mortal conquest.

"Where are they all coming from?" Stone shouted incredulously.

"It's the tunnels!" Williams answered, having dashed to the window to take in the spectacle. "I can't believe I was such an idiot! In the Forties, the gestapo took over the Embassy building and used a system of tunnels underneath it to spread their network, then when the Communists took over the KGB ran espionage from there. They were supposed to be abandoned and sealed after the Revolution, but…"

He marched to the laughing Myska and gripped him by the lapels, lifting him, chair and all, into the air with a show of age defying strength. Slamming him against the wall and letting him drop back to the floor, Williams cuffed him hard across the face.

"Well this is a fucking game changer, isn't it? And you, my little basket of shite, if you place any value on the unfairly small objects dangling between your legs, you are going to come with Captain Stone and I and help mop it up."

"Where are you taking him?" enquired Abelard, desperation in her voice.

"Out there," Williams gestured to the street, "we've got a fucking invasion to prevent."

"I've got a bad feeling it's too late for that."

All eyes turned to Stone who stood, facing out of the shattered window into the smoking chaos below, the same incredulity spreading onto the faces of Abelard and Williams as they joined him.

On the street below, ignored by the panicking figures fleeing the scene, the archaic shell of the T-54 creaked and groaned into reluctant life. Decades old caterpillar tracks began to turn, crushing debris beneath them as they slowly inched the obsolete machine into animation, its movements becoming more fluid with each passing second as its painful manoeuvres became a steady rumble.

"Way too late," Stone continued, his voice steeped in trepidation. "There's no need for an invasion; they're already here."

The turret on the ancient vehicle twisted slowly upwards until it pointed directly and deliberately at the building the trio of observers stood in. Though he yearned to disbelieve what was happening before his eyes, Stone had seen combat enough to know all too well what came next.

"GET DOWN!"

He bellowed his command to his comrades and threw himself back from the window to the floor, dragging Abelard along with him and whispering, even as the room collapsed around them, burning lamentations to the sound of shell fire and crumbling concrete, before something heavy thumped against the back of his head and consciousness slipped swiftly away.

TWENTY-THREE

THE PODIUM WAS PREPARED; a simple boarded stage set before the grand statue of St Wenceslas, which shared the domination of the Square with the imperious, domed National Museum behind it. A lectern had been placed centrally on the stage and Černý prepared himself to make good use of it as the car slowly rolled up the length of the Square. Stepping from it as it stopped, the aged hero paused, allowing himself to savour if only for a moment the long-held love of his people, before heaving his frame onto the platform, Radoslav alongside him.

The timing of the ceremony was hardly appropriate, given Svobodova's current excursions at the border, and the cancellation of the World Leader's visit in the aftermath of Czechoslovakia's expulsion from the international clubs, but Černý was determined to pay his own tribute to the fallen. The bright sunshine robbed the occasion of any excessive degree of somberness, but the atmosphere was still one of respect, just as Černý had hoped. This should be a sober occasion, where the memory of sacrifices old and recent were honoured and cherished and the hush of the crowd, bar infrequent and instantly quietened shouts, pleased him. His speech laid out on the lectern in front of him, Černý preferring to rely on the more traditional tools of speech making, he stood dignified and Presidentially; his people gazing up at him.

He opened his mouth to speak but a noise, as unexpected as it was dreaded, and coming from the far end of the Square, was enough to shake the concentration from him; a heavy, rumbling sound accompanied by the squeak and grind of decades old metal components biting and shifting against each other accompanied by the revving of grimly determined engines.

Disbelieving his eyes, he tried time and again to blink truth into them, or stop them from taunting him with their display of the horrors of the past. But this was not the past and the truth was only too evident. The noise increased, coming too from other directions all around the square and the crowd now began to look around, sharing the President's confusion at the unexpected events

Stepping back from the microphone, Černý gestured to Rado, busily talking into his radio.

"Commander," said the President, still transfixed on the horrors rolling towards him, "I ordered these monstrosities cleared from the Square before the ceremony."

There was no answer Rado could give other than taking firm hold of the old man and ushering him back towards the podium steps, but the route to the car was already blocked by half-panicking, half-cheering figures.

Černý cursed as the still closing tanks ensured the nightmare of his youth continued to be re-lived. And it was a nightmare, surely; a visitation by the horrors of yesteryear, forcibly playing out in front of a powerless, sleeping mind. Or else the wandering mind of an old man, teetering on the abyss after a lifetime of pressure, affording him a fearsome glimpse on the senility to come by reliving past terrors before his waking eyes. But these were not the victims of yesterday fleeing the streets, and these were not the events of the past, and as he watched, he hoped and prayed that madness has taken hold of him, rather than be forced to accept the dawning of a fresh hell for his people.

He had seen these looks before, so many years ago. The first wide-eyed stares of wonder at the steadily rumbling machinery, and the excited innocent laughter at the grand military display playing out in the streets for their pleasure. Until the sudden and final realisation that the tanks were rolling inexorably towards *them*, that the faces of the soldiers who rode and marched alongside the metal hulks were devoid of warmth, focussed instead on the unstoppable march towards *them*, coming for *them*. The dawning of that understanding took longer this time, common sense and the survival instinct numbed by decades of infotainment, reality television and the blissfully ignorant misbelief that such a fate could never conceivably happen to *them*. But slowly, painfully, he watched genuine reality twist the faces of the crowds; their whoops of joy and cheers of giddy inebriation at the entertainment unfolding before them degenerating into the panicked clutching of children to breasts and impotent protestations. Childlike joy and innocent escapism crumbled away with the sound of rolling caterpillar tracks and stomping boots, replaced with the knowledge that the weapons did not dance for their pleasure, that this was not some far away trouble in some far away land. This was happening here and now; their forced participation as extras in a show which threatened to prove compulsory viewing for the rest of the world. And as they screamed and shouted and cried their powerless rage to the wind, he knew that they at last realised the folly of their belief in their own imperviousness; that their safety was based on nothing but paper promises and that the designer clothes and expensive sunglasses with which they adorned their suddenly fragile frames were insufficient to shield them from the cold when the world blew its hardest. And that it could, after all, emphatically happen to *them*.

TWENTY-FOUR

STONE AWOKE WITH A CRY, heaving air thick with the dust of ruined concrete into his lungs and shaking his head free of the temptation to sleep. Mentally checking himself and feeling only superficial pain, he scanned his surroundings before inching to his feet.

The room he had stood in was devastated beyond recognition. The cacophony caused by the exploding shell and falling rubble had resulted in a room covered in the shattered remains of its upstairs neighbour; the whole floor now a study in crushed plasterboard, splintered wood and twisted metallic beams. By some miracle, the shell had hit home one or two levels above Myska's office, saving its occupants from the direct hit which would surely have killed them, instead showering them with debris.

His senses returning, Stone looked to check on Natalie's condition and turned to his side where he had thrown her, to help her up. She wasn't there. Spinning around, he eyes quickly searched for her, the sickening tell-tale sensation of anxiety gnawing its way to residence in the pit of his stomach. She was nowhere to be seen; Williams was there, unconscious and breathing awkwardly, lying in a crumpled heap on the floor away from Stone, his battered old coat caked in a layer of plaster dust. Across the room from him, the chair used to restrain Myska was on its side, minus its traitorous occupant. He had taken her.

Bounding over to the stricken Williams, the Captain pressed his fingers to the older man's neck, searching desperately for a pulse and striving vainly to rouse him, slapping the deeply lined cheeks and repeating his name.

"Williams? Come on now Williams you old bastard, don't die on me now."

It was no use, though the pulse throbbed faintly, the stick thin body remaining resolutely limp in Stone's grasp.

Cursing, he felt a buzz against his leg and reached into his pocket to fish out his phone, his heart leaping for a moment in anticipation that it was the Professor calling; it was a false hope, with the unwelcome name of Jonathan Greyson appearing on the display; Stone pressing it to his ear in annoyance.

"Stone, it's a fucking invasion! The tanks…"

"She's gone Greyson," he interrupted, his voice the very essence of angered frustration.

"What?"

"I said she's gone! Natalie's gone, Myska took her!"

"You let him…"

"No I didn't fucking let him!" Stone bellowed his defiance at the politician, "We were shelled, I was knocked out. When I came round she and Myska were gone. Williams is still out cold, he needs medical attention."

"So do a lot of people, he'll have to wait."

"You can't abandon him!"

"I can't prioritise him either!" Greyson's own voice was dripping with disheartened anger. "The City is down, Stone, occupied! There are tanks rolling up Wenceslas Square and the President is trapped there. It's 1968 all over again!"

"The whole thing was a Red Flag Op," Stone said, searching almost pathetically through the rubble for any possible clue as to Myska's intent as he spoke. "The bombing, the concert; everything was designed to make the Russians victims, to give them an excuse to invade."

"They're issued a press statement denying any hostile intent, saying they simply want to 'aid their Czechoslovak friends' in bringing to justice the perpetrators of violence against the Russian people.'"

"Bullshit," Stone spat, "they've taken the Ukraine and now they're taking Czechoslovakia, without even having to go through an invasion to do it. They already had the equivalent of an armoured division on the ground and with the Army at the border they can take the Capital unopposed and with minimal casualties."

"The media are calling it 'The Velvet Occupation'…fuck!" With each word Greyson's voice conveyed a deeper understanding of the severity of the crisis. "With Prague held to ransom Mirushka will have no choice but to accept whatever terms thrown at her, this country's about to be dragged thirty years back in time without a shot being fired! I have to get to the front, find some way through this…"

"Don't be so damn stupid!" Stone shouted, chastising the politician's recklessness. "What you need to do right now is disappear, get yourself hidden."

"But…"

"No buts! If you go pissing around at the front now then you'll only drag Britain into the mire too, and the last thing we need is to be mixed up militarily with the Russians."

"But, Natalie!"

Stone froze at Greyson's use of the name and the desperation in his voice when he uttered it, allowing silence to descend between them.

"I have to find Natalie," Greyson repeated, with what sounded like tears in his voice.

Stone resented the man's plea, this belated show of affection that had it come sooner might have spared her the pain of divorce. That thought too sparked a renewal of the jealousy Stone had begun to feel and he cursed his own illogicality before responding to Greyson.

"I'm already on it," he growled, "but there's not much to go on. You stay hidden while I try and find where she is."

"She has to be at the border," Greyson forcefully opined. "If Myska was working with the Russians that's where he's heading, he'll be trying to get across to the Ukraine, trying to renew terms of his own."

"They tried to kill him," Stone snapped, his brow settling into well-worn furrows. "The shell they aimed at this place rather suggests he's outlived whatever agreement he had with them; why would he flee to the front?"

"Where else can he go?!" the politician was insistent. "If he stays in Prague he's as good as dead; it won't take long for his involvement to come out, the people will lynch him in the street. The Russians are his best bet, particularly with my ex-wife to use as a bargaining chip!"

Stone was forced to agree with the logic, not least because it offered him a lead, and he began to make his way out of the ruins.

"What about the occupation? What do we do?"

"I haven't a fucking clue," came the answer. "At this point it might even be a case of damage limitation, trying to clean up as much of this shit as we can without becoming officially involved. I'll think of something…"

"Make it bloody good," Stone snapped, hitting his stride, "I'll try and pick up their trail and check in with you when I can."

"Good. Captain Stone? Lincoln?"

"Yes?"

"Find her."

"I will."

"Find her and bring her back to me."

The line went dead, Greyson's last words echoing in Stone's ear in an unanswered loop, accompanied by the rhythmic thud of his own jealously.

"Oh, I'll bring her back alright," he muttered as he reached the street, still heavy "with the dust" and debris of the two explosions, "but it sure as hell won't be for you."

Though chaotic fear had claimed Wenceslas Square, the main perpetrators were confined to the centre, the entrances and alleyways closed by raised turrets and readied arms. Those who had managed to flee the scene had simply kept running, some unable but most unwilling to join the fight, some tripping and stumbling through a potent mixture of alcohol and fear. Others scrambled aimlessly, dragging confused children who themselves clung to adored stuffed toys, hoping for some safe and unguarded path from the country. They would be lucky to find one. The EU, whose open borders had been long decried by so many now stood resolutely closed against their former member, while the airport was secured by the tanks and all flights grounded. To the East lay only the path to the Ukraine, currently occupied on respective sides by the Czechoslovak and Russian Armies, each eyeing each other with a horrendously nervous and tense hostility.

Rado had fought tirelessly to get Černý to the car and away, but hampered both by the President's own refusal to leave his people and the mass of fleeing public and invading soldiers, his task was a fruitless one, until an eventual rifle butt to the head sent him crashing to the ground. Černý himself remained defiantly at the podium, appealing for calm and order and condemning the occupation taking place before his very eyes.

A line of tanks had taken a running position down the center of the square, with others blocking access at each of the openings and roads running from it, backed by squadrons of soldiers who had taken position around the periphery of the square and were slowly hemming the public into the middle, where they could be more easily contained. This act itself was enough to cause claustrophobic anxiety, leading only to a still more violent response; rifle fire and tank shells firing into the air as a consequence from young and nervous soldiers uncertain how to react to the barrage of abuse and projectiles heading in their direction. Two such soldiers were heading to the podium itself, their objective Černý realised, undoubtedly to secure him, but as they approached, a small boy of no more than ten years and likely, he thought, of Romani background was doing his best to run for safety, squeezing and pushing through the crowd. Scared anger was on his face and he carried a handful of small rocks and pebbles with him which he threw into the face of the leading soldier as he ran past, eliciting an array of profanities and orders to stop.

With nowhere else to run, he sped up the steps of the podium, where Černý instantly knelt down to shield and protect him, noting the raised rifle in the offended soldier's hands.

"Стоп, руки вверх!" the soldier and his colleague were shouting, which Černý knew only too well to be an order to stop and give up. Attention returned toward the President and his new protectee as he vocally defied the aggressors from the still working microphones on his podium, while the twin soldiers reached the steps, one with his rifle still drawn and aimed at the child.

With a sickening horror, Černý realised at once what was about to happen, as the jostling crowd heightened the young soldier's nerves; a single but powerful cry issuing forth from the gun's mouth and screaming towards the boy. Before it had been fired, Černý had dropped to his aged and frail knees in front of the boy, whose shouts of protest mixed with those of the crowd. It was a small bullet, only a very small one, but it was enough to pierce the old man's flesh and he staggered forward on his knees a few inches before collapsing into a semi-consciousness. He could feel the young boy lifting his head and cradling him; the warmth of his body an honest comfort, and likewise he could hear the shocked and muted apologies of the soldier who'd fired the shot. But the sound that brought tears to his eyes and more pain than the hot metal in his body which twisted and burned within him, was the unmistakable and heartbreaking sound of Prague descending into leaderless pandemonium.

TWENTY-FIVE

"NATALIE!"

Eight long hours had passed by the time Stone caught up with them, and in truth, he was amazed that he'd been able to find them at all. After extracting himself from the ruins of Myska's offices, he had taken advantage of one of the many abandoned vehicles in its car park and sped off in what he'd feared would be a fruitless pursuit of his lover. Greyson's advice that Myska would surely head for the border was all he'd had to go on, but even then he'd been driving blind. The main access route between the two countries was at Uzhhorod, but there too was the Czechoslovak Army, and Stone surmised the other official crossing points he was aware of, such as Chop or Pinkovce, would likewise be officially monitored. If Myska was to make it across the border then it would have to be at an unmanned point and Stone had no idea where that would be. He had no choice but to keep driving and hope for some divine inspiration.

Resisting his eyelids attempts to droop, he'd pressed his foot down harder on the accelerator and carried on, what traffic there was heading in the opposite direction, worrying that his search was doomed to failure but not allowing such thoughts to deter him from trying. His focus had been eventually rewarded in the simplest way possible, with a pinged text message on his phone which he'd swiped immediately open: Co-ordinates. Map co-ordinates sent from Natalie's phone! Slowing down only to feed them into his phone's map application, he'd given an ecstatic cheer for his lover's resourcefulness and accelerated again; driving until he had run out of road and was forced to follow the signal on foot. The border was sixty miles long, but Stone had guessed that if Myska and a reluctant Natalie were likewise on foot when she'd sent the message then they couldn't be too far away, and the flashing marker on his phone had agreed he was close to the location she'd sent.

A tall, green, double meshed fence straddling the countryside marked the border with occupied Ukraine, and as he approached, he'd seen a section large enough for a man to crawl through precisely cut from the structure, the late afternoon sun glinting off the severed edges of metal.

Easing himself through, he had quickly assessed the terrain of his new country; this part of the border dissecting a green forested area, a tall standing pillar protruding from the ground a few yards from him, decorated with the blue and yellow of the Ukrainian flag, the only indicator of the country's identity. He'd known that the military build-up was taking place not far from here and he could hear the distant rumble of heavy artillery, the stomping of booted feet and the bellowing of orders, so much so he had felt a peculiar pang of homesickness. Ignoring it, he'd carried on the couple of miles into enemy territory, keeping low and deathly quiet to avoid sentries, and straining his eyes for any sign of his quarry; a perverse excitement building steadily and relentlessly in his gut as the thrill of the chase returned to him and he was reminded why he'd volunteered for so many actions in his long career.

It was a passion that had almost overwhelmed him when he had finally spotted the crouching Myska a couple of hundred yards ahead of him, partially obscured by trees and peering over the top of a grassy ridge. Resisting the urge to rush the politician and beat Natalie's whereabouts from him in a manner of which Williams would have been proud, Stone had approached him with all the stealth of his profession, swiftly and deathly quiet. As he'd drawn nearer, Stone saw the weapon the politician held more clearly, recognising it as the shining silver frame of a Tac-50 A1 sniper's rifle; a powerful weapon of war, extraordinarily accurate and utterly deadly. Stone knew the normal field of effectiveness for the weapon to be some nineteen hundred yards, and he'd heard tales of confirmed kills from as far away as twenty-six hundred, but Myska's unconfident grip had leant the gun an erratic quality.

Myska had been inching slowly up the ridge, the rifle cumbersome in his grip and Stone had almost been upon him before he could see clearly what the would-be gunman was struggling to aim at. In the valley below the ridge, some eight or nine hundred yards away, dressed in combat fatigues and surrounded by all manner of officialdom, was the Russian President himself; grand, imperious and oblivious to the threat above and behind him.

"Stop right there you bastard," Stone hissed, shocking the politician, who had dropped the rifle in surprise and spun in the dirt towards the Captain, "where is she?"

Myska had been silent, simply shaking his head at the sight of Stone and scrambling backwards on the ridge.

"One chance," Stone had growled as quietly as he could while still allowing the threat to carry in his voice, "tell me where she is and if you're lucky I'll drag you back to Svobodova alive."

"She's right here."

Abelard's voice had come from the trees behind Stone and he'd turned in surprise to see her step slowly out, her eyes red and watery and a silenced gun in her hand.

"Natalie?"

Stone had squinted in surprise at her emergence, the gun only heightening his incredulity.

A silenced bullet shot forth from the gun in her hand, sending the fleeing Myska to the grass, his fear now a permanent expression.

"I told him if he ran he was dead," the murderous woman said.

TWENTY-SIX

"OH, LINCOLN I'M SORRY, I'm so, so sorry." The beautiful Welsh lilt in her voice with which she had seduced him days earlier now teetered on the edge of despair, as tears began to hinder her words. "I never was Natalie. I didn't want you to find out like this Lincoln," she said, "not like this."

Any plan Stone might have had to rush her and take possession of the weapon was hindered by his ossification at Natalie's, this *woman's*, actions, and he remained rooted as she began to compose herself and sniff back her tears, her gun arm strong and steady. Even the dependable rationality of his military brain was failing him; the sight of his lover gunning down a defenceless man, however corrupt he may have been, burrowing into him with vicious relish. And what the hell did she mean she's 'not Natalie'?"

Catlike, he gauged her movements as she turned from the man she had murdered to point the gun, level and steady, in the Captain's direction; the tears she blinked back shed not for her victim, it seemed to him, or even herself, but that he was there to witness the scene.

"I didn't want you to find out this way," she lamented sincerely, "this wasn't the plan; you found me too soon."

"Too soon?"

He held his hands waist high and palms out, his body language open and receptive and his voice as calm as his inner turmoil would allow.

"What plan? Natalie what's going on?"

The name slipped out from habit, inviting a fresh wince from the woman before him who filled her lungs with air and sighed.

"Professor Natalie Abelard was dead five minutes after she arrived in Prague."

The woman's voice lost in an instant the Welsh infusion which Stone had so enjoyed, and with it all traces of the warmth he had relished in, replaced not with frosty disdain, but with a rigid intransigence alien to the person he knew.

"Dead?" Stone struggled to adapt to the confessions of his mystery lover, "If you're not Natalie who the hell are you and what's going on?"

"I'm a plant," the woman answered with sadness in her voice, "a double put in place by The Institute for European Harmony to oversee the final strategy."

The breath heaved out from Stone's lungs, as though her words were a killer punch to his solar plexus, delivered as punishment for his having given in to his feelings for the woman now pointing a gun at him. And though he knew the situation demanded he retain his senses, the temptation to give in to the whirling emotional turmoil in his chest was steadily growing to become too much.

"I..," he tried to begin, shaking his head, "I came to save you..."

"I know," she nodded, her eyes still damp, "but now I need you to save the world instead."

The ludicrousness of the statement brought Stone back into a semblance of rational thought and he laughed; a hoarse, tense laugh, necessarily restrained through the proximity of a man this faux Abelard apparently wished to see dead.

"Save the world?" he mocked, "you and your Institute friends? From what I'm told of you lot, the only thing you're interested in saving is your own influence."

The jibe seemed to hit home and the sadness in her expression twisted into resentment.

"We're not the bad guys Lincoln," she insisted, "we're saving the future!"

Stone was incredulous. "Saving the future?" He laughed, hard and without humour. "Saving it from what, from who?!"

"From you!"

She hissed the words at him, her body shaking with emotion and fighting the urge to scream her condemnation for the whole valley to hear, but the gun remained steady in her arms and pointing at the Captain.

"From you and everyone like you! From the everyday idiots in the street, behind desks, in shops, on buses and a hundred other places who would let it fall without a fight, who don't understand the realities of what this world is about!"

Stone remained quiet, absorbing the imposter woman's outburst and making no attempt to interject.

"Europe has been fracturing for years, people in every country, in every Member State neglecting the good and the strength of the Union and why? Because there was nothing left to fear anymore. No Cold War, no imminent invasion from dreaded Eastern Forces, no nuclear threat on the horizon. But they were too fucking stupid, to realise that there's always a threat, always, but sometimes threats don't come dressed in army fatigues and carrying a gun. Climate change prevention, scientific advancement, intelligence sharing, humanitarian development; without us, all those things go down the shitter never to be seen again! But people are too stupid to realise that by themselves, so we give them a little help. We let them see what would happen if Europe wasn't there, we give them a small glimpse of the chaos which would engulf the world because we love Europe, we love them enough to do it."

She was as passionate as Stone had ever seen her, even more so than their first day together in Old Town, and with her weapon still pointed at his chest, he realised he could best by time by engaging with her philosophy.

"I get it," Stone replied honestly, "I really do. You give people a taste of what they think they want; a world where there's no need for Trident, no need for Europe, and then hit them with what something like that might actually mean in a world where there's no safety in numbers anymore."

"Exactly," answered the fake Abelard, "but a lesson like that demands a sacrifice."

"Czechoslovakia."

"Yes," she confirmed. "People had grown lazy, without the fear they closed their minds to the bigger picture. The only way to open them was to reintroduce fear into the equation. The loss of Czechoslovakia is to be the catalyst of that fear. That was his masterplan."

"Whose, The Child's?"

"Jonathan told you about him then? Yes, The Child. He knew that the only way to stop Europe from crumbling apart was to take it as close to the edge as he dare, and he is a particularly daring man…"

"He loves Europe enough to bring it to the edge of destruction," Stone mused, remembering their first real conversation and wishing this was still some philosophical debate with a drink in the gentle warmth of the Old Town Square.

"And build something better from the raw materials," the fake Abelard concluded.

"How?"

"Fear is the easiest thing in the world to spread, particularly in a world that insists on feeding on the poison the media provides; anti-Muslim, anti-foreigner. Add one of the tin-pot populists coming to prominence and the fear multiplies ten-fold."

"Myska, or someone in his organisation, uses drugs to brainwash potential terror suspects into blowing up targets, thus boosting his own popularity; but underneath that he's working with the Russians to lay the groundwork for an invasion that will sweep Svobodova from power and hand the country to him. Only the Russians played him; they tried to shell him."

"It wasn't just the Russians playing Myska," she said, shaking her head, "we were playing them both. We knew Russia wouldn't just stop once they got to the Ukraine, not with this President in charge. And as we had little hope of preventing an invasion we decided the next best thing would be to encourage once; one on our own terms which we could control. As far as our late friend Mr Myska was concerned, this was all about pushing out Svobodova and getting the Far Right into power throughout the continent; Czechoslovakia out of the Union, out of NATO and under Russian occupation, all because of those naughty Muslim immigrants blowing everything up. It was Europe's worst nightmare and the Right's dream come true all at the same time."

"You wanted to draw the fascists out, make them play their hand," Stone picked up, quickly analysing his mystery lover's tale.

"Precisely," she confirmed. "The extremists have been poisoning the EU for as long as most people can remember; the populists and the press have always been keen for the bombs to start falling on other countries, but none too keen to clear up the mess afterwards, even if having refugees to scapegoat has given them a useful political tool to strengthen their position across the continent. People's fear of cultural change, of overpopulation, their resentment of cuts to services, low wages and rising inflation; it's so easy to blame it all on the immigrants instead of the governments who failed Europe's people for generations."

Stone nodded his understanding, "And it got to the point where ordinary people were so unhappy, so angry that they started to believe the lies and the Far Right started growing, winning elections, deciding referenda."

"Instead of an annoyance they became a problem, a challenge," the faux Abelard conceded. "And when faced with a challenge one can either bury one's head in the sand or stand and fight."

"The Institute stood and fought."

"What other choice did we have? We couldn't lose the continent to the likes of these people; Europe was beginning to splinter, we'd tried for years to hold it together until we came up with a new strategy: let it fall."

The beautiful simplicity almost brought a smile of admiration to Stone's face and he recalled again their conversation in the Square on their first day together.

"Or bring it as close to collapse as you dare."

A small smile of recognition flashed across her own features as she continued.

"In the old days, we paid the likes of Gaddafi to hold back a migrant surge across the EU for fear of how people would react to an influx, for fear of how the extremists would take advantage of a new wave of immigration to fuel their own agenda. But no matter what we did they kept on spreading their poison and more and more people started to believe it, or use it as an excuse. And so we had to call their bluff, and to do that we had to sacrifice some pieces to find out the full strength of their attack, and then we could wipe them off the board for good. And as it turned out, it was considerably easier, not to mention cheaper, to pay a wannabe Nazi to take advantage of a migrant crisis than it was to pay a dictator to prevent one."

"The Institute gets Myska involved in what he thinks is a Russian put up job and starts bombing key targets in the country, weakening Svobodova's support and antagonising the Americans. Europe and NATO make good on their threat to withdraw membership, Russia, thanks to a certain well-timed film production, occupies the country by stealth under the guise of 'restoring order' and… what? Svobodova is swept from power to be replaced with Myska who negotiates a Russian withdrawal and emerges as the strong leader of a cowed country, hostile to all outsiders and galvanises a Far Right resurgence across the Union?"

"That was the plan," the woman smiled, "at least as far as Myska understood it. What we didn't tell him was that following a swift and unexpected 'regime change' in Russia, his own links to the bombings were about to be exposed and the extreme Right's credibility throughout Europe torn to shreds."

"Nice plan," Stone commented, "the only drawback being Myska's dead and from where I'm standing, and if the Ukraine is anything to go by, Russia doesn't much look like being in the mood to withdraw."

"Well that's where you come in Captain," she acknowledged, brushing away the last of her tears, "you're about to become an assassin. Go pick up the rifle."

"Excuse me?"

"Pick it up I said!" she hissed her command through gritted teeth. "You're right, the only way to get Russia out of Czechoslovakia is to replace the President. He's become unpredictable, vainglorious; he has to be stopped."

She gestured at him with the gun and Stone didn't believe for a moment that she wouldn't kill him if she had to, but neither did he want to kill the President, despite seeing the logic of her argument. He had to keep her talking until he could find some way out of this.

He knelt to where the rifle had fallen and picked it up, the sensation akin to shaking the hand of an old friend; snake crawling on the ground to a comfortable position on the ridge. His emotions were still rattling inside and he felt a peculiar dizziness taunting his vision and nausea in his gut.

"It was all a lie, wasn't it?" he asked, surprised by the hollow sensation her betrayal had left within him; a biological reminder of an emptiness he didn't wish to return to. "I dreamed about bringing you home, introducing you to my boy, of maybe trying to be a family."

He felt a lump rising in his throat as his disappointment gave way to bleakness.

"But it was all just bollocks, wasn't it? You, me, us; every wild night and makeshift breakfast, each cross word and awkward apology. Every casual display of affection to every utterance of love, it was all just more Spook bullshit."

She was silent for a moment, her body delicately shaking though her gun arm remained strong, until finally she answered him.

"The only lie I told was my identity," she quietly stated, "every thought and every emotion were mine, just spoken through someone else's lips, that's all. And I wasn't under orders to seduce you."

Her words struck a tiny match in the darkness of Stone's mind and he turned towards her, all anger gone from his face.

"Then please," he said, gently, "for the sake of everything we went through, however brief it was, whoever you were pretending to be and whoever I thought you were; please just tell me your name."

The veneer began to crack before Stone's eyes, if only slightly; her face which she had frozen into professional intransigence beginning to thaw into the beginnings of a smile.

"I meant it when I said I loved you," she began, her features warming with every word, "my name is…"

No name came, only the loud crack of a neck broken with breathtaking alacrity, followed by the soft impact of her body as it crumpled and fell inelegantly to the ground.

Shouting his defiance, Stone dropped the weapon and scrambled clumsily over the grass to where she lay, shaking his head and repeating his question in anguished insistence, even as tears began to leak from his disbelieving eyes. There was no response she could make and she lay there, silent and un-moving, her own eyes wide with indignant surprise and her mouth open, revealing white teeth and the tip of a pink tongue, upon which rested the name that Stone would never now hear.

TWENTY-SEVEN

THE GRAND COUNTRY HOUSE, once home to one of the ancient families of Bohemia, sat beautifully a few short miles from the border and Miroslava Svobodova waited impatiently in it for her counterpart to arrive, though she was in no way eager for the violence which must surely follow to begin.

She had heard, as had the world, of the Russian attack on Prague, the so-called 'Velvet Occupation', and every second she waited for negotiations to begin was another dagger in her soul. She stood in the opulence of the drawing room, the windows of which offered what would typically be spectacular views of the greenery stretching over the border, but which were now marred by the mechanical build-up of war.

Without warning, the double doors opened with swift and unceremonious efficiency, the slow but unmistakeable tap of well-soled shoes on ancient stone echoing around the building's spacious chamber until they stopped several paces away from her. Her wait had not helped her nerves but neither had it weakened her resolve and she straightened herself, ready to face the Number Two Man to the President who had held Russia in his palm for so many years.

Spinning confidently on her heel, her hand outstretched in a gesture of friendship, she started at the sight of the person before her. The figure's eyes burned with the same ferocity as those of the one she had expected, but this man was neither balding nor stocky, though his visage projected an even more sinister nature. He stood tall, though a little too forcefully stretched as though straining to resist the natural culmination of the decades on his back, while his hair was as white as the Tatra mountains in the dead of winter and the wide brimmed trilby which sat on top of it, along with the voluminous overcoat hanging on his shoulders, as black as the clear spring nights of her youth.

He removed the hat in her presence, revealing in full his deeply lined and distressingly thin features, and stood silently for a moment across from her, withered yet imperious, as though some macabre artist had painted flesh on a skeleton and dressed it in expensive finery; a spectral portent of doom.

She knew at once who it was, though she had never seen him before and more than once she caught herself from stuttering an opening, as though all other meetings in her career had been but rehearsals and she had now forgotten her lines on the opening night.

"It's you," she said finally, her voice still confident but unable to mask her surprise, "the one Peter told me about. You're The Child."

The slightest suggestion of a wince crossed the wrinkled face, disappearing almost as soon as it arrived.

"Really, Madam Prime Minister," the elderly voice replied, the strength of its inflection as strong as ever it was, but its delivery undermined by the wheeze of a chest devoid of the hardiness of youth, "you must learn not to believe everything people tell you; my childhood days are, alas, too far behind me to remember."

"The Lost Child of Lidice," she pressed, unwilling to concede to him the dominance of the conversation his demeanour expected, "torn from your mother's arms in 1942 and taken to be raised by Aryans until the day you killed them after learning the truth and fled to the West in fear of your life."

Personal cruelty was not how Svobodova operated and she took no pleasure in giving in to it now, but she recognised the necessity of displaying her strength to the twisted creature confronting her, for she knew he would respect little else and she held her stare defiantly as his eyes drilled into her own.

"I came to you today out of courtesy," the old man responded after an eerie silence stretching what seemed like an eternity. "I would hope in return to receive the same."

"Of course," she nodded sincerely.

"You will know of course by now that Prague is already occupied by Russian forces, and you are intelligent enough to have realised that the terrorist attacks your country has suffered recently were simply the ruse required to get them there. I understand as well that President Černý has suffered a gunshot wound and is gravely ill. This was not anticipated and is deeply regretted."

He delivered his words as though he were a newsreader dispassionately commentating on the affairs of the day, Svobodova almost bemused by his coldly factual pronunciations.

"Shortly, your own Deputy Prime Minister, who incidentally is the one who betrayed your efforts to bring in Professor Abelard and Captain Stone, will announce an invitation to the Russian Armies whom you see through the window to enter the country and assist in restoring order. I come to you to advise against the issuing of any counter order for your forces to engage; to do so would only invite needless deaths and a prolonged conflict which would benefit no-one."

Svobodova gave a cynical and quiet laugh at the state of play and the issuing of yet another ultimatum against her.

"And then we all go back to normal?" she sarcastically replied.

"Not quite," The Child answered, ignoring her inflection. "Due to an imminent change in the leadership of the Russian Federation, the occupation of Czechoslovakia will be initially brief, although you may well find yourself behind a renewed iron curtain. Those are the facts, there are no other terms to discuss. I await your answer, Madame."

She remained silent for a moment, taking in the figure from across the room before she finally broke the quiet.

"You won't believe this," she began, "but I suspected I would see you here today. It's funny but I think I've been waiting three years, ever since reunification, to meet with you, but now that you're here, all the questions I wanted to ask, I can't think of."

She shook her head, laughing at her apparent absent mindedness.

"Except for this. I only knew Peter for a short time," Svobodova said with sadness in her voice, "but sometimes I feel like I knew him his whole life. He told me so many things, about The Institute, about you. And in all of that, everything he told me I could never understand why? Why do you hate us so much?"

She crossed slowly over to where he stood, in all his ghoulish noiselessness. Her resentment was deep and grew deeper as she approached him, but though she yearned to, the feeling refused to evolve into hatred, pity instead claiming her sensations, and she reached up to place her hand deftly upon his shoulder, meeting only the tiniest of flinches in response.

"Is it because we let you down? After Lidice, the other survivors, the other children, they were all found when the war ended they were all brought home, all of them except you. Is that why you hate us? Because we forgot you, we forgot one of our own...?

The Child twisted his head up to meet her eyes with a speed which defied his age, causing her to step back and recoil her hand as though his shoulder was forged from hot steel.

"Your concern is touching, Ms Svobodova," he intoned, "but misplaced, and the premise you proceed from is false. Though in frustration I may have claimed hatred of your country, the truth is I hold none, only the same affection I hold for all of Europe."

He stepped around her, his gaze fixed on the view of the war machines waiting at the border for permission to kill.

"My heart belongs to Europe. It has done since the day they took me from my mother's arms and so it will remain until the day it stops beating."

"And yet you are willing to sacrifice so much of it?" Svobodova responded.

"What moral significance would a sacrifice have if it holds no personal stake?"

"But surely you still have some national pride in Czechoslovakia?"

"National pride?!" Anger filled the aged voice and he gestured out through the patterned glass windows where the massed ranks of armoured vehicles and regimented troops were visible in their tense stand-off.

"I watched destruction roll across the continent in the name of National Pride! My father, my uncles and their friends were stood against a barn and shot, my mother rotted in a concentration camp, my friends scattered throughout Germany; I watched Europe destroy itself all in the name of national pride!"

The rage, so untypical of the delivery Svobodova had experienced, shook the ancient frame with a ferocity that startled her, but still she pressed on, determined to exploit any chink in his aged armour.

"You claim the noble motivation of preventing war, yet here you are today inviting one just to further your own goals; what moral high ground can you possibly claim to stand in?" She shouted her question with a rage all her own.

"This is not a war," he shook his head, his vice returning to its quieter state, "it is a taste, a reminder of the things that could so easily happen again if Europe continues on its current path. How long do you think the Far Right can survive when the next ocean of refugees contains waves of white faces, running in the opposite direction?"

Svobodova narrowed her eyes as The Child laid out his reasoning, the frail master conspirator narrating his plan without pride or malice.

"Do you think, when the world sees Czechoslovaks today fleeing into Austria, Hungary, Germany, that fear will not take hold? When British refugees begin flooding the Channel Tunnel as they desperately seek shelter in a closed Europe enforcing its boundaries, do you think they will still praise their politicians for 'taking back control'? How safe do you think the barstool patriots in Germany and the armchair racists in France will feel when it hits home to them that they live in a world where their freedom can disappear in the time it takes for them to drain their beer?"

"You would sacrifice Britain, too?"

"Britain has sacrificed itself," he retorted contemptuously, "through its willingness to believe the lies of charlatans and buffoons and whoring itself to the highest bidder in the name of unbridled capitalism."

"But there's no way NATO would stand by and watch Russia invade Britain!"

"Who mentioned the Russians?" The Child quizzed, the confusion in his voice apparently genuine. "And invasions are so 'yesterday'. Britain will one day discover that, as with any prostitute, the decision to walk the streets when the night is at its darkest carries a great risk."

"You mean...?"

"Thanks to the British government's own greed, the Chinese now sit commandingly in their nuclear web, well within the borders the UK were so keen to 'take back control' of. God forbid that web were subject to attack; the Chinese can be so very protective of their assets, often militarily so."

"But NATO, America..."

"Would happily surrender Britain to its fate rather than risk a full-scale confrontation with China, don't you think?" No cynical smile appeared on the aged, lined face, and no trace of malice brushed his voice, which imparted its message coldly and hard. "But we in The Institute will ensure the sacrifice is not in vain. The people of Europe will see what happens to those left out in the cold; Britain occupied, Czechoslovakia on the edge of a new Iron Curtain, and they will clamour to ensure they are not next. Europe will unify, the extremists will be purged and our integration will renew apace, ready after a suitable interval to open dialogue with the new Russian Leaders shortly to take office; a new era of unity to reach far into this century and beyond."

"A unity paid for in unnecessary blood and pointless war."

"Not war!" He raised a finger, as though insulted by the suggestion. "Peace, paid for by the suggestion of war; a reminder, the briefest of glimpses to the people of the horrors that came before, in the days when Europe was divided through blood and tears and perverted notions of 'national pride.'"

For a moment, Svobodova had no words to speak, responding only in open mouthed silence.

"And you tell me you are not driven by hatred."

"Hatred?" The Child frowned, as though the concept were alien to him, "No, Ms Svobodova, my motive is love."

She would have laughed were his words not so earnest, or his expression so pained at her condemnation. Instead, horror was her only reaction at the old man's passionate sincerity.

"You and I have no children, Ms Svobodova," he said, a statement not a question, "no babes in arms to nurture and cherish; instead we channel our parental affections elsewhere; you into your country, mine into the Union. Europe is my child."

"Then why would you hurt it so?"

"Hurt it?" The abhorrence twisted deeper onto his features and he shook his head at her claim. "Do you still fail to understand why I travel this road? Are you still so blind to the love behind my actions?"

Cracks threatened the strength of his voice, as though the passion behind his oratory was too great for his ageing body to any longer contain or express, and despite herself, Svobodova felt a pang of sympathy as a tell-tale dampness played in the old, fading eyes.

"My life, the life I should have had, was taken from me. I died with them that terrible day but still I am here; soulless, empty. And for what purpose other than to ensure that Europe never falls to such monstrous evil again? I have no interest in personal glories or private empires; I hold no secret accounts filled with stolen millions, there are no palatial mansions crammed with looted art I call home. I am a simple civil servant, working for the good of all the people of Europe, not a dictator greedily marching across the globe and consuming it as I go. Though I resent this continued existence I have used it, every day of it since I learned the truth, to bring and hold the continent together in peace."

The sincerity of the elderly figure's words was unmistakeable, yet Svobodova struggled to accept their veracity, shaking her head gently at his protestation while the thought of her long dead lover teased her memories.

"You claim to be a man of peace, but you have destroyed so much, taken the lives of so many…"

"And I mourn the passing of every one of them, whether they fell by my hand or through the ramifications of my arrangements; I accept responsibility and grieve them as I would my own family, I feel their loss as I would my own limb, however necessary it was. But it was not through destructiveness, never that; no, if I am guilty then let the charge be that I cared too much."

"What?" Svobodova frowned in incredulity.

"What father would stand by while his child played carelessly in the busy street, ignorant of the speeding cars bearing down? Which mother would let her curious infant reach out to touch the flame without pulling them back to safety? You call me a monster but I administer only the necessary discipline of a loving parent, I admonish, I chastise, only to bring my previous love back on the right path, to spare them the hurt, to ensure them a future of unbroken peace."

The Child faced her with a yearning on his aged face, as though desperate that she show some slight acceptance of his logic or understanding of his cause, and his eyes scanned her face searching for it.

"What parent could do more?" he quietly asked.

TWENTY EIGHT

Williams stood behind the fallen figure, Stone raising his cloudy eyes to soak him in as a potent cocktail of emotions bubbled inside him. The Scot simply returned the glare, un-intimidated and unfazed, even if noticeably more bedraggled than usual, his clothes evidencing the aftermath of the tank shell back in Prague. The bony, skeletal fingers of his left hand clutched intently at his right arm, his face evidencing pain of some sort.

"You didn't have to fucking kill her!"

Stone hauled himself to his feet, as if ready to swing a blow to William's head; stopping when the familiar click of the old man's knife sounded in front of his face. The spook had dropped his unscathed arm to his pocket and now stood with a grimace of obvious discomfort masked by the wrinkled features, which nonetheless scowled with considerably more tiredness than Stone was used to.

"Don't be fucking dense, of course I had to kill her," Williams burrowed his eyes under their considerable brow. "You don't honestly think she was going to let you go, do you?"

"I was getting through to her, she was going to tell me who she was…"

"It doesn't fucking matter who she was!" Williams' own temper erupted as he chastised the soldier for his emotional display. "All that matters is she wasn't who she said she was and if I hadn't just saved your arse, she'd have handed it to you the moment you pulled the trigger, wake up man!"

Fighting for clarity in his crowded mind, Stone processed the information, and felt a sickness stir inside him as realisation struck home. He wagged his finger in silence at Williams for a moment, almost too nauseated to voice his suspicion, before finally opening his mouth to condemn him.

"You knew," he said, "you knew she was an imposter."

"Well seeing her stood behind you with a gun pointed at your head alongside Myska's ripening corpse gave me one or two clues."

"No," Stone ignored the sarcasm, his distaste deepening with each moment, "before then; you knew, didn't you?"

An unfamiliar twinge of discomfort flashed briefly across the lined face; a subconscious acceptance, Stone imagined, of the condemnation he aimed at him. A tense pause followed before Williams closed and pocketed the knife, returning his hand to his obviously injured right arm and holding it there.

"I always knew The Institute would try and get plants close to Svobodova." He began his admission non-apologetically, but without the usual shamelessness with which he typically spoke. "I'd been telling him that for years, but I must admit even I was surprised when I figured out who it was. The more I think of it though, the more Abelard was the obvious choice…"

"So you did know?"

Williams stared.

"Yes."

"For how long?"

"I had suspicions early on, but it wasn't until last night in Smokin' Hot that I was sure. Did you never wonder why she refused to be in the same room as him?"

"They were divorced," Stone replied defensively.

"Oh yeah, well that must explain it," the Scot rolled his eyes in exasperation. "You said she went back from the bar to get her roots done; Abelard was a natural brunette."

Stone laughed, coldly, at the matter of fact revelation.

"So where is she? The real Natalie, what happened to her?"

"I did some digging," Williams answered, the frigidity returning to his face as he reapplied his customary insensitivity to his words. "A Jane Doe was brought in to Prague Community Hospital the day after Abelard was due to arrive. Homeless apparently, bit of a scruffy cow; she'd overdosed on a mixture of cocaine and strychnine and died on the toilet at Florenc."

Stone's mind instantly replayed the memory of their first meeting with Svobodova, when the politician had despaired of the regular violence at precisely that location and Abelard, or the woman who had stolen Abelard's life, had shuddered at the news of another death coincident with her arrival. He had admired this woman, loved her for who he was convinced she was; aching for her loving words of comfort and yearning for her physical affections, even allowing himself to dream of the day he could return home, his hand tightly in hers as his son met and embraced her for the first time. And now to learn, as he stood on the cusp of his last battlefield, that each kiss had been a new falsehood, each caress a macabre proxy given on behalf of a woman his lover had helped to murder, caused new levels of revulsion to rise in the soldier's chest. The callousness, from whichever side these bastards claimed to be on, appalled him, all of them deserving of his condemnation and his utter contempt. The thought that this dead mystery woman had got just exactly what she deserved threatened to break into his head.

"It looks like they intercepted her as soon as she arrived in the City and replaced with a double, whoever she was."

Williams, as so often, spoke without malice, merely the unabridged honesty of a man with no time for niceties, and he looked down at the fallen woman with disdain in his big, cold eyes.

"And what about Greyson?" Stone pressed, hoping his suspicions were wrong, "did he know too? Did he know the woman who'd shared his life was lying dead on some mortuary slab because of the mess he'd dragged her into?"

"What does it matter if he did? It wouldn't change the job he had to do."

"You pair of absolute bastards," Stone snarled, his righteous indignation catching up with runaway emotions, before Williams snapped in angry response to the reaction.

"Oh for God's sake man, you're bleating over a woman you never really met! While you were whispering sweet nothings into the ear of whoever this murderous bitch was, which by the way wasn't a particularly nice thing to do with the ex-wife of the man paying you, the real Professor Abelard was long since away with the fairies with a tag on her toe! Is that tragic? Of course! Is it unfair? Absolutely! But does it change the necessity of the work we were doing or the need for us to go on doing it without distraction? No. Fucking. Way."

It was William's turn to shake his head, his frown betraying his incomprehension at Stone's sentimentality, while the stricken Captain knelt down by the crumpled body, fighting to forge a path for his mind through the chaos which was jealously squeezing it. Brushing the threat of dampness from his eyes he stretched his lungs to their full capacity, drawing in the fullest and most refreshing of breaths. Looking into the dead eyes which gazed a sightless and unbreakable stare back at him, he reached slowly forward and touched them sadly closed.

"Goodnight," he whispered.

Straightening himself up, Stone turned to look at his vantage point on the ridge, Williams stepping alongside him in grim accompaniment.

"So what happens now?" Stone asked, the bitterness in his voice impossible to fully disguise. "I sincerely hope your Machiavellian repertoire extends to finding some way for us to quell the occupation?"

"As it happens, it does," Williams answered blithely. "It involves you turning around, picking up that rifle and getting your mind back on the job; you've got a President to kill."

"You're mad!"

"No," Williams snarled, trying to keep his voice as low and quiet as necessary, "I'm trying to stop a fucking invasion! Your girlfriend was doing the right thing for the wrong reason," Williams hissed, "Prague is crawling with Russian troops and as soon as they have it secured, the bald fucker down there with the delusions of grandeur is going to give the order for a full-scale invasion of the country; if we take him out now we can stop it happening, if we don't then it's bye-bye Czechoslovakia for the next twenty years!"

"You take the damn shot then!"

"I can't!" Williams hissed, gesturing to his weak arm. "I couldn't lift the rifle, let alone aim it! You're a soldier, man, come on!"

"You're talking about assassination," Stone argued, "that's not the same as fighting in a battlefield."

"Of course it is!" Williams countered, "Assassination is just a fancy word for shooting someone. For fuck's sake man, if you don't take the shot, Myska wins a posthumous victory and Russia takes one more step towards a conflict with Europe, a real one. You say you want to make a better world for the kids? Well, let that bastard walk away and you've shoveled an extra layer of shit onto their lives instead; do this and save the fucking world, man!"

Stone returned to the ridge and picked up the discarded rifle. The President was still in conference below; a succession of advisers approaching him in his vantage point close by to his troops. Williams' logic was sound, the Captain realised that; this President had proven himself an opportunist, taking quick advantage of the political dispute in Ukraine and now had arranged clandestine operations in a neighbouring country for the purposes of conquest. By taking him out now, Stone would save lives, but would lose forever his veneer of honour and nobility in battle. But his son's future…

He slid the rifle into place, keeping his head down low and lining up the President in the crosshairs with an expert precision; there was no way he could miss.

"You win, you bastard," he whispered to Williams as the shot thunderously tore around the valley and the President slumped forward with a hole in the back of his skull. "You win."

"I told you I'd expected you," Svobodova said to The Child as the old man regained control of his emotions, "And I'm glad you're here, I have a counter proposition for you."

"I have little time for games, Ms. Svobodova," intoned The Child, heading back towards the ornate doors, "you have nothing with which to bargain."

"Don't I?"

The certainty in her voice caused him to stop and turn towards her, eyebrows raised in query.

"You have brought Europe just close enough to the edge that you can still bring it back. What if instead I were to give it a push?"

He eyed her with a fierce intensity, speaking slowly and with suspicion.

"There's no way you could."

"Isn't there?"

From her handbag, she pulled a tablet, selecting a file and holding it out to The Child, who took it and looked ashen faced at what it displayed: a man, a young man, dressed in prison overalls talking at length to an investigator, answering questions and giving details about his arrival in Czechoslovakia and what led him to try to blow himself up in the Old Town Square.

Abdul Salam.

"The late Mr. Salam," The Child acknowledged, more uncertainly than it would seem he was used to being, "I'm afraid the words of a dead terrorist will do little to sway me."

"I'd agree," Svobodova nodded sagely, "were he dead."

The eyes grew fiercer still as she deposited the tablet back inside her bag and continued.

"You see, when America began to insist on our giving up Mr. Salam to their custody, Captain Stone and Mr. Williams had been on the verge of a breakthrough of such significance that I couldn't allow him to simply disappear off to one of America's TV show trials. They'd learned that since his arrival in the country, Mr. Salam had been repeatedly drugged with a potent mixture of cannabis and LSD; a cocktail through which one is alleged to enjoy a unique sensory experience, or so I'm told. It also has the effect, should someone take it in ignorance, of producing what can be interpreted as a 'Spiritual Journey'. After learning so much it was inconceivable that I could simply hand him over; we needed the name of his contact, we needed to know the extent of the plot, in as much as he knew it. And so, I arranged a little incident of my own."

For an instant, Svobodova was almost sure that the aged, skeletal features offered the twitch of a smile, before The Child responded.

"So you deceived the good Captain and his friend?" he quizzed, taking any opportunity he could to twist the conversation even slightly his way. "They risked their lives to save a man who was never at risk?"

"And neither were they," she insisted forcefully. "The operation was meticulously planned and has given Mr. Salam the benefit of collecting his thoughts constructively and discussing them at length without the pressures of the watching world upon him; an opportunity which he has grasped with both hands."

"Has he now?"

"Yes. And while the world has focused on the diplomatic fall out and military escalation, my operatives have located the man who guided Salam on his spiritual quest."

The Child went paler still, choosing, it seemed, not to respond until Svobodova had said all she had to say.

"I must admit I'd thought it would be someone linked to Myska's Party, but I suppose that was never wholly likely. Instead I was surprised to discover that he belonged to The Institute for European Harmony; a paper trail exists connecting him to your Brussels office no less."

"One man," The Child began, "in any organisation is easy to disown and to discredit; his capture is of no consequence. Your efforts would achieve nothing."

"Wouldn't they?"

"No."

"You're not sure…"

"No! You have nothing but wild fantasies and conspiracy theories from the mouths of terrorists; no rational person would take such claims seriously."

"Oh, I think they would," Svobodova countered, "especially when corroborated by the statements of so many of Myska's Party Executive, who are even now in custody awaiting interrogation. That wouldn't just be idle talk and speculation; there would be facts, checkable, verifiable; the kind of facts that can turn theories and fantasy into reality. Europe would begin to ask questions, of The Institute and everyone connected to it; what is this 'institute? Who does it influence? What relationship did it have with the bombers? Is it true they armed them and set them to work across the Union?"

Emboldened, Svobodova walked closer to The Child, not with an accusatory face or a gloating demeanour, but an expression of kind and sincere concern.

"If you think Europe is ungrateful now, try and imagine what it would be like if it began to think that of its leaders."

The Child was quiet and still and Svobodova saw the definite glint of a tear in one eye. When he spoke again, there was a weakness to his voice, as though his energy for the fight ebbed away with each word she spoke.

"You would do that?" he asked softly, "destroy Europe and everything it stands for, solely to avenge yourself on me?"

"No," she shook her head, her expression still one of sincere worry. "I love it enough to try to save it. But you, and your Institute, are taking it away from us brick by brick."

She stopped the recording and returned the tablet to her pocket.

"Everyone is so very keen to deliver me their ultimatums; the things I must do for them to survive. Well today I issue one of my own and you are welcome to listen. The occupation is to end, now. Russian forces are to step away from the border and Czechoslovakia's membership of the European Union is to be revived with immediate effect. If not, while you may well get rid of me you will store greater problems for yourself in the future as this film and those like it will be spread online and e-mailed to countless journalists across the globe, all of whom will question an EU Conspiracy to murder civilians. Not wishing to be immodest, I suspect this is an occasion when the world would like to hear my side of the story."

"You misunderstand my intentions," stressed The Child. "I have given my life to Europe, nurtured it, watch it grow strong through cooperation and inter-reliance, achieving so many marvellous things, together in unity. But now, at the end it blindly seeks to tear itself apart, willingly giving in to the Nationalism of the past and revelling in its ignorance of history. I cannot let it end this way; my actions here will safeguard Europe's future, safeguard its people!"

"Wrong!" Svobodova screamed in response, "you're destroying it! Yes, Europe is crumbling and it's doing so through the same fear with which you seek to save it! Men and women like Myska have come to the fore in ever member state, spreading their hatred; and why? Fear, fear of the outsiders, fear of the non-Europeans, fear that those different from us can never adapt to live like we do. Do you expect to fight fear with fear?"

Her insecurities danced around at the back of her mind despite the display of strength and she pressed on while he staggered on the ropes.

"If Europe is falling anyway, at least let it be from something other than fear; then at least we can re-build it again as what it was supposed to be: tolerant, cooperative, progressive and free! Think about it, tell me deep, deep down, isn't that the Europe you want to see? A Union which doesn't react to terrified children fleeing bombs by pulling down the shutters and telling them to die elsewhere. A Union that doesn't claim to want to tackle terrorism on one hand, while selling arms to the same terrorists on the other. A Europe whose member states don't constantly look to find the fault in each other, but who works to become greater than the sum of its whole. But if that's your goal too we won't get there with fear."

She was so close to him now; enough to hear the laboured wheezing he was fighting so hard to supress, as though his soul was yearning to thrash a response, and his lungs were burning to provide the oxygen to do it.

"You're trying to build the peace by laying the foundations for war; and where those foundations exist, someone will always find a way to construct a reason to fight, no matter how 'in control' you feel you are, even you! Europe, for all its many, many faults has kept us safe from each other, from ourselves for decades; you have helped keep that peace, maybe more than anyone else. Don't now be the one who causes us to lose it."

Vice President Bok of the Russian Federation strode purposefully from the makeshift office set up behind the lines, towards the command tent where his Generals waited for their orders to advance. Everything had gone as The Child had explained, from the occupation of Prague to the single shot felling the President, which had surprised all except for Bok as it flew on its journey.

He had taken full advantage of his foreknowledge by throwing himself on the President's body, secure in the knowledge that no further shots would be forthcoming, earning himself the title of hero for his troubles. Relishing the praise his actions earned him, he allowed his mind to wander forward a few months when, after this invasion business was behind them, he would take pride of place at his own medal ceremony and decorate himself for his bravery.

Approaching the tent, he grimaced to see the imposing figure of Konstantin, the late President's Foreign Minister, already on the scene, straightening up as Bok approached, with the Generals behind him coming likewise to attention.

Bok detested Konstantin, who had long rivalled him for power and who continued to argue for cooperation over conquest. He allowed himself a brief smile at the thought of his rival's imminent posting to Siberia, as he finally reached the tent in time for the sun to begin its dip over the two countries.

"Gentlemen," he began, "we cannot afford to mourn for long, it is imperative we avenge ourselves of our loss in the only way honour dictates. Synchronise watches; I hereby give the order to advance the Army through the border with extreme prejudice and proceed to designated targets. Thank you all and good luck."

Not a soul moved and Bok frowned in anger, staring at each of the faces in turn, some of whom looked back at him with an obvious contempt.

"I said…" he began, before Konstantin stepped into him, his face fierce and accusing.

"Mr Vice President," he said, "The government has been made aware of a rather interesting video…"

It was a clatter of boots running towards the podium on which he lay that broke the quiet in Černý's ears.

The sound of protesting had long since stopped, along with the quietened screams and the silenced tears. They were still there, but noiseless and deathly still, as though a People had finally done in practice what so many called for in theory and come together as one, sitting en masse in the middle of the now orderly Wenceslas Square, where they had sat since the extent of his injury became obvious.

Chaos had greeted the sound of the gun, until Černý had clambered to the still functioning PA system and begged for his People's ears, chastising them for giving in to the violence which had claimed the minds of the people standing against them and urging them to resist by showing them instead their love of peace. He stayed with them, refusing to accept the medical evacuation his captors offered, committing instead to those trapped in the Square that he would stay with them in peace until all were free to leave or until God showed him a different route. Then he had sat, weak and bleeding, the young boy whose life he had saved attending him, while the people sat with him, where they were in the Square, some with their eyes closed, some praying; all holding hands together. Though they were quickly fenced in by the occupying regiment, there was little need for them to be. None would leave without the others.

He tried to raise his head towards the approaching feet, or at least towards the Colonel who shared the platform and to whom the sound of boots was heading, but his strength, at least physically, had long since left his frame.

Moments later, the Colonel came into view, crouching down alongside him wearing a look of embarrassed regret on his experienced face. He spoke softly and in Czech to Černý, who smiled in response and gestured to the microphone; the eyes of the Square levelling on the Colonel as he moved to it.

No grand speech came, no magnificent oratory. Instead he called his men throughout the Square to attention, surveying them all and issuing the final command of his brief occupation.

"In good order," he said, in beautifully accented Russian, "regiment will disengage and fall back."

Laughter, applause, cheers and a thousand other symptoms of shock broke out, sporadically at first before the entire wave of people, of every colour creed and background in the country erupted together in joy, embracing the moment and each other in an outpouring of love as the armoured units began to slowly and unexpectedly pull away and begin the long journey back to the border.

"You did it!" the young boy cried to Černý, tears in his eyes, but the President shook his head. They had done it, his people, risen above their squabbles and differences. And even if it were only for one day, it was a day they had shown the invaders and the world their resolve and their solidarity. As the sound of cheering eclipsed the retreating creak of aged war machines, he knew that at last, the People were ready for the challenge, as he was ready to pass it on, and as he smiled widely and closed his eyes for the final time, a flush of excitement warmed his final moment; he couldn't wait to see what they would make of it.

She saw on his ancient, lined face that he was desperate to answer, desperate even to approve of her vision, but before he could speak, the double doors creaked open and an inoffensive but immaculately suited operative strode purposefully into the room towards him. The disturbance served to restore the customary steel to The Child's face and he turned away from Svobodova, inclining his head to the newcomer who wordlessly presented him with a printed dispatch which he took and instantly imbibed.

The pregnant silence was every bit as nerve wracking as when he had first stepped through the door to confront her; that curious mix of eager anticipation and cold dread, but The Child made no attempt to break it, simply reading and re-reading the note again and again.

An age passed before he dismissed the news bearer and, stood, so solitary and abandoned in the middle of the cavernous room that she moved to place her hand on his shoulder, stunning him back into activity. He stared closely at her through his clouded and damnably tired eyes and she wondered for a moment if would ever say anything to her again, until finally, his jaw creaked open once more..

"Madam Prime Minister," he began in his rich, deep inflections, "it would appear, that the occupation is at an end."

TWENTY-NINE

THE HIGH MESHED FENCE came gloriously into view, granting Stone and Williams a renewed vigour as they ran and scrambled towards the safety it offered. Not a word had passed between them since Stone had taken the shot; the pair immediately going to ground as the pandemonium which greeted the President's death was unleashed, before picking themselves up and making for the lines, desperate to keep one step ahead of the detachment which was now surely on their trail.

It was as they took advantage of their timely dose of adrenaline that Williams tripped and keeled over, gripping his ankle in pain.

"Come on, you old bastard," Stone hissed, "you don't get away from me that easily."

Though he stooped to help the old man up, Williams resisted his aid, hauling himself up and continuing the journey, limping as he went.

"Let me help you," Stone offered, "they'll be right on our tail by now."

"Aye," Williams agreed through gritted teeth, "the knights coming to avenge the King."

"And what does that make us? Bishops?"

"Fat fucking chance," sneered Williams. "Like I told you before, we're the pawns. You know, most people, most non-chess playing people that is, don't realise all the subtle elements of the game, like opening moves or terminal gambits. Some don't even realise that there are different types of pawn."

"Are there really?" Stone replied, unsure that he wanted this conversation right now.

"Absolutely. You see, everyone assumes pawns to be the weak pieces you sacrifice at the start of the game, but not all of them are. Take you and me for example, we're both pawns but we've made it all the way through to *Endgame*. I mean, don't get me wrong, every good pawn knows that one day they'll be hung out to dry like all the rest, but sometimes, just occasionally, a pawn can join with the King, an 'Advanced Pawn' they call them, and he can help put the other side into check – fucking – mate. And the truth is, Captain, that today, *this* pawn is advancing on its own."

While the amused half-smile still sat on Stone's face at this older man's bizarre words, Williams spun around, a glint of metal in the sun betraying the presence of the gun in his hand before the silenced shot tore through the soldier's calf.

Stone crumpled to the ground, clutching his leg, a cry of pain and surprise bursting from his throat while Williams, no longer limping and his seemingly injured arm now holding the gun that had fired the shot, stood over him, a look of regret on his face.

"You won't believe me," he said softly, "and nor will you even care, but I wanted you to know I'm sorry, this was never my intention."

"You traitorous bastard!"

"No," Williams shook his head, "not traitorous. I'm doing this for Britain, for the World…"

"What?"

"You have to die so everyone else can live."

"Don't talk bullshit, what the fuck is going on?!"

Williams took a deep breath and bowed his head a little, as though he were preparing himself for the confessional, but his eyes remained unmovably on Stone's.

"I knew," he said, simply and quietly.

"Knew what?"

"Everything. I knew that Myska was working with the Russians on the bombings and I knew there was a pretty good chance they'd be trying to topple Svobodova and lay the groundwork for an invasion. And I knew that The Institute wanted Czechoslovakia kicked out of the international clubs and that there must be a reason for that. And then I found out that an invasion by the President who'd already taken out the Ukraine would provide just the opportunity for The Institute to replace him with someone more sympathetic to their goals. But it was just me and Greyson, so after that we had no choice but to let the whole thing pan out and see what little changes we could make here and there."

The pain in Stone's leg was becoming unbearable but the angered resentment burning in his chest hurt him more.

"You knew?" he hissed. "All this fucking time?"

"Where do you think Greyson's been all this time?" Williams shook his head sadly. "He hasn't been 'keeping his head down in Prague', he's been busy scuppering the deal and making one of his own."

"What...?"

"Bok was an Institute man," Williams said, exasperatedly, the next 'Iron Man of the East' who'd keep Czechoslovakia part of a new Eastern Empire. But aside from a bit of sabre rattling now and then would keep out of The Institute's way in Europe and let them screw the rest of us as hard as they like!"

He shouted the words, all pretence of hiding gone and speaking loudly as though trying to justify his actions more to himself than to Stone.

"And so Greyson got in touch with his old mate from this neck of the woods, Konstantin, and in return for a passage to the Premiership, generously provided by some of the recordings I've made in recent weeks, Konstantin would be waiting to seize power when the President went down, get Bok into custody and withdraw from Czechoslovakia. In return, when Greyson takes over as Prime Minister he'll withdraw British troops from Syria."

Though the intensity of the pain continued to throb, Stone sneered a cynical laugh at Williams' revelation.

"Prime Minister?" he laughed, "Prime fucking Minister? This, all this has been about Greyson's fucking job title?!"

"No," Williams snapped, "it hasn't! Greyson doesn't want the fucking job but that makes him the only one fit to have it! And after the current PM, along with all the other political leaders in Europe who voted in favour of Czechoslovakia's suspension, have some difficult questions to answer, and Konstantin publically praises Greyson as the instigator of the Syrian peace talks, he'll be drafted to fill the vacancy before you can say 'stitch up'. But for the deal to work, the President's killer has to be punished."

"Just like that," Stone shook his head in despair at the ease with which the wool was pulled over his eyes.

"Just like that," Williams repeated. "I'm sorry Captain, but after Brexit, Britain needs friends, wherever it can find them; and what better way to do it than by ending yet another pointless fucking war and saving hundreds of thousands of lives? And at the same time ending an occupation and preventing God knows how many years of oppression? And instead of hordes of young soldiers being sent in to die at the hands of distant politicians, the whole conflict can be solved with minimal casualties: the Aggressor, the Victim and the Man in the Middle; You. You're the Flower on the Shrine, Captain, you're the sacrifice for the sake of lasting peace."

The inequity burned within Stone as fiercely as the wound in his leg, filling him with an insatiable rage. He tried pushing himself to his feet, only for the still bleeding wound to pull him unceremoniously back down.

"Fix this." Stone hissed the words through gritted teeth.

"It is fixed."

"Fix it again!"

"I can't!" It was Williams' turn to lose his cool, his voice at once bellowing out to the world and pointing straight at Stone.

"Is that what you think I am? Do you think I'm Spy Jesus?! I'm not Spy Jesus! I'm not Espionage Moses! This situation is as 'fixed' as it's ever going to be, you just ended up with the shit end of the stick when the music stopped playing; someone had to, and believe me, I know that one day it'll be my turn; but here and now it's yours."

"Why are you doing this?"

"Because there has to be a reason!" Williams bellowed the words, his arms outstretched and passion etched onto his features. "There has to be a fucking point to all this; all the things I've done! It's not enough anymore to just pick the least shitty option and hope for the fucking best, there has to be some greater good, or else why go on? I've been beating on the chest of Britain's decaying corpse for years, trying to spark some kind of life back into it, and all I hear is its final breath wheezing faintly out of it, for years! Nothing! No sign of life! All the false dawns, all the Chosen Men and Anointed Women and not a spark amongst them! Just Hard Right lunatics and Ultra Left morons, all of them using me to do the fucking dirty work for them in the name of some greater good that even they don't really believe in! All of them failed, just leaving an ethically dying people who weren't even worth saving anymore. But then, Greyson came along, someone who knew how to play the game but who had his own idea of the prize. And I heard a heart start beating again. All of a sudden, there was a reason again; someone who understood that the dawn might be the most beautiful part of the day but it isn't the end of it, you have to keep going, keep pushing. Greyson will do that, and as long as he does then it's all worthwhile again."

The aged spy's soul searching offered no comfort to the distressed Captain, whose mind turned, as ever, to thoughts of his boy and his own reason for carrying on.

"It shouldn't end like this, I need to speak to my boy, my son…"

"Your son?"

"Let me talk to him on the phone, now, I have to make him understand, I have to…"

"Lincoln…"

Whether it was that Williams had used his first name, or the almost delicate manner in which he did so, Stone stopped and looked up at his scruffy, traitorous comrade.

"Lincoln, your son's dead."

He spoke the words quietly, delicately even, but they burned through Stone more ferociously than any wound in his career, even the throbbing caused by the bullet in his leg a mild irritant by comparison and he shook his head violently at them, clenching his eyes closed hard and hissing back through gritted, grinding teeth.

"No. No, you shut your fucking mouth you traitorous Scot's bastard! Shut your fucking mouth!"

"He's dead, Lincoln," the uncharacteristic gentleness in Williams' voice continued to tear viciously into the stricken Captain. "He died in your arms, months ago, in the London attack with the others. That's when you had your breakdown…"

"No," Stone was sobbing, staring at the blood on his hands ass though he were back there on the pavement cradling his broken boy and howling with all his ferocious might.

"That's why you were the perfect choice," Williams continued sadly, "the disgraced soldier, supposedly responsible for the flight of the very terrorists who would go on to kill his son, and who, unable to handle the guilt, would uncover evidence of Russian and far right complicity in the attacks, until one day going rogue and taking the President down with a rifle."

Williams held up the phone he had shown off in Myska's office; now playing a video clip of the Captain, stretched over the grassy ridge and firing a shot, zooming closer seconds later to the falling body of the President.

"If it's any consolation," Williams said, "a lot of people are going to remember you as a hero for this."

The anger was still inside him but directed now at himself instead of Williams, his mind clearing just sufficiently to take in the Scotsman's words.

"Not the right people though," he exhaled, fighting to control his tears, "not the right person. I spent so many years, his whole life, trying to make him proud of me, trying to prove myself worthy of being his dad. Trying to be his hero…"

Williams own head shook in sad response.

"You still don't fucking realise do you?"

Stone opened his wet eyes to see William's own betraying a tell-tale glisten as the aging, aching man spoke.

"You always were his hero, Lincoln, you were his father."

A sound in the distance behind them stirred the pair, both men realising that their Russian pursuers were close at hand. Williams reached into an inner pocket and held out his hand to Stone; a small white pill.

"I have to go," he whispered almost apologetically. "Here, there's no point you suffering needlessly; take this and you won't feel a thing."

Stone, his eyes puffy with emotion but his crying contained, looked at the pill and shook his head.

"I was always ready to die for my country," Stone smiled, "I just always thought it would be on the battlefield, as a soldier."

"This is a battlefield," Williams answered, his own voice cracking, "just a different type. And you'll always be a soldier. Goodbye Captain Stone."

Williams turned and ran, reaching the fence and easing himself through the cut-in hole, before melting into the densely wooded trees on the Czechoslovakian side and turning back to watch.

The pain in Stone's leg engulfing him with every fresh movement, he willed himself through the discomfort and strained to stand on his good leg while the wounded one hung limply beneath him. The rumbling and shout of military voices was almost upon him and he knew there would be no warning shot. Through the dense trees, on the other side of the border stood Williams, his one time Guardian Angel turned Harbinger of Death, ghoulishly waiting for Stone's end to come. The scrawny, wrinkled figure stood erect and Stone saw him move his arm in a swift movement, bringing his hand against his head, the tips of his long fingers brushing his temple in respectful salute.

Stone smiled at the gesture. He felt no rage towards Williams, no malice. All that was gone, replaced only with the eager desperation to hurry on his way and hold his boy again; he was waiting for him, Stone knew that. Rasti's words the previous night had proven that to him, and neither the pain from his wound nor any number of bullets could ever numb the elation building in him at his impending reunion. The noise was voluminous and accompanied now by the loud shouts of voices, screaming unfamiliar Russian accented words at him. Turning round to face his end, Stone neither acknowledged, nor cared about the rifles facing him, neither did he flinch when they loudly signalled their readiness; instead he could see only his boy, stood smiling brightly at him, his arms stretched out wide to accept his father's embrace.

"Hello son," Stone said, tears of joy running down his scarred, weathered face, "Daddy's home."

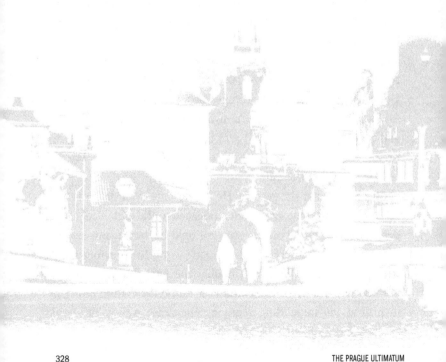

THIRTY

A FRESH PAIN ACCOMPANIED EACH STEP the aged body made, as though time and the earth itself had conspired to punish him by making his final journey longer. Finally, he wheezed to a standstill before the frozen metallic ranks of children before him, his frail hand reaching out to rest on the shoulder of the tallest, while his fading eyes moved to take in all of the faces gazing silently at him.

"You've been ages Marek," he heard one of the children's voices say in his mind. "What took you so long?" asked another, younger voice, filled with the innocent grumpiness of infancy.

"I'm sorry," he said to them aloud, his voice breaking with emotion, "I had work to do."

"What work?"

"Important work," he replied softly, "to make sure what happened to us couldn't happen again. I had to make sure we were safe, that Europe was safe."

"You were gone a long time," replied the grumpy voice.

"We missed you," whispered another, still younger.

"It was a long job," he answered, "but one that's for others to take up now. I missed you too, all of you."

"Did you really miss us Marek?"

"Every day," he answered, "but now I'm back, at last."

The voices were quiet for a moment, as if mulling over his words.

"Can you play with us now?" the young voice finally asked him.

"Yes please," he smiled, "if you'll let me?"

"Of course we'll let you," said an older boy, "how long can you stay?"

"Forever," he said.

The voices cheered and spoke at once, urging him to hurry up and join them and he laughed tearfully as he consented to their joyful requests. Finally, he dropped to his aching knees at the feet of the statue, though the pain no longer registered; and with his hand holding tightly the crucifix around his neck, the Last Child of Lidice went to join his friends.

"Are you proud?"

Greyson had not been fool enough to expect a warm reception but neither was he prepared for the question as he approached Svobodova at her favourite cemetery; the politician stood with her back to him, staring down at some ancient, illegible lines on a crumbling stone grave. The early morning was unseasonably cold, with due clinging to the grass and a slight breeze adding to the chill with which Greyson had awoken that day.

"We came out of it as well as could be expected," he said from his position behind her, "the Russians have withdrawn, Konstantin is in charge and your opponents are discredited forever. You even managed to get Czechoslovakia reinstated in the EU and NATO; it's as much as we could have hoped to achieve."

"And yet the victory brings with it no joy. You lied to me Jonathan."

"There was no way I could prevent the occupation," he said defensively, "all we had was a bit of intelligence, Williams and me; we had to let it play out and crisis manage it as we went along. And while we're on the subject you weren't exactly open about Salam were you? What's going to happen to him?"

"He'll be tried and serve his sentence under an assumed identity," Svobodova said dispassionately. "If only you'd trusted me I could have resolved the whole situation without bloodshed; instead Karol, poor Captain Stone, even your own wife, all dead..."

"We couldn't just relay on Salam," Greyson shook his head, "there were too many variables. Look, I know you're angry, but we could have been standing here now waist deep in deaths in the midst of a new oppression, but instead we're not. You can't change the world, Mirushka," Greyson sighed, "not all at once. It doesn't want to be changed. All you, I or anyone can do is try to do the best we can in our piece of it."

"You didn't trust me enough even to let me try. It was my country at risk, not yours, you had no right to intervene, to go behind my back..." She hissed the words bitterly, the pain in her voice only too evident.

"There was more than just Czechoslovakia at risk," Greyson shook his head sadly, "the whole of Europe could have fallen back forty years. I had to act. And now, instead of a war and countless lives lost, Europe's peace is secure and you have an ally on your border."

"While an innocent man lies dead in a Ukrainian ditch, put there by the very people he fought for."

"Better one man than a hundred, or a thousand."

"One is too many. You should have trusted me."

Greyson, fighting hard to blink back the dampness in his own eyes, took a step closer to Mirushka and placed a hand softly on her shoulder.

"You brought a second flower today?"

"It seemed only right," she said. "Captain Stone has no grave to mourn beside, and while half the world hail him a hero and half castigate him as a murderer, it is appropriate that I acknowledge privately the man he really was."

"You know," he began, looking down at the flowers she had laid, "when I was learning to drive, my old instructor told me that I could be the best, the safest and most skilful driver in the world, but I'd still never be able to guarantee I'd be safe on the road, because I'd have no control over how everyone else drove their cars."

He turned her into him, his voice sad, his words sincere.

"Just because you and I want to drive a straight, honest path, it doesn't mean everyone else on the road wants to do the same. Sometimes, we're forced to drive more defensively than we'd like, forced to take a detour or two, to make sure we reach the destination intact."

"And abandon our passengers on route?"

He dropped his eyes for a moment and she followed them earnestly, as though desperately searching for a spark of the man she knew.

"I didn't want him to die," Greyson's voice began to crack and he struggled to contain it.

"But he did."

He dropped his arms from her shoulders and continued to stare at the ground.

"Two years," he muttered.

"What?"

"I'm heading back to Britain to accept the Premiership, but

we've a General Election in two years; either I'll be voted out or if we win I'll resign."

"Why resign?"

"Because I want you to believe that I didn't do this for power. I did it because I believed it was the only way."

"Oh, Jonathan…" She shook her head sadly.

Greyson looked over to where his official car waited and he leant forward to kiss the top of her head, softly and sincerely.

"Just two years, you'll see," he whispered as he turned and headed to the car.

"Your father would be proud of you," said Svobodova, coldly, her damp eyes not moving from the flowers on the shrine.

"No," Greyson answered, stopping briefly to look sadly back at her over his shoulder before heading finally to his car and to his destiny. "No, he wouldn't."

AUTHOR'S NOTE

CAPTAIN LINCOLN STONE'S MILITARY CAREER is certainly unusual and, in truth, I am probably guilty of stretching its boundaries a little far. Even if he were a fresh-faced youngster at the time of the Falklands War, he would certainly be in the twilight of his career now, and very unlikely to still be leading troops into combat. While the career progression from Private soldier to Captain could well take place as described, most such promotees would find themselves assigned Quarter Master or administrative duties.

The brief cameo of Captain Stone's father, the young Corporal Thomas Stone, owes something to anecdotal magic. My own father, also named Thomas, was a Corporal and Signal Gunner in 4RTR (C Squadron), in the Fifties, stationed in Berlin. As a young child, I remember listening with fascination to his tales of his time in the Regiment, and never more intently than when he described the almost supernatural discomfort of sentry duty, when the ghostly calls to 'Tommy' came whistling from the East. This story is in part a tribute to him and to the Armed Forces, to whom I offer the utmost respect for their willingness to lay down their lives in defence of others. I am exceptionally grateful to Major General (Retd) Sir Laurence New CB, CBE for his kind correspondence and for taking the time to answer my questions on an oft overlooked period of history. For those interested in finding out more of the historical Royal Tank Regiments, I urge you to visit the website maintained by Sir Laurence, at http://www.4and7royaltankregiment.com.

While the good Captain's military journey is fictional, the incident for which he drew international derision is based on a real life event which took place in the aftermath of the Kosovo War, which history recorded as 'The Incident at Pristina Airport'. The incident involved a potential flashpoint between Russian and NATO forces at the airport, with General Sir Mike Jackson, the British CO, famously refusing the order of American NATO Commander, General Wesley Clark, to block the runway, an act which would have served to antagonise the Russians, with the (reported) words, "I'm not going to start Word War Three for you." I offer Sir Mike my apologies for appropriating his famous words and lending them to Captain Stone.

One of the officers present that day, was a young Captain by the name of James Blunt, who went on in life to make rather serviceable use of his voice. Also present was the current Labour MP for Barnsley, Dan Jarvis; at the time a Major and adjutant to General Sir Mike Jackson. I am extremely grateful to Mr Jarvis for sparing me the time to share his recollections of that day as I researched this book. In the absence of books detailing the incident in depth, interested readers may wish to view the salient facts at **https://en.wikipedia.org/wiki/Incident_at_Pristina_airport**.

I am grateful as well to journalist and broadcaster, Peter Hitchens, for his kind permission in allowing me to borrow his "Hotel California" reference to Britain's relationship with the EU. While I profoundly disagree with Mr Hitchens on the European issue, I am open-minded enough to recognise a good soundbite when I hear it.

The fast exit of the film director from the scene, as he realises the severity of the situation, is a nod to a couple of incidents during the real Russian invasion of August 1968. Robert Vaughn, the famous actor and erstwhile Man from UNCLE, was present in the city during that time, filming the movie The Bridge at Remagen. It was during filming that Warsaw Pact forces began the invasion, compelling cast and crew to flee the scene in taxis. Vaughan would himself in later years play himself in a Radio 4 dramatisation of the event.

Likewise, Sixties band The Moody Blues were in Prague at the time, promoting their second album, The Days of Future Passed. Little did they know as they filmed a video for Nights in White Satin on the Charles Bridge, during the afternoon of 20th August, that the Russian tanks were about to roll in. By the evening of the same day, The British Embassy had pulled the band from the City, to be returned home by the RAF. A quick search on YouTube for Moody Blues, Prague, offers an intriguing glimpse of this piece of history.

Williams, MI6's forgotten man in Prague, owes his name to William the Conqueror, to whom history granted the less than flattering title, 'William the Bastard'. I wanted a name which reflected such a characteristic, and as Alan B'Stard was taken, I dipped into history instead. I trust His Late Majesty will forgive my impertinence. For the eager traveller, William's tale of the discovery of the cave system recounted during the interrogation scene is true, and the caves can be visited today. Likewise, the underground tunnels connected to the present day Russian Embassy are genuine and, as Williams again recounted, were utilised in the past by both the Gestapo and the KGB in the maintenance of their networks.

Of less historical note, but just as interesting (at least to me) is the beer garden of the bar in which Stone, Williams and Greyson discuss strategy, and the puma who cameos in the scene. The bar is real as is its occupation by pumas, and both have attained legendary status in the City.

Captain Stone makes reference to Nicholas Winton, in the course of his conversation with the shop assistant, and his story is very much worthy of study, particularly in this new age of refugee crises and immigration bans. Sir Nicholas (as he became), was instrumental in the rescue of 669 mainly Jewish children from Czechoslovakia, on the eve of the Second World War. Eventually dubbed 'The British Schindler' by the press years later, Sir Nicholas was keen to acknowledge the role others played in the operation. His story is a fascinating one and those keen to learn more may like to read If it's not possible... the Life of Sir Nicholas Winton by Barbara Winton.

As I write these words, Europe and the World are at a crossroads, with Nationalism rampant and fear a constant reality for many. Since the Referendum, Britain, with every day that passes, feels less to me like the warm and welcoming home I grew up in, and instead increasingly cold, nasty and an altogether more unpleasant place. As a parent of children with mixed British/Slovak heritage, I fear for the future when, no longer able to blame foreigners for their failures, the Powers that Be look for other groups to scapegoat. Likewise, I will forever lament the opportunities and chances ripped from future generations as a consequence of Brexit, and loathe the lies and deceits peddled to bring about that result.

In a Radio 4 interview, back in 2014, Sir Nicholas Winton opined with regard to humanity that, "I don't think we've learned anything... the world today is in a more dangerous situation than it has ever been."

With the revived claw of Hard Right Nationalism joining the spirit of anti-intellectualism and fear in scraping across the continent, and the occupant of the White House dangerously unpredictable at best, I am regrettably inclined to agree with him.

ACKNOWLEDGEMENTS

I AM INDEBTED to a great many people in the writing of this book, first and foremost my spectacular wife, Miroslava. To her and my children, Timothy and Georgia, I owe sincere thanks for their love, support and for putting up with the cantankerous old grump I become when in the grip of the writing bug. That thanks extends also to the rest of my family who have so often walked on egg shells around me as deadlines drew ever nearer.

For permitting me the usage of names and/or visages, I am eternally grateful to Peter Lowe, Rasti Vojtovic and Lincoln Taylor, and I owe a special thanks to Jamie Marshall, for his steadfast support and superb photographic efforts.

Many have given me invaluable assistance in the research of this book, for which I am extremely grateful. In particular, I express my gratitude to Major General (Retired) Sir Laurence New CB, CBE, former Assistant Chief of the Defence Staff, and a former Colonel Commandant of The Royal Tank Regiment, for his very kind and informative correspondence about life in 4RTR in the Fifties. Thanks also to Dan Jarvis MP, for taking the time to discuss with me his recollections of a fateful incident in the aftermath of the Kosovo War. I am grateful also to journalist and broadcaster

Peter Hitchens for kindly permitting my appropriation of his 'Hotel California' remark.

For sharing with me their personal memories of the Russian Invasion of 1968, I offer my thanks to Suzanne Bojtos and Jirka M. Similarly, I offer sincere thanks to those friends and associates in the Armed Forces, who have taken the time to share their experiences and motivations with me: Richard McAvoy, Pete Barrett, Pete Jefferson and Darren Bell. Thank you all.

No list of acknowledgements could be complete without including my writing comrades in Urbane Publications, and its Founder, Matthew Smith. At Urbane, I am daily thrilled to be part of a genuinely supportive collective of writers, all of whom I respect and admire, and grateful for the trust, respect and support shown me by Matthew. Cheers boss.

And thanks also to you, for picking up and opening this book; it really does make the whole thing worthwhile. I hope you enjoy...

THE PRAGUE ULTIMATUM

THE PRAGUE ULTIMATUM

Years after marvelling at the stories of the 1968 Spring and the Velvet Revolution, James found himself sat in a Prague Blues Bar falling in love with the city in person. A graduate of Politics and Modern History, and a long-standing blues DJ for Modradiouk.net, James's affection for the atmospheric, dark and seedy Cold War thrillers of old was reawakened by his growing affection for this cobbled land of gothic secrets and his writing bone began to itch. James's career has covered a myriad of roles across the public and private sectors including high level technical recruitment and business development, to his current role within HR Consultancy; and it was a bad day at the office which persuaded him to finally act upon his long-held dream of writing. The result was his 2015 debut novel Escape to Perdition, which reflected his love both of central Europe and the espionage genre and was met with wide spread acclaim. James has also written for The Prague Times and his work has been featured by Doctor Who Worldwide and travel site An Englishman in Slovakia. He is currently developing a number of projects across a variety of media. A diehard Whovian, Man City fan, rum drinker and Christian, James is an unrepentant member of the 48%.

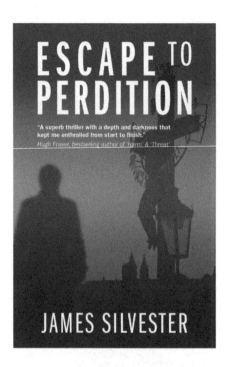

ESCAPE TO PERDITION

PAPERBACK, £8.99,

ISBN: 978-1909273795

"Readers who enjoy intelligently written, tautly plotted and disturbingly executed political thrillers will love 'Escape to Perdition' and may well find themselves affected by it as did I"

Linda's Book Bag

PRAGUE 2015. Herbert Biely, aged hero of the Prague Spring, stands on the brink of an historic victory, poised to reunite the Czech and Slovak Republics twenty-six years after the Velvet Revolution. The imminent Czech elections are the final stage in realising his dream of reunification, but other parties have their own agendas and plans for the fate of the region. A shadowy collective, masked as an innocuous European Union Institute, will do anything to preserve the status quo. The mission of Institute operative Peter Lowes is to prevent reunification by the most drastic of measures. Yet Peter is not all that he seems. A deeply troubled man, desperate to escape the past, his resentment towards himself, his assignment and his superiors deepens as he questions not just the cause, but his growing feelings for the beautiful and captivating mission target. As alliances shift and the election countdown begins, Prague becomes the focal point for intrigue on an international scale. The body count rises, options fade, and Peter's path to redemption is clouded in a maelstrom of love, deception and murder. Can he confront his past to save the future? This is a high-quality page turning thriller and perfect for fans of Le Carré.

Urbane Publications is dedicated to
developing new author voices, and publishing
fiction and non-fiction that challenges, thrills and
fascinates.

From page-turning novels to innovative
reference books, our goal is to publish what
YOU want to read.

Find out more at
urbanepublications.com